DEFEATING THE DEMON LORD'S A CINCH

IF YOU'VE GOT A RINGER

VOLUME

3

TSUKIKAGE

Illustration by bob

YEN ON

New York

Translation by Caleb DeMarais
Cover art by bob

This book is a work of fiction. Names, characters, places, and incidents are the product of the author's imagination or are used fictitiously. Any resemblance to actual events, locales, or persons, living or dead, is coincidental.

Defeating the Demon Lord's a Cinch (If You've Got a Ringer), Vol. 3

TSUKIKAGE

DARENIDEMO DEKIRU KAGE KARA TASUKERU MAO TOBATSU
Vol. 3
© Tsukikage 2017
First published in Japan in 2017 by KADOKAWA CORPORATION, Tokyo.
English translation rights arranged with KADOKAWA CORPORATION, Tokyo through Tuttle-Mori Agency, Inc., Tokyo.

English translation © 2019 by Yen Press, LLC

Yen On
1290 Avenue of the Americas
New York, NY 10104

Visit us at yenpress.com
facebook.com/yenpress
twitter.com/yenpress
yenpress.tumblr.com
instagram.com/yenpress

First Yen On Edition: March 2019

Yen On is an imprint of Yen Press, LLC.
The Yen On name and logo are trademarks of Yen Press, LLC.

The publisher is not responsible for websites (or their content) that are not owned by the publisher.

Library of Congress Cataloging-in-Publication Data
Names: Tsukikage, author. | Bob (Illustrator), illustrator. | Kerwin, Alex, translator. | DeMarais, Caleb, translator.
Title: Defeating the demon lord's a cinch (if you've got a ringer) / Tsukikage ; illustration by bob.
Other titles: Darenidemo Dekiru Kage Kara Tasukeru Mao Tobatsu. English
Description: First Yen On edition. | New York : Yen On, 2018– | v. 1: translation by Alex Kerwin. | v. 2–3 translation by Caleb DeMarais.
Identifiers: LCCN 2018023883| ISBN 9781975327354 (v. 1 : paperback) | ISBN 9781975327378 (v. 2 : paperback) | ISBN 9781975303709 (v. 3 : paperback)
Subjects: LCSH: Fantasy fiction.
Classification: LCC PL876.S853 D3713 2018 | DDC 895.63/6—dc23
LC record available at https://lccn.loc.gov/2018023883

ISBNs: 978-1-9753-0370-9 (paperback)
        978-1-9753-0383-9 (ebook)

10 9 8 7 6 5 4 3 2 1

LSC-C

Printed in the United States of America

CONTENTS

Defeating the Demon Lord's a Cinch
(If You've Got a Ringer)

Part Three

Let's Begin

Golem Valley.

This battlefield boasts the highest level of difficulty in the entire Kingdom of Ruxe.

The unforgiving valley terrain is inhabited by incomparably fearsome golems originally brought to life by an ancient mage. Even the most experienced mercenary is unable to pierce their rugged bodies with a blade. Golem Valley is famously used as a training ground by the Kingdom's royal knights for this very reason.

A warrior should be between levels 40 and 70 to level up in this grueling location. However, for the Holy Warrior, who has been conscripted with the task of vanquishing the Demon Lord, gaining additional prowess even a moment quicker could make a difference. There is no way Naotsugu Toudou can avoid passing through the valley.

The Holy Warrior has been summoned to defeat the Demon Lord Kranos, and she has powerful allies with her: Limis Al Friedia, a mage; Aria Rizas, a sword master; and Glacia, their pet glacial plant. Seeking a new party member—a priest—Toudou and company visited a village named Purif, near the Great Tomb.

There, Toudou met a young girl named Spica Royle, a priest-in-training.

Defeating the Demon Lord

Toudou's party had a noble mission in mind in their search for a new priest. Yet, when Spica learned that their efforts had not borne fruit, she rushed headlong into the Great Tomb all alone in an attempt to train as a priest.

Toudou took on the various ghoulish creatures that ran rampant within the Great Tomb in order to save Spica. After safely rescuing her from danger, the party encountered a priest consumed with his occupation of purging the world of the legions of darkness: Gregorio Legins. Toudou got the idea to ask him to train the party; however, Gregorio's training turned out to be beyond harsh, consisting of endless battle with the undead, hinging on one thing only—divine protection.

Battling the undead in Yutith's Tomb pushed the definition of fearsome to its limit. A massive army of innumerable undead continued to appear, yet Naotsugu Toudou, the Holy Warrior, refused to be frightened. Spica Royle also grew exponentially, and the party managed to complete Gregorio's training.

However, after they finally escaped the tomb unharmed, Gregorio's final test awaited them—to show Gregorio himself their newly honed abilities. Upon learning that Toudou is the Holy Warrior, Gregorio felt it necessary to show her just how it feels to battle a vastly more powerful opponent like the ones she's bound to encounter before long.

Going up against Gregorio, a level-83 priest, was an incredibly trying fight for the far-weaker Toudou, but she managed to put her experience in the Great Tomb to use and show him a sufficient amount of her newfound strength.

Toudou matured even further after battling a much-higher-leveled opponent. She realized the importance of gaining further levels, leading her to choose Golem Valley as the party's next destination.

However, as Toudou and the party prepared to set off on their next journey, Spica came to a sudden decision. She wasn't strong enough to help the party on their quest to vanquish the Demon Lord. She wanted to train further under Gregorio's tutelage.

"The overdone sense of justice is a crime."

Toudou accepted Spica's valiant decision and promised to meet her again before they went their separate ways.

After some time on the road, the party finally reached Golem Valley. No matter what hardships may await, Toudou will not halt her advance. Why, you ask? Because that is proof of a true Holy Warrior's resolve.

Defeating the Demon Lord

Prologue

Thus, the Priest Agonizes

"Uuuuuuuuggghhh, why…why did I ever ask for Stephenne? Whyyyyy?"

We had just arrived at Golem Valley, yet, in my room at the inn, I was already holding my head in my hands. Not because providing support for the Holy Warrior, Naotsugu Toudou, is particularly taxing. It's because the newest party member, who I had specially requested, is already posing a massive threat to our mission.

Stephenne Veronide. As a holy caster who specializes in communication magic, she is extremely talented and will prove highly useful as a supporting member.

In hindsight, I should have expected that she might get lost and be late to join the group.

The previous communication support member assigned to the party, Amelia Nohman, was also extremely talented, and as such, I hadn't anticipated Stephenne to be like this.

In all seriousness—who could've predicted that such an elite holy caster would be so…completely and utterly klutzy?

Mere moments after we arrive in town, Amelia heads off to find Stephenne, looking positively irked as she prepares her tools for communication magic. These items are utterly imperative in order to communicate with the Church headquarters.

The signal immediately picks up, and the line connected by the operator is far more crystal clear and void of distortion than when Stephenne does it.

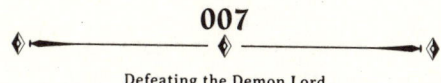

The stern voice of my superior, His Eminence Cardinal Creio Amen, soon resonates deeply from my earring.

"Another problem with the Holy Warrior, Ares?"

"No, it's Stephenne—"

"I have absolutely no intention of hearing any complaints on that matter."

Creio stops me in my tracks before I can even get a word out.

Yeah, I know. This is all my fault. When I asked for Stephenne to be sent our way, Creio initially stopped me, claiming she's a bit of a trouble-maker. Yet, I persisted, saying we needed to test her abilities first.

However, this isn't exactly a vacation for me, either. If it is, this is one messed up vacation.

There were so many things I wanted to say before the transmission got connected, but the only thing I can manage now is "What's…her issue?"

"She's Stephenne Veronide. Ah, Ares, I know what you're trying to say. No need to speak it. She is truly exemplary. Exemplary—but just a touch on the quirky side."

"…Just…a touch?"

I've met my share of mercenaries who had their own idiosyncrasies, and I've obliterated several followers of darkness with more than a few screws loose, but I have no idea if "quirky" indicates whether or not this'll be a piece of cake.

And really, I was prepared to cut her some slack, to an extent. Communication magic is simply that valuable. But really—*to an extent*. I mean, this is in no way normal. She couldn't even walk behind and follow her superior.

Creio's voice shifts in response to my question. His tone is gentle, as if he's giving me a lecture.

"Ares. Stey—oh, that's her nickname—is just a pitiful little girl."

"…Sorry, but that's not quite the answer I was looking for."

"I see. Well then, this will be a long story, but have you heard the surname Veronide before?"

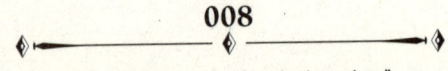

"The overdone sense of justice is a crime."

What the hell? I just said that wasn't the answer I'm looking for, and here you are carrying on!

"Creio, there is only one thing I want to ask. I know you just assigned her to us, and I'm sorry—but she really doesn't seem cut out for this job. I want to send her back. You were right from the beginning, and I understand why you tried to stop me. This is on me. I was in the wrong here, so I'll send her back. That's possible, right?"

Forget lost—I'd rather she wasn't here at all. But I can't just forget about her now that she's scattered to the winds.

I've rambled on in my appeal, but Creio's response is calm.

"Of course that's a possibility, Ares. I had anticipated you'd ask as much."

"Very well. In that case—"

Deal with Stephenne. That's what I thought to say, but then I realize— *Deal with her...how?*

Even if I want to send her back, this region is only inhabited by merchants and mercenaries looking to level up. The unforgiving terrain means that the Church only has a small presence. Giving Stephenne over to them will prove difficult.

"...Can I request someone to come get her?"

"The only person capable of coming to Golem Valley at the moment is...Gregorio. Would that be all right?"

An extreme option—the most extreme of all...

Just what would happen if the most utterly insane man I've ever met were to come into contact with the most troublesome woman I've ever met?

...Wait, wait, wait, wait. Relax. Let's just calm down. I cast tranquility to soothe my muddled thoughts, take a deep breath, and sit down.

First of all—that won't happen. Absolutely not. Okay, I'm calm. I clear my throat and scowl at the door.

"Creio, let's have a productive discussion. Would it be a problem if Stephenne dies?"

"Calm yourself, Ares. It seems you are still upset."

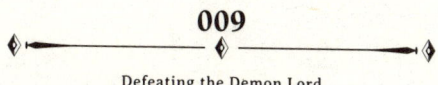

He's right. It's not like her dying would *not* be an issue, and even so, I can't just kill her.

"She had two attendants with her. A man and a woman… Barnard and Vilma. What happened to them?"

"They left Stephenne with me in Purif and ran off in a hurry. Shit—I should've realized then!"

I had no idea. I hadn't even fathomed that such an annoying human being could exist. At this point, I can easily forgive everything Toudou's thrown at me. At least he doesn't go and get himself lost!

"The two of them have looked after Stey since she was a child. You could say they're Stey specialists. When she became the new operator, they had no choice but to look after her then, too."

Creio says this with such indifference. I don't think I've ever heard anything more upsetting in my life.

Getting booted from the party for being a male, learning that Toudou is afraid of the undead—could my luck get any worse lately?

"Give it to me straight, Creio. All I want is to return Stephenne. Amelia's at her wit's end, too."

"Ares Crown—"

In response to my desperate plea, Creio's voice is devoid of emotion, as if he wants to wash his hands of the entire situation.

"I will take her back anytime. If you bring her to the Church head-quarters, that is. I'm very grateful to you, Ares. You have completed all your assignments thus far with the weight of every adverse situation imaginable on your shoulders. I expect nothing less of you this time."

You think I get a kick out of shouldering so much adversity?!

"My head's been hurting a lot lately. My hair might turn gray from all the stress."

"Ha-ha-ha! Nice joke. Your hair is already gray."

"It's…*silver*."

The transmission abruptly cuts out. Just when I thought Toudou was starting to become a bit more manageable, this has to happen. Does God

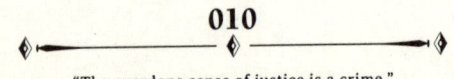

"The overdone sense of justice is a crime."

hate me or something? I mean, I hate God, so on some level, that makes sense.

Just then, I hear someone's exhausted voice from outside the door. I guess…Amelia managed to find her.

"Ares… I'm back."

"Ow, my hand… That hurts—"

It's Amelia and a raven-haired sister whose hand is turning white from being squeezed so hard.

Stephenne Veronide. She's the newest addition to our party…and already nearly dead meat.

Her long black hair accompanies two equally dark eyes. She's two years younger than Amelia and a whole head shorter. She's also maybe just a bit taller than Limis, but her breasts are obviously much larger. Her facial features are sharp, and her black hair and dark eyes are a rarity, so they stick out in a crowd. But what sticks out above all else…is her clothing.

She's wearing a black-toned mage's robe, in a pattern I've never seen before. Her robe is much shorter than Amelia's—practically a miniskirt. Okay, it *is* a miniskirt.

Her pale legs stick out like she's showing them off. If she weren't wearing earrings, the telltale sign of a priest, I wouldn't have believed she actually is one.

Long story short—the newest party member is a piece of work. You could say that I should've kicked her out the second I laid eyes on her, that my sense of impending disaster is lacking—but really, what can I do about it?

She must have realized I was looking—her body stiffens up, but she also smiles, as if trying to entreat me.

"I'm—I'm so sorry. I was following behind Amelia, but before I knew it, she just…disappeared."

No, Amelia didn't disappear. *You* did.

She moves toward me, probably to explain herself. When she realizes her hand is still being squeezed, she looks up at Amelia with doe eyes. Amelia sighs deeply and releases her death grip.

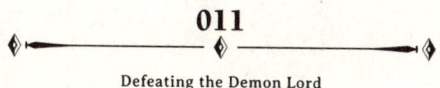

Stephenne perks up noticeably and takes a step toward me—before falling flat on her face. A brilliant swan dive. She didn't slip on the floor or trip on anything in her way. She simply flopped onto the ground with a thunderous crash, without a chance to brace herself whatsoever.

Amelia is silent. Hell, I'm silent, too. Still lying on the floor, Stephenne begins to sob. Her skirt completely flies up, putting her white panties on full display. I look away from the disgraceful sight and speak to Amelia.

"You shouldn't be letting her wear a miniskirt. It's completely inappropriate for a priest, not to mention immodest behavior for any human being."

"It's not like I wanted her to wear one. If it's not this short, she keeps tripping over it and falling."

"She's tripping even in the miniskirt!!"

"She causes trouble the moment you take your eyes off her... Ares, this is all your fault for picking her without consulting me first."

Amelia looks up at me, seemingly irritated.

Yes, it is my fault. In every respect. I should have consulted with you first... So I'm begging you, help me!

Immediately before her arrival, I realized I'd forgotten to tell Amelia about our new recruit. I mentioned it to her casually, and Amelia—whose face is usually expressionless—reacted unexpectedly. Her eyes went wide as saucers. She seemed dazed, not too different from how she looked when we met with Gregorio.

"...Do you know her?"

"...She's my junior. But let's just leave it at that."

She sighed and continued exasperatedly, "There are many things I'd like to say, but first and foremost—Ares, you really are extravagant."

"Extravagant...?"

I must have been visibly flustered by her statement. Amelia heaved another immensely deep sigh and went on.

"What is it about me, Ares? Me, li'l old Amelia, the dynamic, high-level,

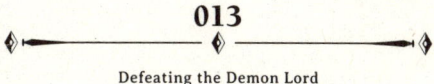

Defeating the Demon Lord

good-natured, charming, cream of the crop among holy casters, the same girl who knows you so well, who you've completely forgotten about, the one who works so hard to assist you. What is it about me that you, Ares, in your infinite knowledge of magic and use of holy techniques, are so dissatisfied with?"

"It's your God-awful sense of humor."

That, and your failure to pick up on the TPO—time, place, and occasion—when things get serious, and how you end up making light of the situation.

Amelia cleared her throat in response and stood up straight, opening her mouth to speak again.

"…Well, let's just leave it at that, Ares."

"Oh, we're leaving things at that, too, are we…?"

Come to think of it—should my subordinate really be the good-natured, charming, li'l old Amelia?

As I pondered the question deeply, Amelia—who knows me so well and is so dynamic—put that dynamism to use and ignored my fretting glance, continuing on.

"Ares, let's pretend for a moment that you never became a crusader—forget about your location and your goals, and all that. You would've attended school, right?"

I suddenly couldn't find my words, and Amelia further elaborated with a stern look on her face.

"Okay, so let's forget the fact that you've got mean eyes and that you're vulgar. You still have the latent potential to rise to the upper echelon of the Out Crusade. You're book-smart and athletic. You're also more or less good with others, and I don't know which one of your parents you look like, but you're not exactly hard on the eyes, either."

"Get to the damn point."

"And, well, it's hard to say whether you would really fit in with your classmates, but people tend to flock to high-class specimens like yourself. Just like they do to me, the charming, good-natured, smart li'l Amelia… Or to Spica, for being, you know, unfortunate."

I wondered if Amelia has a grudge against Spica. Not to mention, she

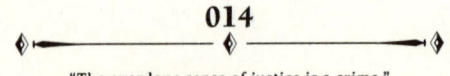

never has anything good to say when she's this talkative. She wouldn't drop the stern face, clear proof that she was trying to read my mind.

"There's a person in the middle of all of it. At a glance, they look extremely accomplished, there's always people around them, they're smart, they're pretty fun to talk to, their quality upbringing is obvious from their choice of words, they're extremely friendly and affable—and as a bonus, they're super easy on the eyes, almost like the kind of character you'd find in a romance novel—"

I didn't see any problem with what she was saying so far.

Amelia seemed to realize that I still didn't understand what was going on. She inhaled sharply and gave it to me straight.

"—the girl with the one fatal flaw... The klutz."

What the hell was she talking about? In moments like this, all I can do is stare at Amelia in shock. When I finally realized that her words held far more meaning than their face value, it was already too late. I've learned two important things from this.

First, before adding someone to the fold, make sure they aren't just skilled, but that they don't have any fatal flaws, either.

Second—I realized that I am indeed indulgent, to the point that me and my lack of satisfaction have to be punished by li'l old Amelia and her disastrous sense of humor.

...Yeesh, Amelia, try a bit harder to stop me next time.

First Report

On the Newest Recruit's Problems and Plans Moving Forward

"This place really feels like a foreign country, don't you think?"

Toudou and her party have arrived in First Town, a small village at the entrance to Golem Valley. It also just happens to be the region's biggest town.

The homes are converted from boulders, which make up for the scarcity of workable land. It's unlike anything Toudou has ever seen before. Nearly everyone in the streets is a mercenary or merchant wielding a sword or staff.

The village itself can be traversed on foot in a matter of hours. After enjoying what the town has to offer, Toudou returns to the inn, a far less classy lodging than anything in the Kingdom's capital. Even so, it has everything a weary traveler needs. The toilet and shower rely on magical implements, and the room's size and amenities are nothing to sneeze at. The doors and furniture are wooden, but the walls and floor are hewn from cream-colored boulders. To Toudou's eyes, it's almost painfully fresh.

Aria lays down her sword and changes out of her armor into casual wear. She notices Toudou's gaze and says, "This place has quite the local flair. Around here, rocks are the only available resources."

"Hmm... I wonder how they make all this?"

"They likely use earth-based elemental spells, I bet. There are...a lot of earth spirits nearby."

Limis takes off her robe and sits on her bed. Her contracted fire spirit, Garnet, nods in agreement from its spot perched atop Limis's head.

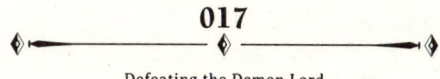

Toudou suddenly closes her eyes upon hearing Limis's explanation. When Naotsugu Toudou was summoned as the Holy Warrior, she received the divine protection of the Three Deities and Eight Spirit Kings along with their associated elements: fire, water, earth, wind, wood, metal, darkness, and light. The divine protection from these sovereign spirits gives her a heightened sense of awareness toward all spiritual beings. If she concentrates hard enough, she can recognize any spiritual power resonating in the area around her.

"Everything's explained by magic, huh?"

"If it wasn't for the spirits around us, the world as we know it would not exist. I can't even imagine the kind of world you came from, Nao."

"We didn't have spirits in my world, but if the miracles of spirits and gods did exist there, maybe it would've turned into a place like this…"

Toudou's words are filled with an indistinct nostalgia. That said, she can't return to her world at this point, so there's no use in wondering *what if*.

Aria notices her expression and attempts to change the topic. "Golems are well-known for their rigid armor. Magic works on them far better than swords do, I've heard."

"Hmm… I can cast a few spells, but not enough to be truly useful."

Two months have passed since the party set out on their journey. Toudou has been fighting with a sword the entire time, but it's not like she's neglected other pertinent skills.

She's learned elemental spells from Limis, and she can also use basic-level holy techniques. However, she's barely had a chance to actually cast anything.

Toudou recites a chant quietly to herself, and a small flame appears on the tip of her finger. It's hardly adequate for real combat, and Limis manages a fatigued smile.

"Hmph. No matter how much divine protection you have, if you don't contract with any spirits, you'll never be able to cast powerful elemental spells."

Toudou becomes sullen. Even after two months, she still hasn't managed to enter a spirit covenant. An elemental spell's power is directly

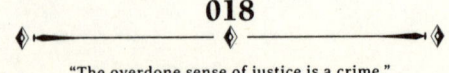

"The overdone sense of justice is a crime."

proportionate to that of the spirit you enter a covenant with. Therefore, one can't afford to simply contract with any old spirit.

"At any rate, we're here to focus on raising our levels. None of us would stand a chance in our current state against a monster as strong as Gregorio. We need to reach level thirty, then our resistance will increase significantly."

Recalling the strong conviction hidden within the face of the young female priest they left in Purif, Toudou responds cheerfully, "…We have to keep up with Spica. Let's work hard to get our level up!"

Toudou's party knows the golems are a handful, but they aren't exactly chumps, either.

She realizes that Limis, who is sitting on the bed, doesn't look like her normal self. Her skin has always been quite pale, but it now has a sickly pallor, and her movements are somehow languid as well.

"? Limis, are you feeling tired?"

"…My body just feels a bit…heavy right now." Limis is always sharp, but her response is listless.

Aria looks at her with concern. "Are you okay? We've really been pushing ourselves lately…"

The Great Forest of the Vale. Battling the undead in Yutith's Tomb. Add to the mix the time they've spent on the road, and the party has barely had time to catch their breath.

"Maybe we should've taken some time to rest."

"Yes, we should have… Mages have comparatively less stamina than the rest of us…"

It's true that Limis's stamina isn't up to par with the party's vanguard.

Limis appears faint as Aria approaches her gently and puts her palm to Limis's forehead.

"…You seem to have a bit of a fever."

"…Should I cast recovery on her?"

"No… This is likely a result of her stamina being simply depleted. She just needs to take a thorough rest."

Toudou stares at Limis with intense worry. She's much smaller than

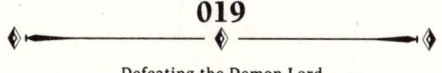

Toudou, yet always tough as nails and full of composure. Right now, she looks utterly helpless.

Limis barely opens her eyes and whispers with a nod, "I'll be fine... I'm just a bit tired."

Her voice is frail and limp. Aria strokes her head with pity and says to Toudou, "Let's keep an eye on her for two or three days. It could just be that she's exhausted. Plus, Limis is the lowest leveled of all of us..."

"Yeah... You're right. I really hope...I get better soon."

Limis's head wobbles as she slowly lies down on the bed. She gropes among the covers on her hands and knees and sinks into them, giving one last glance at Toudou.

Garnet leaps down from Limis's head and curls up near her pillow.

"I'm gonna...sleep."

"Sure... Take it easy. Is there anything you need?"

Limis shakes her head slowly back and forth and closes her eyes.

"I will look after Limis. Nao, please inform the Church that Limis is incapacitated."

"Yes... Understood. I'll see if we can get her a doctor, too."

"Now that I think about it, perhaps we should've done that before we left the village. Let's make sure we get ourselves into top shape here."

Toudou looks down at the small mage who will be relying on them for some time, and then quickly stands up to leave.

§ § §

Before anything else, we need to consider our system moving forward. The three of us gather in a single room of the inn to speak face-to-face.

Up until we reached Purif, Amelia and I had functioned together, joined at the hip. In general, I conducted all the fieldwork, and Amelia was my backup—a relatively flawless setup. But adding any hindrance throws a wrench into all that.

"Amelia, mind if I leave everything with Stephenne to you?"

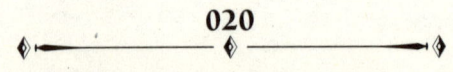

"The overdone sense of justice is a crime."

Amelia is totally silent at my query and looks miffed. Finally, she replies, "......You'll owe me big-time."

"Sir... Um, I mean, Ares... I did actually come here to work, you know— Uh, never mind, forget it."

Stephenne had started to interject, but Amelia shot her down with an icy gaze, and she trailed off.

...Yet, when I think about this rationally, Amelia was completely right. Every single thing about this is all my fault.

"...Stephenne, I have to ask—what is it you're capable of?"

"Ares?!"

Stephenne's eyes widen at my question, and she immediately beams at me.

"Ares, please call me Stey. All my friends do."

"...*Stey*. Just what are you capable of?"

"Ares, you look a bit crazed... Are you all right?"

Cut the chitchat and answer me!

Stey begins to count off the things she can do with a huge smile on her face, practically in singsong.

"I can clean, I can do laundry, and I cook!"

"...Looks like she's got you beat, Amelia."

Except not. That's not the kind of capacity I'm talking about.

The heck? Amelia said the same thing before. Are housework skills really that crucial for holy casters?!

Amelia is glaring at Stey like she's going to strangle her to death. This is bad.

I can't tell if she realizes how Amelia's looking at her or not, but Stey keeps talking with the same dumb smile on her face.

"And also... I can cast most basic holy techniques. You can count on me if you're ever injured!"

"Most... You mean through intermediate level?"

Holy casters are a truly elite breed. A priest who can cast intermediate-level holy techniques is extremely valuable.

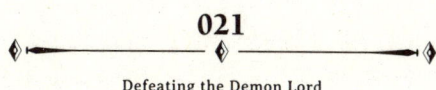

Stey's expression remains interested as she cocks her head to the side like a small animal and says, "? Um, no, I mean advanced level."

"...What the heck, Amelia? She's more talented than you."

"Ares, would you mind keeping the commentary to yourself?"

But, I mean... Seriously. What the heck? Pondering my options, I glance between Amelia and Stey.

Sisters of the faith generally don't lie. That means that Stey, who got lost in five seconds and tripped on absolutely nothing, is an extremely talented cleric. Most likely the top 1 percent.

I scratch my head wildly. I can't believe that Stey being an extremely valuable priest is what's torturing me right now. She smiles like she truly believes in the goodness of this world from the bottom of her heart... Or to put it coldly, she looks like she's got nothing going on upstairs. Maybe that's the kind of thing the God of Order is into?

As I try to convince myself this is all normal, Stey drops an even more explosive bomb.

"Also... Ummm—I'm about level seventy."

"...What?"

Seventy? Did she just say she's level 70?

There is simply no way... Dumbfounded, I put my hand out to touch her head and gauge her level. I can hardly believe my eyes when I catch sight of the amount of life force inside her.

"No goddamn way... Level...seventy-two?!"

Amelia is level 55, so that puts Stey a whole 17 levels above her. A 17-level spread is highly unusual.

More than anything, she's a higher level than can be reached here in Golem Valley. She could probably make it all the way back to Church headquarters herself!

Damn, Amelia—you're losing to your friend Stey on all fronts. And Amelia is definitely a high-class professional herself...

As I remain dumbstruck, Amelia waves a hand in my face and tells me, straight-faced, "Ares, I know what you want to say. That being said... It's impossible."

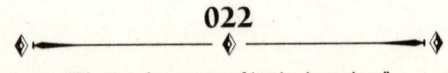

"The overdone sense of justice is a crime."

"And why is that?"

"The only reason Stey's level is so high is because it was determined she'd probably end up dead otherwise."

"I don't...understand this. Seriously, I just don't!"

"You don't have to understand... Just accept it."

What sort of world exists where someone needs to be level 72 just to keep from dying?!

Stey is clearly unperturbed by our frantic back-and-forth as she stares out the window.

...You're telling me this klutz is more than double the level of Toudou, the Holy Warrior?!

"Ares. Take all your expectations—and toss them aside. Don't deem her as capable based on her abilities alone."

"Hey, my expectations are long gone— What do you say we dispatch her to join Toudou and the others?"

"Ares... Do you intend on destroying the Holy Warrior's party?"

"...You're right. Terrible idea."

I should definitely listen to charming, whip-smart, li'l old Amelia.

I heave a sigh and look back to Stey. But she's not there.

"...I see... So this is how she disappeared."

Her need for secrecy must be as high as her level. Without me realizing, she's moved to the window and opened it, gazing down below.

How dare she stand up while I'm talking to her! There's no chance she'd hack it in Toudou's party.

Amelia rushes over to Stey and grabs her by the nape of the neck.

"Eep?! A-Amelia?! Please, I'm not a child!"

Stey struggles against Amelia's grip as she tries explain herself. *So don't act like one, then!*

In all honesty, I can't be bothered to look after her any longer. My job is explicitly limited to supporting Toudou and his party in defeating the Demon Lord.

"Amelia... I'm leaving all matters regarding Stey in your hands. I'm going to focus on the issue of getting Toudou's level up."

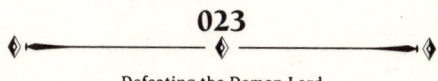

"I have one condition: Buy me a drink soon."

"Ooh... Amelia, I wanna drink, too! I can really hold my liquor, Ares!"

This must be what they mean by "God does not give with both hands." It seems the God of Order has bestowed every gift possible unto Stey but has forgotten one thing, the most critical gift imaginable... Like, order.

Amelia puts her hand to her forehead, a rare gesture for her, and begins to speak in a dark tone. At that very moment, I feel a strong sense of camaraderie with her.

"Ares, you must never give Stey alcohol. One sip and she completely loses it."

Amelia is the same way—absolutely wasted after one sip—so I wonder what she means by "completely loses it." If anything, maybe a good stiff drink would send her around full circle and back to reality. If she could manage that, I have a host of ideas on how to make use of her.

"...Amelia, we haven't seen each other in so long. Don't you think you're being a bit mean? I was really looking forward to this, too."

Stey pleads with Amelia and clings to her tightly, looking up at her with puppy-dog eyes. Calmly, Amelia gives Stey a single command.

"Stey... *Stay*."

"Y-yes, ma'am!" Stey instantly springs upright to attention.

Wait a minute. Is Stey's nickname actually—?

Forget it. Let's just ignore that for now.

I can't think too hard about it, or I might keel over from the stress.

Keeling over after vanquishing the Demon Lord is one thing, but there's no way I'm letting this klutz get the best of me.

Golem Valley is essentially designed for the purpose of leveling up; the elevation is high, and there aren't any other towns nearby. The valley is within the realm of the Kingdom of Ruxe, but it's a remote region, and the royal household hardly meddles in affairs here, although it's within reach of their sovereignty.

The townspeople around here change drastically every few years for this reason. Mercenaries and monster hunters don't settle down in

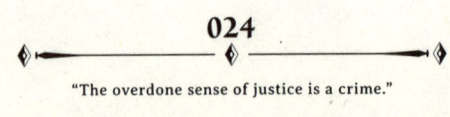

"The overdone sense of justice is a crime."

one place anyway, and anyone sent to this harsh terrain on assignment to manage the town comes begrudgingly. There's a constant flux of people—I hardly recognize anyone still here from when I last came to level up.

The only things that haven't changed are the town's layout and the priests who oversee the local churches. I head for the only church in First Town in order to formulate a plan.

My mission to support the Holy Warrior from the shadows is a top secret one. Nobody can learn of my actions, and the Church is one of my few allies along the way. The father who supervises Purif's churches is just your run-of-the-mill aged cleric, but the priest in charge of the churches here in Golem Valley is an esteemed woman well-known throughout the entire Church. In a sense, she's a bit like Golem Valley's elder.

I'm here to review the state of affairs, replenish supplies, and potentially communicate information to Toudou's party through the Church. I require nothing else.

I need to remain vigilant regarding any demon movements. This region is famous for leveling up. In the Great Forest of the Vale, a similar area, fearsome followers of darkness laid a trap for the Holy Warrior. If the same demons have extended their reach to Golem Valley, it would come as no shock to receive word of abnormal disturbances here, too.

Mercenaries and monster hunters are by nature the most perceptive about such information. However, I've decided to head for the local church instead, as Golem Valley's lead cleric is one of the few veterans around here.

She had already been in charge for more than twenty years by the time I first visited Golem Valley. She's watched over this place for longer than anyone else in history, and her presence alone is enough to loosen the lips of any mercenary or hunter.

The church is located in the town center, next to the headman's estate. It's a relatively small building compared to that of the Vale Village, but the front doors are wide open, with merchants, priests, and wounded hunters lined up at the entrance.

I know the ropes around here. I shoot a sidelong glance at the crowd gathered at the front and head around to the back door. It's unlocked, and when I step inside, I'm greeted with a familiar scene that's remained unchanged for the past several years.

The cramped study contains a few bookshelves, a dirty wooden desk and chair, and, quite unnecessarily, a bed and sofa. A large man is crouching with his back to me, casually pulling books from one of the shelves.

He must have heard the door open, as he suddenly turns back to look at me. Everything in here looks pitifully tiny next to him. Actually, everything in here really *is* tiny. Even crouched down, his head is well above the bookshelves.

He wears a gray robe that covers his entire body. His shoulders are twice as wide as mine, and he's almost double my height. Even among the legendary mercenaries of yore, there are few human beings who meet his incredible stature.

His arms and crossed legs are thick like tree trunks. Even completely still, it's not hard to imagine the incredible power he possesses. He doesn't look like a priest at first glance; his head is massive in comparison with his body, his dark brown hair cropped close. The earrings hanging from his ears show his rank.

It's been a while since I last saw my friend, the half giant Wurtz Beld. I immediately state my purpose.

"Wurtz, long time no see. I have something to discuss with the madam. Take me to her."

"Ares… I see. So it's true— You're the one in charge of *that* mission."

Wurtz's brown eyes widen in surprise, his voice sonorous even at a whisper.

Carina Capp—that's the sixty-something-year-old sister who still oversees the churches in this region. In fact, she's renowned as the warden of every church in all five of Golem Valley's villages. She was assigned to this area at the very beginning, back when there was only one church here, and has continued to maintain this house of worship as

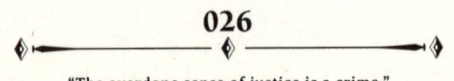

"The overdone sense of justice is a crime."

a sanctuary to all mercenaries who enter. The local inhabitants refer to her respectfully as "Madam Carina" or simply "madam."

Though mercenaries flock to Golem Valley to raise their level, it's also part of the Ruxe royal knights' curriculum for leveling up. For this reason, Madam Carina's influence within the Kingdom of Ruxe cannot be overstated.

The madam looks exactly the same as the last time I saw her a few years ago.

She is both wide and tall in stature, bearing the number of wrinkles you'd expect from a woman of her age. I would be hard-pressed to say her expression is soft, yet her large eyes shine amid the wrinkles, emitting a powerful life force. She doesn't have a single gray hair in her vibrant purple mane, and earrings that indicate the same episcopal level as myself hang from her ears. Truthfully, she looks more like a witch than a priest.

She has refused orders of promotion to the Church headquarters on multiple occasions, instead choosing to remain on the front lines—the "Great Mother."

I approach the madam and stop about one meter in front of her. She looks down at me with the utterly nostalgic, slightly intimidating glance I know well.

"Madam, please forgive me for intruding. I presume you've received word from His Eminence, but I'm here regarding the same matter."

Madam Carina most certainly knows about the Holy Warrior. At any rate, I'll need her help before I get started on anything around here. She remains silent until I finish speaking and then twists her lips into a wry smile.

"Heh-heh-heh. You haven't changed, young Ares. Not so much as a greeting, eh? Of course I've heard the rumors. Apparently, you've been doing incredibly well. That boy I once knew—I hear they now call him Ex Deus. Is that so?"

Her dry old voice rocks my brain—a voice that can only be taken for malice upon first meeting. Most are completely helpless at the sound of it. I smile at the madam and shrug my shoulders.

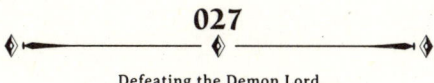

"All thanks to you, Madam. And that nickname of mine isn't something I came up with myself."

"Heh-heh-heh. You've also attained the gift of gab, I see. Though you haven't shown your face here even once ever since."

The madam puts her palm to her lips and stifles a laugh. There isn't a hint of concealed rage beneath her soft expression.

Madam Carina looks intimidating, but she's a genuine intellectual. It would normally be presumptuous for me to evaluate a priest who is far more experienced than myself, but that is simply how well I know her. I get to my point without hesitating.

"I do apologize for that, Madam... However, I would still appreciate your assistance."

She slaps the armrest of her chair and cackles in response.

"Always the workaholic, eh? Heh-heh-heh... Quite remarkable that you would come through my doors yet again, already in need of this old woman's help... God certainly works in mysterious ways."

She couldn't be more correct. In this age of all-out demonic warfare, warriors are not guaranteed to live long based on their prowess alone. Crusaders have a particularly high mortality rate. The madam said that I haven't come back to see her once, but when I last left this place after leveling up, I told her my good-byes.

Surely, meeting again under these circumstances is adverse fortune.

But what of it? I'll take advantage of any situation thrown at me, whether curious fate, or adversity, or whatever comes my way. As the madam continues to grin, I dive right into my plan to beef up Toudou and his party.

After going over the fine details with Madam Carina, I receive word that Toudou has contacted the Church. It's already dusk by the time I return to the inn.

The madam has agreed to help me, so I'm feeling pretty good. I call on Amelia and Stey from the next room and commence a strategy

028

meeting. Amelia looks exhausted, quite unlike her usual self, probably because I asked her to train Stey.

"Limis is incapacitated, I'm told."

"...What? Is she okay?"

"It's likely exhaustion—the party will keep a close eye on her. The long journey has worn her out, I expect. It's very common."

Golem Valley is prone to inclement weather. Due to the high elevation, the air is thin and the temperature low. There is no shortage of people who fall ill here.

"I'm concerned, too, but this gives us a window to reposition ourselves."

There are so many things that still need doing. I spoke with the madam about raising Toudou's party's battle prowess, and I've also asked her to check if any strange occurrences have reared their heads recently in Golem Valley.

This bit of downtime is a blessing from the heavens. Now's the time to tackle a number of the problems we've been putting off.

"Amelia, I need to speak to Glacia. Call her over for me."

"...Do you plan to dispose of her?"

"No. That's my last resort. Though if Spica had joined the party, I might've had to."

Glacia, a demi-dragon, had been lured into the Great Forest of the Vale by some demonic force when we encountered her. She's an evolved glacial plant, currently taking human form as a member of Toudou's party. This girl, with her dark-green eyes and hair, is one seed of worry at our current juncture.

Dragons, by nature, are incompatible with humans. Glacia probably never should have joined Toudou's party, but the situation wouldn't allow otherwise. It's extremely difficult to manipulate someone who functions of their own selfish accord from the shadows. Gathering information on them and guiding their actions always requires some manner of coconspirator. At the moment, Glacia is responsible for communicating

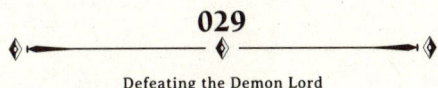

information from within the party, using the same communication magic that Amelia wields on a regular basis. I can't simply get rid of her without an adequate replacement.

"I was just thinking it's time I had a good, long talk with her for once."

It has already been two months since Glacia wormed her way into Toudou's party. Ever since, her stance hasn't changed at all: She obeys orders but doesn't do much else.

From Toudou's group's perspective, they're taking care of a pet that eats its weight in food every meal and doesn't contribute a damn thing, but none of them have ever raised a single complaint. If I was in their party, I'd have kicked her out a long time ago.

While Amelia reaches out to Glacia, I stay busy preparing. I put on a brown overcoat over my mage's robe but leave my mace at home—it sticks out like a sore thumb. Glacia's resistances have dropped significantly since she transformed from a dragon to a human. Using a mace could kill her.

Instead, I put on a pair of thin gloves. My fists alone should be enough to deal with her.

The reason Glacia is on such a tight leash is because of the terror I instilled in her after beating her half to death. However, fear that has been ingrained into someone once will eventually lessen with time. Taking that into account, this is an opportunity to improve her position on things.

"We don't want Toudou following after her, that'd just be a nuisance. Tell Glacia to go to the watchtower."

Violence is a last resort, it pains me to admit. That said, I won't let personal feelings get in my way of executing a mission.

Just then, Stey, who has been entirely silent, raises her hand timidly. Her skin is lily white, and dark circles have formed below her jet-black eyes. Looks like she was up all night being harangued by Amelia.

"Ummm... Ares... What should I do...?"

"The overdone sense of justice is a crime."

"Nothing. Stey, you'll be on standby here at the inn. Standby. Here. With Amelia."

No matter what she does, her klutziness will bring her down. According to Amelia, who I've known for a while now, Stey requires an attendant at all times. Two, if possible, but that would leave us without anyone to cover ground. At this point, she's pushing the limits of klutziness.

When I give Stey her orders, she pouts and folds her hands together timidly.

"...It's just... I was asked to come all this way for work..."

"Stey, what is it you can do for us?"

"I can clean, do laundry, and cook—leave it to me!"

I already heard that yesterday. We can't afford to send her out somewhere. Besides, she's already extremely ostentatious as is. Depending on the situation, she might just cause people to lose their faith in the Church, and that would only adversely affect her, too.

I've come up with the perfect orders for her. "Okay, Stey. I have a job for you."

"O-okay! What is it...?"

With a steely expression, Stey audibly swallows the lump in her throat. She's a knockout in the looks department, and her eyes resonate sincerity. From her appearance, one would swear she's completely capable. It's exactly as Amelia said. On the outside, she looks like a really hard worker.

Between her and Glacia, why does the world have to be so against me? I close my eyes and sigh deeply before giving Stey her command.

"Make us some tea. Cooking's one of your specialities, right?"

"...Is that all? I mean, that'll only take a second."

"After that... Do the laundry. Wash my spare robe, and your own clothes, and Amelia's."

Stey begins to squirm impatiently and asks with pleading eyes, "A-and... When that's all finished?"

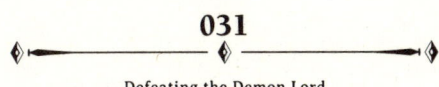

Defeating the Demon Lord

I've already decided. I put on the most serious expression I can muster and point at the floor.

"Clean this room."

"…"

Stey looks at me, completely disgruntled. *I thought you said you were good at those three things?*

She is exceptionally talented. The fact that neither Amelia nor myself can do any of those three things only makes it more so.

"Stey, these are important tasks. This is work neither I nor Amelia are capable of—only you."

"? R-really?"

"Yes, really. I've called upon you specifically for these three crucial tasks. Do you understand?"

Yeah, right, I quip to myself, but the disappointment has already vanished from her face. Stey's eyes light up as she tries to pull herself together before giving an unnatural bow.

"Understood. I will gladly accept your command."

Damn, she actually bought it… This can't be good.

Can brewing a pot of tea really be considered cooking? At any rate, Stey makes me a proper cup with a skilled hand.

Maybe she was actually serious when she said she's good at chores? I'm pretty sure there are a lot of other things she should be working on instead, however.

"Ares, I've reached out to Glacia, so please head over to meet her."

"Got it… Look after Stey."

"…Yes. Be careful."

That's what I should be saying! I start to tell her as much, when Stey lets out a little yelp.

"A-Ares… Oh!"

Stey, carrying a full tea set on a tray, trips over absolutely nothing. This is the second time I've witnessed this same scene in as many days.

The tray and tea set hurtle through the air. The teapot doesn't have

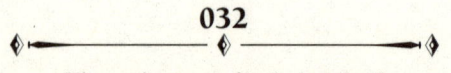

wings, but it comes flying toward Amelia and I, sending a shower of freshly boiled tea our way.

Without saying a word, I grab Amelia, who's gone completely stiff, by the shoulder, spinning her to the side in an instant to avoid the deluge. The teapot and cups fall to the ground with a clamor.

Having completely lost her balance, Stey spins in place a few times before falling right on top of them. As I take in the scene around me, I feel neither contempt nor anger nor compassion. I simply acquiesce.

"I see... So she can't even make a pot of tea without falling over, huh?"

Flustered, Amelia stammers in an attempt to explain on Stey's behalf, "Um... Well... Yes, that's exactly it. Well, n-no, sometimes she makes it all the way..."

And she's *level 72*. This chick's gotta be cursed.

"Take care of Stey and clean this up."

"...Understood."

I let go of Amelia and give her a pat on her delicate back, as if to say thank you.

Stey is crying and sniffling just like she was yesterday. I'm going to keep count of every klutzy action of hers and report my findings to Creio.

Human beings are a species of adaptation. The person I was in the Great Forest of the Vale is a completely different entity from who I am right now. It's only been two months since I was assigned to this role, but I've managed to overcome even Gregorio Legins himself.

Now, I feel like I can approach issues more graciously. Compared to Gregorio, Glacia should be a walk in the park. The moment I arrive at the watchtower, Glacia turns to face me from her position leaning against a railing.

There is still considerable distance between us, which tells me that her sense of perception has not dulled—she's as sharp as ever. Glacia looks stiff as a board, and the way her pupils contract shows just how frightened she is.

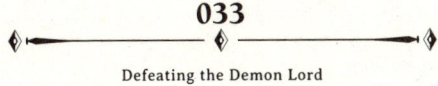

Her current form is eerily humanlike. At a glance, you wouldn't take her for more than a child. What sort of fearsome menace could be created if a demon with malice toward humankind transformed into a similarly accurate human form?

There isn't any sign of Toudou. I walk up to Glacia quickly.

"Sorry to keep you."

Glacia's entire body shakes at the sound of my voice, and her lips tremble as she speaks.

"I haven't been…waiting."

"I see. Let's go somewhere else."

"…"

It seems she's still terrified of me. This should make for quick conversation.

Glacia nods, and I take her hand, cutting off the glance she casts my way as I start walking.

We need a place where we can take our time and chat. If words alone are effective, I'm happy to reach a mutual understanding diplomatically. I'm a human being, after all.

As we walk slowly, Glacia's hand suddenly stiffens. She stops and turns around, gazing into the distance. When she notices I've stopped, too, she turns her snow-white face toward me again.

She'd been looking toward a food cart stopped on the side of the street selling grilled skewers. A delicious, hunger-inducing aroma wafts toward us.

"…I see. You must be hungry, eh?"

"N-no…"

"Come to think of it, I hear you pester Toudou for food all the time."

Glacia opens her eyes wide as saucers and shakes her head violently. Yet, contrary to her actions, her stomach audibly rumbles. There must be a trace of her massive dragon stomach alive in there somewhere.

It's crazy to think that her tiny body could retain such a large appetite but… Hmph. I nod to her and ask, "Why not? You deserve some compensation for your work, right? How many do you want?"

Wow, I've really gone soft. Glacia looks up at me, wide-eyed with surprise.

I am a priest; I'm no monster. The only reason I left Glacia half-dead in the Forest of the Vale is because I had no other choice… I'll do anything necessary with good reason; otherwise, I will refrain. For better or worse, this is all a matter of business.

"C'mon, the least I can do is feed you. How many?"

In response, Glacia tightens her lips and instead looks suspiciously at me. I guess fearing me this much creates some problems of its own.

"Out with it. Time's a-wastin'."

"…A hundred," she whispers back.

A hundred. *A hundred.* The cart doesn't even have enough skewers to begin with, but first of all…

"Hey, Glacia. Don't you think sticking a hundred skewers in your body would hurt just a little bit, even for you?"

"?!"

"Two in your eyes. Two in your nostrils. Two in your ears, and one in each finger and toe makes twenty more… Think you could make it to a hundred? Hey… Don't worry about it, the wounds won't be permanent. I can cast however many holy techniques necessary—I'm among the Church's top class in that respect."

"…!"

Glacia finally breaks and now looks about ready to burst into tears.

Her entire body, including arms and legs, shakes uncontrollably. After staring into her eyes for some time, I notice an odd smell. The ground is wet when I look down; a small puddle has gathered there between her legs.

Smiling, I clap the trembling Glacia on the shoulder without giving her a chance to look down for herself.

"It's a joke, Glacia! Sure, I dole out punishment, but I don't resort to violence without any rhyme or reason. That's a waste of effort."

Violence can be pretty addicting, and it'll eat up your stamina. But I'm a priest, and I remonstrate such ideals.

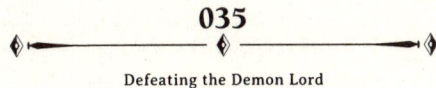

Glacia looks up at me with tears in her eyes, and I whisper once more, "Okay, Glacia. I'll ask you one last time. How many do you want?"

"Go on, dig in."

"…Okay."

We enter a local café. I watch Glacia sit down before shoving the skewers of meat toward her.

Glacia chomps onto one like someone's threatening to take it away. First order of business is to give the informant her reward. I'm such an excellent boss.

Glacia tears into the skewers ravenously and devours the first in seconds. She now has a bit of sauce on her cheek. I hold the remaining nine skewers in my hand, but I'm not hungry, so they're all for Glacia.

With a death grip on her now empty first skewer, she says, "…I ate it."

"Number two, then."

"?! …Okay."

I hand Glacia skewer number two. Her eyes grow huge for a second, but she soon starts eating.

I have no intent to harm her, but she won't stop moving around as she eats. Three, then four—before long, I'm just holding empty skewers. They're made of hard yet supple bamboo, but above all else, they're cheap, and you can fit a lot of them in one hand.

I fiddle with one of the skewers, bits of meat still clinging to it, and ask, "Were they good?"

"…Yes."

That means…it was worth spending money to keep her placated.

Yet, Glacia remains timid and silent, averting her gaze. I haven't scolded her or punished her, but as I watch her in silence, her face pales even further. She opens her mouth a few times but quickly snaps it shut after I shoot her a glare.

The hands on the clock tower are ticking away the time. I wait until the minute hand reaches a quarter of the way around the clock face

before finally opening my mouth to speak. The steam on our cups of tea, which I ordered when we arrived, has long dissipated.

"Have you rested long enough after your big meal?"

Glacia nods with unexpected enthusiasm in response. In that case, I'll get right down to business. I take a skewer and grip the pointed end with my finger, testing its flexibility. I can feel Glacia's eyes on me.

"Are you full?"

"...Y-yes."

"I see. That's good."

I grip the skewer with my other hand and suddenly smash the pointed tip into the table. The bamboo skewer pushes almost halfway through the hard wood. Glacia cries out softly.

"Glacia. This meal was...payment."

"Pay...ment?"

"That's right. Payment for your work up until now. And, it's prepayment for any work that you do from now on."

As she stares back at me fearfully, I calmly and carefully explain things to her, a demi-dragon born and raised in a culture completely different from that of humankind. She may look like a human being, but she's not. Asking her to be autonomous would be a mistake.

Glacia did nothing when Gregorio attacked Toudou, but I can't blame her for that. However, moving forward, the battles the party is bound to face will only heighten in intensity. Toudou and the others are still weak. There's a definite possibility that my support won't reach them in time. In crises like that, the only person who can help them is Glacia, but she's not pulling her weight.

I have no intention of shoving common sense down a dragon's throat. Thankfully, I know just how to negotiate in these kinds of situations.

"Until now, you've been working without payment. Of course, I think saving your life is an irreplaceable form of compensation, but it's not enough. Right?"

If I'm wrong, then why else would she be telling us "I'm hungry" over and over again?

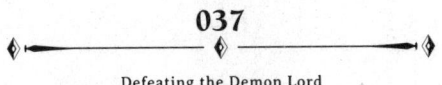

"N-no… Well…"

Glacia shakes her head back and forth. We appear to have piqued the other patrons' curiosity, as they keep peering over at our table, so I take a moment to glare daggers at them so they'll back off.

I continue speaking to Glacia, who looks like she's just witnessed the apocalypse unfold right in front of her.

"That's why I decided to give you this payment. And you accepted it. In other words, when your next task arises, you have to produce results that are equal to that payment."'

"…"

In all reality, Glacia's position is entirely enviable. At the moment, all I'm asking of her are regular updates on Toudou's party, though she is capable of much more. What's more, the accuracy of her updates is all over the board.

Up to this point, I've only ever requested intel from Glacia, so I forgive her for not doing more. It's all water under the bridge. That said, I can't afford her taking advantage of me. She needs to understand her position as we move forward. She needs to make the messages she sends my way as clear as possible.

At times, she'll need to move of her own volition and collect information proactively. If the situation demands it, she'll need to enter battle on Toudou's behalf, and in the worse case, she'll need to lay down her life for him.

I pick up another skewer and point the sharp end at Glacia, and she shoots bolt upright in her seat.

"Glacia, look at this skewer. This is the remnant of the prepayment that you received for your work. By itself, it's just a piece of garbage, but I don't waste anything—not even garbage. Do you know what I'm gonna use it for?"

Glacia shakes her head furiously. Terrified, she replies, "…I d-don't wanna know."

"Too bad. You *need* to know, Glacia."

"The overdone sense of justice is a crime."

I stand the bamboo skewer on end and explain, with the sharp end pointed at the ceiling.

"This skewer is punishment. Glacia, you've received prepayment for your work from this point forward, but even if you don't produce results, I can't get the meat from these skewers back from you. Because you devoured them."

Before I realize it, Glacia is again shedding tears from her emerald-colored eyes. I pay it no mind and continue.

"So I'm gonna use these skewers as punishment. I paid for your services. You received the payment, which naturally entails responsibility on your end to produce results. If you fail to meet my expectations, then—"

I roll the skewer in my fingers and point the sharp end directly at Glacia's eye.

"I will skewer these into you. One. By. One."

"?!"

I can hear Glacia's heart thumping in her chest from across the table. The throbbing rhythm resonates like the early morning church bell, only it indicates nothing but fear. Glacia's eyes move to the ten skewers I hold in my hand. I continue to hammer my point home.

"Listen, Glacia. These are bamboo. Bamboo skewers. You're a demi-dragon. At worst, a metal sword wouldn't be able land a dent in you. So I wonder, Glacia—you think these skewers could pierce your skin as it is now?"

"…"

Glacia swallows the lump in her throat and her eyes bulge. She's probably thinking hard about what I said.

I still remember our battle in the Great Forest of the Vale very well. Her defenses are incredibly tough.

After about one minute passes, Glacia's expression relaxes slightly. She must have reached a conclusion. I immediately swing one of the bamboo skewers, the sharp end barely visible thanks to my level-93 prowess.

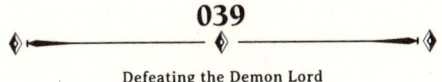

"?!"

Glacia's eyes are wide as saucers, and her just-relaxed cheeks stiffen once more. She slowly puts her hand to her cheek, and one of her pale fingers comes back stained with red. Dragons have an extremely high recovery rate; a small scratch will heal in no time. I show her the bamboo skewer tip—there isn't even a drop of blood on it—and smile softly.

"......Okay, now that I have your answer... Let's get to the main point."

"...O-okay..."

Glacia must finally get the picture, as she answers through gritted teeth.

Apprehension and preparedness. These are what Glacia is missing. Leave it to me—I'll make sure she understands the grave nature of our mission.

Having finished my negotiations with Glacia, I return to the inn to see a haggard-looking Amelia in a hunched-over position, along with a panicked Stey. I take a brief glance around the room. It's in rough shape: The table has been flipped over, the bed stripped bare, and the sheets lie in a rumpled pile on the floor. There are cracks in both the windows and the light fixtures, and an overturned basket sits among the shattered remains of a teacup... What the hell?

"...I have to ask: Did a war break out in here or something?"

Amelia turns her face toward me and smiles with exhaustion.

"...That's one way to put it, I suppose."

I don't recall asking for a snappy comeback.

Stey looks toward me with a bright sparkle in her eye, as if she's found a clue to solving our current predicament. That sparkle is probably the most that's happening in that head of hers.

"N-no, Ares. This is... I was just cleaning up, and—"

I get it. You don't have to say anything. It's all my fault.

If you think about it logically, Stey couldn't even carry a tray of tea without falling. How could she possibly clean up anything?

My expectations for Stey now further lowered, I make a mental note to place klutzes within my top-three most-hated things in the entire

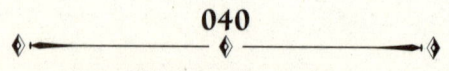

"The overdone sense of justice is a crime."

world. Just then, she tries approaching me to explain further, and I mimic Amelia by yelling, "Stey— *Stay!*"

"Yessiiiiir!"

In what seems like a conditioned response, Stey immediately straightens herself up on the spot, her expression frozen. Upon careful inspection, I realize that she's soaked from head to toe like someone threw a bucket of water on her. Every curve of her body is clearly visible through her drenched clothing. How in the hell does this sort of thing even happen?

I walk past the stock-still Stey and sit down on my bed.

"Whoever trained Stey to do that is a genius."

At any rate, we should be able to reduce the average number of times she trips and falls using this command. Really, the fact that she's been trained this well so far is mind-blowing. I have nothing but profound respect for the marvelous progenitor who made it all possible. There's gotta be a way to teach her more commands!

Stey scratches her cheek bashfully.

"Oh... Eh-heh-heh... W-well, I'm not *that* much of a—"

That wasn't a compliment. Even dogs know stay!

As Stey remains standing straight at attention, I thrust my finger at her and make an announcement. If I don't make things blatantly obvious, she'll probably end up making the wrong decisions.

"I'd been highly considering turning you over to Gregorio, but that would be unfair to poor Spica, so I won't!"

"Th-thank you very...much?"

She truly has no idea what I just said. Her head is cocked askance.

Amelia is unusually disheartened and looks slightly ill. I give her a directive.

"All right, Amelia. We'll have our meeting in your room. I'll book a new room, and any damages from this one will come out of Stey's pay. I don't even want to know what happened here, so don't include this in your report. Any questions?"

Amelia stands up shakily at my instructions. Stey raises her hand ever so slightly.

041

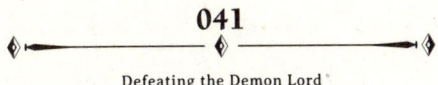

"Um... But I'm not receiving any payment..."

"...Noted. Anyway, I don't know why you're sopping wet, but please, before anything else, change your clothes."

"Oh... Y-yes, sir. I'll change right away!"

Stey's only strong point is in her responses. The next second, Amelia's face instantly regains its color and she jumps toward Stey, grabbing her arm.

I see what's happening. Stey was seconds from taking her clothes off right here and now. Even though Amelia stopped her, Stey looks completely oblivious as she blinks repeatedly.

Now my head hurts, but for a different reason than usual... I sigh and say to Amelia, "Li'l old charming, loyal Amelia, please help this girl get changed."

"...Understood."

There's no way I can entrust Stey to the madam. She's simply too much of a pain.

"Toudou's party's target level to reach in Golem Valley will be sixty."

"...That's over twice their current average level..."

Having finished getting Stey into new clothes and relaxed significantly, Amelia looks at me wide-eyed, yet calmly.

"Yes. Of course, that's provided nothing particular goes wrong, but keep in mind that Golem Valley is by far the most efficient place for leveling up in all of the Kingdom of Ruxe."

Monsters in this area have high life force, and they don't use the particularly troublesome attacks that cause status ailments, making them easy to fight. The environment is extremely harsh, but that in and of itself makes for excellent conditioning. Golem Valley is the final training grounds for the Kingdom's royal knights. For that reason, if you can make it through this area, you're essentially qualified to protect the Kingdom.

"What was the average level acquired here again?"

"Reaching level sixty shouldn't take long. If you push yourself, you can reach about sixty-five."

Sticking it out even longer leads some all the way to level 70, but it's not very realistic or efficient in terms of time.

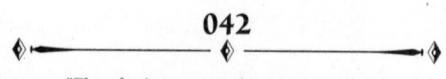

"The overdone sense of justice is a crime."

Amelia cocks her head to the side and looks up at me.

"Can I raise my level here while we're at it?"

Amelia is level 55. Golem Valley is a fine place in terms of leveling up, but it doesn't match up well for her. In order for Amelia to raise her level, she'd need to kill golems by herself, but they're incredibly troublesome opponents for priests.

Blunt-force weapons are effective against them, but Amelia can't generate destructive force with her frail arms.

Her face remains calm. She's got bona fide talent as a priest, but I've never taken her for the battle-proficient type.

"Can you swing a mace?"

"...Most likely not."

"Can you cast any attack magic?"

"...Nothing that will damage a golem."

In that case, there's no other option than for me to bring a golem near death and let Amelia land the final blows. A golem's weak point is the core hidden in the center of its tough, armored skin. The core isn't particularly hard, so if we can break down their armor and render them immobile, it would be easy for Amelia to kill them, too, but that demands a lot of time and man power. Plus, we would need to repeat this process with many, many golems.

"...It'll all depend on Toudou, then. If we have some leeway, we'll work on your level a bit, too."

I would like to raise Amelia's level, and this is not the last place we will raise Toudou's. I don't intend to put Amelia in the vanguard to bear the full brunt of any hostilities, but I need her level to be high, or I'll have concerns when it's crunch time.

Amelia nods slightly. Sitting in a chair next to her and holding her knees, Stey raises her hand again. She has changed out of her soaking wet robe into an indigo dress—one of Amelia's, judging by how off the sizing is. Apparently, Stey had just washed all her other spare robes and didn't have anything to change into.

I did order her to do the laundry, but why would she wash clothes

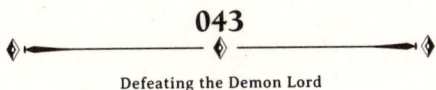

she hasn't worn yet? Damn, is she only capable of following *exact* orders, to the letter?

She's quite smaller than Amelia, and the dress is baggy on her. The chest, however, is overly tight. Stey doesn't seem to mind, as she plays with the sleeves and cocks her head to the side.

"Ares, my level is—"

"...Seventy-two is plenty high. If anything, I wish you could spare a few and share them with Amelia."

Her level is a complete waste of experience. It'd really be great if they could actually switch.

Stey's eyes widen in response, then beams and pokes Amelia in the arm.

"Hey, Amelia, should I give you some of my levels?"

"...And how would you do that?"

Techniques to split life force or experience do not exist. How the hell does she plan to do it?

Stey takes a moment to think up a response to Amelia's question before clapping her hands together softly and chuckling shyly.

"Oh... You're right. Levels can't be divided up, can they? Ha-ha!"

"...Amelia, she's messing with us."

"...Sorry to break it to you, but she's completely earnest."

Amelia doesn't look angry at all and simply sighs. I can see she's clearly used to this.

It really is a shame, though. I'm particularly disappointed that I have no idea how to make use of Stey. The only thing I was after was a low-level, agreeable new intern who could use communication magic...

In that moment, I realize something and look at Stey. She tends to suck the oxygen out of the room, so I'm forgetting the most crucial aspect of her being here.

"...By the way... Can you even use communication magic?"

"? Of course I can, but—?"

Stey looks at me in befuddlement with her dark eyes—just a hair

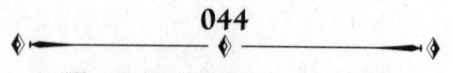

"The overdone sense of justice is a crime."

darker than Toudou's. The entire reason I requested Stey was because I need a party member who can use communication magic. Up until now, I couldn't contact Amelia from my end whenever she and I split up, but with Stey, that will change. This is a huge merit to her existence. I have a bad habit of focusing on the risks over the rewards.

"I see... You might be crazy, but at least you know the basics."

"Hee-hee... I get that a lot."

If that's the case, although I intended to have Amelia keep an eye on Stey, it looks like I'll be pairing up with her after all. I ruminate while looking at Amelia. At the least, she won't go off and get herself lost.

I expect I'll be suffering a heavy dose of mental exhaustion, so I just won't think of Stey as a human—I'll think of her as a communication device. That solves it.

Amelia is staring at Stey, wondering just what she finds so fun about all this, when she says with disappointment, "I have a feeling that this will end up very uncomfortable for me."

Now the real issue at hand is how to keep this ditz in tow.

...I'm thinking a collar and leash.

Should I treat this issue in terms of efficiency or morality? As I seriously ponder the question, the ditz in question playfully teases Amelia, who's wavering on the spot.

§ § §

In reality, Amelia Nohman doesn't actually hate Stephenne Veronide. Stephenne is quite genial, and Amelia isn't so cold that she would turn away someone who so continually fawns over her.

Above all else, Stey has something that Amelia doesn't: a bubbly personality and natural sociability. These traits set a perfect example for Amelia, who has never been good at expressing her emotions. In fact, Amelia has already learned a thing or two from watching Stephenne. But that's not to say that Stephenne is the sort of person suited for vanquishing the Demon Lord.

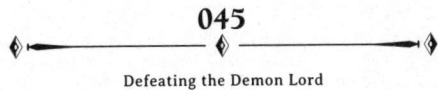

045

Amelia speaks to Creio via transmission as she watches Stephenne sleep soundly.

"Creio, are you planning on killing her?"

"She won't die. Amelia, Stey is highly capable. She is high level, her holy techniques are powerful, and she can even cast magic. The Church is certainly a wide-ranging organization, but you won't find anyone else like her."

His Eminence's voice is the same as always, even in the middle of the night.

Amelia knows Stey is capable, yet, she clicks her tongue softly before asking, "What about her character?"

"…Amelia, this was Ares's decision. I gave him thorough warning myself."

Amelia hadn't the slightest idea what Ares meant when she first heard him talking about a "new member." As far as she's concerned, there isn't anyone on earth less qualified for this position. She's heard all the particulars, but thinking about it logically, this couldn't be more of a mess.

Sure, holy casters are valuable, but there are plenty of holy casters in existence. How is it that out of all those people, it was Stey who got picked to be Ares's operator and sent all the way to Golem Valley?

"…Creio… You did this on purpose, didn't you?"

"I don't understand what you're getting at."

"It's rather obvious if you take Ares's personality into account, including the reason he asked for another communication magic user, and the fact that Stey had the highest potential to be chosen as an operator candidate. Quite frankly, there are a number of more suitable holy casters that you could have chosen."

Amelia makes a fairly plausible point, and her boss remains silent for a moment before responding.

"…Amelia, you may not be aware of this, but—Stey has something that Ares needs."

Something he needs… Like the ability to relieve stress?

"…Perhaps, but she also has plenty of things that he doesn't need."

"The overdone sense of justice is a crime."

"May you receive Ahz Gried's blessings, Amelia."

Creio's harsh tone is the last thing Amelia hears before the transmission is cut. In spite of his supplication, the only thing Amelia feels welling inside of her is an intangible black mass of emotion. It's something close to murderous rage, she realizes as she pushes it down. Just then, a dark shadow rises from the bed in front of her.

Stey is sleepy and languid, looking around the room with half-closed eyes. When she finds Amelia in the dark, her eyes indicate a smile. Amelia sighs at how predictable her junior holy caster is, and Stephenne stands up on shaky legs.

Her thick sleeping gown is far different from her usual miniskirt mage's robe—it actually comes down to the ankles and can't be taken off unless several of the buttons are undone.

This sleeping gown was specially ordered, developed through trial and error based on the number of incidents Stey had caused while half-asleep. The many buttons are intended to prevent Stey from stripping down to the nude in her sleep, the long hem implemented to trip Stey into consciousness when she sleepwalks.

Stephenne stumbles toward Amelia, nearly falling down, but manages to stay upright.

"...Huh. How is it that you're not falling down, despite being half-asleep?"

She'd definitely be facedown on the floor right now if she were fully awake.

"Umph... A-Amelia..."

Stephenne finally makes it to Amelia's side and falls into her, clutching at her with both hands. Ares would have sidestepped her, no doubt, but Amelia stands her ground and accepts her embrace.

Stephenne's breasts, which are ludicrously large in proportion to her height, smoosh into Amelia's face. There isn't any strength in Stey's arms, but her entirely body is perfectly soft as she leans into her superior.

Amelia looks down at Stey, still perpetually dozing, and speaks to her. Her voice is much icier than when she just talked with Creio.

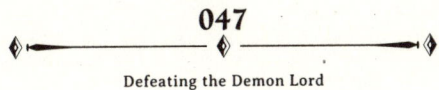

"If you did this to Ares, he'd kill you."

"...Okeydoke..."

"Are you really sleeping?"

"Mmph...," she babbles sleepily, clearly lying. It's so obvious, it's not even funny. But upon further inspection, it seems that, for better or worse, Stephenne is being honest. Completely innocent. An elite priest like her does not tell lies.

She needs to stay away from Ares. Amelia clenches her fists with renewed conviction.

§ § §

I walk along, grabbing Stey, our communication device, by the hand. Upon informing Amelia of my plan, which I thought about all night, she responds, "Ares, do you enjoy pushing people's buttons?"

"U-um, Amelia... Your face is twitching." Amelia's blunt comment and icy expression cause Stey's voice to tremble.

Wow, to say a thing like that about your junior ... Well, I can't really blame her. But I'm well aware of this plan's shortcomings. It's all for the sake of efficiency.

I explain my idea again, but Amelia's face doesn't change one bit. Instead, she repeats, "Ares, do you enjoy pushing people's buttons?"

"But I...was asked to come here..."

Stey pulls on Amelia's sleeve, looking at her with puppy-dog eyes. Amelia shakes her off without a word.

"Look at it this way, Amelia. It's not as bad as Gregorio—Stey won't try to kill Toudou or anything."

"You sure are tough, Ares..."

"Worst-case scenario, I'll tuck her under my arm. She's tiny and won't impede my movements at all."

"You sure are tough, Ares..."

"When I need both hands... Like when I need to fight... She'll make do, somehow."

"The overdone sense of justice is a crime."

"...Yes, sir! I will!"

Stey beams brightly, her fists clenched in determination, but Amelia glowers at her like they're sworn enemies.

"You sure are tough, Ares..."

A mammoth wrought-iron black gate stands at the only entrance to the interior of Golem Valley. Several meters high and over a meter thick, the metal gate looks like it leads straight into hell.

Golems are humanoid effigies operated by mages. Rather than a soul, they are powered by magical circuitry and energy.

Creating a golem requires advanced sorcery that is still present in the modern age, and many high-level mages employ them as convoys or assistants. Golems do not possess thought, and they function only according to the magical circuitry embedded within them. They are utterly obedient to their owners, and as long as their magical energy doesn't run out, they have an infinite life span, allowing them to operate forever—truly valuable magical beings.

However, despite being incredibly valuable, their capacity for good or evil is entirely determined by their creator. In the past, before the Kingdom of Ruxe was officially a country, there existed a fool known as the Doll Master.

The man was a fool, sure, but also a genius.

He was a mage. Just as his nickname states, no one has been able to surpass his mastery of golems. He was a legitimate savant, and also quite perverse, they say. He obsessed over the golems he created, loved them. If that was the end of it, people would have known him only as a man who obsessed over his dolls. However, after creating many golems, the genius managed to forge an entire new system.

It was one in which golems could create new golems, known as the "mother system." This mage used it to try to create a paradise filled with the golems he so adored—a place where golems, who are in principle created to satisfy the whim of their creators, could become self-aware.

The Doll Master was also highly gifted in aerial magic, and he visited

a series of valleys rich in the magical stones used as the golems' cores. This was where he created several special golems, called mother golems, which included full versions of the mother system within them. These special creatures followed his system to the letter and autonomously proceeded to create other golems ad nauseam.

The man further endeavored to establish a system by which the golems would never need maintenance and could function indefinitely. It was a self-defense system, one which draws depleted magical energy from the surrounding air. Most mages would have given up trying to devise such a method—it's essentially playing God. Yet, the man was unmistakably a genius.

Months and years passed, but the golems showed no signs of ceasing functionality. Even when the Doll Master died, they continued functioning for tens, then hundreds of years. When the Kingdom of Ruxe Survey Corps entered this series of valleys, the golems were still functioning, and they had acquired extensive amounts of life force. As such, the Kingdom determined the valleys to be both extremely dangerous and valuable. To this day, the series of valleys dominated by freely roaming hordes of golems is known as Golem Valley.

The region's paths and caves have all been created by the golems over many, many years. To mankind's benefit, the vast majority of golems are limited in their abilities to destroy man-made structures. That's why this single gate provides enough protection.

Golem Valley's gate is a thick iron wall. The security forces here were established in anticipation of fending off the portion of golems that do have the tendency to destroy man-made structures. Their level, experience, and equipment are in accord with their valor, and they are not outdone by anyone—even the most seasoned veteran mercenaries that come to this place.

"Wooow!! I've never seen anything like this!"

Stey looks up at the gate and jumps up and down. Who jumps up and down in a miniskirt?!

Next to her, Amelia—who has been in a foul mood ever since I

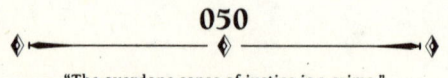

"The overdone sense of justice is a crime."

told her we would indeed be working with Stey—looks up at the gate, expressionless.

"Even the royal capital's gate in Ruxe isn't as sturdy as this one," I comment.

The majority of the Kingdom's cities are protected by barriers cast through holy techniques, as opposed to physical gates.

"...Yes, that's because holy technique barriers don't work against inanimate monsters."

"Ooh... I didn't know there are monsters that barriers don't work against."

Stey should have learned all about that during training at the Church, but she's completely in awe at Amelia's statement, her eyes sparkling.

I look back at Stey and Amelia behind me and remind them, "Amelia, don't you dare let go of Stey's hand."

"...Yes."

"Ares, don't worry! I'll be fine," Stey responds with meaningless overconfidence.

Amelia sighs and grips her hand with force. The three of us pass through the mammoth gate and enter Golem Valley.

The valley's construction is simple. There are two main routes: through the cliffs on the outside, or through innumerable caves in the interior. It's said that the outside route is easier to battle on. There's a danger of falling from the cliffs, and the path is narrow. This generally prevents larger golems from appearing.

Since the outside route would be a complete death trap for Stey, we'll be making our way through the caves using the interior route.

After walking for some time, the mercenary parties we saw everywhere in the town are nowhere to be found.

The surface of the craggy boulders is rugged and impairs walking considerably. Stey, who constantly falls on flat ground, nearly wipes out with every other step. Amelia helps her up each time. Just as I thought— it's a death trap.

Before too long, we reach the mouth of the first cave.

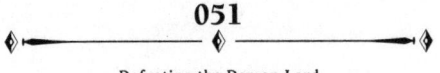

A dim light emanates from the cave, which had been excavated as an easier route through the boulders. There is an ample field of vision inside.

Most of the caves were dug out by golems and were thus excavated at a size that accommodates them. Even with three people standing side by side, there is still room to spare.

It's said the faint light shining within the caves also stems from the golems. The only sounds resonating within are the wind and Stey's constant tripping.

I've entered Golem Valley one step ahead of Toudou and his party in order to show Amelia and Stey the behavior of this area's monsters. Although we've entered their domain, Stey is still acting like she's taking a stroll through town.

She smiles from ear to ear as she says to Amelia, who's still holding her hand, "Hee-hee, Amelia, it's like we're out for a picnic!"

"...Please be more alert."

Unbelievable. I...really should have thought this through.

The air inside the cave is cool and dry. After walking for a while, Amelia stops suddenly.

"A powerful monster is approaching."

"Got it."

I can't feel its presence just yet. Golems are not living beings, and their presence is therefore quite weak. Conversely, because they function off magical energy, mages can detect their cores quite easily.

Stey looks around nonchalantly and casually adds, "Ohhh, you're right. There are three of them."

The moment she finishes speaking, a golem appears. Three meters in height, its body mimics human proportions, although it's made of ochre-colored boulder. Two black rocks are buried in the space where a human would have eyes.

Golems have long arms in comparison to humans, nearly reaching the ground when standing, with five corpulent fingers on each hand.

These are rock golems. The boulder covering their outer body is

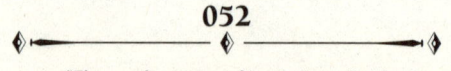

strengthened by magical energy, and they possess immense upper-body strength and rugged defenses. This is the most common type of golem. Their weaknesses include water- or earth-based elemental magic. Blunt-force weapons are said to be most effective against them, but the holy sword Ex should be able to cleave through their rugged outer shell with ease.

"These are rock golems. The appropriate level for defeating them is thirty to thirty-five."

"…Will Toudou be able to defeat them?"

"They're not particularly aggressive monsters, just huge, tough, and powerful. He'll manage."

I hold up my hand and call Amelia and Stey back. At the same time, one of the golems surges toward us. The ground shakes, and the approaching golem brings its fist down for a massive strike, which I quickly sidestep to the left.

The golem's chest is left wide open, and I smash my mace into it, flinging its massive body across the cave like a scrap of paper. It smashes into the remaining two golems, crushing all three of them against the wall.

The entire cave shakes with a thunderous roar. The golems' cores must have been destroyed, as their life force flows into my body. I smack the butt end of my mace's handle on the ground a few times and turn back toward Amelia and Stey. I don't even need a buff to wreck these golems.

"See, that's all there is to them… They're not that strong."

"Three golems with a single blow… You're a brute."

"Rock golems are the weakest monsters in this entire area. You could say this is just a primer."

Amelia remains astringent, while Stey manages her most high-pitched squeal.

"Woooow, amazing! Ares, you're so cool!"

"…That's enough. Stey, just make sure not to get lost. Don't get distracted."

"I'm fine…! I'm holding Amelia's hand, don't worry!"

Stey raises her hand with Amelia's, fingers interlocked conspicuously,

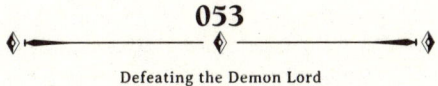

as high as she can to show me. Amelia has apparently lost all emotion; her expression remains vacant. These two really seem to embody the big sister, little sister dynamic.

We fight against most types of golem near the town to test their reactions.

Golems aren't naturally occurring in the wild, so this is my first time fighting against them in quite a while. I'm not expecting any problems.

We call it a day at the appropriate time and start to head back to town. Even with golems that dwarf her in size running rampant, Stey refused to stop whooping it up all day long. Her cheeks are flushed and her breath is ragged.

She practically skips toward me and looks up at me with stars in her eyes.

"Amazing! Ares, I didn't know you're so strong!"

I guess she's complimenting me, but when I think about the near future, I just can't pretend to be flattered. She definitely needs to remain more alert. She'd be absolutely useless if she were even just a bit less capable.

Amelia taps me on the shoulder wearily.

"Ares, should I start acting a little more like Stey?"

"I'm not sure what you're implying here, but don't even think about it."

"I see…"

One is already too much to handle. If Amelia starts bouncing off the walls, too… I won't know where to turn.

I continue to chide Stey as she frolics carelessly to and fro on the path back to town. By the time we arrive, the sun has already gone down.

The timing is perfect, so I take both of them to the local church. It's time to meet the madam.

We are shown to the madam's room, the same place I met her the other day. It's filled with rustic furniture, quite stark in contrast to a

"The overdone sense of justice is a crime."

typical sister's room. There is a glass shelf littered with liquor bottles of indiscernible origin, and the photos pinned to the wall of the madam with various mercenaries are most likely all of individuals who have visited this place.

I recognize a few members of the Out Crusade in the photos, and there is one of Creio at a young age, too. These photos are proof of the long history that Sister Carina Capp has accumulated in her time here.

As always, we find the madam seated deeply in her chair. Her eyes are alight as she stares at the two girls behind me.

"Welcome again, young Ares. Are those your new friends?"

"Yes. This is Amelia Nohman and Stephenne Veronide."

"Heh-heh-heh, bringing two young girls with you on assignment— you've really ranked up, Ares."

"Guess I can't really call Toudou a womanizer anymore, can I?"

She must not have enjoyed my retort. The madam's spirit seems dampened as she snorts.

Her personality burns brightest when she becomes sardonic, and even though she playfully calls me *boy* when it's just the two of us, she's obviously behaving differently in front of my two cohorts. I guess she's fond of me.

Amelia's face has stiffened at the madam's welcome, but when I urge her forward with my chin, she approaches Carina. Amelia holds the hem of her robe and bows graciously. If she weren't so expressionless, it would have been perfect.

"My name is Amelia Nohman. Madam Carina… Your reputation precedes you."

"Yes… I've heard about you as well, from His Eminence."

What has Carina possibly heard about Amelia…?

The madam simply nods two or three times and continues in a hoarse yet affectionate tone, "Make sure to help out your compatriot there. No matter how high her level, she's completely helpless by herself."

"…Yes, that is precisely what I have been assigned to do."

On cue, the high-level but totally helpless Stey flits toward Amelia

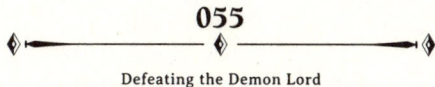

and stands next to her. Stey beams at the madam and then bows deeply, her head nearly touching her stomach. Although she is standing straight as an arrow, in the next moment, she staggers and falls right on top of the madam.

The madam doesn't look bothered and catches her effortlessly. With her face still in the old woman's lap, Stey whispers, "…I'm Stephenne."

Are you serious?! At least get off her lap before you introduce yourself!

I step forward to pick Stey up, but the madam sighs deeply and says with exasperation, "…Stey, you have not changed one bit."

"Madam… Don't tell me you already know her?"

The madam sweeps back Stey's hair with her fingers. At a glance, the two of them practically look like grandmother and granddaughter. Then the madam looks at me and says something unexpected.

"Ares. This girl…is the daughter of someone you also happen to know: Veronide."

"Vero…nide…?"

Come to think of it, Creio mentioned as much, but it went in one ear and out the other: "*…Have you heard the surname Veronide before?*"

Powerful holy techniques and an abnormally high level. Thinking about it rationally…that's definitely not normal.

As I furrow my brow and wrack my brain for a clue, just then, the highly useful li'l ol' Amelia informs me.

"Ares, *that* Veronide. Stey is the daughter of Sylvester Veronide… I thought Creio had already told you…"

"Syl… Sylvester…?"

Having been given the details, I finally remember, and I swear I can hear myself go white as a sheet.

"Yes, one of the cardinals of the Church of Ahz Gried. She's Sylvester Veronide's daughter."

The daughter…of a cardinal?! Unfathomable… Are there no decent people left in the Church? Give me a break.

I shut out the doubts racing through my mind and decide to file a complaint with Creio about this.

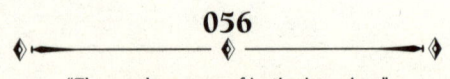

"The overdone sense of justice is a crime."

§ § §

She is dreaming.

It's a dream of fire. A devastating flame, a flame that is cognizant, tearing through the darkness.

The only things within that darkness are the flame, and a blond-haired girl—Limis Al Friedia.

The air shimmers, and an extensive swath of magical energy spirals in the sky.

It is a spirit, one of the greatest powers reigning over this world, and the source of an elementalist's power.

The seething flame is inviting Limis, and she is reeled in, extending her fingers toward it.

—Just then, Limis awakens.

A ceiling that she's never seen before enters her field of vision. There is no light, and the room is blurry and dim. In her confusion, something hot brushes Limis's cheek; it's her covenant spirit salamander licking her with its tiny tongue. It peers at her, and when she meets its dark-red eyes—the origin of its name, Garnet—she finally remembers where she is.

Limis slowly gets up, her entire body languid. A strange sensation burns in her chest, and she presses her hand against it.

She sputters out a cough and puts her palm to her forehead. It doesn't feel like she has a fever anymore. Garnet chirps and climbs up onto her arm. She speaks to Garnet in a low voice.

"Ohhh… I remember now. I was…intoxicated," she whispers, now aware of her own condition. Exhaustion isn't the reason that she fell ill. Well, there's no doubt that her body ran out of energy from being tired, but the real reason is that her body overreacted to the earth spirit energy ubiquitous in Golem Valley. It's a phenomenon commonly referred to as "spirit intoxication."

As an elementalist, Limis has a strong affinity for spirits. That means she sometimes draws them in from the air and incorporates them into

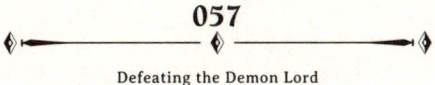

herself. Homologous spirits form a shield, so a proper elementalist who has contracted with all eight spirit types should never experience this phenomenon. However, because Limis has only established a covenant with a fire spirit, she's had this happen to her on more than one occasion thus far.

Garnet glowers at the air around them. Limis sighs and strokes its head with her pointer finger.

"Garnet, don't be so intimidating. A lot of earth spirits inhabit this area."

Status exists, even among spirits. Those that float through the air, invisible, are generally diluted and weak, but they too will retort if threatened. They will also lend their power to those with divine protection who ask for it.

Garnet flicks out its tongue and climbs up Limis's body, diving inside her clothes from the neck. Limis twists her body slightly and takes note of her condition. She feels listless—clear proof that she's still affected. It will take her a few more days to get back into full form.

She's not technically sick, so she can still move around, but if she doesn't take her time and get back to full health, there's a high chance the same phenomenon will reoccur. Besides, it'd be a sad sight if she were to pass out in the middle of a battle in the valley.

...I have to...apologize to Nao and the others.

Limis hears footsteps outside her room. She gazes blankly at the door and shakes her head.

"Sorry I worried you guys."

"Not at all, we're just glad you're okay. Seriously..."

Limis feels terrible, but Toudou smiles gently at her. All four members of the party go outside to chat and walk around the town. They head for the weapons shop.

After getting a full day's rest, Limis has healed up enough to walk without stumbling. She won't be able to leave the town until she's fully recovered, but she can certainly prepare in the meantime. The group is

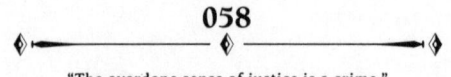

"The overdone sense of justice is a crime."

headed to the weapons shop to repair Toudou's shield, which cracked in her battle with Gregorio.

The blacksmith has close-cropped hair. He looks down at Toudou's cracked shield—the Shield of Radiance—and grumbles with a furrowed brow, "…This'll be a real tough fix…"

The shield Toudou acquired from the Kingdom is made of a special metal alloy called blue metal. Unlike the holy sword Ex and holy armor Fried, this shield did not belong to the previous Holy Warrior. However, blue metal is highly resistant to physical and magical attacks and is well-known for its use in the equipment of first-rate mercenaries.

Toudou's shield is said to be able to withstand dragon's breath, but now its surface is riddled with thin fractures. It's not completely broken, but continuing to use a cracked shield is out of the question.

Toudou doesn't do well with men, so Aria—who's also highly knowledgeable regarding weapons and armor—responds to the blacksmith.

"Does that mean there's no chance of repairing it? If so, we'd like to purchase a replacement."

The style of swordsmanship that Toudou studied at the royal castle—that of the Pramia school—is predicated on the use of a shield. Without one, Toudou's battle methods will change dramatically, and she can't simply learn a new style of swordsmanship at this juncture.

Aria is reminded slightly of how difficult it was when she switched her own sword-fighting style. She narrows her eyes and soon has a bitter look on her face as the blacksmith sighs. He raps his knuckles on the shield's outer surface.

"Nah, it's not like it's impossible to repair it. Hey, where'd you get this shield anyway? Blue metal is a grade below mythril and orichalcum, but this is a valuable piece. We don't have the materials here, much less the equipment to work on it. Plus, this shield's been imbued with high-level magic, some of which has left traces behind. The operative procedure'd be a bit messy, and I'd need a specialist mage to work alongside me if we're gonna fix 'er up."

Toudou was staring at the weapons and armor hanging on the wall,

but when she hears this, her expression darkens slightly. Aria coughs once loudly and rephrases her question. "Where could we possibly bring it to get it fixed?"

"If you've got the time and money to fix it, you're better off buying a new one. You should ask the blacksmith that sold it to you. 'Sides, we simply lack the proper facilities."

The cracks cover the entire surface of the shield, almost like a decoration.

The blacksmith carefully traces his fingers over the shield and looks up at Aria with suspicion.

"Just what were you fightin' against anyway? Blue metal's highly impervious to slash attacks, blunt damage, and magic. It ain't easy to beat it up this much. Not to mention, this one here's got traces of magic to boost its hardness and a barrier cast on it. No golem round these parts could land a dent in it, even with a straight-on attack."

"...Well, you know... Things happen..."

Aria obscures her words—she can't possibly tell him it's from battling a priest. Toudou's shield was originally in Aria's family's possession, just one of the defensive armaments that the Rizas clan had held for generations. She couldn't believe it—this brilliant shield has seen her family through many battles and was never damaged once. A scratch is one thing, but for a magically reinforced shield to have cracks across its entire surface is simply unheard of.

For this reason, Aria was actually relieved when she heard that it was Gregorio who'd caused all those cracks. If the shield had been of just slightly poorer quality, or if Toudou had been a split second slower in raising it, she might not have made it out alive.

The blacksmith points to a shield hanging from the wall. The mercenaries of First Town are high level and have a corresponding amount of gold. Even for Aria—who has seen innumerable valuable weapons and armor in her day—these are not shabby selections.

Yet, the blacksmith does not sound particularly enthusiastic. "We've got a few shields available here, but to be honest...nothing on that level."

"The overdone sense of justice is a crime."

"But it's filled with cracks…"

"Even cracked, it's still better than what we got."

Toudou takes the shield back from the blacksmith. Her gaze is locked on to it, and the blacksmith says to her, "Blue metal is hard and lightweight. It's cracked, and none of its magical buffs work right now, but as long as you don't take any crazy hits, it shouldn't break down any further. You oughtta take it to the capital or a larger city to get it fixed as soon as possible."

"…I understand. Would you mind if we took a look at what you have to offer as a spare?"

It's typically impractical to carry around multiple heavy items, but Aria and the party possess a magical implement that allows them to stow items out of sight, so that won't be a problem.

The blacksmith shoots Aria a curious look and replies simply, "Look as long as you like. Prices are next to the items."

Aria and Toudou examine each shield thoroughly. The weapons shop mainly sells exactly that—weapons—and there are consequently only a few shields available. Mercenaries tend to travel light, and shields aren't in high demand.

Toudou's choices are already very limited. She takes a shield approximately the same size as her Shield of Radiance down from the wall and, upon hefting it, lets out a low groan.

"…So heavy."

She hoists it easily up and down a few times, but there is definitely a huge difference compared with watching her hold the Shield of Radiance.

"I'm not surprised… Blue metal isn't as airy as mythril, but it's still very light."

"Mm… Even if I'm only gonna use it in battle, it'll take some time to get used to, I think…"

Toudou isn't all that strong to begin with, and her stamina isn't on the same level as other male mercenaries. The reason she can move around so well is partially thanks to her resourcefulness, but her use of light equipment is also a factor.

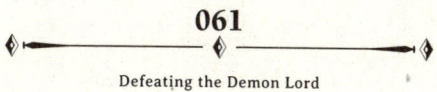

The thick black shield certainly looks sturdy, but when Aria takes it from Toudou, she quickly furrows her brow.

Even for Aria, who had originally used the Pramia school style of sword fighting, the shield is definitely on the heavy side.

"Golems are known for their heavy attacks, so a shield of this thickness could be just right."

"Will it feel lighter as I gain levels?"

"It will to some extent, yes…"

Leveling up doesn't make one all-powerful. Stats that an individual is gifted in from the start will grow more quickly, while those they aren't suited to will grow slowly.

The reason that Toudou has high growth potential, as a female, is due to her agility regarding magical energy and explosive power. The strength and agility needed to wield a shield are not her forte, so they grow much more slowly.

Toudou shakes her head as she hefts the shield again. She can hold it just fine, but it just feels different in her hand. Aria inspects the shop's remaining shields with Toudou in the corner of her eye, but all that's left include a tower shield—which conceals the user's entire body—or smaller shields of approximately thirty centimeters in diameter. None of them feel just right.

"…We might have to proceed with this shield for now, after all. We can figure out how to repair it once we return to the capital."

"Well, might as well buy this one, too… Better safe than sorry, as they say. Damn—it's expensive as hell!"

Toudou is absolutely blown away by the price tag. The Kingdom provided her with a thousand lux to spend on preparations for vanquishing the Demon Lord… She received another ten million for all the necessary implements, including weapons, armor, and travel supplies, but the shield in question is listed at one hundred thousand lux by itself.

The blacksmith must have heard Toudou, because he's glaring daggers in her direction. Toudou grins sheepishly and looks back at the price tag.

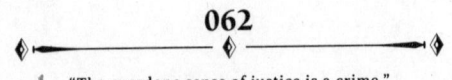

"The overdone sense of justice is a crime."

"The shield must be so expensive because there isn't much demand. That said... They're still cheaper than the weapons."

Typically, weapons and armor are leagues more expensive than other everyday items. Toudou's holy sword Ex is no exception. Aria's magical sword Lightning Howl is similarly invaluable, no matter how many gold coins one proffers.

"Yeah, but it's just a metal shield...," replies Toudou, unconvinced.

Aria and the party have been burning through their gold reserves at a steady pace for the past few months, so the price of the shield is hefty. But as the saying goes: You can't spend the money when you're dead.

Toudou scowls and grumbles to herself. Just then, a voice calls out to the two of them from behind.

"Hey, Aria, Toudou! Come here!"

It's Limis. When Toudou catches her gaze, she puts the shield back on the wall and walks toward her.

Limis and Glacia are in the weapons corner of the shop, which includes all varieties of armaments aside from swords. There are spears, gauntlets, and axes—many weapons that most mercenaries don't really use.

"I thought you were going to look for mage weapons?"

"Yeah... Well... I've seen them already. But forget that—take a look at these!"

Limis points at a selection of weapons on the wall. There is one behemoth among them. The massive black metal handle is as thick as Limis's neck, and as long as she is tall. But it's the head of the weapon that stands out even more. It's about one meter wide and half a meter tall, shaped like a box, and without adornment. It radiates pure heft.

It's massive and unrefined, completely distinctive among the other weapons.

"That's a war hammer, but it's way bigger than most. Maybe it's for fighting golems?"

Aria opens her eyes wide and sizes up the weapon. It's the type rarely used by mercenaries or knights. If anything, a priest who can't wield a blade might use it, but she's never seen one this massive.

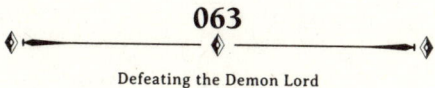

Its size guarantees it will be hard to swing, and the hammer head is extremely heavy—the balance must be terrible. Using it effectively demands umpteen times more physical strength than the black shield they were just looking at. It's the most impractical weapon possible. It must have been on the wall forever, with no one to buy it. However, given its massive size, the listed price is actually quite low.

"Who knew a thing like this existed... So what are you gonna do with it?" asks Toudou, and Limis looks down from the war hammer. There stands Glacia, who's seemed different ever since she went out by herself yesterday evening. She gazes up at the war hammer.

Limis puts her hand on Glacia's head and strokes it, then she adds with a bewildered look on her face, "She says she wants it."

Unexpected, indeed, but Glacia hasn't changed at all. She may not be totally enamored with Aria and the others, but for some reason, this mysterious girl has stuck by their side.

Aria can't believe her ears and asks Limis, "...Wait—Glacia said that?"

"...Yes."

"...She does know she can't eat it, right?"

The war hammer easily dwarfs Glacia's entire body. What could she possibly want with it?

As Aria wonders in doubt, Glacia turns her emerald-eyed gaze on her. She's obviously trying to hold back an extraordinary feeling as she opens her mouth, and to say she sounds innocent would be a misinterpretation of her emotions.

"I'm...gonna fight, too."

"The overdone sense of justice is a crime."

On Toudou's Party's Increasing Battle Prowess

Although easily describable as "golems," there are many different categories therein.

For example, the golem that I defeated earlier to test my mettle was a rock golem. They have four long limbs, enabling them to complete intricate processes, and they're quite quick.

There are golems that are purely defense-oriented, with supremely hard armored bodies, and there are types that spew fire to attack.

Their progenitors, the mother golems, develop these creatures in accordance with their environments. Without exception, they are powerful weapons of war that should be feared at all costs. One reason why it's so difficult to come up with a battle plan for this region is due to the sheer variety of golems present. Another is the area's renown as a training ground.

Toudou and his party must know this. Far below me, the four of them walk along the cliffs looking anxious.

Their formation is as follows: Toudou in the lead; then Aria, furrowing her brow; Limis, who has recovered; and Glacia bringing up the rear, looking sullen.

The only thing different than usual is the massive metal hammer strapped to Glacia's back. It seems she negotiated well and got them to purchase a weapon for her, just in case she needs it. At any rate, it's good to see her caring for a change.

"Oof... The wind sure is strong up here..."

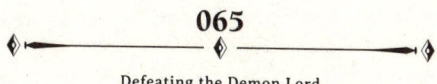

I am observing Toudou's party from a cliff ten meters above the path they're traversing.

I'm keeping a firm grip on Stey, the dead weight, while following Toudou's movements.

I refocus my senses. Although I keep a close watch on Toudou, the path we're traveling isn't safe by any means, either.

Golems are different from demons. They will attack even if their opponent clearly outmatches them in prowess. And above all else—

"Oh, I know! Do you wanna play a word game?"

As I pull her along by the hand, Stey proposes an idea with unnecessary cheer.

Amelia proposed a similar idea in the Great Tomb... Are word games making a comeback or something?! Hell no, I don't want to play a word game!

"That's a shame."

"You're a shame, Stey."

I can't be sure of what she actually feels in her heart of hearts, but she giggles all the same.

"I get that a lot."

"No surprise there!"

I'm trailing Toudou's party, keeping an eye out for monsters and keeping the other eye on Stey. I can't let up for even a second on all three, and it's a serious burden.

Stey comes closer to me while I hold her hand. She looks up at me and says, as if consoling me, "Let's do our very best, okay? Okay, Ares? Right?"

"...I'm trying."

There's no way...absolutely no way I can let go of her for even a second. I carve this mantra afresh in my mind as I look down on Stey, who is quickly becoming overly clingy with me.

Sylvester Veronide. There isn't likely a single person in the entire Kingdom of Ruxe who doesn't know his name. He's a native of the Kingdom, a merchant who converted to the priesthood of the Church of Ahz

Gried and rose through the ranks to become a top executive member—one of the Church's five cardinals.

Of course, I know his name, too. I just didn't connect it with Stey at first.

He's supposedly the least qualified cardinal in history, yet the Church very much depends on him.

My superior, Cardinal Creio, oversees the Church's military power, and similarly, Sylvester manages its treasury. Well before I became a priest, Sylvester was a preeminent merchant within the Kingdom, and when he converted to the faith, he distinguished himself as invaluable among the inner Church members who had a paltry understanding of economic concepts.

He claims he's a priest, but without money, his faith would dissipate. Everything costs money—his robe, his mace, his scripture book. Sylvester managed to instill a mercantile aspect within the faith-based Church and completely overhauled its financial affairs, which were previously in a state of disarray. He is not well liked within the Church, but his influence is undeniably massive.

How could a man of such great stature and an untrained sister possibly be related? Yet, that seems to be the truth. They're father and daughter.

Sylvester should be an old man by now. I feel like their ages are too far apart to be parent and child, and both Amelia and Creio should have told me about them from the beginning. Furthermore, Stey ought to mention such pertinent details when she introduces herself.

In most instances, this would be unfathomable. The daughter of a cardinal has more value than Aria or Limis. There's no way Stey should be allowed to participate in a quest to vanquish the Demon Lord, especially considering she has more than a few screws loose.

I called Creio to enter a formal complaint, but his response was simply another thorn in my side.

—*"Ares, Stey is just a pitiful little girl. Sylvester has given up on her entirely."*

Creio spoke with such compassion, and it made everything crystal

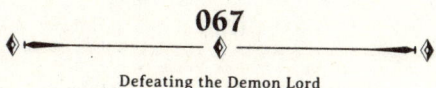

067

clear for me. It's simple: Everyone's thrown in the towel when it comes to handling Stey, and now that towel has flown my way, into my hand—that's all there is to it.

—*"Anyway, she has redeeming qualities. Even Sylvester knows this. Ares, I'm confident that you'll be able to...handle her well."*

Creio's kind words looped in my mind over and over—to the point that I haven't been able to sleep since yesterday. But I can't just ignore Stey. In the end, I decided to take her along myself, just as was planned initially.

Thankfully, even though she might seem hopeless, walking along while holding her hand isn't a problem at all.

"Ummm... Ares? You can let go of my hand now, okay? I'll be careful."

"No chance."

I'm sure Stey's intentions are pure, but she truly doesn't know her own place, and I bluntly refuse her request before continuing to track Toudou.

I hold Stey's hand with my left and swing my mace with my right, obliterating the monsters that sporadically appear.

"You really are a worrywart, Ares!"

"Shut up."

The path that Toudou and his party are traversing is vastly different from ours. It's one taken by the majority of mercenaries who leave town. They haven't run into many monsters thus far, but just now, a few golems appear in their way.

There are three of them, each about the size of a human head. At a glance, they look like small spheres with limbs, just as their name indicates: ball golems. Their shape emphasizes speed over resistance or power, and the claws on their arms and legs allow them to climb cliffs with ease. They generally travel in packs of five to fifteen.

Toudou and his party notice the ball golems approaching a few seconds after I do. Toudou takes out his fractured shield and draws his sword. Aria takes a step forward and lines up with him. Limis grabs Glacia by the

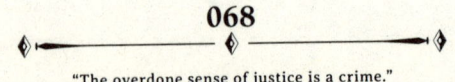

"The overdone sense of justice is a crime."

arm and drags her to the rear. It looks like they're not letting Glacia get in on the action just yet.

And the battle begins.

Ball golems are particularly mobile, but in terms of strength, they're some of the lowest-ranking monsters in this area.

Their bodies are made from ore and relatively hard, but it won't be a challenge for the holy sword Ex to pierce their armored shells.

A ball golem flies at Toudou in a flurry, and he blocks it with his shield. He's knocked slightly off his feet from the attack but quickly stands strong again. He brings his sword down on the ball golem, but a second before impact, it uses his shield as scaffolding, clambering up and flipping backward off it.

Toudou's holy sword whiffs through the air. In the ensuing gap, another ball golem flies in to attack, but Aria stands in its way. Her magical sword Lightning Howl slashes through the air like a streak of lightning and hits the golem head-on. The piercing shrill of metal against the golem's body rips through the valley.

"Get 'em ! Get 'em!"

The ball golem is smashed and bounces off the ground. Aria's blade made a direct hit on the golem, but its armored shell has only been damaged—it's not dead. However, it launches itself off the path to the cliffs below. Life force can't be absorbed from it now.

"Get 'em! Get 'em!"

The third golem hurls itself at the golem that had used Toudou's shield as scaffolding. When it connects, it turns the golem itself into a springboard and rapidly gains speed.

The golem unpredictably stops on a dime, and Aria steps in to slash at it from the side. The golem smashes against the cliff wall, but its cohort still remains. It refuses to leave an opening and hurls itself against Aria, now open on her flank.

Aria is completely unprepared for the lunge attack and is knocked off her feet. She stifles a scream as she smashes into the cliff. She isn't

069

heavily damaged, but depending on the direction of the lunge attack, she could have easily fallen to the cliffs below.

"Go, go, go!"

Toudou screams Aria's name and unleashes a slash attack on the ball golem, already preparing for another lunge attack. Because it is preoccupied, it has no chance to escape. The holy sword Ex screams with fury as it cleaves the ball golem in half. Toudou doesn't even stop to watch it fall to bits and runs to Aria's side. She is groaning in pain.

However, there is still a monster in their midst. The ball golem that was smashed against the cliff wall by Aria's slash attack now rushes toward Toudou, who has his back turned. The moment before it smashes into Toudou's back, a flame is unleashed from behind, engulfing the ball golem. It's burned to a crisp and falls to the ground.

Toudou reacts far too late and turns around quickly. Limis shrugs her shoulders, skeptical, and holds up her staff.

Stey, who has been supporting the party with her lackluster cheering, now gives a shout of joy.

"Wow! They did it. The Holy Warrior is the real deal."

"Stey, get in touch with Amelia. It's time for plan B."

"...Huh?"

Are you completely blind? You might think Toudou's the real deal, but that was obviously a close call.

Ball golems are a drop in the bucket. Plus, there were only three of them—quite smaller than the packs they usually form. If that low number is already causing them damage, then there's no way they'll survive Golem Valley.

Toudou and his party are far less accomplished than I thought. Compared to the undead foes of the Great Tomb, Golem Valley is old-school hard knocks. There aren't that many bothersome powers at work here—just pure brute strength. However, they still came out on top. The reason the battle was tough is simply due to their lack of experience.

After engaging a number of golems in combat, Toudou and his party

"The overdone sense of justice is a crime."

return to town with exhaustion on their faces. Most of their battles went the same way as the first—clearly an indication of Toudou's present capabilities.

I'll need to ask for the madam's involvement after all. I'm glad I spoke to her beforehand.

"This doesn't look very good, does it?"

"No, it's not as bad as you think."

Stey—easily the most annoying, helpless person on earth—puts her finger to her lips and cocks her head to the side. Because she falls down so easily, I ended up holding her hand the entire damn time we were out.

I explain to her, a bit dejectedly, "Toudou's level is still low. That's why he's having a hard time. If his level goes up and he learns some new techniques, he'll iron out the kinks."

Toudou is still in his beginnings as the Holy Warrior. He has potential. With training, his growth will be exponential. There's no turning back now.

§　§　§

"…Training?" Aria asks Toudou, blinking.

They have just finished eating dinner and are mulling over how difficult today's battles were.

Golems are far more difficult than they expected—on a completely different level than anything they've fought thus far. The footing of the valley's cliffs is horrendous, and the fierce, cold wind pierces their spirits. Myriad varieties of golems encroach at all times.

The biggest difference between these battles and past ones is that Aria can't slay any of the golems in a single fell swoop. Until now, both Toudou and Aria were able to slaughter nearly every enemy they encountered with a single blow.

Aria's sword, Lightning Howl, is one of the most powerful blades in the entire Kingdom, a magical sword imbued with the power of lightning. In theory, even a golem's robust armored shell should not be able to withstand a single blow from it.

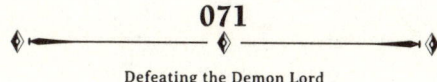

Part of the reason she cannot cleave golems in half with a single blow lies in her lack of experience, something Aria herself knows all too well. As someone who doesn't use a shield, being able to slay her enemies with a single slash is a point of deep pride for her. She needs to enhance her swordsmanship skills.

Toudou is just barely able to slay the golems with one blow, and they have sidestepped her attacks a number of times. She remains committed to becoming stronger.

Limis, who is dead tired from today's march along the bluffs, rolls around on her bed.

Toudou looks to her and begins to discuss a message she received from the inn's proprietor earlier. It had to do with the town headman they'd met upon their arrival.

"Yeah… There was a message from the town headman. It appears there's a training ground nearby for those who aren't used to the monsters in Golem Valley yet… He said they provide lectures on how to fight golems."

"…I see. I didn't know they had such a thing…"

"Hey, why don't we take them up on it? Though I doubt it'll be much use for me, personally," adds Limis.

"…Yes, I suppose so."

Aria stares at her hands. They still sting from attacking the rock-hard golems over and over. She's felt it before, in training, but never from wielding the magical sword Lightning Howl. Aria lifts her head up and looks right into Toudou's dark eyes.

"Let's ask for training right away… Raising our levels is foremost, but the golems here are far stronger than any undead. We will have to reconfigure the battle plan we used in the Great Tomb."

—He's huge.

Next to the town headman stands a massive man two heads taller and shaped like a boulder—no, more like a mountain. He's clothed in a

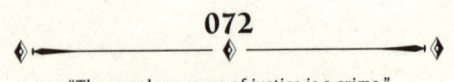

"The overdone sense of justice is a crime."

gray priest's robe and has the mark of a priest hanging from his ear, but Toudou simply can't imagine him as one.

Aria and Limis are also flabbergasted. The only one unfazed is Glacia, the tiniest of them all. The hard-faced town headman next to the statuesque man nods in a boastful manner.

"This is Wurtz, a former mercenary who now works for the Church as a priest. Although he's quite busy with regular duties, he's made time for the Holy Warrior's training today."

The man named Wurtz nods placidly in response. Behind Toudou, Limis mutters quietly, "Is he a gigas?"

The town headman groans. He slaps his forehead in exaggerated fashion and shakes his head from side to side.

"No, no, no, Lady Friedia. He is a courageous warrior with giant's blood running through his veins. Wurtz, sir, please pay her no mind. She means no ill will… She's simply a bit sheltered."

Limis is miffed, but before she can speak, Wurtz nods deeply and comes to the front of the group. A single step shakes their entire environs. Wurtz approaches Toudou and extends his arm toward her slowly. He's wearing white gloves on his massive hands.

"Wurtz Beld. It is a true honor to meet you, Holy Warrior."

"Ah… Y-yeah…"

Wurtz's voice is so unexpectedly gentle that Toudou's eyes go wide as saucers. Aria's and Limis's do the same. Toudou reaches out timidly and shakes Wurtz's hand lightly. He nods deeply and turns to Limis.

"Gigas are a type of monster. They resemble humans, but they are different. Though they are highly intelligent beings, their fighting instincts and savage nature are far more prominent. My ancestors were the most formidable type of monster on this planet."

"And they're different now?"

"No… They're still that way."

Wurtz's brown eyes are ablaze at Toudou's question. They are the eyes of a predator set apart from humankind.

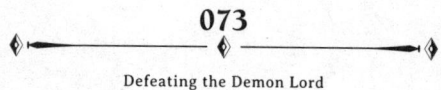

"Yet, within the gigas, there were a few with a strong sense of reason. They chose to live with the weaker beings. It's an ancient tale. The grandchildren of those who chose to live with humans—including myself—are now known as giants. That is why…you should not confuse giants with the gigas. You will invite unwanted strife."

"I-I'm so sorry… I didn't know."

Limis quickly bows her head. Clearly amused, the town headman curls his lips into a sneer.

"Heh-heh. Wurtz is especially intellectual among giants. At any rate, many of his ilk are extremely hot-blooded and fearsome."

Wurtz closes his eyes and speaks with great emotion. "I was once the same way. But…I have changed. That, Holy Warrior, is why I laid down my sword."

Just as he says, Wurtz only carries a ceremonial mace on his waist and does not have an actual weapon. In all honesty, with muscles evolved to that level, it doesn't matter if he carries one or not.

"I am level sixty-five. I haven't gained a level in quite some time, but… I know how to fight in this region. Since you seem to have only just arrived here…I may be able to assist you. Though I'm not very familiar with the art of sorcery…"

"…That's fine. We'll wield magic of our own accord, so…"

"I see… Not a problem, then."

Just then, the door swings open. The town headman gleefully greets the individual who enters.

"Ah, Madam Carina. It's been so long. We've been waiting for you."

Madam Carina. Toudou and Aria have heard the name before. She's the most famous person in all of Golem Valley, a matron of many legendary tales.

"So you're the Holy Warrior, eh…?"

The woman who appears before them looks starkly different from what Toudou had expected. She has vibrant purple hair and skin creased with wrinkles, appropriate for her age, but her eyes burn with a distinct fire. She looks like a witch.

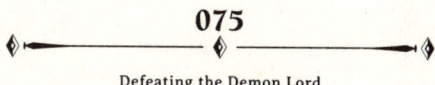

This may be the town headman's house, but she is leagues more dignified and impressive than him.

Even the overwhelming Wurtz somehow looks small next to her. She's half his height but still dwarfs him with her stately presence. Toudou is speechless. The witch bares her teeth and grins at her, laughing.

"I have heard your tale. Even without a priest, you've been quite active all throughout the Kingdom, haven't you?"

"Huh...? Um... W-well... I suppose..."

Carina nods with satisfaction and stares directly into Toudou's eyes, announcing with a grand gesture, "Yet, for the Church this is a cause of great regret. This is a fine opportunity, as we were the ones who requested you train here. Once your training is complete, you'll be the strongest warrior on earth."

"Strongest...on...earth?"

"That was a joke. You are still weak. It's a great inconvenience to us. We need you to at least be capable of slaying golems with ease."

Toudou stares wide-eyed as Carina, having said her piece, turns on her heel. She walks briskly to the door and goes to open it before yelling at Toudou, who is frozen stiff.

"Just what are you doing?! Get yourself to the training grounds, now! You get yourself ready, too, Wurtz."

"Understood, Madam."

Wurtz nods and thrusts his chin at Toudou, directing her outside. After receiving some words of encouragement from the town headman, the party quickly follows after Madam Carina.

"To begin, we'll get an idea of your present abilities."

"Uh—okay."

The training grounds are at the highest point of the village in a wide-open area, over one hundred meters in all directions. On one side of the cliff is a wall full of innumerable holes. The other three sides are hemmed in by a tall fence that prevents anyone from falling off.

The wind howls fiercely as Wurtz stands, looking the exact same as

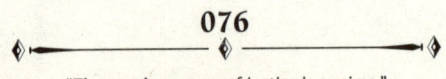

earlier. The only difference is that he's switched his white gloves for a thick pair of gauntlets, and his boots have been replaced by a sturdy pair of greaves.

Toudou's equipment, however, has not changed. The only difference is the steel longsword hanging from her belt—the holy sword Ex is not used for training purposes.

Live combat training. The steel longsword is much heavier than what she's used to, and she furrows her brow as she asks Carina standing nearby, "Four versus one—are you sure?"

"If you're uncomfortable, you can go one-on-one. But at your levels, I think this should be just right," she replies casually.

Toudou's eyes grow wide. Training that uses a many-to-one formulation is only feasible in extreme cases of discrepancy in prowess. Toudou has been treated with care by Carina until now, but this is putting a real thorn in her side.

"...Can I take the exercise on by myself, for starters?"

Carina gazes at Toudou and cackles, expelling hot breath.

"Heh-heh-heh, fine by me. The Holy Warrior should have a certain measure of foolhardiness, in my view."

Foolhardiness...

Toudou repeats the word in her head. She clenches her small fists as Limis and Aria look on with worry. Carina shouts to Wurtz, who has his eyes closed as if asleep.

"Wurtz! Take care not to...kill this young boy, eh? He still doesn't know how to unleash his true potential!"

"...But of course, Madam. I'm not...the same as before."

Wurtz opens his eyes and stares silently down at Toudou. Emotion smolders in his eyes and sends shivers down Toudou's spine. In that moment, Toudou almost instinctively shuts out all the emotions that have bubbled up from what others have said to her.

Toudou takes shallow breaths and psyches herself up. She draws her sword from her belt in a single fluid motion and manifests her shield, riddled with cracks, in her left hand.

She's always been adept at concentrating. Her field of vision is

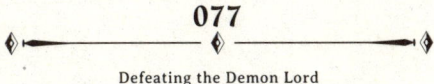

completely clear, and the only thing that remains is the towering man in front of her.

Unlike her fights with the golems, she now only has one opponent. He's level 65. Toudou has no intention of losing to him without putting up a real fight.

"How will we determine the winner?"

"The first one unconscious is the loser. No killing allowed. We want you to give it everything you've got, young warrior."

"…Got it."

Toudou has had only two weeks of official swordsmanship training, but she's honed her skills along the path in her quest. The steel long-sword is the same length as the holy sword Ex, and although slightly heavier, it's not cause for concern.

Toudou stares at the massive boulder of a man in front of her, calculating.

The gap between them is ten meters. Wurtz's arms are far longer than hers, but he's unarmed, so there isn't a big difference in their reach. It's plain as day that Wurtz dwarfs her in size, but that's not an explicit advantage for him. He has a wide field of vision but, in turn, larger blind spots. For Toudou, small in stature, sliding in to take advantage of them shouldn't be difficult.

A powerful gust blows through. The chilly air sends a cool bead of sweat down Toudou's body, and Carina raises her voice to begin the match. Toudou takes a preemptive stance. As she steps in toward Wurtz, his expression changes drastically. His eyes burn bloodred, and his unaffected countenance morphs into something demonic. His vicious howl rips through the air.

"OUUUGHHHHHHHHHHHHH!!!!! DIEEEEEEEEEEEEEEEEE EE!!"

§ § §

I suddenly feel a subtle ripple in the air and lift my head up.

"They're at it already…"

078

"The overdone sense of justice is a crime."

Even here, far from the training grounds, I can feel the impact of the same spell that Toudou cast in the Great Tomb—Howl. Wurtz must have used it during training. The spell's power decreases drastically with distance. The average human would never be able to reach this far.

Wurtz, a half giant, has a mix of human and giant blood. As a result, he's inherited a fine balance of both races' powers. He can level up, just like a human, but has the sheer physical strength of a giant.

In general, anyone with the mixed blood of a human and a demi-human is a formidable warrior. Wurtz is a fine example. A giant's Howl is nothing like a human's. The fact that Wurtz's reached all the way here speaks to this fact. To distinguish from a normal Howl, this version is often called a *Gigas Howl*.

This was one of Wurtz's foremost techniques—before he became a priest. It seems that even a few years passing hasn't robbed him of his true nature.

One of Toudou's party's biggest problems is their lack of a single high-level member. The capacities that increase with leveling up are not simply limited to physical strength. There's a knack to unleashing the amount of power relevant to one's level.

The reason I've asked the madam to train Toudou is so that he can learn how to harness this power. Wurtz is already a seasoned veteran—he'll temper Toudou's battle readiness, for certain.

At that moment, the weapons shop owner returns from behind the counter.

"Sorry to keep you. I searched high and low, but…this's the only one we got."

He produces a thumb-tip-sized bullet with his gnarled fingers and places it on the counter. It flashes silver-white and has a unique glint—it's a mythril bullet, a rarity in this world. I've heard of such a thing, but forcing the rare element mythril into disposable artillery is not a sane course of action.

"We rarely see mythril weapons brought in here. This is the only one we got, and it's only a sample."

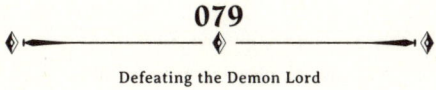

079

I observe the bullet on the counter. What I'm really after is something I can use as a medium for a prism, so anything mythril will do, but this can hardly be called a bullet. Mythril is, by nature, a metal that requires extremely high precision technology to process.

"Do you have a gun that can fire this?"

"Nope. Even if there was one, the bullet can't be recreated. It was made for hobbyist purposes."

The weapons shop owner spits out the words distastefully. Mythril, with its incredible effectiveness against demons, is supremely rare. In our current era, when the Demon Lord has invaded once again, the price of a gram of mythril is the highest among any known metal.

I originally used a mythril knife as a medium for prisms. I had spares, but I lost four in the battle with Zarpahn, and I currently retain two for personal use. Creating a barrier requires four separate items as mediums. Using my mace and this bullet makes four exactly. I would be left empty-handed in that case, but until the Church can replenish my mythril knife stock, this should suffice in the meantime.

"…Okay. I'll take it."

"You're a curious one, too."

I place some coins on the counter. It's an extraordinary price for a bullet, but necessity knows no bounds. If anything, I'm extremely lucky to have found this piece.

The blacksmith counts my coins and looks up at me. "Anything else you need?"

Prompted by his question, I remember what Gregorio used when we last fought.

"Yes, perhaps… Do you have any heavy-duty demon skins?"

"Demon skins? What the hell for?"

"I'm gonna stretch it tight, wrap my mace in it, and whip it at someone's face."

"The hell're you on about?"

The owner looks at me as if I've got two heads. Well, I guess there's no reason a weapons shop would have one anyway.

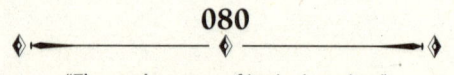

"The overdone sense of justice is a crime."

Demons are God's natural enemies. I wouldn't be able to procure demon skin from the Church even if I tried. There must be somewhere else...

I ponder the issue as I step outside and happen to run into Amelia and Stey. I asked them to speak with the local mercenaries and merchants and see if anything unusual has happened here recently.

Stey looks at me and breaks into a smile, running toward me. She's more and more over-friendly by the second.

"Oh, it's Ares! Good work today!"

"Did you find anything out?"

"No, not particularly... It seems that nothing major has happened here lately," Amelia replies.

"Hmm... I see."

That matches the intel the madam provided me. No formidable monsters have appeared, and nothing out the ordinary has happened. However, "nothing out of the ordinary" feels far more ominous than "the world's falling apart" at this point in time. There's a reason, something gnawing at me, which prompted me to ask Amelia to conduct a survey, even though the madam already told me that nothing is amiss.

Golem Valley is the foremost area for leveling up in all of the Kingdom of Ruxe. If I were the Demon Lord, I wouldn't choose to dispatch demons to the Great Forest of the Vale only to completely ignore this place.

"Continue to survey the area, just in case. In the end, we'll at least have a specific grasp on how the monsters are distributed and their tendencies for spawning."

"...You're quite the worrywart."

I've asked the madam to look after Toudou and company. This is a matter of having the right people in the right place. We won't leave any stone unturned.

My resolve freshly renewed, Stey tries to get a peek at what I'm holding in my hand.

"Oh? Whatcha got there, Ares?"

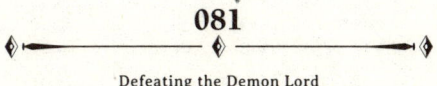

"…It's a piece of mythril I'm going to use as a medium for a barrier. I finally managed to find one."

"…I can't believe they had any for sale," Amelia pipes up, curious.

These days, demand for mythril is exceedingly high, and even putting a request in through the Church doesn't guarantee you'll actually get any. It was the last one in the weapons shop, and it was only there because the shop had no gun to fire it with.

Compared to Amelia, Stey—who asked me about it in the first place—looks completely perplexed.

"I mean, it's still not enough. I don't want to give up my mace as a medium if I can avoid it."

Especially here—we'd be screwed. My mace, Wrath of God, was developed using the full extent of the Church's technical engineering. It's irreplaceable. If it falls to the cliffs below, I will have no choice but to climb down after it. For that reason, I'm relieved that all I lost in the battle with Zarpahn were a few mythril knives.

Suddenly, Stey's dark eyes stare at me earnestly, and she cocks her head to the side.

"So you need mythril?"

"…That's right. I've made a request to the Church, but…"

As the words leave my mouth, I hear a snapping sound, like something being torn off.

My eyes bulge out of their sockets. Stey beams from ear to ear as she rips the top button off her mage's robe, the robe that's so damn short it can't possibly be something an actual sister would wear. Without the button, her robe pops open slightly, and I can see the white swell of her bosom.

"…What are you doing?"

"Here you go, Ares!"

I'm staring at her with ice-cold eyes, but she takes my hand and places the button inside.

The white button is inscribed with a pair of scales. I squint and hold it up to the light for observation. Suddenly, I feel my face freeze. *A white button inscribed with a pair of scales.*

"…Whoa… It's…myth…ril…"

"Huh?"

There's no mistaking it. The original luster has worn out from being handled, but it is undoubtedly holy silver.

I look Stey over from head to toe again as she smiles bashfully at me. Black miniskirt. Knee-high socks. Her black robe has buttons numbering one, two, three, four… Wait, she's even got some on the sleeves?!

Stey shyly repeats what I've already heard from Amelia.

"My robe is…custom-made!"

"Amelia, strip her bare. Her robe's…fitted with mythril."

"Huh…? Um, okay."

Amelia knows the robe is custom-made, but she must not have known everything about it, given how she's staring blankly, mouth agape. Well, I can't really blame her. There's no way I would have noticed without being told, either. What dumbass decided to make buttons out of something as exceedingly rare as mythril? Since its trademark luster has been rubbed off, it's impossible to tell unless you look very closely.

Now that I think about it, when Amelia complained to Creio about Stey being dispatched to us, he said something about how Stey has something I need… Did he really mean—?

"U-umm… But… I don't have anything else to wear!"

My face dead serious, I grab Stey by the shoulders and give her an order.

"Stephenne Veronide. I'm giving you an order, one that you and only you are capable of doing."

Stey gulps audibly.

"What… What is it?"

"…Your father, the cardinal— Ask him for a spare robe."

"Huh? …Ask Papa?"

Stey's tense expression finally relaxes. I guess she was expecting a different demand.

"…Yes. Ask your papa."

"Well… Okay, I guess."

Defeating the Demon Lord

Stey wrings her hands restlessly and pouts, looking displeased. I've never met Sylvester, but he's most definitely spoiled Stey rotten. There's no way a normal father would give his daughter a mythril-laden robe. Not to mention, Stey claims this robe is approved under Church regulations, but he obviously made that happen, too, given the mythril-tinted circumstances.

He really is a big-time former merchant... The guy's absolutely loaded.

I clench my fists and peer deep into Stey's eyes before adding, "And make it three."

The second they arrive, I'll strip them all bare.

Am I sure I'll make good use of her? Yes, indeed. I'll make plenty good use of her...

"Ares, you're evil..."

Amelia's whole body quakes from having realized my intentions, and her face is full of terror.

§ § §

Giants possess the highest physical capabilities among all demi-humans. Wurtz, who is mixed with human lineage, doesn't have the same level of sheer strength as a pure giant, but his power is amalgamated with the merits of a human being. Therefore, because Wurtz is blessed with incredible physical strength and the ability to level up, he considers human beings synonymous with frailty—at least, he used to.

His magic-infused Howl is full of murderous intent, rocking the earth and tearing through the sky above. Whenever he enters his battle stance, the blood rushes to his head. He sees red flashing in his mind, yet he doesn't take a step forward. Instead, he simply peers down at the tiny human in front of him.

A thin adolescent with black hair, named Naotsugu Toudou. Only level 29—and the Holy Warrior.

Howl cast by a predator such as a giant strikes primitive fear into the hearts of most living beings and renders them immobile. Losing the

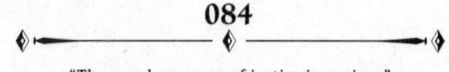

"The overdone sense of justice is a crime."

ability to move during battle is on par with suicide. Against an ordinary human being, this fight would have already been over.

However, the adolescent in front of him has only stiffened a bit, and his appearance has barely changed.

"The Holy Warrior... So this is the Holy Warrior... Hmm."

Wurtz has heard the rumors, but he never imagined he would be tasked with training the Holy Warrior himself. Wurtz nods deeply toward Toudou without saying a word. He has true capacity.

The capacity to become a true warrior lies in one's ability to overcome fear. Conquering the fear of death, and having the courage to march onward—possessing those qualities outweighs any latent talent. Increasing your level might heighten your abilities, but it doesn't strengthen the workings of your inner spirit.

The rippling air ceases, and Toudou's tense expression fades.

Wurtz breathes heavy, hot breaths and cools the fire addling his brain. Toudou asks suspiciously, "Why...didn't you attack me when you had the opening?"

"This is...training, Sir Holy Warrior. But make no mistake... I do not take you lightly."

"Take me...lightly?"

Wurtz quells his heightened combative instincts and smiles.

"Indeed, Sir Holy Warrior... In the past, I fought another who was able to withstand Howl as you just did. Back then—I attacked the moment I cast Howl and...took a severe counterattack. Ever since then... I've remained vigilant."

"...I'm...only half your level."

"Level is merely...a standard. Even with our vast differences, Sir Holy Warrior, nothing is for certain."

Wurtz takes a single step toward Toudou, enough to cause the ground to rumble. His gauntlets creak from the force of his clenched fists. Toudou's brow spasms, his expression stiffening once again.

"That is why...I will not let my guard down around you. My arms, my legs—my entire body howls for me to unleash its power. However,

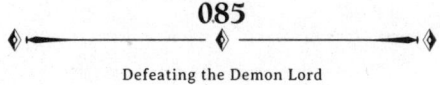

I am keeping it under control. It's a matter of reason—and proof of my cowardice. Laugh all you want! Giants are known for their dauntless courage in the face of formidable foes, but as for me—"

There are approximately two meters between Wurtz and Toudou. Toudou steps in closer, to the point where he can draw his sword and make a direct hit. Wurtz looks down at the weakling in front of him and grins fiendishly.

"—I refuse to take the chance of losing, no matter how slight."

Wurtz's remarks spring Toudou into action, his eyes wide as he draws his sword. In the same moment, Wurtz lunges forth like a cannon-ball and smashes his fist down toward him.

This is bad. The moment the thought crops up in Toudou's mind, Wurtz's fist rains down on her like a boulder falling from the sky.

Toudou herself has ample confidence in her own prowess, but she's not conceited enough to think she can easily defeat someone of such a higher level. Find the enemy's blind spots. Counterattack. Stopping to aim will leave her unprepared. She must put her sights on the minute openings that occur in the course of being attacked.

That is Toudou's plan, but she was completely shell-shocked by Wurtz's statement. A massive fist raining down on her. She thinks about meeting the fist with her sword but at the last second lunges to the side to avoid his attack.

"?!"

Despite having evaded his fist, the resulting impact of Wurtz's strike sends Toudou rolling. Her ears ring and her vision blurs. Wurtz does not pursue Toudou as she bounces along the ground.

"Ugh... What the hell was that—?"

"Your decision to evade was...a sound judgment."

Toudou was hit with the force of the impact of Wurtz's strike even though it hadn't connected. She would have been knocked off her feet had she tried to counter with her own blade, and there's no way she could've blocked him with her shield.

"The overdone sense of justice is a crime."

Toudou quickly realizes she's misjudged the difference in strength between them. Their bodies are on a different scale, along with their level. And just as Wurtz said—it would be negligent to think there are any blind spots.

The man in front of Toudou is a far more accomplished warrior. Toudou stands up and staggers, raising her sword and shield once again.

She simply can't receive his attacks. She would need to sidestep every single one. Toudou purses her lips, and Wurtz smiles, his voice mellow.

"You knew our difference in strength, yet, you still chose to attack me solo. I admire your spirit. Let us begin, young warrior."

"Bring it!" shouts Toudou.

The next moment, Wurtz vanishes into thin air.

Life force. Toudou has heard the words so many times since coming into this world.

Wurtz Beld is double Toudou's size and more than twice as heavy. When the mountain of a man towering before her suddenly disappears, Toudou realizes in the next instant that she's suspended in the air. She didn't even have the chance to blink.

She saw his first attack coming, but the second blow is on another level. Wurtz was still reining in his strength, so Toudou only took a small amount of damage, but if this were a real battlefield, she would have been grievously injured. Toudou stares up at the sky, sprawled across the ground, faceup, body splayed out. Wurtz speaks to her in a deep voice befitting his massive stature.

"Holy Warrior. You don't yet understand yourself. The reason you're laid out right now is because you, as a pure, unadulterated level twenty-nine human don't understand…what it is you're capable of."

"You mean…my technique is lacking?"

Toudou has learned swordsmanship, magic, and holy techniques. Every other apprentice knew her as top of her class.

Of course, she still lacks experience, but she has self-confidence. Toudou herself knows she's grown during the course of her party's quest.

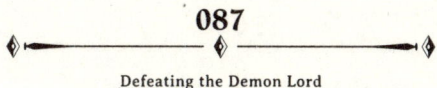

Wurtz receives Toudou's jet-black gaze and shakes his head.

"No, Sir Holy Warrior. The opposite."

"The…opposite?"

"Yes. Level is only a measure of your acquired life force. You must never forget this, Sir Holy Warrior."

Wurtz stomps both feet on the ground, and in the next instant, he disappears.

Limis and Aria are wide-eyed on the sidelines—Wurtz has teleported to just a few meters away from them. Toudou can move quickly, too, but escaping someone's field of vision in an instant is not typical. Wurtz continues to speak to Toudou, who's flabbergasted.

"You, Sir Holy Warrior, must know thyself. Your level is only indicative of what you're capable of in this world. Before you raise your level, you must come to understand just how different you are."

"How different I am…"

Wurtz's words remind Toudou of her showdown with Gregorio in Purif. Gregorio hadn't done a thing to her, and yet, she had been unable to move even a single finger. He had said something similar.

"Toudou, there are so very many things that I, far above your level, can do that you cannot."

"Indeed, young warrior. You are still so unaware of what you can do, the things you have become capable of."

Wurtz nods deeply and rests his kind eyes on Aria and Limis before continuing.

"These are things you must discover through live combat. Now, then—who's up next?"

Toudou raises herself up off the ground. Just as Aria takes a step forward to announce herself as the next candidate, a small, silent shadow darts out in front of Wurtz and raises her hand.

"Hmm…?"

"I'll…do it…"

Glacia's long, dark-green hair grazes the ground. Wurtz's massive

bulk completely dwarfs her. Her left hand drags the gargantuan metal hunk—the war hammer that was purchased for her—behind her.

Toudou's eyes fly open as Wurtz observes her with his gentle eyes.

"Glacia?!"

"......Very well."

Wurtz clenches his fists and drops his shoulders. Even staring up at his gigantic body, Glacia is unfazed. Both Limis and Aria start to call out to her, but they hold their tongues when they catch a glimpse of her fearless expression.

"Come at me whenever you're ready."

Glacia slowly raises the weighty war hammer aloft. Watching her lift it with her arm—thinner than the handle itself—is nothing short of an incredible joke.

Of course, Glacia tested her ability to lift the war hammer before purchasing it, but Toudou is still wide-eyed at the immensely improbable scene playing out before her.

Wurtz's expression changes. He realizes that Glacia still has plenty of strength left over.

"Hmph... Surely, you are not human."

Glacia refrains from answering and brings up the war hammer with ease—like wielding a twig.

Glacia is an absolute powerhouse. When she lived in the Great Forest of the Vale, she didn't have a single enemy. She was bigger than everyone and simply more powerful. Back then, she lived a quiet life, with nobody to ever challenge her prowess. Yet, right now, all that is meaningless.

She chose the war hammer because it was the biggest weapon. Glacia knows her own strength.

She looks up at the giant man in front of her. His body is extraordinarily massive and his battle prowess exceptional. Yet—he's nothing like that deranged priest.

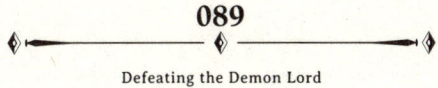

Glacia had been no match for the priest. He's an insurmountable foe, though it pains Glacia to the core to admit it. Of course, even she knows pride, but pride goes out the window when it comes to that man. Her only choice regarding him is to show her hand and feign allegiance.

Glacia stomps on the ground with all her might. Her body feels light next to the incredible weight of her war hammer, but she takes advantage of the fact and brings it down on the ground in front of her with full force. She intends to crush anyone who stands in her path.

The war hammer thunders uproariously, but Wurtz has already sidestepped the blow. Glacia lifts the war hammer again, like a feather, and stares at him.

"Here I come!!" Wurtz roars, stepping forward. Glacia brandishes her weapon and says a little prayer to herself:

At the very least, don't let my efforts go unnoticed.

Having finished her first day of training, Toudou lays sprawled out on her bed and sighs deeply. Wurtz's movements defied all common sense. His muscles are like steel, his speed dizzying.

In the end, having gone through a number of battle simulation exercises, Toudou was unable to land a single blow on Wurtz.

"He defies...the law of physics. Even with my magic... Not that it'd make a difference."

"Giants have a particular aptitude for combat. But he is truly something else...," replies Aria, a grim look on her face—just like Toudou, she couldn't land a single blow.

Toudou stares at the ceiling as she whispers, her voice brimming with raw emotion, "The world is full of powerful beings..."

Everywhere she's visited thus far, Toudou has only met people far more highly leveled than her. She couldn't lay a finger on Gregorio back in Purif, and in the Great Forest of the Vale, she lost consciousness after getting involved in a fight against a demon.

Toudou sighs dejectedly, and Limis sits down next to her on the bed.

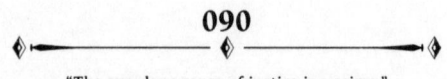

"The overdone sense of justice is a crime."

"What are you talking about, Nao? You're the one who has to become the most powerful of all of them."

"...I wonder if I can."

Limis meets Toudou's gaze as she stares up from the bed.

"You have to. Even Glacia's giving it her all."

Glacia, standing around absentmindedly, hears her name and looks at Limis. Her deep green eyes flicker; it's impossible to read what she's thinking. However, she's the only member of the party who could go pound-for-pound with Wurtz. He evaded her attacks, and hers alone, so seriously.

"Glacia used to be a demi-dragon, so it's not far-fetched to think that she could fight... But why so suddenly?"

"It's a good thing, this sudden burst of motivation. Are you worried or something?"

"...I suppose you've got a point..."

As usual, Glacia looks wistfully at Limis and Aria, giving no indication of answering their question. Toudou thinks for a second and then perks up, saying, "Well, looks like I'll have my work cut out for me if I wanna keep up with Glacia..."

Although she wasn't able to land a single hit during today's training session, she was told that her movements were improving little by little. In truth, Toudou herself can feel her movements becoming quicker as well.

Yet, Wurtz's form is tremendous, and going head-to-head with him is like standing on the precipice of death.

Toudou continues to aimlessly stare at the ceiling, stifling the profound exhaustion wracking her entire body.

§ § §

"For the record, I have to ask—is he still alive?" I ask right away.

I'm visiting the local church for a report on the training session. Shocked, the madam responds, "What on earth are you on about?"

I guess…Wurtz must have learned how to control himself. I wasn't actually that worried since the madam was also present, but at the end of the day, giants are hotheaded. In the heat of battle, they tend to forget everything else.

Wurtz looks up at me and says in his typically unaffected tone, "He has…talent."

"So he lost?"

"Ares… If you were level twenty-nine, do you think you could defeat me?"

Fair enough. The half giant is already far superior to Toudou in physical prowess, and on top of that, he's over twice his level. In all honesty, there's no way Toudou would stand a chance against Wurtz. Neither would I.

"Yeah, but I'm not Toudou."

He's the hero. I'll be damned if I'm lumped together with someone who has the protection of the Three Deities and Eight Spirit Kings.

Wurtz gives an affected nod in response. His eyes seem to be staring into far-off space.

"That's correct. You are not the Holy Warrior. He is…committed to fighting fair and square."

Fair and square, huh…? That's a wonderful thing. The people will never recognize a cowardly hero. No need for the Church to spin things, either. That's all predicated on the Holy Warrior's success, of course.

"He has a lot of potential for growth. If he trains hard…he could be very powerful."

"Perhaps, but he doesn't have the time to lollygag."

I already know that Toudou has massive potential. I want him to level up and become powerful as quickly as possible, to slay the Demon Lord. I'm really pulling for him, here.

The madam contorts her lips into a smile and chuckles before chiming in.

"Impatience is a sin, boy. Human beings are resilient. We won't easily lie down without a fight."

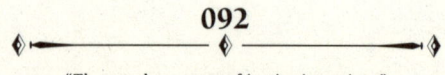

092

"The overdone sense of justice is a crime."

"Madam—it is my responsibility to get Toudou to slay the Demon Lord as quickly and safely as possible."

"This I know full well. Yet, this Holy Warrior is rather…peculiar."

The madam puts a well-used, luxurious pipe to her mouth and sparks it, puffing away.

She may be referring to someone else, but the madam is plenty peculiar herself, as is everyone around me.

Wurtz continues, talking rapid-fire. He's in incredibly high spirits. Purple smoke wafts gently toward the ceiling and disappears out a vent.

"I will be of service to the Holy Warrior as long as he's here. However, once he learns the bare minimum, we should really move on to leveling him up. At level twenty-nine, there's a limit to how much he can learn in training."

"Thanks… I appreciate it."

This means I can leave Toudou and his party's battle prowess up to Wurtz. It's a perfect arrangement, since I can't make my presence known.

I've struck gold—or not quite, but these connections are working out… Whoa, we're actually doing pretty well.

Has my luck turned around…? There's always a snake in the grass, however…always.

I let the potential vision of reality go for now and turn to Wurtz, asking jokingly, "By the way, you had a chance to train everyone, right? Who showed the highest potential?"

Wurtz screws up his face and grumbles for a moment before telling me.

"Glacia."

"…I forgot to tell you, but she's only in the party for internal information-gathering purposes. You don't need to train her."

That was *not* the answer I'd hoped for…

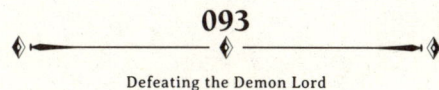

093

Third Report

On Fixing the New Recruit's Weakness

It's been approximately two weeks since the party has arrived in Golem Valley. The situation is progressing extremely well.

Pruflas Wrath, God of War—one of the sources of Toudou's divine protection—is known to bestow Their divine protection only to someone who possesses the attributes of a refined warrior. It didn't take Toudou any time at all to adapt to the newfound physical strength he's acquired through training.

From a protruding cliff, I observe Toudou on the training grounds leagues below. His eyes are closed and he's breathing deeply, cyclically. This alone shows how profoundly he's changed since beginning Wurtz's training.

Wurtz waits for an ample period before entering the training grounds. He has a single doll strapped to his back. It's slim and looks a lot like a human being. Its armored shell is riddled with scrapes but has been polished to a shiny dark gray. This kind of doll resembles a metal golem and was created by a mage for training purposes.

Metal golems are the strongest enemies in the entire area. They're smaller than rock golems but more powerful and extremely agile. Their armored bodies are made from a special metal that is very hard and resistant to magic. As an added bonus, they can even attack with weapons.

This special metal golem created for training use is weaker than its wild counterparts, but if one can face off against it easily, other golems will be a breeze.

Toudou's eyes open wide. Aria, Limis, and Glacia are watching him

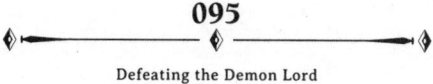

from a short distance. Wurtz puts the metal golem on the ground and looks at Toudou.

"Today, you'll be facing this thing here."

"Yes, sir."

"Even previous Holy Warriors struggled to hold their own against it. The recommended level for defeating one of these is…about fifty. It doesn't have any special abilities—it's just lightning quick, solid, and powerful. Also highly resistant to magic."

"Understood."

Toudou's expression doesn't change. He's only staring incessantly at the golem, not looking nervous at all.

"Okay—do you want to fight solo again today?"

"…Yes. I'll try."

Toudou's answer hasn't changed since the first time Wurtz asked. A mercenary obsessed with winning would have opted to fight as a whole party. This is further proof that Toudou is less of a mercenary and more of a knight who values a fair match. Another one of his qualities.

"Very well."

The metal golem made for training grinds and creaks as it stands upright. Its head turns slowly toward Toudou. After checking that everything is in order, Wurtz retreats to stand beside Aria and the others.

To tell the truth, Wurtz has a tendency to make reckless statements. Toudou likely understands this by now, but when Wurtz says the appropriate level is 50, he means level 50 battling as a party. And the appropriate level for a real metal golem is much higher than that.

Per our faith, we priests cannot tell lies, but in truth, anything outside of a bald-faced lie is fair game.

Toudou brandishes his training sword and shield and slowly circles the golem, encroaching on it. The metal golem launches toward him without warning.

"You should come back here when your level is higher. This should be enough training for you at your current level."

"Pant, pant… Yes, sir. Thank you…very much."

Toudou and Aria look up from where they're standing, bent over with their hands on their knees, breathing raggedly. The metal golem doesn't have a single scratch. It's fairly obvious how things turned out. Even as a whole party, they're not at the appropriate level. Miracles don't occur so readily.

Yet, keeping that in mind, their results were actually quite impressive. Toudou couldn't land any fatal blows, but he definitely lasted a long time against the metal golem. Aria managed to endure the golem's fierce attacks while at the same time avoiding taking any serious damage. Both party members have grown to the point where they can hold their own against a metal golem, albeit for a relatively short period of time.

If I'd had the same training at their level, I would likely be at my wit's end.

"You should be ready to take on wild golems. The only reason that you, Sir Holy Warrior, couldn't defeat this opponent was simply because you still lack the ability. It's nothing to beat yourself up over."

"Yes, I…know."

Toudou has to wring the words out of his mouth, and he bites his lip in frustration. He couldn't bring down the metal golem, but the experience he's gained over the past few days is invaluable.

Wurtz continues to give advice on their tactics, and I turn on my heel to leave. I can say with confidence that Toudou is getting along exceptionally well.

I have my own business I must attend to.

I crumple up a letter I just received, then sigh deeply in an effort to quell the indignation and anxiety wracking my mind. The letter contains the results of Amelia's survey on any strange occurrences within the region.

There are five towns within Golem Valley, but they're all connected by a series of networks: mercenaries, merchants, and the Church. As they all have different points of view, the information that can be garnered from each is also different.

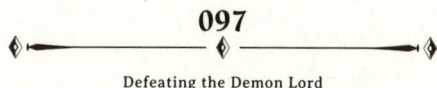

In my spare time, I'd worked to gather what information I could from all three networks. My feelings must be fairly obvious, as Amelia opens her mouth to speak.

"Did something—?"

"Did something happen, Ares?"

We've ranked up—hitting a gold mine of veritable net worth—but Stey doesn't seem to realize it at all, as she approaches me hesitantly.

"No... It's...nothing."

"...Huh?"

"There's absolutely nothing... This is unbelievable."

I go over each and every town rumor in my head, every slightly odd occurrence, but I can't come up with anything.

The report doesn't mention anything unusual, just peace and harmony. How is that even possible?

"...*Ahem*. Isn't that...a good thing?"

Amelia clears her throat softly and looks blankly at Stey after getting cut off.

She's right. It *is* a good thing—under normal circumstances. However, this quest to defeat the Demon Lord has been plagued with problems up until now. Is it reasonable to think that nothing could go wrong this time? No chance in hell.

I stare at the massive klutz standing in front of me. She is a legitimate problem, but not a serious one. She slows us down, but she does have her merits. There must be something else headed our way—perhaps from the outside?

I've entrusted Amelia with reporting back to the Church headquarters for the past several days, so I ask her, "Amelia, where is Gregorio right now?"

"He's still in Purif, I'm told."

"...Any signs of him coming this way?"

"...Not particularly. Actually, I'd say it's entirely unlikely. Spica's still alive for the time being anyway."

"The overdone sense of justice is a crime."

Amelia is blunt, as always. Entirely unlikely, is it? Then where the hell is our problem gonna come from?! If something's coming our way, then it'd better happen sooner rather than later. Otherwise—we'll have no choice but to prepare ourselves for the next one!! Is that what you want?! Is that *really* what you want?!

No—it's useless. We can't let our guard down. Remember everything that's happened so far, Ares Crown. The second we let our guard down, they'll be planning their next attack.

"Ares... You're exhausted. Why don't you take a rest?"

"Amelia's right, Ares! You work too hard. She's always talking about how you're such a workaholic."

I hate to worry them... But I'm not insane, and I'm not tired, dammit.

Honestly, I just wish something would happen right this second. It feels like I'm in the calm before the storm, and I can't afford a second to relax.

"No—not now. They get back to leveling up tomorrow. Something will happen—something unexpected."

But what will it be? Will Toudou...die? No, wait. That can't happen. I won't allow it.

Given the trends in our previous problems, this one will be something far more...off the wall.

"Please calm yourself, Ares. Deep breaths, deep breaths."

"...Psh. I've heard enough. Bring me a spear or a pistol."

"Ares?!"

We're completely prepared. As long as all our preparations are in order, there won't be any issues. No matter what happens, I'll drive right up the middle and pull through.

Stey looks up at me shyly. For starters...I'll begin with her.

"Hmm... Maybe what Ares is saying is complicated, because I don't really understand."

"Amelia. Booze. Bring me booze."

"Wha—?! Wh-why all of a sudden?"

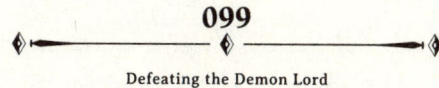

You should know. I'm gonna get Stey drunk and determine what kind of problem that creates. We still have the time. If I figure the problem out now, it'll be easier to deal with if it happens again.

I'll smash every possible problem ahead of time—smash them to smithereens.

§   §   §

Toudou hasn't been outside the town for a while, and she's in a peculiarly quiet mood.

She passes through the mammoth gate and walks through the valley without an iota of the anxiety she felt coming through here the first day.

Two weeks of constant training. Her actual level hasn't increased, but she now understands how important it really was. Level is simply a measure of one's authority in this world. As a result, having a high level gives you more possibilities.

The flow and sound of the wind, previously unknown to Toudou, provide her with information. She can sense things beyond her field of vision, what lies unseen farther down the road. Now she knows why she lost to Wurtz in their first fight.

After just a short period of practical training, Toudou's body has adapted to her newfound abilities. The sights she now sees, and the stage she's reached in life, are completely different. Anything that gets in her way doesn't stand a chance.

Up ahead, beyond a curve in the road, Toudou senses the presence of a ball golem. She draws her sword.

Just as she anticipated, a ball golem appears from around the bend. It lunges forward on a trajectory Toudou could not perceive previously. Five golems approach her rapidly, and she steps out to face them.

Although Toudou's level hasn't changed, she can now predict her opponents' movements. Just what did she do in these situations before?

This golem is less than half as fast as Wurtz, her instructor for the past two weeks. Toudou switches up her gait to match the golem's

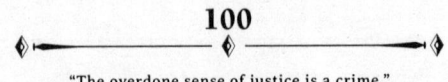

rhythm, which is on a straight beeline. At the very least, it won't stray from the same trajectory when it's airborne.

When the ball golem comes past her, she brings the holy sword Ex down on it and cleaves it in two with ease. Without stopping to confirm its demise, she slashes through the remaining four golems behind her. Five golems, and five slashes from the holy blade. The sound of their carcasses hitting the ground echoes throughout the valley well after the fact.

Toudou is a completely different person than before her training. Seeing this, Limis says in bewilderment, "…You really ripped through them no sweat."

"Maybe, but this is a holy blade, after all. I was pretty surprised myself, but at this rate, I should be able to start leveling up."

"We'll have to express our thanks to Wurtz."

Toudou gives a small nod in agreement. Training was brutal, and losing repeatedly had her at her wit's end, but now, she knows only gratitude.

Toudou collects the ball golems' remains to be used for magical tools, and the party continues forward on the path. Wurtz told them to return for additional training when they hit level 30.

Today, they're heading for Second Town. Along the way, Toudou and the party slay innumerable golems and soon arrive at their destination. From this short trip alone, Toudou has already reached level 30.

It feels like power is welling from deep within her body. Leveling up always causes that sort of sensation, but this time is unlike anything she's ever experienced. Toudou closes her eyes and exhales deeply before opening them.

"So this is…level thirty…"

"Congratulations."

"Nice going, Nao!"

As they ventured off to Second Town, Aria had reached level 28, and Limis 20—the greatest improvement of everyone—perhaps because they'd annihilated everything around them. They both offer words of congratulations to Toudou.

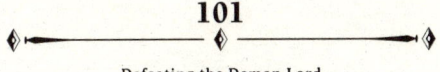

She's heard many times before that reaching level 30 is just one obstacle. However, having finally reached it herself, she can definitely feel a significant difference. At the same time, it's a clear indicator of all the things she was previously incapable of.

Toudou looks to her fellow party members, both of whom have yet to reach level 30—a fact that brings her great frustration.

"We all need…to get stronger, as quickly as possible."

"I agree…"

"We can make it happen here… Though not being able to perform the level-up ritual repeatedly might be tricky…"

Toudou's limited holy energy means that she can't perform the level-up ritual in succession. She must look dejected, because Aria quickly approaches her and pats her on the shoulder in consolation.

"Don't worry, your holy energy will continue to climb as well… And I'll need to remain diligent and avoid injury as much as possible."

"That's right, Aria. Besides, the less holy energy you expend on being injured, the more you'll have left over to level up…"

"That's irrelevant—we all need to conserve our holy energy as much as possible! You never know what'll happen on the battlefield."

Limis and Aria start to bicker. Toudou says again, this time in a whisper to herself, "We all need…to get stronger."

Toudou has finally reached the bare minimum level, but there are still so many other things she must take care of: practice her magic, temper her swordsmanship, boost her amount of holy energy. They should even be able to improve their battle formation, too, now that Glacia is an active participant.

Toudou is casting her eyes downward when Limis quickly interjects as if suddenly remembering something.

"Oh, by the way, Nao—I feel like I should learn healing magic, too. I've been thinking about it for a while now, but I finally got the necessary tools to learn… Well, I can't cast any spells yet, but—"

"H-hey! Are you listening to me?!" exclaims Aria, stunned by Limis changing the subject.

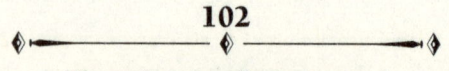

Toudou's party is doing everything they can. Looking at Limis and Aria, Toudou breaks into a smile.

Defeating the Demon Lord. It would be a daunting task if she were on her own, but with her party's support, nothing will throw them off their course.

§ § §

"So he's finally at level thirty…"

Golem Valley is packed with mercenaries. In particular, as you venture deeper into the valley, their numbers continue to increase. The bar at the inn in Second Town, where I've chosen to meet with Amelia, is chock-full of them.

"We're slightly behind our original schedule, but it's not a problem. It won't be too long before we can stop monitoring them."

We'd been observing them from above again today, just to be safe, but Toudou and his party have made leaps and bounds since their training began. They'll only get more efficient at leveling up from here on out.

Beaming ear to ear, Stey raises both hands up and gives her own opinion, sauce still covering her lips.

"Toudou was soooo awesome! He took down that ball thing like *fwoosh*!"

"I personally think that Ares, who's still somehow managing to drag you all over Golem Valley, is the awesome one here."

Amelia spits pure venom with a completely deadpan look. Hey, all I'm doing is pulling Stey along by the hand. In any case… Moving on…

Amelia must have realized what I wanted to say, even though I haven't opened my mouth. She launches into her report.

"Just as you asked, Ares, I've gathered some of the rumors floating around Second Town."

"Did you find anything out?"

Double-check and triple-check and quadruple-check. I've left the survey of Second Town up to Amelia's trusted footwork. She's far better

than I am at getting information out of strangers. I look toward her with anticipation in my eyes, but she only shakes her head briefly.

"As expected, there are no rumors of anything out of the ordinary. Everything is peaceful."

"There's really...nothing? ...Seriously?"

Every last piece of information we've gathered since arriving in Golem Valley indicates that nothing is out of place. As I groan, the corners of Amelia's mouth turn up ever so slightly as she smiles.

"Yes, really. Isn't this how things usually are?"

She's absolutely right. But I'm still not convinced.

As I'm vexed over the situation, Amelia follows up with a one-two punch. Pointing at Stey, she says, "Isn't Stey more than enough trouble for you right now?"

"...Hey. Just one question. How'd you two get so close anyway?"

No matter which way I look at it, Amelia's being particularly cold to Stey.

It's an honest question. Stey answers cheerfully, "Amelia used to sit next to me at the Church headquarters!"

"...I also taught her how to be an operator." Amelia sounds dead tired.

She took her sweet time getting me connected back when she was the operator, so really, Amelia, you should've done a better job of teaching her... At least, that's what I want to say. But I'm sure teaching her took a hell of a lot of effort, so I decide to hold my tongue.

"Stey...causes trouble the second you let your eyes off her. It was extremely vexing."

"I see... Just like right now?"

I point to Stey. Next to Amelia, she's ordering a drink from the waiter. I gave her alcohol yesterday as a test and subsequently wasted no time in enacting a full-stop alcohol ban.

"Yes, exactly like—Stey, no! I thought I told you no drinking!"

"I'm not gonna drink it! I'm just ordering, that's all!"

Amelia grabs Stey by the cheek as she pouts. For the record, drunk

Stey is just like drunk Amelia. I know I said they're like sisters, but I wish they didn't resemble each other quite *this* much.

I clear my throat and decide to change locations, knocking Amelia's hand off Stey's cheek.

"For now, we'll continue monitoring Toudou a while longer, at least until everyone is around level thirty. Personally, I think we should keep an eye on them for longer, but Cardinal Creio is of the opinion that I'm being overprotective."

Having to keep my superior's wishes in mind is an incredible nuisance. Well, at the very worst, if I'm not around, the party should be able to use Glacia as a tank to buy some time. I'll persuade her to take the initiative and be their shield.

"Keep up with the survey just in case. If you notice anything at all, let me know."

"I have a proposal."

"Tell me."

"Would you consider switching my role with Stey's?"

The hell is she talking about? Her job isn't particularly difficult. All that's required is to make snap decisions, think for yourself, and not get lost.

But Amelia's expression is dead serious. She's not joking around when she looks like that.

"And why is that?"

"You and Stey together, exploring dangerous locations—I can hardly stand the thought of it."

"Well, I can't stand the thought of Stey on her own. Proposal denied."

It's not that I absolutely can't understand where Amelia's coming from, but it's too late for such concerns.

Stey's eyes are wide as she looks between Amelia and me. I'm used to her shenanigans by now. Don't overthink it, and if something goes awry, I'll take the situation by force. As long as I stick to these two rules, we'll manage somehow.

Amelia looks at me with reproach.

"I'll be worried sick."

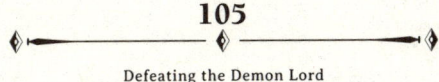

"Be sick, then."

I'm already fully aware of Amelia's impudence. She's tough—she'll be fine.

It would appear that Toudou and party have heeded Wurtz's advice and are proceeding to focus on training and leveling up alternatively. After leveling up for two days, they'll mix in a day of training. They're using First Town and Second Town as bases in turn.

Perhaps thanks to Wurtz's training, Toudou's now leveling up with such efficiency that her previous progress seems like a total joke. She's already reached level 33, and Aria and Limis have made progress as well. They can defeat low-level golems easily now, without facing any real threat.

Everything's going quite smoothly, yet, I'm still gripped by an unknown sense of dread. The door to my room opens a crack.

Stey sticks her head in, wearing a robe now adorned with wooden buttons, and announces casually, "Ares, it's morning!"

"Yes... I'm aware."

Having traveled together for a little while, I'm fully used to Stey by now, and I guess she feels the same way about me. There's not a lick of worry on her face. Maybe I should try being that carefree.

"Did you compile every type and number of monster Toudou's party has defeated so far, like I asked you to?"

"Yep! I have that here for you."

"You always look like you're having so much fun."

"Oh? Do you think so?"

Stey tilts her head to the side curiously and hands me the report she's holding. I flip quickly through the pages and inspect it. This is a bit like a record of Toudou's growth—the report includes his level-up pace as well as the type and number of monsters he's encountered. This data will also prove invaluable for educating future generations of Holy Warriors.

There don't appear to be any glaring issues with the contents. Against all odds, this klutz seems to possess legitimate administrative skills. As I

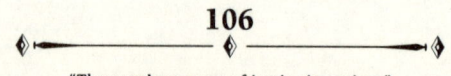

"The overdone sense of justice is a crime."

take my eyes off the papers for a moment, I realize that Stey is looking up at me, biding her time.

"Oh, thanks for this. It's a big help."

"! You're very welcome!"

"Seriously though, you always look like you're enjoying yourself."

"That's because I love working!"

Sister Stey's reply is full of cheer. She really does seem to enjoy it. Back at the Church headquarters, she was probably deemed too useless for anyone to give her real work. That doesn't seem like a productive topic, so I decide not to pursue it further.

"All party members are leveling up steadily. I'd like to resolve any and all fundamental issues as soon as possible."

"Fundamental...issues? What do you mean?"

For example, Aria's complete lack of magical energy. Or the fact that Limis has only entered a covenant with a fire spirit. There are so many issues that I've been putting off. I can't tell if Stey understands me or not, but she decides to chime in.

"I mean, sure, Aria seems to be having the hardest time in battle..."

There's nothing that can be done about Aria's lack of magical energy, so we must simply leave that to the course of events. I sigh and continue.

"There's also Limis. The fact that she's only contracted with a fire spirit is a huge problem."

"Ohhh... Yeah, that's pretty rare, huh?"

Can Stey think like a mage? She sure looks like she does, as she's agreeing with me.

"It's not especially rare for an elementalist to only have a single contracted spirit, but...do you know why it's a problem?"

"Hmm... Well, individual monsters have strengths and weaknesses to specific attributes..."

Stey looks a bit subdued as she answers, but she definitely seems to understand the general principle.

"That's right. Elementalists thrive when they exploit an enemy's elemental weakness."

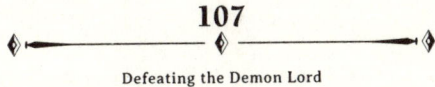

For example, glacial plants have a high resistance to all elemental attributes, but when it comes to water-based attack magic, they're practically immune. Conversely, they are the weakest to fire-based attack magic, compared with the other elements.

Although Limis is probably better off than Aria, this is still a major thorn in her side as an elementalist. But there's still something here that defies my expectations. I had originally planned on using Golem Valley as a training grounds for Limis.

"The majority of golems are highly resistant to fire. I knew that Limis would have a rough time here. At the very least, I knew she'd be way out of her league and wouldn't be able to one-shot any of the monsters here. However, she's now able to one-shot everything she confronts."

Limis's growth has far exceeded my expectations. This isn't normal, even for someone from a prestigious line of elementalists like the House of Friedia.

I stare intently at Stey, and her cheeks flush bashfully. *Quit it.*

"How is that possible?"

Stey closes her eyes and grumbles softly to herself before quickly opening them.

"Hmm, well, the most important thing for an elementalist is, above all else…the degree to which they establish a deep emotional bond with their spirit, so…"

So it is possible… No, this isn't a matter of possible versus impossible. It's already happening.

The difference between Limis's problem and Aria's problem is that Aria's simply cannot be solved, whereas Limis's still has the potential to be rectified. I don't know why Limis has only entered into a covenant with a fire spirit, and I've never heard that she's only capable of a single contract, either.

For that reason, I've decided to give Limis a taste of reality—show her the severe limits of only establishing a covenant with a fire spirit, and get her to look at things with a fresh perspective.

"Um, Ares? You look perplexed."

"The overdone sense of justice is a crime."

"…Not yet. Limis has yet to face off against a volcanic golem."

"A volcanic…golem?"

Volcanic golems are some of the strongest monsters that inhabit Golem Valley, with nearly perfect resistance to all fire-based properties. They aren't especially rare, so the party will definitely encounter them the deeper they progress into the valley. Just how will Limis react when she meets an enemy wholly unaffected by her magic attacks?

"…Well, most mages are girls anyway, so I'd be able to replace her more easily than Aria."

"Don't worry. I'm sure Limis will be just fine!" Without a shadow of doubt on her face, Stey makes a claim she can't guarantee.

A highly compressed burst of fire from the *Flame Lance* spell rips into the trunk of the rock golem, whose body is a few meters thick. The lance melts the golem's chest and comes out the other side, obliterating its core and burning it to ash.

Limis is currently level-23, but at this rate, she'll match Toudou's level in no time flat. Not to mention, as unlikely as it seems, Flame Lance is low-level attack magic. Even a level-23 elementalist can cast it in succession, and although some mages have trouble aiming it accurately, Limis never misses.

The House of Friedia has a long lineage of powerful mages. I have a newfound appreciation of this fact.

A strong rear guard entails a thriving vanguard. Toudou's party is functioning like a well-oiled machine right now.

Perhaps they've gained another level? I hear shouts of joy. There's no sign of stopping Toudou and company's battle march now.

"The golems in this area no longer pose a threat. Our last day of monitoring the party may be closer than we think."

I had intended on observing them until every member reached level 30, but at this rate, there's no need for any further concern.

"You might be right… Wait… In that case, does that mean you won't need me anymore?"

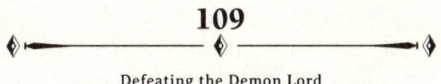

Stey is teetering on her feet, and her eyes go wide at my statement. I look back at her wearily. Hmm... Keeping the future in mind, perhaps a bit more discipline is at hand while there's still time.

I've been pondering for a while now; it's time to employ the Stephenne Veronide improvement strategy.

Currently, Stey is my subordinate. I have an obligation to make sure she's useful. That's why I've been thoroughly prepared from day one.

A bitter, cold wind buffets my body. Toudou and the others are far down the path, and judging from the sounds of battle, they aren't having any problems. There aren't any signs of other mercenaries nearby—just the right day to pull off the perfect crime.

The thin yet sturdy chain in my hands jangles as I drag it along and address Stey.

"Stey, are you ready?"

The chain is connected to a metal clasp on Stey's right ankle. It's a special-order physical restraint.

Stey must feel uncomfortable. She's bent over with her finger pressed to her lips, head tilted.

"Ummm, Ares, I've seen this thing somewhere before."

"It's used to transport criminals. I can vouch for its strength. Even if your leg gets sliced off, it can't be removed."

"Wooow, that's incredible! ...Huh? Why's it on me, then?!"

"You're asking me this now? You put it on yourself."

"Um... But that's because you told me to!"

Stey doesn't quite get what's going on yet, and I sigh. She's just a bit lacking.

"Stey, you don't have enough of a sense of danger. At least, I sure can't see it."

"Um... Sense of danger?"

"That's right. Honestly, I can't hold your hand and lead you around forever. I mean, I thought I'd only have to do that for a short amount of time, but enough's enough. I'm done."

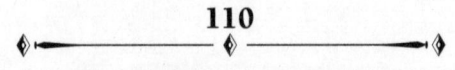

"The overdone sense of justice is a crime."

I don't exactly have pity on her, but for Stey to remain this way her entire life isn't exactly good for her, either. Many different people have tried to get her to change over the years, with no luck—but I haven't tried yet.

Stey is bewildered by the situation, and I cast a buff on her just to be safe. It'd be a real pain in my ass if she died.

She must have decided to stop thinking too hard about it, as she grins shyly.

"Um... Well... Thank you very much??"

"You are quite welcome."

I put my arm around Stey. She must be taken aback, as her arms and legs flail wildly.

"Wha—A-A-A-Ares?! Ares?!"

"Bite your tongue."

"?!"

With that, I toss Stey off the cliff into the depths below. Her scream trails into the sky before disappearing in the clouds. The chain in my hand pulls taut, and in the next moment I can hear Stey smacking into the cliff wall.

I am hopeless. This is the only way I know to impress reason onto someone.

I wait for some time before pulling the chain up against the cliff face. Before long, Stey appears, flapping about like a freshly caught fish. She has tears in her eyes and a red spot on her nose—probably from smacking into the cliff face.

"Ugghhh... Owww..."

"Don't lie. You're level seventy-two, and I put a buff on you. There's no way you're in pain."

She's apparently not bothered that her skirt is upside down and starts to throw a tantrum, punching the ground repeatedly.

"Is...is that...all you have to say?! After doing something so awful all of a sudden—"

"No, there's more."

111

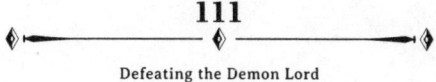

"...Huh?"

The daughter of a cardinal. If she hasn't changed under his tutelage, then I have no choice but to take drastic measures.

I grab Stey by the collar and pull her up, then walk back to the cliff's edge to dangle her over the expanse. There's a thin path a few meters below, and farther down lies a drop with no end in sight.

Even if the chain breaks, she'll probably land on the path below. Probably.

Stey stares into the void in horror for a moment but then suddenly turns to look at me, her smiling face twitching convulsively.

"Umm... Ares? ...Th-this is...a sick joke, right?"

"Down you go, one more time. Stey, this is not playtime, and I'm not just doing this to let off steam."

I'm gonna show you what happens to a massive ditz on the battlefield.

"Waaaahhh! Ameliaaa!"

The moment she sees Amelia, Stey trips over her own feet to bury her face in her chest. However, despite Stey's sorry state, Amelia's expression doesn't change one bit. She simply receives Stey's embrace and looks at me.

"...What did you do to her?"

"Just some klutz-reversing training exercises. But they were worthless. It's truly a mystery."

To be perfectly honest, she did stop falling off the cliff after the first time, but soon after, she was back to her usual clumsy self.

Stey moans, "Ughhh... Ares, I *haaate* you!"

I remove the chain I've been wearing as a belt and show it to Amelia.

"I chained her up by the leg and held her over a cliff."

"Ares... That's pretty medieval of you."

"Maybe, but it didn't work at all."

Stey retreats behind Amelia and uses her thin body as a shield before whimpering, "*Sniffle*... I—I told you I'd b-be just...fine!"

Seriously—where does she get that unlimited source of self-confidence?

"We'll continue the exercise tomorrow."

"Huh?! There's m-m-m-m-more?!"

This is my chance, while Toudou and the others don't need my involvement. I'll stick to Stey's side, exhaustively, until we reach common ground.

Stey rubs her face against Amelia, tears still in her eyes, and Amelia gives her a little smack without even looking at her. It was a light tap, but Stey still staggers and falls to the floor. That was harsh...

"To be honest, when I heard you and Stey would be working together, I didn't know what to think, but..."

"But what?"

I didn't know what to think myself.

"...But I am very relieved. It's only natural that you'd keep work and pleasure separate."

Amelia smiles gently and pours some tea from a teapot. The sound of Stey crying, facedown on the floor, combines with the sound of tea trickling out of the pot to create a peculiar harmony. I think I might be losing it.

"...How is your monster-spawning-rate survey going?"

Amelia sighs as she responds. "It's a wash. None of the mercenaries remember the number and type of monsters they've killed."

I've asked her to conduct a detailed survey on the spawning rates of the monsters in this area. If there's nothing out of the ordinary from the data she's collected...then we have no choice but to delve even deeper.

The majority of mercenaries do not keep a record of the number and type of monsters they've defeated, so we'll need to dig up legitimate records by greasing some palms and paying off each party we encounter. It's an absurd task. I'm not sure if Amelia's up to it.

"...Ares, you really are a worrywart."

"The more you and Wurtz tell me that, the more worried I become."

If it's needless anxiety, then so be it. But we have time right now, and we're in no position to cut corners.

"The overdone sense of justice is a crime."

*   *   *

I haven't had any luck with Stey, but in contrast, Toudou is excelling, both in training and in leveling up.

"Not bad. He's holding his own."

I'm in Wurtz's room at the church. He hands me a letter containing the results of today's training and grunts.

Wurtz Beld is a former sword master, but he never utilized refined swordsmanship techniques. Rather, his fighting style was closer to the Berserker style of swordplay peculiar to a giant's immense physical strength and high level of battle lust.

It's been a number of years since he converted to the priesthood, but I suspect he can't quell his true self—not yet. Having just finished a training session with Toudou, Wurtz struggles to hold back a smile.

"I'm aware. He has divine protection, after all. Not to mention magical energy, and the ability to use holy techniques. Summoned Holy Warriors have always displayed immense capacity, despite coming from different backgrounds."

"Courage, Ares. On the battlefield, it's the most crucial thing—the will to move forward when your legs are frozen stiff. No matter how strong, without courage, you cannot become a true warrior. He has it."

This is just like Wurtz—the giants venerate warrior heroes. I can see how he and Toudou are a good fit.

However, that is far from the most important point right now. Now that Toudou's surpassed level 30, it's time to decide how we'll get him to develop going forward. People act according to their own individual wits. In what aspects will Toudou grow the most, and in what aspects should we most heartily reinforce that growth?

In the end, Toudou has to make the decision for himself, but we can subtly show him the possibilities.

It's been over three full months since we began the quest to defeat the Demon Lord. Before too long, we have to produce some form of tangible results, and if we do, investors will come flocking to our quest.

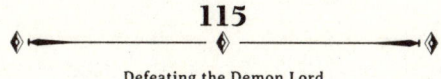

This will give Toudou increased financial support. Defeating the Demon Lord is all business.

Wurtz gauges my expression and laughs dryly before sharing his thoughts on Toudou's training sessions.

"He is quite weak. He's also low in stamina, but on the other hand, he has high magical energy and his movements are nimble."

"Does that mean he's not cut out as a sword master?"

"…His lack of attack power will be compensated by the holy sword Ex. It's not impossible for him to become a sword master."

I can sense doubt on Wurtz's face as he speaks. A giant's chief attributes are brute strength and endurance—the two most important qualities for a sword master. At the very least, one must possess both.

"However… The Holy Warrior's physical strength and stamina are…likely lower than Ms. Aria's."

I know that Toudou is lighter on his feet than Aria, but I was unaware that he's even weaker than her—a female. This is truly vexing. Among human beings, the males are larger than their female counterparts and are subsequently stronger in general. I've always thought Toudou was frail, but I figured it was just because he never trained his body.

His leveling up isn't exactly convincing, either. Given his disposition, his abilities aren't increasing as quickly as I'd hoped. Given the fact that he's still falling behind Aria at level 30, there's a chance that he's simply built that way. It's a high chance, and there's nothing to be done about that.

"Lower than Aria…? What a pain in the ass."

"It's not a matter of life and death, but…it will cause him great trouble moving forward."

The holy sword Ex and holy armor Fried are enchanted with weight-reducing magic, making them feather-light. Call it silver lining, perhaps, but without that, Toudou would probably move at a snail's pace under all his equipment.

The majority of Holy Warriors thus far have been magical sword masters. They've largely relied on swordsmanship—not as mages who

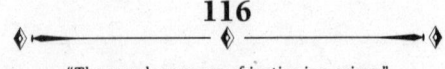

"The overdone sense of justice is a crime."

can use swords, but as sword masters who can also cast magic. Until the existence of the supremely powerful holy sword Ex, there was no reason to do otherwise.

However, if Toudou doesn't even have the strength of a female sword-wielding counterpart, then he may just have to embrace both roles equally.

I hammer all this information into my brain. I have to figure out what Toudou needs, and how best to provide it for him...

We continue to discuss Aria and Glacia, who have just begun training. Aria and her complete lack of magical energy have a host of problems, but it seems Glacia is the most stable of them all, from what Wurtz has to say. We're really running short on saving graces.

After reviewing all the training results, Wurtz lets out a heavy sigh and eyes me suspiciously.

"Ares... Don't burn the candle at both ends."

"...I want them to focus on leveling up. Let's reduce the number of training sessions and focus our efforts on leveling the party up."

"Yes, I understand. May you receive the blessings of Ahz Gried, Ares."

The real struggle begins when the demons make their first big move. Until then, we have to ready ourselves as much as we can.

In the middle of giving my usual report, Creio stops me.

"Ares, Stey's father—Cardinal Sylvester—wants to speak with you. He contacted me."

"Creio... Tell him I'm indisposed. I'm not here."

Has Sylvester found out I'm treating his daughter like a gold mine? Even if he has...I'm prepared for this. Everything falls on Sylvester's head—he's the one who tossed Stey onto Creio. I've just made use of what was presented to me.

"And also, tell him we need more funds. Stey's involvement has proven more costly than expected. Chains and padlocks don't come cheap."

"You should have received more than enough funds."

"Money is different from people. You can never have enough. He's used plenty on his precious daughter's gear—I'm sure he won't mind."

"Ares... You're truly unbelievable...," Creio says in astonishment.

"Here's my report. I have no intention of playing babysitter. I'm providing support for the quest to defeat the Demon Lord, and at the same time, I'm training my subordinate who everyone else has given up on. Don't you think I'm a model crusader?"

"...Ares, there is a limit to what even I can accomplish."

Opposing a cardinal with an iron grip on finances is an exercise in futility. But all will be forgiven if I can simply produce results. Even if I have to tie her up in chains and throw her off a cliff—no matter how much she cries or screams.

The thinking comes later. I feel really sorry for Creio.

"Please, Your Eminence, bear with me. Please do not interfere... Oh, by the way, there's something I wanted to tell you."

"...And what is that?" Creio's voice is dry as kindling. I continue to speak, reaching out to jangle the freshly polished chain in front of me.

"You have to draw a straight line."

"...What?"

"With silver chalk, on the ground. A single line."

I've experimented. It's not like I'm simply torturing Stey for fun.

"And then, I made Stey walk the line. About ten meters. What do you think happened?"

"...What, pray tell?"

"She walked the whole line without falling. This would be pretty normal for the average person, but for Stey, who trips all the time when walking, running, or simply standing— What the—? Shit, he hung up!"

The transmission has been cut. I click my tongue—but I might have hung up if I were him, too.

Stey still trips a lot, but the experiment wasn't entirely meaningless. I wrap the immaculate chain around my wrist and open the door to

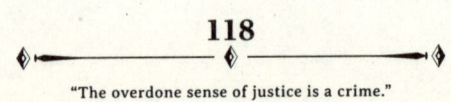

"The overdone sense of justice is a crime."

Amelia and Stey's room. Stey is still lounging limply in the corner in her pajamas, but when I enter the room, her whole body shudders.

"C'mon, Stey! Let's go!"

"Eeeek! Amelia, Ares is being mean to meee!"

I move quickly to the corner where Stey is babbling nonsense and hoist her up by the abdomen. She squirms and tries to resist, but let's face it—given her tiny frame, it's pointless. She eventually gives in, realizing that it's no use putting up a fight.

As I start to carry her out the door, I glance down at her meek little face.

"Stey, did you rat me out to your father?"

"Huh...? Wh-wh-wh-what are you talking about?"

"Well, it's no use! Even if he ordered me to stop, there's no way I'm easing up! I'm the one in the right here, so blab to him all you want!"

"Whaaa?!"

Stey's eyes go wide as I dangle her in midair.

I've recently realized that once Stey is focused on the issue at hand, she forgets everything else. What a dumbass!

The notebook I've been keeping on Stey since we began these exercises is full of worthless information.

"Stey, I'm not training you because I enjoy it or anything."

"Whaaaaaaa?! You call that training? Putting a chain around my ankle and pushing me off a cliff?!"

"That's right."

"A-and...getting smashed against the cliff?"

"Indeed."

"And pointlessly walking a straight line over and over again, too?"

"That, too. What was going on in your head when you obeyed all my orders? I explained everything at the beginning."

Stey bats her eyes repeatedly and says quietly, "I thought it was... your hobby."

"...Dammit, that's actually kind of funny."

Quit it with the sudden curveballs!

119

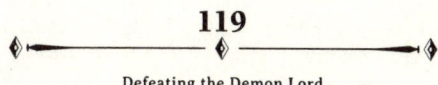

Defeating the Demon Lord

While still holding Stey, I give an order to Amelia, who's been silent so far. Maybe it's because I've made her work solo so much lately, but she does not look like she's in a great mood.

"Toudou has training today. I'm going to beat Stey into shape, so I'll leave him and the party up to you. "

"...Perhaps it's time you gave up on Stey's training?"

"No. Not yet. I haven't exhausted all my options."

Today we're going bungee jumping without a rope.

"...Also, she's still in her pajamas. I think you should at least let her change before taking her with you."

Amelia holds her head and sighs. She must have picked up my habit. I am truly sorry.

I meet Stey's eyes. Her cheeks flush as she tells me, slightly embarrassed, "Y-yeah, she's right. I can't go out looking like this, that would be mortifying... I'll get changed, so please just wait here..."

"...After all the times you've had your panties on full display, now you're suddenly embarrassed by pajamas?"

"...WHA—?????!!!!!"

Stey's voice cracks and her whole body stiffens. In the next instant, her entire face reddens and she begins to protest, voice shaking.

"O-o-o-o-oh really, A-A-A-A-Ares?! Huh? I've... I've never shown you my panties!!! No way, no how!"

"Did you think I couldn't see them when you were hanging upside down off the cliff?"

Her skirt is ultra short to begin with. They were on full display.

"!!!???????"

I know she has a screw loose, but how could she not even realize this?

Stey's eyes dart all over the room—she's trying to escape the embarassment.

"Wha... Why... Whyyy didn't you tell meeee???" she demands tearfully, now beet red.

I guess she *can* feel shame...

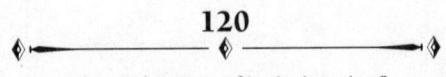

"The overdone sense of justice is a crime."

"It's too late. I've seen your panties so many times, I know them at every angle."

"…P-please, just kill me now."

She must really be embarrassed. Seriously, though—I got an eyeful the very first time she tripped. Hanging her upside down is beside the point. However… I can use this to my advantage, too. My voice is gentle when I address Stey, who remains frozen in place.

"Stey. The next time you trip and fall, I'm going to make a detailed report of your panties. So you better not fall over."

"HUH?! You… You're kidding, right? You, kind Ares, would never do such a thing… Right?"

"It's not like I want to… But say your reputation is on the line, or you incur serious financial damage from flagrant rumors… Then I, kind Ares, am prepared to do whatever it takes to see to my precious subordinate."

The blood drains from Stey's face before returning to a flat norm. Training's a bitch.

"Ares… You are the worst. I am beyond dismayed."

Amelia spits an acrid barb my way to end the conversation.

After a few more days of putting Stey to use, I managed to produce a result.

"She has my seal of approval."

"Seal…of…approval?"

Amelia looks taken aback. Even Stey herself seems perplexed.

Stephenne Veronide is the most annoying woman in the entire Kingdom.

I conducted a number of experiments. I tried threatening her, sweet-talking her. I included the color of her panties in my report to Creio, and I chained her up and dragged her around. I even threw her off the cliff without the chain.

In turn, she tripped, got lost, forgot to wear panties, forgot the

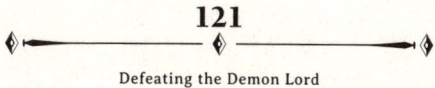

incantations for holy techniques, forgot the tools that I asked her to prepare, and so much more. The fact that I took the compassionate route and didn't stick her with any chicken skewers shows that I am the true, kind Ares so often spoke of.

I sit through Amelia's ice-cold gaze. We need to trace this problem back to its roots and come up with a plan.

Toudou's leveling up is going well. His training is also bearing fruit, and he's no longer experiencing problems in battle.

Naotsugu Toudou, level 37. Aria Rizas, level 29. Limis Al Friedia, level 28. With the benefit of Glacia's support, the party is steadily making their way through Golem Valley.

I pat the stack of papers with Stey's research data and continue on. It's the thickest report I've compiled since coming to Golem Valley.

"I'm switching things up. Amelia and I will do our work here in town. Stey, you will tail Toudou and his party on your own."

"Ares... Has the stress finally gotten to your head...?"

"Wh-what does that mean, Amelia?! Hey—!"

Amelia's rude comment prompts Stey to totter to the front of the room. She squeezes my hand and fawns on me. I can feel heat coming off of her pale fingertips.

"Seal of approval!! A-A-Ares, do I...have your seal of approval?"

"Yeah, you do. I've got nothing more to teach you."

Even if I did, it wouldn't make a difference. If I've learned one thing from training her, that's it.

"You won't chain me up—"

"No, I won't."

"You won't push me off the cliff, without any chains—"

"Yeah, that's all over."

"I—I can't believe you actually did those things to me..."

Tears well up in Stey's eyes—she must be recalling all the horror I put her though. Behind her, Amelia's cheek is twitching imperceptibly.

I take a box that just arrived from the Church out from underneath the desk and open the metal clasps. There's a black leather bangle inside.

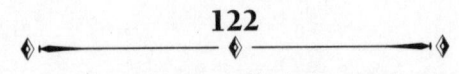

"The overdone sense of justice is a crime."

In a sense, this black bangle goes against the creed of the God of Order, for reasons that are difficult to explain.

Stey rubs her bloodshot eyes with her sleeve and asks, "? What's that for?"

"It's proof of my seal of approval. Put it on your wrist."

I lob it at Stey, who lunges hastily to catch it. She stares intently at the chic design before asking me, "Proof... Are you s-sure?"

"...Yes. Secure it safely to your wrist, so that it never comes loose."

"U-understood."

Stey secures the bangle tightly on her right wrist. Her cheeks relax, and she lifts her arm, flaunting her new accessory.

"Hee-hee—does it look good on me?"

"Stey, don't ever lose it. That's an order. Aside from bathing or sleeping, don't you dare take it off."

Even just one of these bangles is insanely expensive to manufacture. It's called a Dizast's Bangle, and it's made from the skin of the eponymous calamitous demon that once laid waste to a number of villages. Needless to say, it has a shady history. It's not cursed in any way, but any normal priest wouldn't touch it, even with a gun to their head.

For the record, the Church does not keep the skins of demons—sworn enemies of God—in their possession. This is from Gregorio's personal collection. It's leftover from the demon leather upholstering on Gregorio's weapon—Pandora's Coffin—and I had to cut a deal with him to acquire some. That son of a bitch.

"Okay! I'll be careful with it... Huh?!"

I double-check that Holy Bind is still in effect. Pulled by the invisible chain, Stey starts to lose her balance and looks puzzled as I release the chain without a word.

"Stey, your role is to trail Toudou and track his movements without getting noticed."

"Y-yes, sir! Roger that!"

"If anything happens, update me accordingly."

"Yes, of course. I'll be in touch!"

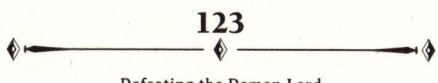

123

The only thing she's good at is replying...

"Got your handkerchief? Your potions? No dillydallying. There's no one to save you if you fall off the cliff now, got it? Don't even dare trip—you'll die!"

"I'll...I'll be fine! Gosh, Ares, you're such a worrywart... I'm not a child, you know!"

Embarrassed, Stey's cheeks flush. She sticks out her chest proudly—nope, definitely not a child.

Amelia looks like she's about to say something, but she remains silent.

"O-okay, then—I'm off. Hee-hee... I'll do my best at my new job!"

"Wait a second, Stey. There's one last thing I have to ask before you go."

"Oh... What is it?"

I take out a pen and piece of paper and hand them to her. To give her some sense of the danger ahead, I say gravely, "Write your will before you leave. Your father will be beside himself."

I can hear Stey tripping outside the door, but I bite my lip and let it pass. Amelia has been standing around without making so much as a peep, but now she sits down in front of me, looking serious.

"Ares."

"Yeah, I know you've got something to say."

"Should I trip and fall from time to time, too?"

"......"

I stand up silently and look out the window. I can see Stey leaving the inn with a skip in her step. She's lightly equipped and isn't even carrying a mace. At the last minute, she turns around and nearly stumbles, having noticed me in the window. As she waves her hand and smiles, she loses her balance and falls right on her ass.

Bystanders stop to stare at the girl who fell over so suddenly. Her cheeks flush red, clearly embarrassed, and she stands up, smiling from ear to ear, waving at me one last time. She heads toward Toudou and company's inn on shaky legs.

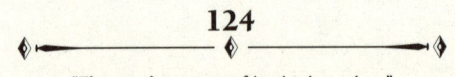

"The overdone sense of justice is a crime."

Amelia is standing next to me before I realize it and asks softly, "I thought she stopped tripping?"

What the hell were you just watching?

"Did you really?"

That's beside the point. Amelia might be legitimately worried—she sends a reproachful glance my way.

"…All right, we're heading out, too."

I gather the pack I've prepared. Just as I start to change clothes, Amelia asks curiously, "? And just where are we going?"

"To follow Stey, obviously."

Stephenne Veronide is my first-ever errand girl. Today, she's going to prove her worth.

Stephenne Veronide has an unparalleled capacity to strike anxiety into the hearts of strangers. If pressed to determine just exactly what causes such feelings in people, the largest contributor is definitely her absurdly unreliable gait. Just beholding it is cause for concern—she dizzily floats along, as if her feet never touch the ground at all.

"Ares… Don't you think this is a bit reckless?"

Stey must be elated at having been told she's got my "seal of approval"—her gait is more unsteady than ever.

There aren't a whole lot of girls in Golem Valley, and among those few, Stey sticks out like a sore thumb in her miniskirt.

Everyone on the street is staring at her, but she is completely oblivious.

A strapping older man running a sandwich stall hollers at Stey, "Hey there, little lady! You look like you're on cloud nine."

"…Heh-heh… Actually, I just got my seal of approval."

Stey cheerfully answers the hard-faced man—who looks a lot like a mercenary himself—without a trace of timidity. *Quit wasting time! You just left ten minutes ago!*

"…Seal of approval? Well, it's great that you're so happy, but watch where you're walking or you'll trip."

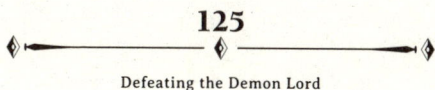

"? I'm walking just fine, thank you very much."

"...No, it's just that... You seem a bit unsteady, and—"

"Um, what? No, I don't."

Stey can't be more obviously unstable, and the older man furrows his brow. He's probably used to slinging sandwiches to weatherworn mercenary veterans. This has to be his first time encountering a human being of Stey's nature.

Stey eyes the sandwiches out for sale with a glint in her eye and starts rummaging around in her pack for her wallet. Her face turns white as a sheet. Has she forgotten it? *Stop playing around and get to work!*

"...Ares... This is the definition of reckless."

"No, you and everyone else have been too easy on her."

Eventually, Stey looks down dejectedly and starts to walk again.

I am legitimately worried, but Stey has experience trailing Toudou alongside me. She can do it.

"Just checking, but Stey can use detection magic, right?"

"Ares, you cannot work as an operator without knowing detection magic. Operators use communication magic to search for contacts to speak with and to establish a connection with them."

Stey stumbles to and fro, across both sides of the road, before finally reaching the inn where the party is staying. The second she arrives, Toudou and company burst out of the door. They look radiant—perhaps due to how well things are going lately?

Stey's expression turns just a touch serious, and she manages to hide in the shade of the building. From my vantage point, she looks extremely conspicuous. Thankfully, she's put some distance between herself and Toudou's party, and they don't notice her.

"She doesn't stand a chance."

"Stey probably knows this already, but just in case she's found out, she needs to feign ignorance. Tell her now."

Amelia falls silent and connects to Stey through transmission magic before swallowing a lump in her throat and looking up at me.

"The overdone sense of justice is a crime."

"...Okay, I've told her... She doesn't seem to have any idea of how to do that."

"..."

Toudou and the others head out of town, and Stey follows them. We take up the rear and leave First Town behind us. Toudou's party chooses the low route—known to be shorter—while Stey chooses the high route, where she can keep an eye on them. It's the same path Stey and I used to track Toudou the first time.

Amelia and I decide to follow Stey along the path she's chosen. Gripped with suspense, Amelia twists the hem of her mage's robe as she stares at Stey.

The roads in town are relatively unkempt, but they're nothing compared to the paths outside it.

"Don't worry. If something happens, I'll cast Holy Bind and grab hold of her."

"...But it won't catch her unless it touches her bangle, right?"

"What's your point?"

"I just think it seems like a pretty small target."

There are about fifty meters between us and Stey. She's wearing the bangle on her right wrist. It *is* a small target. However, for someone of my level, hitting it will be easy, provided that nothing distracts me.

Stey continues teetering down the narrow path, completely unaware of both how worried sick Amelia is and that we're even following her.

Stey kicks a rock, and it tumbles down the cliffs below. Given how many times she's tripped in just the past few days, it's nothing short of a sign of true accomplishment that she's walking without hesitation now, all by herself.

Stey is rocked from side to side each time the wind blows. Actually, she's all over the place even without the wind. If she sticks to the left and keeps her hand on the wall, she could find a bit of support, but she doesn't show any intention of doing so and instead walks brazenly right down the middle.

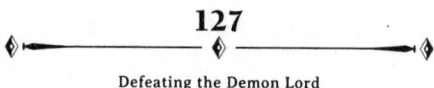

In that moment, a rock the size of a human head topples off the cliff face above Stey. It comes crashing down, aiming directly for Stey's head—but she is completely oblivious.

Amelia's eyes bulge out of their sockets. The rock misses Stey by a hair and lands behind her. Incredibly, she doesn't even seem to notice that it fell.

Her sense of danger is so severely lacking, I can't help but laugh. Does she even have eyes?

"Ares, I'm telling you, this is pure recklessness…"

As Amelia hems and haws, Stey stops dead in her tracks. She's walked to edge of the cliff and is carefully peering down below. Amelia gulps and steps out from the shadow we're hiding in. I grab her by the collar and pull her back.

"Ares, it's like she *wants* to fall."

"Simmer down. If and when she falls, it'll be out of nowhere. I'm speaking from experience."

Stey doesn't have a lick of concern for her surroundings. She's probably trying to get an eye on Toudou and his party down on the path below, but I agree—she looks like she's about to jump to her death. *Use your damn detection magic!*

"Ares, don't tell me— Are you trying to get rid of her and make it look like an accident…?"

…I don't even need to. She'll probably take the plunge herself by accident.

I watch Stey intently, and the next thing I know, she's lying down flat on her stomach, slowly crawling toward the edge to look even farther down. So much for having a clear view of Stey at all times… She's some sort of genius.

"A-Ares, if she falls face-forward like that, how are you going to aim for the bangle…?"

Stey's hands are over the edge, and I can't see it. This will definitely make it hard to hit…

"I guess there's no way to prevent her from dying now."

"The overdone sense of justice is a crime."

"?!"

"Just chill out. It's not time to panic yet."

"Your standards have...taken quite a nosedive."

Stey peers down at the path below for a while, kicking her legs in the air, before finally retreating and standing up.

And so the death march begins again. As I start to trail Stey, Amelia tugs at my sleeve. Her dark-indigo eyes are peering into my soul, trying to read my mind.

"Ares... Don't you think this is enough? I really don't think we can leave Stey alone..."

"It's only been two hours."

"That's not enough for you?!"

What does two hours prove? Admittedly, Stey does look like she might die out there. She's riddled with blind spots, and one wrong step could easily take her down an irreversible plunge. Yet, despite all this—

"I'm determined to reveal her limits. If we help her, she won't learn a damn thing."

"This terrain isn't the only thing threatening her safety! Even the most confident person wouldn't think to walk alone through Golem Valley..."

She's totally right. Anywhere outside the towns here is a land of wicked remorse. Mercenaries don't trust themselves out here alone, and when merchants or regular folk traverse these paths, they generally travel with an envoy. Monsters spawn at a relatively high rate here. The reason Toudou and his party are managing to level up here is partially thanks to their equipment and abilities, but it's also because they're not alone.

The only reason I can get around here by myself with no trouble is because of my high level. Amelia wouldn't venture out here all alone, either.

"But Stey never said no."

Amelia narrows her eyes in response. She lowers her voice and whispers to me, like she's telling a secret, "Ares, this is just between you and me, but Stey is... Um... A bit of an airhead."

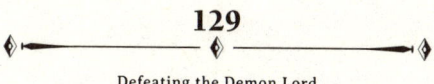

"I already know Stey's dumb as shit."

"…"

I can't even begin to tell you how many times I've noticed over the past few days. Really, truly, I know. Ask anyone—they'll agree.

Airhead. Klutz. A few screws loose. However, thanks to her, I was able to acquire the materials I need. I'll watch after her, for as long as the goods she proffered warrant. She's actually quite accomplished, aside from being so dumb. We can still use her.

Just then, I hear another sound from the cliffs above Stey. I look up—it's not a rock this time.

Three spheres with arms and legs careen down the cliff face—ball golems.

"Um… Ares?"

I pick up a few pebbles and check their shape and size in my hand. Stey doesn't need to kill the ball golems, she just needs to get them to fall to the cliffs below. Amelia looks between Stey and me repeatedly. Stey has noticed the monsters coming to attack her, miraculously, as she leisurely confirms their existence. Then, she's obviously taken aback, mouth agape.

"Ares, hurry!"

"Just cool it."

The ball golems' front claws, made for digging into boulders and stopping on a dime, are pointed directly at Stey as the monsters careen down the cliff side. Stey rushes to sidestep the first one—but she trips over her legs.

Without warning, Stey loses her balance and crumples, causing the golem's claws to whiff entirely. The golem had been aiming for Stey's head at full speed, and now it can't stop its own momentum, plunging down to the cliffs below.

She didn't intend to crumple to the ground, but once she does, the other two golems attack from both sides, and they also miss. What's more, they smash directly into each other and flip backward, sailing down the cliff and disappearing into oblivion.

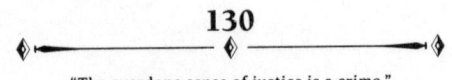

"The overdone sense of justice is a crime."

By the time Stey stands up, wiping tears from her eyes, all three golems are gone. She must have bumped the tip of her nose, which is swollen red. She casts Heal on herself and looks around in confusion and amazement.

She stands there dumbstruck for a few moments before giving up on thinking too hard and continuing down the path again.

Amelia swallows audibly after watching with bated breath. I let the pebbles loose from my hand.

"That was too close… Y-you're still convinced she'll be okay?"

"…No clue. But whether that was on purpose or not—it was incredible."

"How can you be so irresponsible?"

I don't wanna hear that from the person who brought Spica to me solely because she was cute.

That said, luck is just another skill. Cavorting around with me, Stey is completely useless, but alone, she's holding her own. In other words—we can leave her to her own devices.

"W-well… She's surviving, somehow… But only just barely."

It's a wonder that a massive klutz like her managed to make it all the way to age sixteen.

I'm still unconvinced. I think everyone around her just babies her too much.

"Ares, are you seriously trying to spin this in a positive light?"

"I'll inform Creio that Stey is fine to be left on her own."

"Now wait just a minute."

If anything, I have the feeling that the hack who dispatched Stey is responsible.

"I told you, there's no way… Oh, look! Another monster—"

A rock golem appears in front of Stey. These are rarer on outdoor paths—in this case, the golem's wide body takes up the whole thing. If it comes at Stey, she'll have nowhere to run.

The rock golem sends vibrations throughout the valley with each step. Stey's face stiffens, and she looks up at it, retreating a few steps.

131

A blow from a rock golem's bulky arms is a true menace, but they move quite slowly. They were developed to traverse narrow paths with extreme care, so as not to fall to their deaths below.

I guess this time around, Stey won't be able to depend on luck. Just in case, I put on my mask and calculate when I'll need to jump in and save her. I don't particularly want her to recognize me.

It's not the end of the world if she does, but for her to learn that I sent her on a solo mission only to actually be watching her would be… awkward.

Stey continues retreating until her back hits the wall then gropes along it as if searching for something. The rock golem has closed in significantly and reels back its massive arm to strike. Just as I go to step in and rescue her, the rock golem is blown off the cliff.

"…Huh?"

After a thunderous roar, the golem's massive body, over twice Stey's size, careens down the side of the cliff and tumbles far below.

I rub my eyes and do a double take, but that's really what happened. Amelia stares at her petite colleague, wide-eyed in disbelief.

A bundle of gigantic boulder stakes is sticking out of the ground next to Stey. I steady my breathing and gather my thoughts. I've seen this exact same phenomenon before.

"That's an elemental spell… An earth-type one called *Move Earth*."

A pretty well-known one, too. All it does is allow the user to freely manipulate the nearby earth. It's typically one of the more basic earth-type spells, but Stey used it to bombard the golem. I've never heard of such a thing.

"No way… She can cast elemental spells?!"

I've heard earth-type elemental spells are particularly difficult. Using magic requires extreme mental concentration. Being able to do so under duress is the sign of a truly superior mage.

"I've never seen…anything like that. Of course, the term holy caster applies to priests who can wield magic… And there's a possibility that

Stey is also an elementalist... But—," Amelia mumbles, apparently shaken.

I've gone to full lengths to confirm Stey's capabilities beforehand. She never mentioned anything about being able to cast elemental spells.

I take a deep breath and wonder: Did she pull one over on me? Did she lie? I never got that sense from her, but... Perhaps the most likely possibility is that she just forgot?

You just forgot the magic you can cast?! Bullshit!

Stey sits on the ground, regaining her composure, before standing up and darting her eyes here and there across the valley. The massive bundle of stakes blocking the path retreats noiselessly into the earth without a trace left behind.

This is the nature of elemental spells, but Stey's apparent power to destroy evidence spurs suspicion within me.

"Was she pulling one over on us? What's the point of hiding it? Is her klutziness just one big act...?"

But really. If you think about it logically, there's no way someone could be that damn stupid.

Amelia and Creio both testified to her stupidity, so I didn't thoroughly investigate it myself.

Think about it, Ares. The merits and demerits. Everything has meaning.

Amelia recovers from her catatonic mumbling state and looks up at me.

"No... Ares, Stey has always acted that way, ever since I first met her several years ago."

"Several years ago... Are you saying she's been putting on this act since childhood?! She's that cold and calculating?!"

"No... That's not quite what I meant—"

"Was she playing dumb just to distract me? Did she choose to get strung up by a chain and swung around like a dead cat, just to keep up the ruse?"

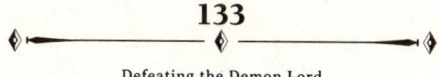

If so, she's got nerves of pure steel. There is nothing more terrifying than a human being with such an ironclad will. I thought she was just a mega-dumbass.

Even so, I don't understand her intentions. Was she just playing dumb until I reported every detail of her panties to my superior? Is that an achievement?

It's going too far to even consider the possibility that she's a pawn of the Demon Lord. That is simply not an idea I will entertain.

I bite my lower lip and squint my eyes, observing Stey. She doesn't appear to be aware that she's being surveilled.

But I've realized something. Ever since we started trailing her, Stey hasn't tripped once.

She's loitered by the wayside, gotten her legs tangled and nearly fallen down, forgotten her wallet and gone white as a ghost, lilted to and fro, lain on her stomach on the ground and kicked her legs in the air like a five-year-old—but she hasn't tripped a single time. The hell?!

Stey's had some close calls, but she hasn't actually tripped and fallen. When I was making the rounds with her, she definitely fell down four or five times, even though we were only out for as many hours. For a second, I'm impressed that she's managed so well on her own, but clearly something's amiss. I really hate to say it, but this is *simply not normal*.

It's increasingly messed up, the more I think about it. Stey is insane.

I try to explain all this to Amelia, and she momentarily falls quiet before showing a rare look of concern.

"You're probably…overthinking it."

"If I'm overthinking it, then that can only mean that Stey is a complete imbecile."

"Stey *is* a complete imbecile."

A complete imbecile… A complete…imbecile?

I glare in Stey's direction, downright confused. The imbecile in question must be relieved to have driven back the golem as she's now all smiles and walking again.

134

In that second, Stey trips on absolutely nothing and plummets to the cliffs below, disappearing from view.

"Oh... Huh...? Ares... Stey's—"

"Sorry. Just gimme a few minutes to calm myself down."

My mouth is dry, and my voice comes out sounding frighteningly dark. I hold my head, throbbing with pain, in my hands. Give me five minutes... No, three will do. That'll be enough time for me to grasp all this.

§ § §

Stephenne Veronide was born into a wealthy family.

Her father used to be one of the Kingdom of Ruxe's most preeminent merchants. After converting to the priesthood, he rose through the ranks in the blink of an eye and was soon recognized as a man of great influence. For as long as she can remember, Stephenne has never had to struggle with money.

Her parents were also blessed in terms of interpersonal relationships, and although they were always busy, Stephenne was never without an attendant to watch over her.

In terms of education, the Veronide family had the highest echelon of personal tutors in the Kingdom of Ruxe on house call, and Stephenne also learned magic from a legendary line of mages.

You could say that Stephenne has always gotten everything she's ever wanted. That said, although she's aware of her good fortune, her only complaint in the entire world would be that everyone around her has always been overprotective.

Her entire life, Stephenne has hardly ever been alone. She typically has two chamberlains attending to her. Even if she finds herself alone for a moment, someone will come to find her, without exception—no matter how much she insists that she's fine on her own.

That's why when Stephenne received her seal of approval, she was

135

overcome with emotion. She finally felt like she was recognized as a human being. In the same moment, she realized that now, especially now, she cannot fail. If she does, there's no way she'll be given a real job ever again.

A feeling of unease Stephenne knows all too well rises within her again. At the same time, the low-level earth spirit she has entered a covenant with—a gnome named Cacao—reacts to the sense of danger she is now feeling. It sinks beneath the quickly approaching ground and plows it soft using smooth, familiar movements.

In the next instant, a powerful shock runs through Stephenne's entire body—a fierce, blinding pain that jolts and numbs her brain. Yet, her spirit familiar has given her a buff, and she takes hardly any damage. She puts her hands on the ground and lifts herself up, slowly.

"…Eek?! Wh-wh-what was that? …Huh??? It's…a girl?"

"Oof… That huuurt…"

Even at level 72, pain is pain. With tears running down her cheeks, Stephenne sits back down on the ground.

Her contracted spirit, Cacao, appearing in the form of a young girl, twirls and flits about near Stephenne's knee. Golem Valley is rife with earth-type magic particles, and so the spirit feels rejuvenated. However, it appears to have no intention of comforting Stephenne.

Stephenne pokes Cacao, who is doing a strange sort of dance, on the cheek, when suddenly—

"Um— Excuse me— Are you…okay?"

—Stephenne's entire body shivers, shocked by the voice seemingly coming from outside her own consciousness. She looks up to see none other than the hero she's supposed to be watching over as part of her job.

The strikingly handsome Holy Warrior celebrated in legend, Naotsugu Toudou, looks at her with confusion, when—

"Just what on earth is going on—? …Huh?"

—just then, Limis peeks her head out from behind him, looking flabbergasted the moment she catches sight of Stephenne. Rubbing her eyes, the transparent blue of pure ocean water, Limis stares at Stey and thoroughly inspects her from head to toe.

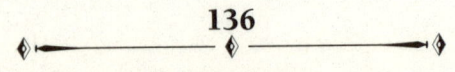

This looks like the person who will surely break Stephenne out of this fix. She beams at Limis and waves at her with gusto.

"Looong time no see, Limis! What a coincidence!"

Limis's expression stiffens at Stephenne's voice. Her fire spirit, Garnet, scrambles from her shoulder to hide inside her hat.

"Wha… What are you doing in a place like this?"

Toudou looks at Limis.

"Wait, what? Do you know her…?"

"Limis, what's going on—? …Wait—Stey?! …Wh-what are *you* doing here?"

Aria also appears, wearing the same stiff expression as Limis.

"What am I doing here? …I'm working, obviously!"

Having run into her two friends she hasn't seen in a while, Stephenne forgets the entire point of her assignment.

The color quickly drains from Limis's face, and she raises her head to look up at the cliffs. Her hat falls off, and Garnet latches onto her hair for dear life. After checking that there's no one up above, she addresses Stephenne with trepidation.

"Huh? Working? By yourself?"

"Uh-huh! Of course I'm by myself, silly! I have a…seal of approval? So, yeah…"

"Wha…what sort of reckless moron sent you out by yourself?"

"You know her?! You seriously know her?! Limis, you're friends with this girl who just fell out of the sky?!"

Toudou is absolutely blown away. Aria struggles to calm down through ragged breaths and explains, "Please relax. We're only…slightly acquainted… She's the daughter of someone famous within the Kingdom of Ruxe."

Hearing this, Stephenne smiles from ear to ear. Aria's expression remains stiff, and she retreats a few paces.

"Let's deal with this calmly. This narrow path is…not a good place for Stey," Aria whispers to Toudou, who's only a bit less shaken than Aria herself. Sweat is pouring down her face.

137

Aria puts her hand out to restrain Stey and shouts, "Stey! Do you have any idea where you are?!"

"Um, on top of a cliff, duh?"

"So why are you here if you know that?! You're gonna fall to your death!!" Aria yells angrily, and Stephenne ponders the sequence of events that brought her to this place before responding, head atilt, "Well, I've already fallen a few times, and I'm still alive, aren't I?"

"Did you power up?!" Limis shudders, her eyes now open as wide as they can possibly go.

Stephenne can't believe the reception she's getting, and she sighs in annoyance. She doesn't know what's going on, and she's certainly been discovered, but her first order of business is to get her new companions to calm down, right now.

Stephenne laughs shyly and takes one step toward Limis—just one.

"Heh-heh... Anyway, I'm just so incredibly happy to see you guys again... Oh—"

Stephenne finally remembers just what she was sent out to do.

Monitor Toudou. Surveillance. What's more, she's supposed to be doing all this from afar, so that no one notices her.

She takes one last hard look at Toudou's face and nods imperceptibly. Sure, she's been discovered and all that...but she hasn't said anything about Ares, so maybe she's still in the clear?

"Well, it's about time I got back to work, so... See ya later, Limis!"

"...Huh?"

"Bye for now!"

Stephenne approaches the cliff face she just fell down from and touches it with her right hand. She quietly recites an incantation, and Cacao, only visible to its contracted mage, casts a spell.

The wall shudders, then forms the shape of a hand and gently grabs hold of Stephenne's body.

She's an elementalist contracted with each of the spirits but has a particularly high affinity for earth. In Golem Valley, which is teeming

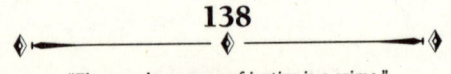

"The overdone sense of justice is a crime."

with that element's magic particles, Stephenne can wield her powers to an incredible extent.

Stephenne's arms obey the spell's command and she begins to climb the cliff face. She looks down at her companions with a smile and waves before saying good-bye.

"Let's go out for a bite to eat somewhere next time!"

"Hey— What the...?!" Limis cries hysterically.

The Holy Warrior stares at Stephenne in utter disbelief as she disappears into the cliffs above.

When Stephenne reaches the top, the earthen hand disappears silently into the ground. She pats the dust off her skirt and takes a deep breath, not able to help herself from breaking into a smile after running into her old companions.

She'd been told to not let the Holy Warrior notice her, which really put a damper on her chances to meet him. But now she finally did, and they even spoke! Stephenne hadn't expected to fall off the cliff only to be discovered by the Holy Warrior, but hey, all's well that ends well. Just as she starts back on the path—

"You seem to be enjoying yourself, Stey."

"Yes! I love my job!"

"That's great to hear. By the way, do you know Limis and Aria?"

"Yes! They're my friends from way back. We lived close to one another!"

"I see. You're friends. Friends are so important in life... So why didn't you tell me?"

"...Huh?"

—Stey whirls around, hearing a familiar voice.

It's her superior, smiling gently. Stey grins back, as if beckoned by him.

§   §   §

139

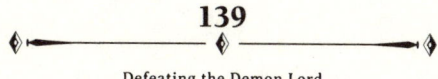

"So... Who is she?"

Aria and Limis have been completely unfocused since their encounter in the valley, and after Toudou rushes them back to the inn, she doesn't waste any time getting to the question on her mind. It's highly unusual for the both of them to be so aloof.

Limis doesn't answer and sits on her bed. She lies down and remains silent for a few minutes before finally saying, "...She's...an old friend."

"Wait, a friend? ...But she fell out of the sky— And what was up with that magic—?"

Limis smacks her hand against her forehead and doesn't say anything else. Instead, Aria glances up, looking just as haggard as Limis, and begins to explain in a somber voice.

"Nao, that girl—Stephenne Veronide—is a childhood friend of Limis's and mine."

"A childhood friend...?"

"Although... She's always been involved with the Church, so her status is different from ours."

Toudou brings the girl's appearance to mind and compares her to everyone she's ever met so far that's connected to the Church. For starters, her outfit is different from any priest Toudou knows. Her short black skirt is practically designed to show off her bare legs; definitely not very priest-like.

"...That was a miniskirt she was wearing, right?"

"How should I know? It's been years since I last saw her... And back then, she was always dressed conservatively..." Limis offers a curt reply, perhaps controlling her agitation by petting Garnet, who sits in her palm.

A look of disgust appears on Aria's face as she adds, practically spitting out the words, "I heard through the grapevine she's working at the Church headquarters... But to run into her in a place like this..."

"Do you guys...have some sort of problem with her?"

Aria and Limis look up at the exact same time and respond almost simultaneously, as if they conspired beforehand.

"She's not a bad person! It's just the timing!"

140

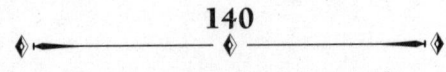

"The overdone sense of justice is a crime."

"I don't hate her, but… We really shouldn't be running into each other here."

Surprised by the force behind their voices, Glacia, who is nibbling on beef jerky, looks up suddenly.

They shouldn't be running into each other here…? What does she mean, the timing is…bad?

Toudou is still perplexed by the situation, while Limis and Aria exchange serious glances.

"So what's she doing here?"

"How should I know?"

"She said she was working… What kind of work?"

"Like I said, I don't know. She did mention a 'next time,' though…"

Aria purses her lips tightly and stomps once on the floor. "Limis, is Stey a priest now?"

"…I dunno. But she definitely seems like one, right? I mean, look at her dad…"

The conversation is flying by—Toudou can't get a word in edgewise. An uncomfortable silence falls on the room again. There are so many things Toudou wants to ask, but the atmosphere isn't making it easy.

Toudou waits, feeling like she's lying on a bed of nails. Aria turns to her and says, "Nao… There's something I'd like to discuss with you."

"…Discuss?"

"Yes. According to our schedule… Starting tomorrow, we're going even deeper into the valley to continue leveling up, right?"

"That's right. Wurtz said we should go deeper if we really want to level up."

The party's average level is already over 30. They've been alternating training and leveling up until now, but Wurtz has advised them to reduce their training sessions and focus on leveling up in earnest.

"Moving forward, we're going to fight stronger golems, and I don't think we'll be able to avoid taking damage. You can cast Heal, and we still have a decent supply of potions. We have Glacia with us, but without a real priest, things are going to get rough."

On the whole, Toudou's party leans toward the offensive side of things. Limis is attempting to learn healing spells through sprite magic, which includes many supportive spells—but at the end of the day, she is an elementalist.

None of them know what Spica has been up to since she broke away from the party for an apprenticeship.

Considering how gloomy Aria sounded, Toudou infers what she's really trying to say.

Aria's childhood friend just fell from the sky. She's alone in Golem Valley—she must be high level.

Spica has a standing invitation to act as the party's priest, but there is no doubt—they severely lack members who can use holy techniques. If they can acquire someone capable now, their level-up rate will improve dramatically.

Aria faces the highest odds of taking damage from golems, given her light equipment and lack of a shield.

Adding a different priest to the party at this juncture makes it feel like they're betraying Spica, who they've promised the position to, but Aria is convinced that because it's for the safety of the party, she'll forgive them.

Aria looks torn, and Toudou nods, offering a warm smile to assuage her anxiety.

"I got it. Let's get Stephenne to join the party."

The following morning, Toudou and company are eating breakfast in the inn's dining hall when the girl they just saw last night appears at the door.

Stephenne Veronide. Limis notices before Toudou and pokes her. Toudou glances up.

Stephenne looks flustered, her eyes darting around the room, but when they land on Toudou, she breaks into a smile. They exchange glances, and Toudou looks her over from head to toe. Seeing her again,

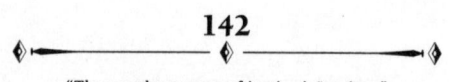

"The overdone sense of justice is a crime."

Toudou still can't imagine she's really a priest. Yet, although she didn't notice yesterday, today she can clearly see that Stephenne has proof of her priesthood hanging from her ear.

Stephenne stumbles between the tables and rushes over to where the party sits. Aria and Limis look irked. When Stephenne arrives directly in front of Toudou, she puts both arms straight down by her side and smiles from ear to ear.

"It's so nice to meet you, Toudou! Please let me join your party!" No introduction, no explanation, nothing.

Aria and Limis exchange doubtful glances. Neither of them were expecting Stephenne's request to be so sudden. Even as a member of the same sex, Toudou nearly swoons at Stephenne's smiling face—she's cute as hell.

"...I'm sorry. You can't," answers Toudou.

As guilty as she feels, she can't simply deny Aria and Limis. Per Aria's discussion the day before: *Sure, it will be difficult moving forward without a priest. But above all else, we absolutely cannot let Stephenne into the party.*

Stephenne must not have expected this refusal. Her smile stiffens, then disappears altogether. Tears instantly well up in her large, dark eyes, and she gives Toudou a look that strikes guilt into her heart.

"But... Wh-wh-why not? Huh?! If you don't let me in, then... Did I— Was it something I did?!"

"I'm sorry. I'm really sorry... But there's no way. You just can't."

Toudou puts her hand over her aching heart and says it once more.

§   §   §

"They sure made the right decision..."

That's the only thing I have to say to Stey, who came running back to us with tears in her eyes.

"Waaah... Wh-what does that even meeean?"

Stey is latched on to Amelia and crying her eyes out. Amelia looks annoyed as she pats Stey on the head carelessly.

143

Defeating the Demon Lord

Stey is a ditz. So much so that she probably doesn't even know what the word *ditz* means. Not to mention she also lacks self-awareness.

Of course, her father knows this, and he pushed his money and connections to the limit to devise an antidote.

From what I've learned, Stey had originally studied in the Kingdom of Ruxe to become an elementalist. Speaking of the Kingdom's elementalists, Limis's family are among the progenitors. It goes without saying that Stey's father knew them.

Sylvester is a native of the Kingdom and thus has a lot of clout there. Limis and Stey are approximately the same age, so I should have considered the fact that they could be acquaintances from the moment I learned he's Stey's father.

But seriously, she should've told me herself...

Stey doesn't appear to have nefarious intentions, but her stupidity is far more of a pain than any ill will. I'm used to detecting animosity, but I can't tell from the get-go if someone's an airhead or not.

The reason she kept quiet about her elementalist training is also pathetic. When Stey was still learning spells, Sylvester instructed her to never tell anyone about them unless it was absolutely necessary—treat them like her ace in the hole.

As the father of a moronic daughter who lacks self-awareness, it's understandable that he wanted to give her some method of self-defense. But seriously, at least make mention of it—to *me*! "Anyone else" shouldn't include her damn boss! This is her job, for crying out loud! Is this dumbass really only capable of doing exactly—*literally*—as she's told?

"I told you to just give up on Stey... She's a waste of time."

"Waaah... Wh-what does that even meeean?"

Amelia's words cut deep for Stey who, for some reason, is nuzzling her head against her. Not exactly a mind like a steel trap.

Toudou rejected Stey's bid to join the party. From one perspective, this is highly fortunate. And the fact that Limis and Aria know Stey can also be used to our advantage. There's a correct tool for every job, as they say.

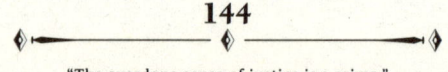

"Regarding Stey's role, I've been thinking... For example, if it looks like Toudou's about to mess things up, we can throw Stey in the mix at that exact moment."

"So, essentially, harassment?"

"I'll patch up anything she can't deal with herself. Of course, it's a pain to imagine how Toudou's perception of the Church might degrade as a result, but..."

Stey stops burying her face into Amelia and looks up at me, bewildered.

"...Ares? What do you mean?"

"On my signal, you'll get close to Toudou and create a diversion."

"Create a diversion...h-how?"

"Don't worry. Just be yourself. All you have to do, Stey, is get close to Toudou and act like you always do."

Stey's capacity to create chaos wherever she may be is staggering. This will work. Stey looks perplexed, but after a few seconds, she smiles. Maybe she thinks I was complimenting her? Phew—don't make me have second thoughts.

"Stey, we'll have you pretend to be a messenger from the Church. If you already know them, it will be a perfect cover."

My strategy for making use of Stey is coming along well. If this turns out to be a success, supporting the party will get a lot easier.

Amelia raises her hand and voices an objection.

"Shouldn't I be the one to go?"

"No, Stey won't put them on their guard."

"Well... Perhaps that's true, but can you trust her...?"

"I've thought this for a while now, but your opinion of Stey is ridiculously low."

Anything is worth a shot... At the very worst, Toudou and his party won't face sudden death, or anything of the sort. Stey might die, but from what I've seen, her spell-casting ability is more than sufficient. There aren't many powerful offensive earth elemental spells, but conversely, there are many that provide excellent defense. Plus, she seems able to cast magic relatively quickly.

145

If anything, this girl might show her true merits in moments of imminent peril.

I beckon Stey, and she stumbles over to me. And falls down. She gives me a perfect view of her white lace panties, and I stare down at her icily. I lightly step one foot on her back and tell her, "Stey. There's no point in me giving you a bunch of orders, so from now on, I'm only going to tell you what you must absolutely *not* do."

"Hnngh… Do you really have to say it when I'm like thiiis??"

I've already paid significant dues thanks to Stey. If this strategy fails, it will be a total loss.

My tolerance is being tested. Just a bit more, now. Just a bit more until I can actually get some use out of her, I know it…

"Ares, you're the type to gamble and lose everything, aren't you?"

"I don't gamble. I have terrible luck."

"You're taking a gamble right now."

Don't call this gambling.

"Ares… Are you trying to cost me my job?"

Creio's voice enters my head thanks to communication magic, and I've never heard him sound so exhausted. He normally doesn't show much emotion, but it looks like this is what happens when I talk about how to best make use of Stey.

"Please don't worry, Your Excellency. The other thing I ask of you… is that you bear full responsibility."

"?!"

"It'll be fine. If Stey becomes a real problem…I'll bury her. I have no intention of letting my priorities get mixed up."

Toudou's existence is paramount. Stey certainly requires delicate handling, but if we manage to defeat the Demon Lord, any strikes against me will be forgiven. All or nothing… That's what we're dealing with here.

I can tell that Creio is speechless on the other end of the line, but I hang up regardless.

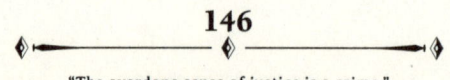

"The overdone sense of justice is a crime."

"Ares, shall I bury her?"

Don't take me so literally. Stey looks at me with absolute despair in her eyes.

"Don't bury your junior."

"If you really want her buried, just give me the word anytime. I will bear this sin, too."

Stey tumbles off her chair onto the carpet and crawls over to me like a zombie, grabbing my leg. She holds on like grim death and pleads, "Ares... P-please don't abandon me! I can still work..."

You can work? Talk about an empty promise. You really do think too highly of yourself.

"Stey, I still have a use for you. I have permission...from Creio."

"Ares, that makes you sound like some sort of villain."

As usual, Amelia pipes up with an unnecessary comment. Just shut up.

Stey must not have heard Amelia. She tries to clamber up my leg and hollers, "Ohhhhh, thank you so much, great and noble Lord Ares!"

"'Lord'? ...You can't seriously be the daughter of a cardinal."

That's unacceptable, even as a joke. Amelia circles around behind Stey and grabs her under the arms, prying her off me.

As she slowly peels her away, Amelia asks, "Are you really entrusting Stey as a messenger? Honestly, I don't know if that's something she's capable of—"

It's true that Stey isn't of much use. If anything, I'd say she's a pile of hot garbage with incredible stats. No—she's a high-powered explosive. At close range, she might be dangerous if she blows up, but even explosives have their uses.

"Stey, I know I just said your role was messenger, but I want you to instill a sense of danger into Toudou and his party."

"...Huh? Sense of danger?"

Stey sits flat on the floor and blinks repeatedly. She wouldn't know what a sense of danger was if it punched her in the face.

§ § §

The Church of Ahz Gried has the Sacred Nation of Ahz Gried as its head sect. It has a great number of believers scattered across many different locations across the world and is one of the largest organizations of its kind.

The scale of the Church has surpassed that of every other major power, and due to its incredible influence, the kingdoms generally keep a respectable distance.

The Kingdom of Ruxe is no exception. However, when a cardinal emerges from within the Kingdom—that is a different story.

One of the current cardinals, Sylvester Veronide, was originally a merchant native to the Kingdom and is extremely well-known throughout its entirety. Money is power. At times, it surpasses even authority. Sylvester is not an aristocrat, yet, his power exceeds that of regular nobility. He has an intimate relationship with high-ranking noble families, including Limis's and Aria's.

Limis ended up meeting Sylvester's only daughter through this connection. She was a cheerful, adorable girl. If one were to describe her disposition in a word, one might choose *innocent*.

Limis's first impression of Stephenne was that she was a bit of a natural airhead, but that changed in the blink of an eye. Stephenne had visited Limis's home in order to receive training in elemental magic.

She was intelligent and possessed high magical energy, and she picked up spells quickly—but the short time she was there was enough to sow seeds of trauma in Limis's mind. She can't even remember how many times she worried for Stephenne's safety during that brief period.

"I can't believe she hasn't changed one bit, after so many years..."

For Limis, Stephenne is like something of a clumsy little sister.

Aria finishes polishing her sword and puts it back in its sheath before frowning. Toudou looks puzzled.

"Okay, but what should we do about her?"

"? We already told her no."

"The overdone sense of justice is a crime."

"…That's all well and good, but… It seems like there's something more going on here…"

"Besides, is she even capable of a job in the first place…?"

Limis and Aria exchange dubious glances as they discuss.

Just then, a knocking sound resonates throughout the room. Glacia, who remains silent as always, looks up and stares at the door.

Limis is suddenly gripped with a horrible premonition, and her shoulders shiver. Aria immediately gets up and presses her ear to the door. In that second, they hear a spirited voice coming from the other side.

"Helloooo? Limis? Aria?"

"Wh-what do you want…?"

Aria's voice trembles with fear, but Stephenne's doesn't change. She replies playfully, "I'm here for work! The Church sent me as a messenger…"

"An assassin from the Church…?! Why would the Church hire an assassin?!"

"Not an assassin, silly! A *messenger*. Open up! Knock, knock!"

Stephenne mimics the sound of knocking on a door. Aria pushes her entire body up against the door and questions her.

"A messenger…? Are you saying that the Church decided to give you the responsibility of an actual job? Who sent you here as messenger?"

"Of course, that's Ar—"

Stephenne's voice cuts off. Her boisterous temperament trails off, and she goes quiet, as if it was all a ruse.

"…Ar?"

"Um, ar… Ar-arrrgh, just who was it, again? I forgot. But really, I'm just here as a messenger!"

Is this for real? Seriously?

An intense doubt surges through the party. Aria makes a face as she opens the door.

"So anyway— Due to that person's orders, I will be representing the Church and acting as backup for your party! Yaaay! Clap, clap, clap."

Stephenne beams as she gives a solo round of applause. All of a

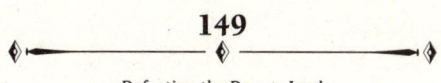

sudden, Limis feels like she's having a nightmare. Stephenne's proclamation has Aria and Toudou at a loss for words.

"…You're our…backup? Are you for real?"

"Heh-heh… That person asked me to… This is the first time I've been given a real job!"

"Who the heck is 'that person'?!"

"If I say their name, they'll bury me. So I can't."

"Huh?!"

Limis is dumbstruck, and Aria taps her on the shoulder. Time to switch players. Aria already regrets opening the door and letting Stephenne in. She pleads, "Stey. I'll be honest. It hurts to say this to a friend, but we just can't have you as our backup."

"That's simply not true. I'm totally capable of working!"

"It's…not a question of capability. It's simply not happening. You can't join!"

Aria is completely sincere, taking Stephenne aback. Regardless, she remains tenacious.

"B-but… If I don't do what I'm told, that person's gonna bury me!!"

"Seriously, who is 'that person'…?"

"I'll be forced to bungee jump without a rope!!"

"What?! W-w-wait a sec!"

Stephenne's shoulders are shaking. Toudou taps Limis and Aria on the shoulder, and they huddle in the corner of the room. She's not particularly keen to make a girl who looks younger than her bawl her eyes out. Toudou drops her voice to a whisper.

"Is this for real?"

"Stey is always so cheery. To see her shake like that… It's not normal."

"She's the daughter of an authority within the Church. Sylvester always doted on her, so…if she's truly that terrified, then…'that person' must be—"

There are only a select few individuals within the Church of Ahz Gried who are superior to cardinals. Aria swallows a lump in her throat. A cold sweat forms on her brow as she continues.

"Could it be…the Pope?!"

"The overdone sense of justice is a crime."

As far as Aria knows, aside from the Saint and the Holy Warrior, the only person who outranks the cardinals in terms of status is the Pope.

The Saint is largely a figurehead and doesn't have any real power. Her presence is perfunctory. Toudou's eyes go wide as saucers. She doesn't have any direct acquaintance with the Pope, but she understands this is not an everyday occurrence.

Aria begins to explain in detail, but Stephenne interjects.

"Ummm... Toudou, may I continue?"

"Oh, uh... Sure..."

Toudou nods, and Stephenne puffs up with pride. It's a distinguished gesture, but Stephenne is baby-faced, so it holds no real gravity.

"So, long story short... Because of that person's orders, I will now be supporting you!"

"...Just how are you going to support us? We already have a prospective priest on reserve."

"Well... Um... Just give me a moment..."

At Limis's questioning, Stephenne hastily shoves her hand in her pocket, removing a crumpled piece of paper. The party is completely flabbergasted as she spreads it out.

"Um... So, for starters, because you're all doing quite well, I don't have any specific tasks!"

"...What the hell?"

"Hmm... Well, this says that I should leave you guys be when you're doing well at leveling up. You don't need my help."

She's right—the leveling-up process has been going exceptionally well lately. It won't be long before every member of the party surpasses level 30. Toudou and company all exchange sighs of relief. Aria had been tensed up, but she also relaxes her shoulders.

Okay then, what exactly does Stephenne plan to do...? Representing the entire party, Toudou proceeds to ask.

"Umm... Stephenne?"

"Toudou, please call me Stey. Everyone does!"

"...Okay. So, um, Stey... What do you plan on doing?"

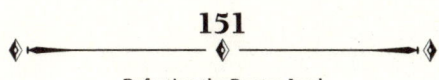

Stey puts the piece of paper back in her pocket and smiles from ear to ear. She assures her, "If leveling up gets tough, I'll join the party temporarily and help you out!"

§　§　§

It's a half-baked, experimental strategy, but it soon produces unexpected results.

The party is en route to Third Town, and their every facet is burning bright with purpose. Toudou is defeating golems left and right without any sign of danger. Aria is resolute on the front lines and is managing to keep her damage low. Limis freely wields her flame magic, and as an added bonus, Glacia is thrashing golems with abandon.

Limis and Aria are showing the greatest prowess, flourishing at a previously unseen level. Toudou is slightly baffled by this transformation, but she is also spurred on by them, and the party's overall battle performance has skyrocketed.

This is the first time they've set out toward Third Town, but they arrive effortlessly, without any holdups.

"Nicely done, Stey."

"Heh-heh... This is what happens when you depend on me."

Stey puffs out her chest proudly. We're now in the bar of the inn we've chosen as our base in Third Town. She smiles brightly and asks, "...Also, Ares. When should I go to help them?"

Stey still doesn't understand the meaning behind her assignment. No matter how many times I explain it.

Her task is not to *actually* help the party, but rather just insinuate that she can.

"You really do think highly of yourself, don't you?"

"I'd like to use some healing magic on Limis and the party, to help them recover."

Unfortunately, healing magic doesn't cure broken hearts. Stey's eyes

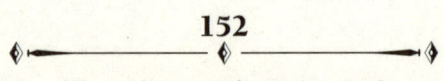

well up as she pleads with me in a saccharine tone. She doesn't think things through when she gets these ideas in her head.

"Stey, meaningless support does nothing for Toudou and his party. You understand that?"

"Um... Uhhh... Huuuh? No, I don't understand."

"...Get it through your head. Or I'll bury you."

I've already threatened her. Can I just give her back already?

Whoever managed to get Stey all the way to level 72 is something else. They have my undying respect.

"O-okay, I understand," she answers readily in a low, dark voice. Her entire body shivers.

There we go. That's the spirit. Don't think about it too much, just do exactly as I say.

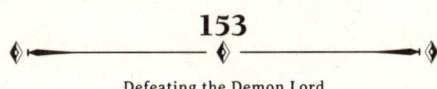

On Discovering Ancient Ruins and Adjusting Battle Plans Accordingly

"Flame Lance."

A short incantation. Garnet glows red-hot, infused with magical energy, and a flash of light erupts right in front of Limis.

Garnet cries out softly, paying no mind to the innumerable drove of low-level earth spirits around it. The light gathers force at once and forms a meter-long Flame Lance in the blink of an eye.

The surrounding earth spirits hum incessantly in response to the opposing spirit's presence. Toudou blocks the fist of a rock golem over twice her size and notices the spell being cast, sidestepping quickly.

The Flame Lance shoots forward. The golem takes a defensive stance with both arms to block the attack.

The Flame Lance blasts waves of phosphorescent fire in all directions as it flies toward its target like a shooting star. The thick lance pierces both arms of the golem, but it doesn't lose momentum. The monster's sturdy arms glow red and melt in seconds as the Flame Lance passes through them, the force of which sends the golem back a few paces.

The Flame Lance refuses to dissipate and strikes the golem's chest before exploding, blasting the monster to pieces. Hunks of debris fly toward Toudou, and she blocks them with her shield.

The golem's core has been destroyed, and its life force pours into Limis's being. She gains a level.

"Wow, Limis… Your magic is truly something else!" Toudou remarks in admiration.

The dry, hot air is blown away by the cool valley breeze and dissipates.

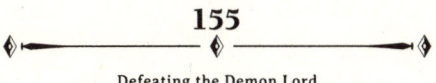

Toudou pokes at the golem's melted remains with her boot. Aria sheathes her sword as she says, "The House of Friedia is among the top class of elementalists in Ruxe, after all."

"If I could just...control the force of it a bit more, it'd be perfect..."

Limis sighs and shows no signs of embarrassment after being complimented. Garnet clutches the top of her staff and flicks its tongue out in disapproval at her response.

The golem has been utterly obliterated. None of the remains are salvageable for sale.

"Whoa, you're not satisfied even with this?"

"It's enough to defeat them, but controlling the intensity and area of effect of fire elemental spells is really difficult."

Casting elemental spells requires entering a covenant with one of the vast number of elemental spirits throughout the world, and borrowing their power to conjure magic. Limis has entered a covenant with Garnet, a high-level spirit that even a low-level mage can use to produce fearsome phenomena. However, spirits of this nature tend to forget moderation from time to time.

Of course, Flame Lance isn't the only spell that Limis can cast. If she casts a lower-level spell, such as *Flame Arrow*, it won't be as powerful, and she still hasn't solved her problem of a lack of basic capabilities.

Limis's breath comes out in white puffs, and Toudou pats her on the shoulder to comfort her.

"Don't worry, Limis... You'll be able to control your power soon. Let's keep up the good work."

Limis stares intently at Garnet as she listens to Toudou. Spirits and humans think differently. She stares into its obsidian pupils, but even as the covenant bearer, Limis can't understand what Garnet is thinking.

"Yeah, there's no use fretting over it... It's not a bad thing to be overpowered anyway..."

Limis quells the impatience lingering tortuously within her and looks ahead. Among all the golems that have stood in her path so far, there hasn't been a single one she couldn't defeat.

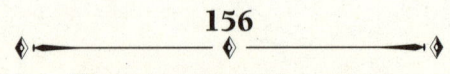

§ § §

Toudou and company arrive at the next town with ease. At this stage, they have no problem defeating high-level golems. Maybe they're most afraid of Stey joining them? As I observe their steady progress, I turn to Amelia.

"Lately, my relationship with Creio has gone south."

"…Why is that?"

"It would seem that he sees putting Stey in direct contact with Toudou and his party as a huge risk."

"…Well, he's not wrong."

Creio is a tolerant man. As long as he gets results, he'll let almost anything slide. He'll even pardon a little unlawful activity and provide me with necessary resources. For him to interfere with Stey's work is a definite anomaly. Depending on the situation, Stey might even be one of Creio's trump cards. She's a truly terrifying girl.

And the girl in question, following behind us, cocks her head to the side, more than likely dubious.

"Ares, could you possibly be…complimenting me?"

"Stey, your sense of humor is even worse than Amelia's."

In all reality, it makes little difference. Is she jerking me around here?

As I continue walking forward with that stupid thought on my mind, I suddenly hear a sharp sound coming from a cave ten meters ahead.

A golem unlike any we've seen thus far takes one step out. For starters, it's a different color from the previous golems. Its body is slim, about two meters tall, with a shiny black-red luster. It looks strikingly human, although there are two black stones stuck in its face in place of eyes. Furthermore, it's wielding a spear with a similar luster to its own.

Amelia takes a step back and furrows her brow, identifying the enemy in a whisper.

"It's a volcanic golem…"

"I wonder why it's appeared here and not near Toudou?"

Volcanic golems are the type I'd expect Limis to have the most trouble with, given their high resistance to fire. The volcanic golem, with its

157

sharp human form, moves smoothly and exposes its entire body in broad daylight.

They are upper-level enemies, but with the holy sword Ex—able to cleave through most everything with ease—Toudou shouldn't find them to be particularly powerful foes.

However, Limis's magic will prove useless against this type of golem. According to Wurtz, Limis is already aware which monsters prove to be the most difficult for her. Even with this knowledge, she'll undoubtedly try to roast them with the elemental spells she's so proud of.

And that is precisely why the volcanic golems are going to play a crucial role moving forward. They will likely become the impetus for Limis Al Friedia to change her ways. The fact that we've come across one first is poorly contrived.

The volcanic golem stops in its tracks and looks toward us with unfeeling eyes.

Let's take care of this quickly. I brandish my mace and take a step forward before suddenly noticing: Rooted to the spot, Stey is staring at the golem, unfazed by its presence. I look down at her.

I know that she can cast elemental spells, but—just how battle-ready is she?

"Stey, take it out."

Given her usual getup, I never thought she could actually fight. But this is Stey we're talking about...

Stey looks bewildered and blinks repeatedly, tilting her head.

"Umm... Ares? It's just, Papa told me not to show my magic too much."

"...You're telling me now? It's too late for that."

The golem slowly encroaches, pointing its shoddy spear at us.

"Stey. Volcanic golems are not weak, by any means. They even use weapons. Don't let your guard down."

"B-but... I just..."

Stey looks at the approaching monster and begrudgingly pouts her lips.

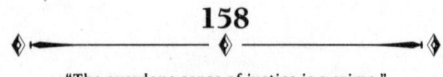

"The overdone sense of justice is a crime."

*　　*　　*

The volcanic golem stomps on the ground with all its might. The sound of the splitting earth rocks the air, and the golem gains speed like a flying arrow. Its spearhead is aimed directly at the back of Stey's unprotected head. Her pupils contract in sudden shock, and I silently grab her by the nape of her neck to pull her back.

I maintain my position and meet the golem's spear thrust head-on. I grab the razor-sharp spearhead with my right hand and stop it. The golem's entire body stops dead in its tracks. It tries to thrust farther, but it's pitiful.

Stey topples to the ground and looks up at me with frightened eyes. I stare at her even harder this time and order her again, "Kill it."

"Uh... Um... *Ground Spike!*"

A boulder spike shoots from the ground and strikes the defense-less golem in the stomach. A loud shriek pierces the air, and the impact causes the spear to fall out of the golem's hand and clatter a few meters away. Ground Spike is a low-level earth elemental spell. Living beings, whether human or monster, are quite weak to attacks from below. The stomach is generally a vital point, which makes this spell quite conve-nient for offense.

However, golems have thick armored shells. The volcanic golem is blasted and topples over but soon jumps back to its feet. With four limbs planted on the ground, it stares at Stey. Its stomach is completely undam-aged. Stey's attack was simply too weak.

The golem leaps into the air from all fours, this time attacking from above.

Just as I start to think that maybe this is too much for Stey, I hear her whisper, "Cacao... A more solid one, p-please."

A massive pillar springs from the earth before my very eyes. This is different from Ground Spike—it's a black, shiny pillar made of metal. It pierces the golem in the stomach, and this time, the monster lets loose a shriek far more piercing than before.

It must be damaged—the golem crawls along the ground toward us. Stey clings to my leg, and her dark eyes are swimming with tears. They're the kind of tears that make you think, *Oh well, I guess I'll help you out a little bit.*

"A-A-A-A-Ares!! Um, a little help, please!"

"*...Kill it yourself.*"

"Unbelievable! Ares, you're a monster!"

Stey's pupils contract fiercely as she watches the golem inch closer. She opens her mouth, and her entire body shivers.

"Ohhh n-n-n-noooo... I... I forgot the spell!"

Truly a piece of work.

Amelia stares at Stey, slack-jawed. Just then, Stey screams desperately, "C-Cacao, make it heavy!"

Only a meter away, the volcanic golem's entire body is suddenly pressed into the ground. Its hands crawl along the earth and dig into it. However, although its movements have been greatly slowed, it's still not stopping.

"Cacao! Even heavier, please!"

"This is unlike any magic I've ever seen," I can't help but grumble, and the golem is pushed down ever farther into the earth, its movements now barely noticeable.

What the hell is this? How can an incantation like that possibly have this effect? Amelia's expression is impossible to read. Suddenly, Stey claps her hands together and gives a cheerful shout.

"Oh, that's right! It's called **Earth Gravity**."

"How the hell could you forget such a short incantation?!"

As Stey recites the spell, the golem sinks into the ground. Its body groans under the weight, and the earth cracks in all directions. It's trying to stand up again, but the immense pressure prevents it from moving at all.

It's true that our environs facilitate earth elemental spells, but completely immobilizing a high-level golem means...

Amelia... Stey might actually be really strong. Even though she should be

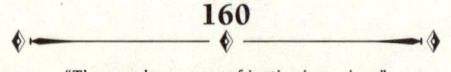

quickly sapped of her magical energy from casting the gravity-manipulating spell, Stey's still flopping around like a fish on a line. She shakes my leg with tears in her eyes.

"Ares... You're scary! That was so mean!"

"*You're* the scary one! Now finish it off!"

The golem can no longer move, but it's alive. The gravitational pull isn't enough to destroy its armored shell. Stey's lip trembles at my reproach, but she manages to pull herself together and put on a serious face.

"Um... Uh... O black star, ruler of all creation! By my sovereign's name, I shall not break the seal here! I ask not of right and wrong, but only to return to nothingness. We who possess all intentions can only despair at our worthless fate– Mmph?!"

I grab Stey by the lips and pull her away from the golem as I stomp its head in.

...What the hell was that terrifying recitation?!

Toudou and company reach Fourth Town without incident. It's border-line ominous how well they are progressing, but I've made every play I can come up with. All I can do now is pray.

I'm gathering together the data I've accumulated so far when Stey sidles up to me, smiling.

"Ares, can I go see Limis and the others?"

"...For what reason?"

"Heh-heh... For fun— Um, I mean, they must be kind of tired, so I thought I'd cast Heal for them," she pleads, smiling innocently.

She's demonic.

This was how she threatened me the first time. I can't let her out in the open now, when things are going so well.

"...No... I have a job I want you to complete."

"...What?!"

Stey beams wholeheartedly. The only possible conclusion is that she

loves working. If she was actually a respectable human, this would be perfect. I can't help but mourn the loss of my previous companion.

"W-well then, I guess... Ares, do you need my help?"

The task at hand is an analysis of the results of the survey we conducted on the unusual occurrences in the region. The survey itself is finished, but the data has not been fully compiled. I pull out a file containing the data that Amelia so diligently gathered from local merchants and mercenaries and put it in front of Stey. It includes recent monster spawning information from Golem Valley, along with their numbers, types, additional information from mercenaries, raw materials gathered from monsters that merchants have bought or sold—a vast amount of data that has been meticulously compiled and totals 125 pages.

"Use this to analyze monster spawning trends and summarize them, including the time, place, and number of golems that appeared."

"...You mean, for all of this?"

Stey flips through the pages as she speaks. There's a lot of data from the past month crammed into these pages. Analyzing it will take a considerable amount of time. My head hurts just thinking about it.

"No, that's not all. Amelia is currently gathering information from the area around Fourth Town as well. You don't want to do it?"

"N-no, I'll do it! I love working!"

"Can you handle this by yourself?"

"Hmm... Well..."

Stey puts her finger to her lips and cocks her head to the side. I still can't get over the fact that based on looks alone, she really could be an honor student.

"Can I ask Cacao to help me?"

What the hell? ...Cacao? I'm aware that it's the name of the earth spirit that Stey has contracted with, but a spirit's job is to aid in casting magic spells. To my knowledge, they don't help with administrative desk work.

"Can it actually help you...? Or rather—can it even read?"

"Cacao always looks over anything I write."

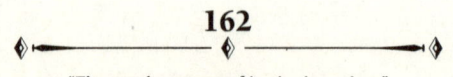

"The overdone sense of justice is a crime."

"You can't be serious."

Stey continues, now slightly boastful. She's staring at the tabletop, although there isn't anything there. Low-level elemental spirits can only be seen by their covenant owners. She's probably looking at Cacao, or whatever its name is.

"Cacao is super smart. She always seems to understand me whenever I talk to her."

"You can't be serious."

The fact that it understands language is impressive, but I'm also floored that she's been talking to it this whole time.

"She also gives me advice on how to improve and points things out for me."

"You're getting advice from an elemental spirit?"

"She's such a good girl! Whenever I fall down, she's always there to comfort me."

"Even though she's like a servant, and you're the princess."

"She's been with me ever since I learned elemental spells! Heh-heh... I guess you could say she's kinda like a big sister."

I think you mean *little* sister.

Stey continues, swelling with confidence, "At any rate, if there's ever work that needs to be done, leave it to me! Cacao's here, too."

"I see. I'm counting on you, Cacao."

"Excuse me?! Leave it up to *me*!"

"...By the way, do you have any other spirits you're in a covenant with?"

"? Of course! All eight types!"

...She's legitimately leagues beyond Limis's capabilities. Level 72, able to cast high-level holy techniques and elemental spells, and has already entered covenants with all eight elemental spirits.

She's a stunner in the looks department, her breasts are huge, and she's extraordinarily cheery. She's exceptionally qualified as a member of Toudou's party. So what kind of karmic affliction does she have that makes her so incompetent?

★   ★   ★

Amelia returns from her survey just before dusk. She, too, is highly qualified. She's smart and attractive. She's a bit stiffer than Stey, but she's highly trustworthy. After receiving her oral report, I take the day's results from her and thank her.

"Thank you for your hard work."

In the end, Amelia couldn't find any abnormalities in play near Fourth Town, either. It may be time to conjure a new tactic. My grounds for searching for unusual circumstances is simply because that's what I would do, if it were up to me.

I ponder the notion deeply when Amelia opens her mouth to speak, clearly tormented.

"Ares."

"Yes?"

"Don't you feel I've been a bit forgettable lately?"

The hell is she talking about all of a sudden? I remain silent, and Amelia continues on aimlessly.

"No, I mean, I believe that you understand me fully, but I'm doing my absolute best. But lately with Gregorio, and Stey being around... Although, comparing me to all these crazy people puts me at a disadvantage..."

"..."

"Gregorio is of a whole different breed, so let's forget him for now. But Stey is a sister just like me... I'm still learning, but I'm no match for an airhead, or, that is, I just can't lie to myself and be like that..."

She sounds like she's getting defensive and sighs heavily. *Uh...Amelia? Are you tired or something?*

"But, Stey is so, well, *Stey*, I figured you'd toss her aside in no time, but it turns out she's actually extremely qualified... To be honest, I completely underestimated your capacity to deal with her."

"..."

"I've had a bad feeling ever since she arrived, but I've ignored it. I still have so much to learn..."

165

"…"

"I really think that I should take up something new. Adopt a new persona, or change my direction… I mean, if I don't grow in some capacity, then I might get snuffed out by Stey. What should I do…?"

The direction you're heading in isn't particularly clear to begin with…

Amelia is clearly not joking around. Her downcast eyes are rife with sorrow as she peeks at me.

"Amelia… Please, just be yourself. Stay the same as you've always been, I'm begging you."

Seriously—your current persona's already intense enough. I was really hoping that I'd get a normal person dispatched to me at some point. It's probably *my* personality that's paper-thin. If Amelia's personality became even more extreme than Stey's, I wouldn't know what to do with myself.

I'm shaking in my boots. Amelia whispers to me, "…Dinnertime."

"Ah, you're right. I'm famished! All right, let's go!"

"You must be tired from dealing with Stey, meow."

"Yeah, that's true. Okay, okay! I'll take care of it! I'll do it, so quit with the meowing!"

"I'm joking. I'll take care of it."

Amelia is dead serious.

§　§　§

Rain mixed in with heavy winds crashes against the window.

Carina has been using the same sturdy, oaken armchair since she first came to Golem Valley. It's old and worn, filled with odd cracks and stains. As she lets her body down into its familiar recess, she sparks her pipe and sighs.

Her body is atrophied from old age and years of duress, yet, as she relaxes against the backrest, her eyes retain a distinct shine. No one would get the impression that she's frail. She knows this full well; local rumors say that she's a witch.

Golem Valley has been developed and cultivated over the decades

Carina has resided here. Originally, it was known for the fearsome golems that inhabited its lands. They were infested with horrible monsters, and the location is on the very edge of the Kingdom of Ruxe to boot. Until First Town was built, no one except overzealous mercenaries hell-bent on training ever visited this place.

When the Kingdom of Ruxe decided to pioneer these lands for the first time, the Church headquarters dispatched Carina here. She was still in her teens at the time and has worked at the church ever since.

Golem Valley is made for leveling up. Mercenaries visit and gain levels, only to soon depart. Others are sent here from the Kingdom for administrative purposes, but they change quickly and often. This includes the merchants and knights who all pass through this place like the ebb and flow of the tides.

Carina has always observed the developments that have taken place here. For example, even if someone leaves the valley and is replaced, she immediately knows who takes over. She doesn't show any signs of her previous voluptuous beauty, but the wrinkles she's gained in return are sheer proof of her experience.

Her husky voice echoes throughout the dimly lit room. She has a magical implement for communicating with the Church headquarters hanging from her ear.

"Ever the workaholic, that boy. Despite his cleverness, he keeps on marching forward, unafraid of failure."

Ares hasn't changed noticeably since the first time he visited Golem Valley to level up so many years ago. Not in his personality, his nature, nor his lack of flexibility. He may have moved up among the ranks, and he's physically matured—but that's it.

On the other end of the transmission, Creio responds.

"Yes, I know. But the Demon Lord we are currently facing is not the Demon Lord of ancient tales. We are continuing investigations on our end, but right now, we need Ares."

"Hmph... You may be right."

Carina looks toward the bookshelf while deliberating. The Demon

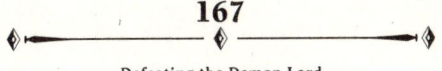

Lord is the king of all demon kind. One has appeared multiple times throughout history, and much of the research into his intentions has been conducted intensively within the Church.

Most of the books on the bookshelf in Carina's private study have to do with the Demon Lord.

As a member of the Church, she has surveyed all of them, and she has exchanged opinions on the matter, but Creio's right. The Demon Lord that has appeared this time—Kranos, the head of a demon army—is certainly making moves that cannot be found in the tales of yore.

In general, demons are exponentially more powerful and capable than humans, and as a result, they are extremely prideful. There was even one Demon Lord who entered humanity's dominion and battled them all alone. No matter how powerful, it requires a staggering amount of pride to take on all of humanity by yourself.

Others have gathered all their fellow demons and taken command of their corps in battle to start a war with humanity, and the infiltration tactics have varied, but the common point among them all is the emphasis on an offensive approach. Demons do not fall back to defend. They are brutal and cunning and look down on anyone they deem inferior, which is why they will always invade directly, regardless of any traps or schemes plotted against them. At the very least, from the demons' perspective, humanity has always defied them. Humans are nothing more than prey to be hunted.

And so, a hero is summoned. The demons' mortal enemy, humanity's only hope—the Holy Warrior—has appeared time and again to defeat the Demon Lord. However, this time, it's been three months since the hero was summoned, but there has yet to be even a single attack on them in earnest. Creio continues speaking, his tone at ease.

"The vampire Zarpahn Drago Fahni managed to cast a web wide enough to reach the Great Forest of the Vale… This is also highly unusual. We've never seen an actual trap laid for the Holy Warrior."

"Hmm… As humanity continues to evolve, it's not too absurd to imagine that demons are changing their ways, too."

168

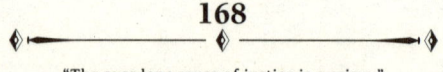

"The overdone sense of justice is a crime."

Battle tactics change. People gain further knowledge of leveling up and develop new magic and techniques.

Golem Valley itself has expanded considerably in the past several decades. The average level of the entire Kingdom of Ruxe has also risen, albeit by a small margin.

Creio responds with sudden passion.

"That's exactly right, Madam. It's highly inconvenient for us, isn't it? But if these events are all the result of Kranos's orders, that means the current Demon Lord is far more charismatic than we've seen thus far. The ideology of demon kind's superiority has been taking root for many years. Leveling up and divine protection are only a drop in the bucket... The ideas behind these concepts are the main reasons why humanity is still alive and well."

There's an innate distinction in true potential between humans and demons. Take the average capability of humans and put it against that of the average demon...the latter will always come out on top. If demons had the same mentality, intellect, conscious thought, and history as humanity, they would have enslaved mankind eons ago. These thoughts often turn to murmurings between intellectuals, but from the perspective of a member of the Church, such an explanation is beyond sacrilegious.

"Madam Carina. I cannot help but feel that we are, at present...in the calm before the storm."

Creio's words remind her of Ares, and Carina stifles a wry chuckle.

"...Heh-heh... The apple doesn't fall far from the tree, as they say. You and Ares are truly alike."

"...We need a Holy Warrior of ultimate strength. Madam, I say this as the head of the Church's military power."

"Yes, I'm quite aware. I've provided everything you asked for. The rest is up to your Holy Warrior and his qualifications."

Researching the Demon Lord will provide all the knowledge necessary to create the most powerful Holy Warrior possible. If the Demon Lord Kranos has no precedent, then Naotsugu Toudou must in turn

169

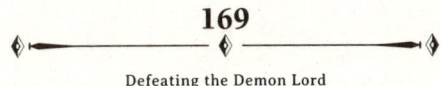

become the kind of Holy Warrior whose likes have never been seen before—no more, no less.

Carina looks out the window while she converses with Creio. The rain has begun to fall with a vengeance, with no sign of stopping soon.

§ § §

The atmospheric conditions in Golem Valley change easily and often.

The party had heard this before arriving, but they didn't think they'd end up soaked in a squall without any warning.

Toudou raises the hood on her coat—the closest thing she has to rain gear—and pulls it tight against the fierce winds mixed with rain. She regrets taking the outdoor route now. Aria wipes rain from her face with a stern look and steels her gaze.

"This is bad—I can't see a thing."

It's not just the rain; the thick fog surrounding them has also reduced their visibility considerably. At this point, they're incapable of moving forward or retreating. They can't see their enemies coming, and if they make a wrong step, they'll fall far to the river below.

Thinking of the potential plummet sends shivers down Toudou's spine. With her pointer finger, she pushes away her bangs, which are stuck to her forehead. Behind her, Limis is plodding along painstakingly and asks in a muffled voice, "What should we do? Continue ahead?"

"Even if we turn back…we won't see any caves for a while."

Toudou compares her mental map with their current location. Even if they turn back or continue ahead, there isn't anywhere for them to avoid the rain. They chose the outdoor route because of its proximity to Fifth Town, but they were completely devastated just trying to put on their waterproof overcoats when the cloudless, sunny skies immediately turned to a downpour.

Toudou bites her lip. Her dark eyes stare into the blank void in front of her. "It's dangerous to continue ahead in these conditions," Aria chimes in.

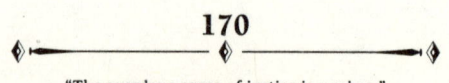

"The overdone sense of justice is a crime."

"Perhaps, but it's also meaningless to stay put—"

"The real problem is the monsters," interjects Limis.

The party finally decides to huddle together close to the wall—to ensure no one falls below—and continues their conversation.

Garnet is riding on Limis's shoulder, its skin now covered in a glossy shine from the rain, and it peeks up at her. Glacia's hair has absorbed a lot of moisture and is gently swaying back and forth. Limis looks down at her and continues speaking.

"Golems are made for this environment! They can navigate these paths without using sight, I'm sure of it."

"Yeah, I guess we can't afford to be ambushed. Besides, I can't get a read on anything in this rain…"

Toudou closes her eyes and attempts to probe their surroundings, but the sounds and sensations of the wind and rain interfere, and she can't grasp anything.

Aria limply lowers her sword to her side and stands on guard. Toudou follows suit and strains her eyes at the path ahead. Limis sighs quietly so that Toudou and Aria won't notice her.

In general, mercenaries are inactive during inclement weather. Donning their heavy waterproof overcoats alone is a waste of valuable stamina, and traversing their environs with minimal visibility is simply too risky. That said, there are some ways to cope with any issues that may arise.

One option is elemental spells. Water-type elemental spells allow the caster to control water. The caster can even shut out the rain completely, or draw the moisture out of the air and clear away surrounding fog, to an extent.

Garnet is a powerful spirit, but there's a limit to how much support it's able to provide. Fire elemental spirits can only control fire. In theory, Limis should be able to get them out of this fix herself. Being completely incapable of helping aggravates her deeply.

Limis looks down and her eyes bore into the earth as she wracks her brain for a solution to the deadlock.

Toudou and Aria stay on their guard while they converse in hushed tones.

"Maybe if I cast a prism, it'll keep the monsters at bay?"

"Living magical beings are unaffected by normal prisms. We would need something more high level... I'm not sure you'd be able to manage it, Nao."

"When do you think the rain will let up?"

"It doesn't look like it will for a while..."

Just as Aria said, the rain isn't abating anytime soon. Toudou, Limis, and Aria look dejected, but conversely, Glacia actually looks more upbeat than normal. Her long, wavy hair moves like a tentacle as she uses it to splash in a puddle.

"Gee, Glacia... You sure look happy. Not to mention... Your hair's really gotten long, huh?"

"...Mm."

Glacia stumbles past Toudou to the front of the party. The handle of the war hammer strapped to her back brushes just in front of Toudou's face, and she quickly moves to avoid it. Aria lets out a wry chuckle at Toudou's quick sidestep, which is far more agile than usual.

"She used to be a glacial plant... A plant-type demi-dragon... Maybe she has an affinity for water?"

"Her hair looks all jagged, but maybe it's sucking up water...like roots?"

Limis touches Glacia's hair. It's glossy and ice-cold; touching it for too long would likely freeze one's hand.

Glacia peers straight into the fog with her dark-green eyes. She seems to know exactly where she's looking, and Limis furrows her brow.

"...Glacia, can you possibly...see through the fog to the other side?"

"......Mm."

Glacia nods imperceptibly. Toudou's eyes go wide, and Glacia suddenly waves her arm in the air. Her tiny hand knocks down a shadow flying through the fog, and a massive crushing sound erupts in the rain.

Dumbstruck, Aria looks down at the object lying at Glacia's feet.

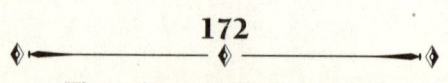

"The overdone sense of justice is a crime."

The familiar sight of a ball golem is sunken into the ground, ripped in half.

"…So there *was* a monster nearby…"

"Incredible…!" Toudou exclaims in wonder.

Aria crosses her arms and stares at Glacia wide-eyed.

The young girl who just happened to join their party is now their glimmer of hope. They can't afford to stay in one place. It goes without saying that no one in the party realized that ball golems were about to attack, except Glacia. They don't have any other options.

"Nao."

"…Got it."

Toudou picks up on Aria's implication and nods. She drops to a crouch—just Glacia's height—and looks her in the face.

"Glacia, we can't see in front of us. Sorry to put this on you, but could you guide us?"

"……Okay."

Glacia nods slightly and starts to walk through the nearly blinding fog without any hesitation.

§　§　§

The rain subsides, and the sky is dyed bloodred. The resplendent view sends a murmur of chills through my bones. I watched Toudou and his party pass through the massive steel gate far below, looking exhausted.

Fifth Town is located in the deep recesses of Golem Valley, and although the valley continues far beyond here, there are no more towns to be found. Not many mercenaries venture past this point.

Amelia is bewildered. "They finally made it… But really, I didn't quite expect them to make it this far in just under a month…"

The group has overcome the sudden inclement weather—which you could call a "Golem Valley baptism"—thanks to Glacia's powers. They defeated a vast number of golems in their path before arriving in

the valley's deepest town. In less than a month—officially, just nineteen days—since arriving here, they've made it this far.

Toudou's party's average level is still far below what's appropriate for this place. That's one hell of an incredible achievement.

I think back on just how much time it took me to arrive at Fifth Town when I came to the valley to level up so long ago. At the time, my level was far higher than Toudou's currently. They rushed to gain levels as fast as possible, but it really paid dividends for them. I put my hand to my forehead and calmly think.

Something's giving me a sense of unease. Oh, that's right…their level.

"What are their current levels?"

"Let's see… Toudou is thirty-nine, Limis is twenty-nine, Aria is also twenty-nine, and Glacia's level is unknown."

Stey manages to count on her fingers for me in response. It's a good thing that Toudou is leveling up quickly. The fact that Limis is now the same level as Aria is largely because Aria can't deliver many finishing blows. As for Glacia, I'm not even sure if she has a level. Everyone should be over 30 in no time. No problems at the moment. Not a one…

The second I think that far, I realize I'm not thinking hard enough.

Abnormalities. There aren't any abnormalities. Not much of anything has happened at all.

Yet, it's impossible there aren't any. It's simply that *I haven't noticed them.*

Toudou and his party are progressing well—too well. I thought this was all the result of their skills and equipment and having Stey tail them, but that's not it.

"Amelia. Among the golems that Toudou's come across, how many were high level?"

"Huh…?"

Amelia is dumbstruck by my question for a second but quickly gathers herself and responds.

"The overdone sense of justice is a crime."

"From what I've seen… None, I don't think…"

Precisely. They haven't come across any. Not a single one. I clench my fists and stare at the gate to Fifth Town. The gate, created from special metal alloys, imparts a sense of dependability and authority.

There's no way they can make it this far. Not at level 39, or 29—no one with that low a level should pass through that gate.

Luck plays a part in which monsters you come across, but it doesn't make any sense for someone at their level to make it all the way here.

I finally get it. The monsters may have increased in number, but that doesn't necessarily mean the stronger ones are appearing more often.

—*They're becoming rarer.*

"…Damn. The Golem Valley I used to know has gone completely soft."

I review the files that Cacao compiled and summarized in a day and a half, and my jaw drops.

"Unbelievable…"

The file includes the data graphed in chronological order. It shows the transitions in monster types and numbers across the past month, but that wouldn't indicate any abnormalities. That explains why the madam and all the local mercenaries didn't mention anything when we asked.

I put my elbow on the table and hold my forehead, mumbling. The clock's second hand thunders in my head, rushing me on with each moment.

"We need a graph that goes back further—but that's impossible. What is going on here?"

It was a massive undertaking to gather data from the past month. Gathering data from the past few years or anything close to it would be impossible—no one will remember that far back.

A more detailed survey would have to be left to the Church headquarters or the Kingdom. So—what exactly should I do now?

The most important thing is keeping Toudou safe, but what I need right now is to investigate what's going on.

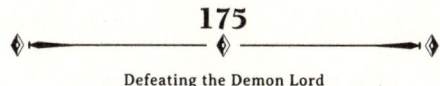

For starters, I need to know if the decrease in monsters recently is the work of demons. I've already told Creio of my suspicions, but without specific proof of numbers, we can't mobilize anyone. Verification will have to be based on my own intuition. That's what makes it such a terrifying prospect. If this is the workings of the Demon Lord's army—

"That's—one hell of a long con."

There's nothing brash about it. It's a massive departure from any of the tactics employed by armies of the Demon Lord in the past.

Fewer golems. This strategy's only possible goals would be reducing the amount of life force that can be gained in larger numbers from stronger monsters, thus slowing their level-up process, or reducing the number of items that parties can gain from defeating them. That would certainly weaken the Kingdom of Ruxe, but this isn't the only place built for leveling up, and it would not have immediate effects.

Would a band of demons even do something like this, given their arrogance? It's entirely too…underhanded.

I hold my head in my hands at the table for some time, but I don't come to any conclusions.

Just then, Amelia and Stey return after having stepped out to speak with some mercenaries.

Amelia sets down her knapsack and immediately begins her report with a stern expression on her face.

"As expected, no one has noticed a significant reduction in monsters lately. However, it seems there haven't been many sightings of high-level golems, either."

"Not many high-level golem sightings… Did they mention their spawn rates?"

"Walking a full day, seeing just one is above the norm lately, so they say."

One high-level golem in one day… I feel like I saw a lot more when I was leveling up here, but my memory is hazy.

Next, Stey—who has been tasked with speaking to the madam—looks up at me and says, "Umm… Since many people are leveling up on their

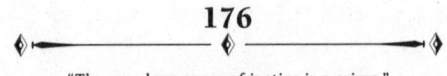

"The overdone sense of justice is a crime."

own, I can't be completely sure, but it looks like the number of injuries over the past few years has gone down a little bit. There are records of all those injured, I'm told… However, it's unclear if this is due to fewer monsters appearing, or increased knowledge of dealing with the golems themselves…"

Fewer injuries. It's thin grounds, but it can be used as a form of persuasion. At any rate, regardless of any possible involvement of the Demon Lord, this could be proof that there's something in the works. We're not shit out of luck—not yet.

"This is our chance. It's good that we've learned these things before Toudou gets into any trouble."

I give another order to Amelia and Stey, who are lined up side by side.

"Amelia, starting tomorrow, I need you out in the field. You'll go ahead of Toudou and his party and investigate the validity of this phenomena and any potential causes."

We now have a specific aim in mind. If golems are truly declining in number, we should be considering the possibility that something's happened to the mother golems that create them. If something has happened, there will be traces left behind. We'll scour the area and come back with evidence. To the extent possible, we'll also eliminate whatever gets in our way.

As I begin to formulate a detailed plan in my head, Stey tugs on my sleeve.

"Ares, what do you want me to do?"

"Cacao needs to meet up with Toudou's party and provide assistance. If something happens, please inform me."

"???? U-um, okay, I guess?"

"Also, Cacao… Make sure you follow up with me."

"???? Ummm… My name is *Stephenne*."

My orders are for Cacao. I can't see her, but I know she's extremely capable—she even helped compile my reports. I'd practically adopt Cacao myself.

I'm going to solve all the problems at hand, while Stey keeps Toudou busy.

177

*   *   *

A piercing crash resounds through the blue sky, and the rock golem, having taken a mace bash to the abdomen, is smashed against the rock wall. As I sidestep the chunks of golem flying through the air, Amelia, who was waiting behind me to stay out of the way, yells curtly.

"Ares! Above you!"

A golem flies in from above, blotting out the sun.

It has wings like a bat and a single silver eye. Despite being made from metal, it can fly through the air freely. Due to the harsh conditions of Golem Valley, this type of golem is deemed one of the most powerful: a winged golem.

Despite the narrow paths, winged golems attack from high in the sky, launching metal projectiles. Warriors who specialize in close combat can't reach them. There aren't many of this type of golem, but they've been known to even fly over the town gates and attack people, which makes them extremely dangerous.

Their armor can't be pierced by arrows, and because swords can't reach them, it's difficult to defeat them without a mage who can cast powerful attack magic... Unless you're high level yourself, that is.

I make a break for the wall. I can hear Amelia swallow a lump in her throat, and then the sound of a bullet landing behind me. I dash up the cliff at nearly ninety degrees. All you need against these monsters are a decently high level and a strong will.

When I race up to the winged golem's height, I flip my body over and jump in the air. The winged golem continues to intermittently fire metal bullets at me, and I repel them with my mace. I fly right over the monster and bash my mace directly into its freakish head.

The golem falls from the sky and lands on the ground. Amelia says to me, wide-eyed, "...That was truly monstrous... Just curious, but that wasn't a normal takedown, was it?"

"If I throw my mace and lose it, we'd be in deep shit."

"...Well, I suppose."

"The overdone sense of justice is a crime."

I survey our surroundings to ensure that no other golems are approaching.

"Don't let your guard down. That was a high-level golem. The monsters are becoming more defensive. It means we're getting close to whatever they're hiding."

"...Judging from what I just saw, defense doesn't appear to have much to do with anything... But understood."

Amelia seems discouraged, but I continue to escort her and beat back the golems that approach us as we continue farther down our path. Before long, the scenery of Golem Valley changes from a reddish-brown hue to a pale gray. At the same time, the path slowly becomes extremely craggy—further proof that most people don't come this far.

Hardly anyone ventures past Fifth Town, and no one dares to enter the mother golems' territory.

The day steadily wanes. A thin sliver of the sun setting behind the horizon emits a soft vermilion light. After continuing down the path for a while, I suddenly stumble upon something incredible and stop dead in my tracks.

I hunch down and feel along the rugged ground—there's a hole in it.

"? What is that?"

"...Footprints... And not from a golem."

The footprint is approximately sixty centimeters long and ten centimeters deep. The outline is weathered and hard to distinguish, but looking at it carefully, there's an obvious difference between this and the surrounding ground.

I gently trace the outline with my finger. There are deep gouges in the spot where the toes would be—four of them. No golem could leave a footprint like this behind—nor could any human.

I examine the nearby ground, but there's only two footprints total—one pair.

Amelia falls quiet for a time and then looks up at the sky. She understands.

"That's right. From the sky. This isn't from displacement magic, like Zarpahn."

The ground here is solid bedrock. Any normal footsteps wouldn't leave a print here. This is an impression left behind by someone or something falling from the sky.

A shiver races up my back. I can see it clearly in my mind's eye.

A tempestuous wind. Clouds rushing through the sky. A brilliant crimson sun and dark shadows to shroud it. And then, a humanlike figure plummeting toward earth from those shadows.

I speculate from the size of the footprint that whoever it is, they're bigger than me but smaller than Wurtz. They're definitely of a stature that is unfazed by falling multiple meters from the sky.

Their giant body is covered in thick, bristling needlelike hair as they smash into the ground like a launched projectile. Their evolutionarily advanced legs hammer into the bedrock and leave two giant footprints. They remain completely unscathed—with a skeletal and muscular system vastly superior to humankind; a simple fall from the sky cannot injure them. The four deep gouges near the front of the footprint are undeniably claw marks.

Pointed ears sticking out toward the heavens. Their vicious howl rips through the blue sky and convinces anyone beholding them that it's all just a hallucination.

"A werebeast—it's a werebeast. A tiger? A lion? Either way, it's definitely feline."

It must be a werecat. Its figure is too immaculate.

Werebeasts are part beast, part demi-human. They possess superior physical prowess on the whole, but unlike followers of darkness, they aren't susceptible to magic.

Due to their feral nature, they will only follow the orders of an exceptionally formidable being. If anything, they are particularly well-known as typical subordinates of the Demon Lord.

"The town's overland route is closed. If it did come from the sky, it

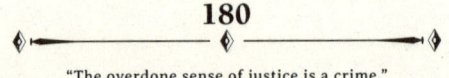

"The overdone sense of justice is a crime."

has to have wings. I'd say there are at least two of them, no more than that."

I investigate the footprint thoroughly, but that's all I can deduce with my scope of knowledge and capabilities. Yet, this is a huge hint.

"Ares, there's another monster."

"Yeah, I got it."

I stand up slowly and stare at the monster with an air of composure. "It wasn't what we expected, but we did find some evidence. Should we fall back for the time being?" asks Amelia.

The sky is already pale and gloomy. It will be fully dark by the time we reach town. If we play by the book, that is.

"Amelia, in order to track this thing, we'll need…patience."

"…You'll protect me, yes?"

"Yeah."

"Wooow, Ares, you're sooo cool. Clap, clap, clap… You're a *priest*, right?"

Amelia's praise is half-hearted and listless. Can she be serious? …Ah, whatever.

I brace myself and raise my mace to swing down on the rock golem steadily encroaching on us.

§ § §

Limis peers at Stephenne from the crack in the door and asks her, unable to hide the agitation in her voice, "…What did you just say?"

"Heh-heh… Ar—Uh… Arrrgh, that one person… They asked me to…to follow after Toudou!"

"What does that even mean?! It's not like we're struggling or anything!!"

Stephenne replies bashfully, but Limis simply shouts at her in anger, her eyes popping out of her head. They're not *quite* on the same page.

"Oh… But how can you be so sure?"

"What?!"

Limis is completely taken aback. Stephenne shoves herself through the crack in the door and enters the room.

Limis instantly reaches out to stop her, but Stephenne evades rather deftly. She reaches Toudou and Aria—whose face looks stiff—and does a little hop.

"Toudou! I've come to help you!"

"Oh... Um... Gee... Thanks?"

"You're welcome!"

"Hold on, hold on. Just wait a minute. Settle down."

Aria rushes in between them, putting her arms out as if holding Toudou back while at the same time restraining Stephenne.

"Stey. Calm down and listen to me. Really listen. We still don't need any help."

"But I can cast Heal!"

"?!"

Stephenne sneaks a glance at Limis. Stephenne originally learned elemental spells at Limis's home. She was told to never let anyone know, but saying it in front of Limis doesn't count since she knows this already.

Cacao dances in a circle at Stephenne's feet, as if cheering her on. Stephenne smiles and continues.

"I can cast elemental spells, too!"

"?!?!"

"...By the way, what level are you again?" asks Aria, her voice subdued.

Stephenne cocks her head to the side but then answers with a bright smile.

"About seventy, I'm pretty sure!"

"C'mooon! This is my jooob, you guys! Someone's counting on me! I'm gonna go with you. *I'mmm goiiing wiiith yooou!* Right, Limis? Right?!"

"Ugh, would you shut up?! Don't touch me!"

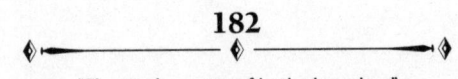

"The overdone sense of justice is a crime."

Limis is sitting in a chair hugging her knees when Stey grabs her by the shoulders and begins to shake her.

"...The last time we met, you were about the same level as me..."

Limis's eyes are lifeless.

"Don't you worry about that, Limis! Your level doesn't define you!" Stephenne tells her sweetly.

"It's pretty convincing when you say it, in more ways than one."

"But honestly, level seventy... Just what did you do to get to that level...?" Aria mumbles dubiously. Only a handful of knights in the Kingdom of Ruxe are over level seventy.

Limis winces as Stephenne continues to wrap her body around her. Toudou smiles wryly and cuts in.

"C'mon, guys... Stey seems to need active work, so what's the harm in letting her join us on a temporary basis?"

"Whaaat?! Nao, do you even realize what you're saying right now?!"

"W-well, I mean... As long as we kill all the monsters, what's the problem? Besides, it'll only be until Spica gets back anyway...," mumbles Toudou, avoiding Limis's stern gaze.

Limis continues to glare at Toudou. When she realizes Toudou's opinion isn't changing, she heaves a sigh.

"...Fine. See if I care!"

"Yaay! Thank you, Toudou! My limbs are now safe!"

"Your limbs...? Wait—"

Something soft envelops the back of Toudou's head. Stephenne hugs Toudou around the neck from behind, and Toudou squeals.

Unimpressed, Limis says, "Stey, you have no shame, as usual."

"Hey—Stey! Y-your boobs are touching me!"

Even reproached, Stephenne's face doesn't change a bit. She keeps her grip on Toudou's neck and head and turns her head to the side, perplexed.

"Oh... Huh? Why should that matter?"

"I-it matters to me! You know I'm a man, right?! You can't do stuff like that!"

"...Huh... What...? Huuuh?"

Stephenne blinks repeatedly and brings her nose to Toudou's lacquer-black hair, sniffing like a bloodhound. Now she's even more confused.

"Umm... You smell like a girl, though."

"...Um... Uh... What?"

"You smell like a girl."

Stey looks completely bewildered as time stops on its axis. Limis's face convulses wildly when their eyes meet.

Toudou starts to sweat cold bullets as her entire body goes stiff as a board.

"I'm a b-boy. A man... I'm a man. I mean, look at me..."

"Um, no? You definitely smell like a girl— Let me see again..."

"Wha— Stop! Nooooo!"

"Stey, get off him! Nao, run away!"

§ § §

"Yes. We're getting along splendidly."

"That's...great."

Stey's report goes in one ear and out the other. Her only role at the moment is to keep Toudou in one place. I don't care about anything else.

"If anything happens, let me know. Make sure you provide Toudou with all the support he needs."

"Of course! You can count on me!"

Now it won't be so easy for the party to move around. Shaking Stey off is no simple feat.

I look toward Amelia. We have real business to take care of. If Stey is going to be the source of even a shred of interference, I can't waste my time on her.

Amelia sits down on a large boulder and closes her eyes as if she's falling asleep.

"Did you find anything?"

"The overdone sense of justice is a crime."

"Not a thing... The scope is too broad... There are a few golems with high life force, but I can't really tell which is which."

Amelia opens her eyes slowly and sighs imperceptibly. Her brow is slightly sweaty, and her cheeks are flushed red. Her moist skin reflects the torchlight. Yet, her expression is distinct.

"I guess detection magic doesn't cut it, huh?"

"The human brain can only process so much information, after all. If I had encountered the monsters in question beforehand, that would be a different story..."

Finding them quickly would have made things so much easier, but I guess we aren't that lucky...

We're huddled inside a small cave to avoid the wind. The sun has completely set, and the star-studded sky is so stunning that it gives me goose bumps.

"Can't we leave this up to the Church?"

"I'll look into a few things, and if there's no sign of improvement on our end, I'll leave it up to them."

Judging from the data we have, abnormalities have been occurring since before Toudou was summoned. Thus, the chance the demons are directly targeting Toudou is low, but currently, our verification is incomplete. The footprint is still not enough. Even if it doesn't directly lead to our goal—their annihilation—we need to know if the owner of the footprint is still in the area.

I catch a glimpse of Amelia's deep, indigo eyes. Bringing her along is a risk, but I need detection magic. I purse my lips, but the ever-prescient Amelia raises her eyebrows and says, "Ares, it seems like you've figured something out."

"...We leave at dawn. Make sure to replenish all your magical energy."

We spring into action with the morning sun, our sights once again set on the mother golems.

I thrash four-legged golems that look like beasts and obliterate ball

golems that attack from above. The monsters' spawn rate in this area is well beyond the capacity of mercenaries currently present.

I stop to ensure the golems we've encountered are all dead and shake off my mace with a sigh. Amelia looks up from her place a step away from the battle, where she's counting the number of slain golems.

"You're right... None of these are high-level golems."

"Yeah..."

Before long, the ground—which had been changing color gradually—turns stark white. We've entered the mother golems' territory.

This area is known as White Plains, due to its geographical formation. The surrounding land has been cleared and would be ideal for building a town. It looks like a snow field dotted with the occasional golem.

"Ares, have you ever been this far?"

"No... But I've seen it from afar. A few years back, there were far more golems here."

This was golem paradise back then. Thinking about it that way, the decline in golems is stark.

Several golems are alerted to my presence and form a faction headed this way. They have numbers, but none of them are high level. I smash through the golems encroaching on all sides as we continue onward. They aren't strong individually, but I can feel them nearly sucking me in as they gather in number. Before long, I can barely move.

If I were alone, I could outrun them and put some space between us, but having Amelia here is complicating things. Nonetheless, we continue deeper and deeper into the White Plains, with no sign of the mothers, or any form of ruins.

"At this rate—we won't—make any—progress!" I yell as I annihilate five ball golems in one fell swoop. At the same time, I fall back and obliterate the ones coming up on Amelia's flank.

Amelia doesn't bat an eye at the golems that attack her and answers calmly.

"...Yes, you're right... Shall we go back to town?"

There is no sign of the mothers, or any high-level golems, for that matter. I suppose there'd be more security if any of the mother golems were nearby.

We're fortunate to have noticed the change in numbers, at least. When we reach the area's entrance to turn back and escape, Amelia says, "Ares... Look—"

I turn around at the sound of her voice. A figure looms far out in the white field.

It's not a werebeast but a dark-gray figure vaguely resembling a human being. It's void of eyes or a nose or a mouth, and it holds two straight swords.

It races toward us at frightening speed with silent footsteps. It's humanlike, yet clearly something inhuman. Its movements are far more natural and smooth than the golems we've encountered, and in comparison, it's most definitely *a living, breathing creature*.

This type of monster possesses the highest life force in all of Golem Valley. I click my tongue and glare at it.

"A metal golem..."

These fearsome creatures' bodies are composed of a special metal alloy. They have superior defensive and offensive capacity, along with speed, and they have no known weaknesses. They're the rarest of all golems in the valley and require the most vigilance.

But we're not only facing one of them. I grip my mace and ready my stance, pushing Amelia behind me.

There are five metal golems, all lined up in military formation like soldiers. It's incredibly rare for high-level golems to form a group. A cadre of metal golems is something that I'm likely seeing for the first time in history.

Five. Metal. Golems. The average mercenary party of appropriate level for the valley would be torn to shreds in an instant.

I steady my breath. There's no escape—I have to bring the first one down in a single blow. I summon all my rancor and murderous intent, boring my eyes into them.

Just then, the metal golems all stop in unison, only ten meters away from us. I instinctively swallow the lump in my throat. Their expressionless, featureless faces turn to us, as if taking note of our countenances.

The golems remain still and silent for more than ten seconds before suddenly turning back as if they've lost interest. They rush off and disappear over the horizon faster than the wind.

A bizarre spectacle. Following them certainly may reveal something, but I can't summon the gumption to pursue such a foe.

Amelia leans in close and whispers, "…What on earth was that?"

"…No clue. But—"

—golems aren't known to possess a flight response.

We saw them gather in a group, even though they don't form factions. Their behavior was like nothing I've ever seen before.

These details will never leave me. We put the White Plains to our backs.

§ § §

"I *told* you…"

The party has taken a room at the inn in Fifth Town, and Toudou hangs her head, wearing a grim expression.

Toudou believes in a person's capacity to grow and develop. That's precisely why she couldn't fathom it—the fact that someone could become more and more useless as time goes on.

Limis is lying limp in bed hugging a pillow, while Aria tends to her sword with a dead look in her eyes. Stephenne has joined the party temporarily, and after going out to hunt monsters with the group, she exceeded Toudou's expectations by a margin.

However, the party can't go on like this. Toudou nods, steadying herself, and speaks to Stephenne timidly.

"Hey… Stey. I don't wanna say this, but…"

"? What's the matter?"

"The overdone sense of justice is a crime."

Toudou takes a deep breath and finally asks what's been on her mind.

"Are you... Um... How should I put this—? Are you getting... clumsier...on purpose?"

"?! Um, n-no, not at all!"

"No, but really, you have to be! At first, I thought we'd bring you along, but then, like, all *this* stuff happens!!"

She trips. She forgets her spells. She gets distracted by her surroundings and bumps right into Aria and Toudou in front of her. She loses her priest's ring. She stumbles and manages to fall off a cliff. At first, Stephenne only seemed like a bit of a ditz, but things escalated so quickly that it didn't take long for Toudou to decide to head back.

Seemingly self-aware, Stephenne's eyes are downcast as she answers.

"I-I'm not doing it on purpose, though..."

"...I guess...you're telling the truth, huh..."

"Yes, it's the truth!!" Stephenne hollers, proclaiming her innocence. Toudou looks lifeless as she watches her.

It'd be better if you were *doing it on purpose*, thinks Toudou. But she can't verbalize the sentiment.

As Toudou purses her lips, Aria looks up resolutely.

"...I think it's best for Stey to leave the party, after all..."

"Wha... You guys...don't need me?"

Stephenne's eyes well up with tears. She looks needy and eager for someone's help, but Aria's expression is stiff.

"Stey... We simply cannot—"

"I'm an errand girl with the Church, you know! They sent me here on official business! You can't just kick me out!"

"...?!"

Aria struggles to find any words as Stephenne pleads. Toudou has already forced one priest out of her party. Though they were never told explicitly, the entire party assumes this is part of the reason they weren't assigned a new priest immediately.

They can't afford to foster any further ill will with the Church.

Limis raises herself from the bed and looks up, exchanging a glance with Aria. Gauging the atmosphere in the room, Stephenne leaps to Limis and latches onto her. Her entire body shakes as she pleads, as if begging for mercy.

"Limis?! Limis! If I get kicked out of the party, Ares is gonna bury me alive!! I'll do better—I swear I'll do better! Okay?!"

"Say what you like, but you're— Um, hang on... Who did you just say would bury you alive?"

"Oh... Uhhh... Um... No one! It's that person whose name I can't say!"

Stephenne laughs awkwardly as Limis stares at her before glancing at Toudou.

Stephenne's dark eyes shimmer in the lamplight. Before Toudou can open her mouth, Stephenne shouts urgently, "In any case!! It's dangerous to fight without a priest! You guys need me, okay?"

She's really desperate now. Toudou stares at her for what seems like an eternity before sighing the deepest of sighs.

It's pretty obvious she doesn't have any ill intentions. In Limis's eyes, that's the most annoying thing about Stephenne.

This quickly proves how incompatible she is with Toudou, who constantly strives to do what is just. The Holy Warrior, Naotsugu Toudou, simply cannot abandon her fellow human beings, including Stephenne Veronide—no matter how incapable she may be.

In the end, Toudou accepts Stephenne back into the party, on the condition that she uphold three promises.

First, her support will be limited to before and directly after battle. She is not to participate in any combat, during which time she must remain calm and on standby at the party's rear.

Second, she must take extra-special care not to trip or fall off any cliffs.

Lastly, once she has accompanied the party and confirmed they are

"The overdone sense of justice is a crime."

leveling up without any problems, she is to report as such to the Church and, at said juncture, leave the party.

The group gets ready to level up. Limis stashes magical energy-replenishing potions in her belt and checks that the flare ruby embedded atop her staff hasn't faded. When preparations are complete, she takes a moment to remind Stey.

"Stey, you better keep your promises, okay?"

"Aww, c'mon, Limis—I know that! With me around, this'll be smooth sinking!"

"…Smooth…*sinking*?"

Stephenne seems utterly confident in this colloquialism. Limis's stomach is already cramping up.

Just then, Aria returns from going out to gather information on what lies beyond Fifth Town. She glances at Stephenne before approaching Toudou and whispering in her ear.

"Nao, just past Fifth Town, there is an area called White Plains. It's where golems spawn."

Toudou's eyes widen subtly, and she asks in a low voice, "Is it dangerous?"

"It seems quite dangerous given the high spawn rate. Lately, hardly anyone dares venture there, so I'm told…"

"Then it's a bust."

Toudou answers without even a second thought, and Aria shifts her gaze toward Stephenne.

"Perhaps… But I imagine it makes leveling up very efficient. Golems with high life force should spawn in droves there. If we can prove to the Church that we're capable of taking down high-level golems, they might be swayed after all."

Toudou closes her eyes and thinks for a moment before quickly shaking her head.

"…No. That's still not good enough. C'mon, Aria… Think about it rationally for a second."

Toudou already understands just how problematic Stephenne can be. In her heart of hearts, she wants her out of their party as soon as possible.

"Do you really think you can fight off an insane amount of golems while protecting Stephenne, who constantly trips and stumbles and falls off cliffs? I know I can't."

Limis's magic will be a huge boost for the party. Aria's not quite strong enough to one-shot golems, but she's got enough power to hold down the front line. Combined with Toudou, they can hold off a number of golems at once. Also, Glacia has been participating in battle lately. The party should be able to take on any foe at this point.

But it's no use, according to the Holy Warrior, who lost her confidence somewhere along the way. Aria looks at Stephenne. She's throwing both her hands in the air and squealing.

"…My apologies. It seems I was mistaken."

"You see? Let's take it easy. I know we can. We'll stick with the safer route. There's no reason to take unnecessary risks. We'll succeed—one step at a time. I…believe in us."

Her lip is trembling, but the Holy Warrior, certain to live on in legend, speaks in a voice thick with emotion.

"I am—the hero."

Yet, courage and recklessness are not the same. Time often demands an effective retreat.

Toudou repeats this mantra to herself and turns her dark, tempestuous eyes on Stephenne.

§ § §

"Don't you think we should get Toudou and his party to sit tight for a while?"

Amelia pours me a cup of tea and sits down at my side as I examine the new data she's collected.

"No… It's too early for that."

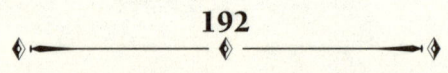

"The overdone sense of justice is a crime."

Before engaging in any sort of business, I always make sure to keep the following three points in mind:

Never lose sight of your goal. Prioritize. Be extremely thorough, to the extent that risk and resources allow.

We cannot afford to hinder Toudou's progress in leveling up. From the very beginning, the Holy Warrior is destined to do battle with demon kind. There is no such thing as guaranteed safety. Asking Toudou to pull back at this juncture will certainly warrant a complaint from the Church.

Balance is paramount. Right now, Toudou can run from almost any enemy without issue.

"Don't worry—that's why I have Stey with them. If something goes wrong, Cacao will be there to intervene."

Amelia looks at me as if I've grown two heads. I pat her on the shoulder and spread out a map. We never were able to find the mother golems in the White Plains. That means there's a high chance they've relocated.

It's altogether too painstaking to search these nebulous lands for them, but we must. The mother golems must have a convoy of guard golems at their side. Our only choice is to narrow the spectrum based on monster spawning trends.

"This is going to be a sobering task."

"Perhaps, but there's no other choice."

The battlefields surrounding us are simply too vast. I don't have the same cunning intuition as Gregorio. All I can do is hustle. Yet, if we can surmise the mother golems' general area, we should be able to find them using Amelia's detection magic.

The most vexing proposition is going up against two or more golems. Amelia could be taken hostage as I'm fighting one off. In that instance, I'd be forced to act rationally and potentially abandon her.

"…It's too dangerous with just the two of us… Amelia, contact the madam. We need Wurtz."

"…Are you expecting demons powerful enough to warrant his help?"

"It's just a precaution."

I take a deep breath and psych myself up. My freshly polished mace absorbs the sunlight coming in through the window and gives off a dim glint.

I can't be completely sure we're on the right path, but I will be giving it my very best. That includes walking into the maw of uncertainty when required. The darkest void holds the purest truth—whether unspeakable wickedness or a golden fortune.

Now, then… Let's get down to business.

§   §   §

They said she had talent. She wasn't jealous—that much was obvious.

A mage's power runs as deep as their blood, a culmination of unbroken pedigree inherited among human beings of boundless magical energy. Limis is a direct descendant of the ancient and honorable House of Friedia, born into this world to become a mage of the highest caliber.

She has innately powerful magical energy, an arsenal of mage skills, myriad prized treasures—and a powerful elemental spirit.

Spirits exist throughout the world, but those strong enough to act of their own volition are highly rare. Limis is low level and inexperienced. The fact that she has entered a covenant with Garnet is proof of her Friedia family heritage.

"Flame Lance!"

Surmising Limis's intent, Garnet fires a blast of searing light.

In spite of the golem's high fire resistance, the Flame Lance completely melts its target into a syrupy puddle. Stephenne claps in amazement at the liquefied mass.

"You're just as amazing as ever, Limis…"

"…This is a piece of cake for Garnet."

"But I feel like you're a lot stronger than before?"

"…Oh, really? And just when are you talking about? Over ten years ago, right?"

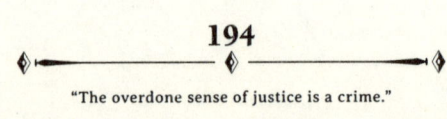

"The overdone sense of justice is a crime."

"...Ha-ha. You're right."

Stephenne hasn't changed at all since learning magic from Limis's family all those years back.

Limis grabs Stephenne with her left hand to make sure she doesn't go astray. Her right hand holds the Friedia clan's prized mage's staff, atop which Garnet rests, wrapped protectively around its gem. Stephenne looks at Garnet with affection and says, "I see you're doing quite well yourself, Gar-Gar."

"Elemental spirits don't fall ill so easily, y'know."

"Well, yeah, but..."

Stephenne gently stretches her pointer finger toward Garnet, but it avoids her stealthily. Stephenne looks genuinely disappointed, and Limis sighs deeply.

Just as they expected, the lands beyond Fifth Town have the highest monster spawn rate they've seen so far. First, there's the slimy, viscous mud golems like the one Limis just melted. Then there's the massive rock golems, covered in a boulder-like outer shell. And finally, there are the ball golems that attack in groups with their small, spherical bodies.

However, the party has already fought all these types before. They're used to them, and above all else, they simply don't take as much concentration.

They need to prove that they're doing just fine, that they don't need someone to watch over them. That much needs to be hammered home.

A single swing of the holy sword Ex sends a rock golem's arm flying, and Aria's blade cuts straight through to a mud golem's core, destroying it. Limis's Flame Arrow zooms toward a ball golem that has lurched forward, piercing its round body. Then, Glacia smashes its companion to smithereens.

Toudou's party is now showing the battle prowess of heroic tales of yore. Stephenne claps enthusiastically, her eyes sparkling.

"Wooow! The hero is the real deal! At this rate, defeating the Demon Lord will be a cinch!"

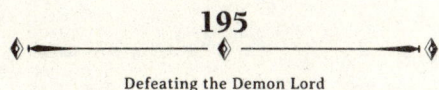

Stephenne says this with earnest sincerity, and Toudou sheathes her sword slightly bashfully.

"We're still pretty new to all this, but I definitely feel how far we've come. Before you know it, we'll definitely show the Demon Lord who's boss!"

Their levels are still low, but they've now got the green light from Wurtz, who gave them training. Limis is empowered by Toudou's strong display of will and pipes up.

"Well? Nothing to worry about, right? Go on and tell that to the Church."

"Umm... But I'm still not sure yet... I'd like to see Toudou fight a bit more."

"...Don't you go forgetting your purpose here!"

"I know, I know! Once I see you guys through to the end, then I'll uphold my end of the deal and inform the Church!"

Stephenne's overconfident attitude comes across limply, and Toudou and company all exchange concerned glances.

Suddenly, Stephenne claps her hands together like she just remembered something and says, "Oh, by the way, Limis, you're still only contracted with Gar-Gar, right?"

She says it with such nonchalance that it causes Limis's eyebrow to twitch. For Limis—no, for the entire House of Friedia—this subject is entirely taboo. The fact that the daughter of the kingdom's most prestigious line of mages has a covenant with only *one* elemental spirit is not widely known.

Limis toys with the idea of going off on Stephenne for a moment, but looking at her ignorant grin, she decides it's not worth it and sighs wearily.

"...You know, don't you? ...I can't enter more covenants. Garnet's rank is...too high."

Garnet's eyes don't emit any emotion. But Limis knows that unlike the innumerable spirits interspersed throughout the world—even the

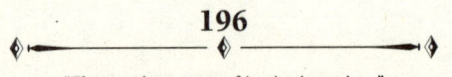

"The overdone sense of justice is a crime."

ones with the capacity for free will—Garnet's intelligence is closer to that of a god than a spirit.

In fact, Garnet is the most powerful fire spirit ever inherited within the hundreds of years of the House of Friedia's legacy.

Already, more than ten years have passed since Limis Al Friedia became the only person able to enter a covenant with that spirit, confined within several layers of magic seals inside the basement of the Friedia estate.

A Full Account of the Golem Valley Survey

A cold wind blows through the valley. Fragments of boulder resonate faintly along the rocky earth.

The wind is fierce, and even if a scent lingers, such as the fur of a werebeast, any trace of it is soon erased.

Behind me, a looming wall of shadow is surveying our surroundings. It's Wurtz, who we made a big deal of having dispatched to assist us. His long mage's robe is bulky from the weatherworn armor he's donned underneath. His pointed gaze pierces through sky far, far away.

From that alone, I can surmise that despite his long hiatus, he hasn't lost his touch.

Wurtz's nose twitches, and he grunts as he screws up his face in thought.

"Hmph... Indeed—it seems that the monsters have declined in number. I haven't been here for quite some time, however..."

"Right? They've practically been obliterated. I can't come up with any other explanation for why their numbers have tanked."

"...It has been confirmed that there are multiple mother golems. It's highly unlikely that they've all gone extinct. If they did, we would see a much greater shift in their behavior."

The extinction of the mother golems would spell the ruin of Golem Valley itself. I confirm my previous suspicions as Wurtz speaks. Amelia, who is staring far into the horizon, draws a short breath before adding, "If it's werebeasts we're dealing with, then they can't wield magic. They're likely using a physical implement to track the golems."

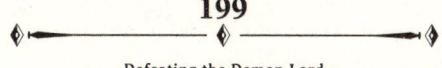

For our own tracking purposes, the data we've gathered so far isn't our only resource.

Werebeasts have incredibly high physical capacities, but conversely, they possess less magical capacity than humans. Their options are limited.

"Golems do not have a strong scent, but— Hmph. That means…"

Half giants and werebeasts have a number of commonalities. Wurtz squints and looks up at the cliffs jutting above.

"The sky…"

"Right."

I follow suit. The sky is so serenely blue without a cloud in sight, it could practically swallow me whole.

"If we're going to search for enemies in this area, we should start with the sky. If I were the Demon Lord, I would send out those capable of flight."

"The ability to fly… That's rare, even among werebeasts."

Only a slim handful of werebeasts are capable of flight. They have exceptionally high mobility and are perfectly adept as scouts, but they lack any significant battle prowess. I've heard they're easily singled out and their numbers have steadily dwindled from war and conflict.

"We'll do as they do and scour the valley from above with a fine-tooth comb. If we see any werebeasts, we'll apprehend them, and if we find the mother golems, we'll observe them."

Maneuvering from above the cliffs will give us a wide vantage, and there won't be any risk of being ambushed.

Wurtz silently nods, but Amelia shows some doubt.

"…Wait a minute. How are we going to get above the cliffs?"

"…We'll climb them, obviously."

The cliffs are steep, but they're only ten or so meters high. Piece of cake.

From atop the cliff, we can see the entire valley in all its grandeur.

Amelia climbs down from my back and furrows her brow at the breathtaking scenery.

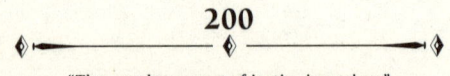

"…This is going to be like finding a needle in a haystack."

"Werebeasts in the sky, mother golems on the ground. Locating them will be up to your detection magic, Amelia."

"…I can hardly wait," she replies, although she doesn't exactly look it.

The valley is expansive, but it's not infinite. At the very least, we'll find some traces.

Amelia continues with a pointed observation. "Also, what if the absence of the mother golems in the White Plains, their usual domain, means they've all been destroyed?"

As we walk forward, I answer her with exactly what is on my mind.

"…To be honest, this was a contingency plan from the get-go. All we know right now is that we found werebeast tracks, the number of golems is declining, and the mother golems have vanished from the White Plains."

Even if nothing is certain, we have no choice but to make a move.

"Imagine that I'm the Demon Lord. Let's say I've dispatched my minions, the werebeasts, to gain complete control of Golem Valley. Suppose my goal is to annihilate the mother golems. Their territory is extremely well-known and can be easily investigated from the outside."

Demons are cunning. They often forgo detailed planning due to their arrogance, but they are more intelligent than humans.

"In that case, they'll definitely attack the White Plains first. Even the demon army is low on numbers, so they'll want as short a battle campaign as possible."

From the data we've gathered, the golems' decline in numbers has occurred so steadily that no one has noticed. Yet, thinking about it rationally, that doesn't make any sense. If they want to drive the golems to extinction, all they have to do is annihilate the mother golems. There isn't a mage left in existence who could possibly recreate them.

Yet, that isn't what's happening here. In that case, we can assume there was one thing the demons didn't think of, and that's just how incredibly capable the mother golems are.

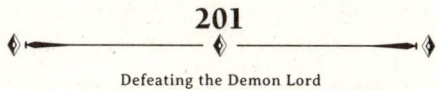

"Currently, there are still some existing golems left. In other words… the mother golems are…trying to escape. Is that correct?"

"Until now, people thought the mother golems would never leave the White Plains. However, the mother golems are the masterpieces of a famed mage known as the Doll Master. I wouldn't be surprised if there were some sort of unfathomable mechanism contained within these creatures… If there are several mothers with the ability to self-replicate, and they all scattered, it'd be a real slog to eliminate them entirely, don't you think?"

"I see…"

In this game of hide-and-seek, we have the upper hand—the mothers haven't been defeated yet. The rest is a race against time. Somehow, we have to put an end to things as soon as possible.

As we continue surveying the land, I see that the path on the cliff below is a different color. If it weren't for my current bird's-eye view, I likely wouldn't have noticed the subtle contrast.

"Amelia, I'm going down to investigate."

I let Amelia down off my back and descend to the cliff below, and suddenly, she cries out softly.

"Ares, take a look at this!"

She points at three small holes in the ground. They're clearly not of natural origin.

"That could be the remains of where a mother generated new golems. I've heard they can cast magic by inserting one of their feelers into the earth."

"Can you tell how long they've been there?"

"I'm not a specialist, so I can't be entirely sure… But I'd say these aren't that old."

For once, Amelia doesn't look very confident. If we can somehow determine these remains aren't very old, that will be a huge push in the right direction. If the mother golems are generating new golems on the move, finding any other similar holes in the ground and connecting the dots will allow us to estimate their course.

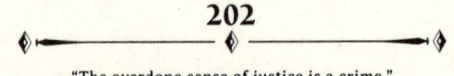

"The overdone sense of justice is a crime."

*   *   *

Stey remains our burden...she's strictly limited to observation, while Amelia, Wurtz, and I continue to survey the valley. We've established a good system, but we need to make the survey as quick as possible. At all costs, we need to avoid the awkward situation of Toudou and his party leaving the valley while we dillydally, trying to find the mother golems.

I'm completely on edge as we search—it's been three days. Yet, these are the times when fate strikes.

Amelia is casting detection magic as per usual when she opens her eyes wide and calls out to me.

"Ares, I see something— It's a beast."

She was looking beyond the cliffs. I focus my senses, but I don't feel anything.

It's doubtful we'll be able to catch it, but once Amelia senses a beast's presence, she'll be able to lock on to its location again with detection magic. As the thoughts run through my mind, Amelia provides more concise information.

"It's about one and a half kilometers out. It's taking the upper path— Wait... What...?"

Just as she starts up, Amelia lets out a cry of shock. She shuts her eyes tightly, starting the incantation again. I keep an eye on her while casting a buff on Wurtz and myself. My limbs swell with power, my senses ring clear. Finally, Amelia looks up again, her cheeks stiff. Her voice trembles as she reports to me.

"It's...gone."

Despite Amelia's tone, I'm not shaken. We've finally got *something* on them. That's an achievement.

Magic is not omnipotent. Detection magic itself is quite useful, but even among its users, there are still professional trackers.

"Did it fall out of range?"

"...No. I suddenly lost sight of it."

This must be a first for Amelia—she's unable to hide her confusion.

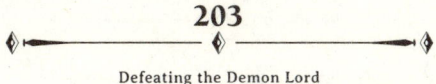

Yet, for all of detection magic's uses, a number of countermeasures have been developed. For starters, a particularly prescient target is able to sense that they are being tracked. If they themselves are a user of displacement magic, they can escape outside the original caster's range, and casting a prism can potentially block the detection magic altogether. Some magical tools can even allow the wearer to slip through undetected, although these are rarer.

If the beast Amelia was tracking really did disappear suddenly, it definitely employed some technique to deceive her.

Amelia is staggering on her feet, perhaps from the shock, and I put my left arm around her while giving an order to Wurtz.

"Let's go after it. Wurtz, follow me. Amelia, I'm counting on you to navigate."

Information is paramount at this stage. Even if we can't directly detect its presence, there will be traces left behind.

I kick off the ground and rush up the cliff in one leap, looking toward the direction Amelia's indicated. The expanse of Golem Valley stretches before me, and Wurtz climbs up a few seconds later.

"Let's go!"

"…Right."

On Wurtz's reply, I take off across the craggy, uneven cliffs. Following Amelia's navigation, we then race down a gradual slope. I can hear Wurtz's pounding footsteps behind me.

Amelia said it was a beast. Lucky for me; I don't have a shred of interest in the mother golems. I'm only interested in our enemies.

The Demon Lord Kranos is formidable. Hats off to him for being vigilant enough to have predicted the Holy Warrior's arrival and then sent out a demon to the Great Forest to meet him.

However—the Demon Lord's minions are not like him. Zarpahn Drago Fahni, who I battled in the Great Forest of the Vale, was foolish enough to fall for a simple provocation—and this is the standard all demon foes succumb to. They are a proud group of intelligent creatures with unparalleled strength. They boast of valor yet quickly fall into sheer

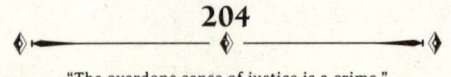

sadism. If the Demon Lord Kranos can quell their true nature, then the calamity brought down by him will eclipse anything our world has seen so far.

But that's not going to happen. Not on my watch. The demons' true nature, ingrained into their very beings for years upon years, will not fade so easily.

Just as humanity cannot gather as one, even in the face of the Demon Lord's arrival.

Just as Wurtz, who now embraces the priesthood, still relishes a fight.

Humankind and demon kind alike are not so quick to change.

"! Ares! The path— It's gone!"

"It is?"

The path we're headed for is no longer. There's now a cliff face roughly one hundred meters away. Amelia's eyes go wide and she yelps—but her detection magic is leading us in that direction.

"!!!!"

Amelia latches on to me tightly, and I take one big leap, not letting up on my speed.

The blue sky draws near. Something wraps around my arm. The wind envelops me, and I hold my breath. My field of vision is enhanced; I can see as far as the horizon allows. The ground is quickly approaching. I subdue any potential impact and land on the ground flawlessly.

Ignoring the cloud of sand erupting around me, I quickly turn around. Wurtz is soaring through the air.

From my vantage point, the intimidating man I know looks more like an insect against the expansive sky. He didn't slow down before leaping, but it's quite clear he won't make the gap. Given his body weight and level, I doubt he'll be able to clear it. I steady my ragged breath, deftly grasp the wire wrapped around my arm with all my might, and pull hard. Wurtz has grabbed on to the other end of it.

As he falls through the sky in a massive arc, Wurtz is drawn toward me at top speed before landing right at my side. His weight and velocity send a massive roar through the valley, practically kicking up a dust storm.

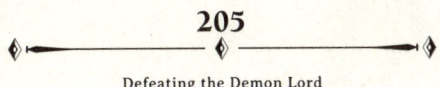

I wait for the dust to subside and remove the wire from my arm as I speak to Wurtz.

"You're reckless. What did you plan to do if the wire didn't attach?"

"You're wrong. The wire didn't attach—*I* attached *it*. Not to mention, how can you say that when you're the one who leaped blindly off a cliff?"

"Makes no difference either way, if you ask me," Amelia chimes in, releasing my arm and standing up shakily. She has tears in her eyes—now that's a real rarity.

Looking around, it's now clear that although we managed to cross one river, nothing has changed in our stark and severe surroundings.

However, the leap was worth the effort. Wurtz's right cheek twitches, and an animalistic grin creeps across his face.

"I can still smell it... It's close, Ares. Really close. It's the scent of a beast."

"Ugh, I can't take this anymore... I wanna go home with Ares. Wurtz, you go and find the beast yourself."

"Hey, Ares—"

"This is just another one of Amelia's jokes. Pay it no mind—I certainly don't."

"Huuuuuh?!"

Amelia begrudgingly recites another detection magic spell and shakes her head.

Wurtz is right. There's still a lingering scent—the subtle scent of a beast. There's a high possibility that it's very close by. Yet, there are also caves and multiple obstructions here. If it wants to hide, it has all the options it needs.

As an unfortunate aside, it's nearly dusk. Okay... Where should we begin our search?

I cross my arms and sink deep into thought. Behind me, Amelia is staring down the cliff face when she suddenly claps her hands together.

"Ares, Ares, I have a good idea."

"..."

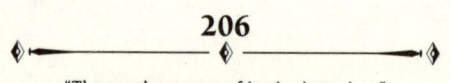

"The overdone sense of justice is a crime."

I don't have any fond recollections of Amelia's sudden ideas. I furrow my brow and look at her, but she has a poker face, as usual—she's a tough cookie, through and through. Didn't she just say she wanted to go home, though?

"You wanna go home?"

"Quit pulling my leg. Yes, I want to finish this as soon as possible, go home, and take a shower. With you, Ares."

Oh boy. Now I really am sorry.

Before I know it, I've fully committed to Amelia's "good idea."

"You spineless coward, running away with your tail between your legs just because you've been followed!! And here I thought werebeasts were superior warriors—you're nothing but a pathetic excuse for a creature! Now I know what to expect of the Demon Lord's army!"

Wurtz's thick voice rolls down from the cliff tops like thunder booming across the entire valley. Taking a direct hit from someone with the lung capacity of a half giant is truly intense. Now I understand why a giant's Howl is so renowned.

We've concealed ourselves in a blind spot below the cliffs. The progenitor of this idea plugs her ears and looks up at me.

"Seriously, Amelia, there's no way they'll fall for a two-bit provocation like this."

"Ares, don't think that everyone else is as dispassionate as you are. There are hot-blooded fools in the mix, too."

"I'm not sure if you're praising me or talking shit. Make up your mind."

Nonetheless, I myself thought this idea might just work. Zarpahn fell for my trick and ended up self-destructing. The demons I've seen thus far are truly hard to wrap my head around.

Wurtz's invectives linger in the air for some time, but nothing really comes of it. As we wait a few minutes longer, Amelia gently puts her lips by my ear and whispers, "...I'm sorry, Ares. I didn't consider the fact that our opponent could be just as dispassionate as you."

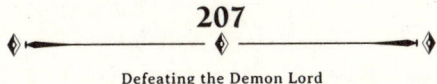

...Amelia, you and Stey really are cut from the same cloth.

When I go to tell her so, a sudden vibration rips through the air. I instinctively grab Amelia tight and bring us into a huddle. Soon, another powerful Howl shoots through my entire being.

"—AAAH—AAAAHH—AHHH—"

It's just barely audible to human ears. This is a faint but vengeful and murderous Howl.

As I shield Amelia, she moves only her lips and speaks to me, barely audible.

"There aren't many people out there as dispassionate as you are, Ares."

"...Oh really?"

Does she hate me? The trivial doubt crosses my mind before Amelia speaks again, this time sounding confident, triumphant:

"Now then, let's get down to business, shall we?"

§　§　§

"Oof... So...tired..."

Toudou moans, clearly beat. Limis and Aria aren't far off, with soulless expressions on their faces. Yet, the task at hand is going extremely well. Stephenne smiles and clasps both hands in front of herself, bowing cordially.

"Great work today, guys!"

Stephenne followed Toudou and the others through the rugged valley terrain all day and watched them fight many battles. She cast Heal a few times, but in reality, she doesn't feel tired at all. She feels entirely fulfilled.

Stephenne has belonged to the Church for a number of years, but this is the first time an assignment has gone so well for her. Usually, her boss or her associates stop her in her tracks, but today, she's successfully carrying out a top secret mission.

"Okay—see you again tomorrow morning! Be sure to rest up!"

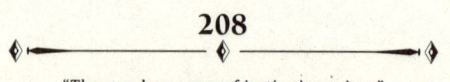

"The overdone sense of justice is a crime."

"...Hey, Stey... I think you've seen enough, don't you?"

It's Limis, signaling the end of Stephenne's tenure. Stephenne imme-diately crosses her pointer fingers to make an X mark.

"No way! You haven't taken down any high-level golems yet. I'm still worried!"

"Ugh... Having you around makes it harder to level up! We're too busy protecting you!" Limis shouts, red in the face. Stephenne looks deeply befuddled.

"? But it's normal to protect a priest who can cast holy techniques, isn't it? Isn't it, Aria?"

Stephenne sounds like she's reasoning with a child, and now Limis is really incensed, like a live wire. Aria notices Limis's face turning an even deeper shade of red and rushes out in front as if to cover her.

"...W-well... Sure, I guess. Limis, calm down. It's no use trying to convince Stey. She says she'll leave if we take down some high-level golems. Just realize this is all temporary, and we'll get through it."

...? I didn't say anything of the sort, did I? Stephenne stares vacantly at Aria and Limis.

She promised to accompany the party, and if there aren't any prob-lems, she'll tell the Church as much and leave them be.

Toudou and Stephenne haven't come to an agreement on the exact length of her stay, and it was originally Ares's idea for Stephenne to join the group. Toudou is not Stephenne's superior.

Thus, Stephenne intends to accompany the party until instructed otherwise by her boss—whether that takes ten, twenty, even thirty more days.

She contemplates whether she should tell them as much, but Aria and Limis look awfully busy, so she holds her tongue.

"Okay, then I'm heading back. See you tomorrow."

"Yeah, see you tomorrow... Oh, Stey. I've said it many times already, but you can't tell anyone about...*that*."

"About what...?"

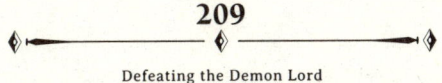

Stephenne is puzzled by Toudou's severe expression and hushed tone. After staring at Toudou's uneasy expression for a few seconds, Stephenne claps her hands.

"Ohhh, you mean about how you're a gir—"

"Hey! Just a… I told you not to say anything, didn't I?!"

Toudou flies at Stephenne and shuts her mouth, looking desperate.

Can't tell anyone… But why? Stephenne simply doesn't understand what Toudou's so worked up about.

For Stephenne, it's obvious what gender Toudou is just from looking at her. Sure, she's a little bit boyish, but her scent gives it away, and even if she was scentless, it would still be easy. Anyone who claims they can't tell she's a girl must have hunks of coal for eyeballs.

"I—I understand! I won't tell anyone! I promise!"

"Are you sure? Are you really, really sure?"

"Yes, I'm sure! Please, don't worry about it!"

Toudou asks again and again, just to drive the point home. Stephenne puffs out her chest and replies with confidence.

Stephenne has been a disciple of the God of Order since she was a young girl. There's no way she'd ever break a promise.

"Oh, Ares, you're back! Um… Did you find it?"

When Ares returns to the room at the inn, the members of the group who've been away for the past few days gather around the table. Ares's scowl is more formidable that usual, but Stephenne still smiles from ear to ear and scurries toward him like a squirrel.

Ares casts a sidelong glance at Stephenne and sighs inexplicably.

"Well, just its voice. I didn't actually see it. I ran out of supplies, hence we're back here."

Stephenne realizes that things aren't exactly going well and decides to assuage Ares's fears by giving a positive report.

"No issues on my end! Everything's *perrrrfect*!"

"Is that so? Well done. Anything else to report?"

"Not particularly!"

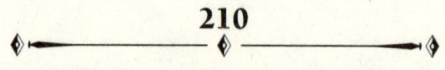

"The overdone sense of justice is a crime."

"...I see. You're the same as ever, Stey... If only Cacao could talk, I'd ask her to give the reports."

"What do you mean by that? You do know that Cacao can't speak, right?!"

"Yes, I know. At any rate—keep it up."

Ares rudely shoos Stephenne away with a wave of his hand and begins to speak to the others, deliberately leaving her out of the conversation. She stands there bewildered for a moment before quickly shaking the back of Ares's chair.

"Umm—Ares? I said everything's going *perfectly*!"

"Oh good, that's great. I'm busy right now, so go and play with Cacao or something."

"You're treating me like I'm a nuisance!"

"Stey, just what the hell do you want from me?"

Ares sighs in exasperation and finally looks Stephenne directly in the eyes. She thinks hard for a moment, then peers down at Cacao, who seems to have taken Ares's instructions seriously and is tapping playfully on Stephenne's boots.

"Umm... I just thought that since everything's going perfectly with my assignment, maybe you would praise me?"

"I said 'well done.' Now scram!"

"You're so grumpy, Ares... Would it be so awful to just give me a pat on the head?"

This is a rare chance for Stey to be praised. She sticks her head toward Ares, and his cheeks begin to twitch.

"How are you so damn shameless? Do you want me to smash in your head like a rotten tomato?"

No, that's not what I—! Just when Stephenne starts to object, Amelia sticks her hand out from the side. She rubs Stephenne's head quickly, like she's sweeping some crumbs off the floor, and motions to the door with her chin.

"Go on, Stey. Hurry up and get out of here. And leave some of that shamelessness behind for me."

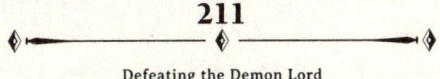

"You're so mean!!"

The conversation starts back up again in spite of Stephenne's shock, as if nothing happened. Stephenne withholds what she wants to say and decides to wait silently next to Amelia.

Cacao floats up gently and starts to do a twirly dance on the table in front of her. She watches it gleefully as the conversation continues.

"Wurtz's provocation definitely reached them. Amelia, your idea was spot-on."

"Yet, they didn't appear… Even though we went so over the top…," Amelia mumbles with her head hanging low. Wurtz, who has remained silent thus far, lifts his face.

"That Howl was rife with bloodlust. It's not so simple to quell the fire of a werebeast's wrath."

"But—"

Amelia interjects, contradicting Wurtz's opinion, and he replies with his own rebuttal. Ares listens for a while with his arms crossed and a stern expression, finally nodding heavily as if convincing himself of something.

"For the time being, I've come up with three options. We'll gather some extra supplies and head out at the first sign of daybreak."

"…Huh?!"

Ares turns to Stephenne with a sharp glance and continues.

"This'll be finished within a few days. Stey, you continue to provide support for Toudou. If something goes awry, don't hesitate to use your magic."

Ares quickly changes the subject, and Stephenne blinks vapidly up at him. His eyes look different from all the other times he's given her orders. Stephenne swallows a lump in her throat.

"We'll lead the way, so you shouldn't be in any real danger. You'll have Cacao with you, too."

"Y-yes! Leave it to me—we'll do our best!"

Ares drops to his haunches and continues, making sure he's heard.

"Cacao, if Toudou runs into a werebeast, or a high-level golem he

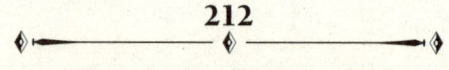

"The overdone sense of justice is a crime."

can't take on, I want you to use earth magic to stop them dead in their tracks, okay? If you can completely bring them down, then by all means, go for it. You got it?"

"Yes… This is one of those huge responsibility things, right? We're on it!"

Ares sounds serious, and Stephenne answers accordingly. Cacao also nods in agreement.

"Wait— You're talking to me, not Cacao, right?"

"Okay, everyone, time's up. Wurtz, you take care of the supplies. Amelia, help me polish up this strategy of ours."

"…Understood."

"Yes, sir."

Amelia, Wurtz, and Cacao rise from their seats.

Feeling like she's not quite on the same page as her fellow team members, Stephenne cocks her head to the side yet again, confused.

§ § §

Hot, ragged breath fills the dim cave like a sandstorm.

The mane swathed around the creature's head is a symbol of valor and strength. Its golden fur, like velvet, covers its entire body except for its head and is supple and strong. It functions as natural armor; an unskilled blade could never pierce it. Its physique may look slender at a glance, but its musculature is of an extremely high caliber, far different from a human being. The thick, powerful tail extending from its rear is standing on end—a sign of anger.

The beast's razor-sharp claws lash into the cave wall, leaving behind gashes yet not making a sound. Sapo watches the gashes increase in number from the corner of his eye before furrowing his brow and swallowing a sigh.

His companion is a kind of werebeast that boasts particularly exceptional battle prowess—the steel tiger race. Known as harbingers of death due to their brute strength, this race of beasts possesses a wild temperament that leads them to destroy anything in their path.

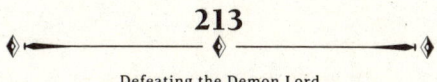

213

He is a supremely capable warrior and possesses the notoriously rough disposition and pride of his kin. His body is approximately the same size as Sapo's, but just beholding his physical form and fearsome aura sends shivers down the spine. His golden eyes burn with an unquenchable flame, sending murderous intent rollicking throughout any area he occupies.

"Curses! Why must I, of all beasts, be toyed with like this by a mere human?!"

His powerful claws tear into the boulder walls with ease. For a were-beast, strength is everything. For Sapo, his companion is simultaneously a source of endless admiration and difficulty. He waits for the were-beast's rage to subside before speaking.

"Felsa, calm yourself. It's clearly a trap."

The steel tiger turns around in response to his name, resentment smoldering in his every last movement.

However, despite their blatant gap in battle prowess, Felsa and Sapo are of the same status. Although Felsa is enraged at falling for a human trick, Sapo, as a member of the blackwing race, cannot fathom turning a condescending eye toward his companion.

Sapo does not look like a fearless warrior on the outside. His slender frame does not contain the muscular tenacity or explosive power that Felsa's does. However, the two glossy obsidian-colored wings sprouting from his shoulders give him the power to manipulate the air around him. The blackwings are just as rare as the steel tigers, and Sapo's abilities as a member of that race will be crucial in order to capture Golem Valley.

Felsa takes a step in front of Sapo. They're precisely the same height, but the natural-born warrior Felsa and the highly nimble Sapo simply impart a different sense of intimidation. Felsa spits in the air and bores into Sapo with eyes that glint of hellfire.

"A trap...? Then we must destroy it! Trample it to bits! Let this impertinent, useless machination be littered with the blood of those who dare minimize my presence!!"

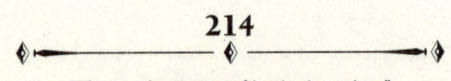

"The overdone sense of justice is a crime."

A shock wave rips through the air and slightly ruffles Sapo's elegant plumage from being so close. Sapo, too, has pride. The blackwings are no match for the steel tigers in terms of sheer strength, but they are still leagues more powerful than an average human being.

For him to say that being treated like an inferior species does not disgust him would be a lie.

Yet, breathing deeply, Sapo endeavors to remain calm in his response.

"Have you forgotten? The task our lord granted to us...is to remain unnoticed and unseen."

Sapo can swallow his anger, his pride, if it's for the sake of carrying out his lord's command. He and Felsa have been entrusted with a top secret mission. The particulars are left shrouded in mystery, but their lord specifically paired the two of them together for this mission: a steel tiger, the most formidable war machine on earth; and a blackwing, a race known for its extreme mobility and wisdom.

Furthermore, they have been gifted two highly rare magical implements that allow them to evade detection. They must not fail. He will meet expectations—this is Sapo's greatest point of pride.

Even on the receiving end of Sapo's sharp glance, Felsa still shows no sign of easing up—his fur bristles angrily.

Felsa only knows how to express his fury through combat. Even using Howl failed to provide him a moment of consolation. That is for cowards. No matter the reason, simply remaining silent in the face of a provocation is an act of sheer cowardice. It is certainly not something the most fearsome warrior on earth would ever do.

If Sapo hadn't stopped him, Felsa would have ended the poor bastard who set this trap already.

"Let's kill them—along with any possible witnesses," says Felsa in a stifled voice.

Sapo detects earnest intent in his companion's eyes and shakes his head, irritated.

"No, we mustn't. They are trying to smoke us out. If we fail to kill them, it'd plague us to our deaths."

"Hrmph… Are you saying that I, the invincible Felsa, could possibly be defeated?"

Felsa bares his fangs at Sapo, ready to rip him to shreds in an instant. His teeth can pulverize a metal golem to dust—the most rugged, solid monster in all the valley. Sapo wouldn't stand a chance.

Despite the chills he feels running through his body, Sapo remains firm in his rebuttal.

Their assignment has dragged on for longer than anticipated. Sapo has already endured this type of altercation countless times.

Based on experience, Sapo remains careful not to provoke Felsa's pride, and comes at him from a different angle this time.

"Come now, Felsa. No human being could ever eclipse your power. Our lord knows this, and that's why he sent you here."

"…Hrmph…"

Felsa's breath eases, if just barely. Sapo seizes the moment.

"Yet, you mustn't forget. We have not yet completed our lord's command."

"Grrr… Worthless golems… Constantly running from their feeble status in life…"

Felsa paws at the ground in irritation, as if he's just remembered something.

Sapo definitely remembers. The day they received their orders, Felsa so confidently declared that they could easily wipe out mankind's golems through the superior power of the steel tigers.

He was not altogether wrong. The golems may be formidable enemies for humans, but against Felsa's claws, able to shred any substance on earth, and his unmatched raw power, they are more like wooden dolls. Additionally, he can avoid his race's one weak point—the rugged terrain—to a certain extent thanks to the blackwing. With the two of them together, it wouldn't take long at all to complete the assignment—Sapo had insisted so himself. He, Felsa, and the Demon Lord all agreed.

The golems' capacity for learning was the outlier. Even with Sapo's

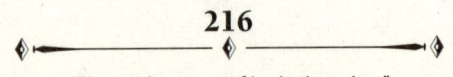

ability to fly, now that the mother golems have broken into multiple factions, he is no longer able to track them across such vast distances. Nor did they expect the mothers to have the capacity of reason to escape so quickly.

However, Sapo is not flustered. Their mission is taking far longer than expected, but as of now, they are still on track.

"Relax. We're nearly done. There are only a few mothers left. We'll soon obliterate them all. Once that happens, what more will a few human beings be? Our lord will laud high praises upon our perseverance and meritorious service."

It would be quite unexpected. Of course, no one should have noticed them yet. Throughout all their years, the two of them have never even met a human. However, this trap most definitely indicates that they've been noticed by someone.

Sapo senses a bad omen. He's received notification from his regular communications that the Holy Warrior has appeared. Felsa is pure, unbridled warfare, but Sapo has valor and discretion in the same package. Felsa would call it cowardice, but Sapo knows this isn't true.

If Sapo is a coward, then their much-revered lord is no different.

"It's a bluff. There's no way they've detected us. They're just trying to smoke us out."

Sapo turns his head and blurts his words out quickly and with little sincerity. They've already made two mistakes.

Sapo, who holds the magical implements that allow them to evade detection, had been separated from Felsa when the spell hit them.

Secondly, Felsa instinctively roared back in response to the cheap trick that ensnared him.

However, this is far from finished. Their presence has been discovered, but they have not yet actually been found.

It's unfathomable that Sapo and Felsa could be discovered here, in these vast lands, by detection magic when they have magical tools specifically designed to evade such techniques. Sapo calculates the chances in his head as he continues.

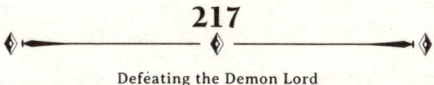

"You must be starving by now. If you don't get something in your belly, you won't be able to function at even half strength."

"...Precisely."

Opportunities to feed in Golem Valley are limited due to the lack of living beings present. Felsa can function for some time on an empty stomach, but if he gets too hungry, his strength is severely hindered.

Sapo stops Felsa precisely because he knows he is reaching the point of exhaustion.

Felsa may be prone to rushing headlong into battle, but he's not stupid by any means. He simply values violence above all else.

Sapo confirms that Felsa's anger has subsided and lets loose a sigh of relief, making sure Felsa doesn't notice. They've been together for some time, but he can't help but feel like prey in the jaws of a predator whenever he has to soothe him.

Felsa's tail, which was standing on end, relaxes slightly.

"At any rate, we don't even know if they're still in Golem Valley. I can't believe they managed to withstand your Howl head-on. They've likely already run away with their tails between their legs—"

The moment the words leave Sapo's mouth—

"Did you really think I wouldn't appear again, you diminutive pissant? You, who lack even the guts to challenge me—you are no warrior! If you mean to flee with your tail between your legs like the vermin you are, then I have no intention of giving chase! However, should you have even an ounce of pride left, then come and fight me, fair and square!"

"..."

—he and Felsa suddenly hear the same voice that provoked them yesterday. Even Sapo, whose hearing is not particularly good, could make it out—there's no way Felsa's sublimely attuned senses could have missed it.

Felsa's tail stands straight up before Sapo can even gloss over what was just said. His fur bristles, and his glowering golden eyes peer straight toward where the voice is coming from.

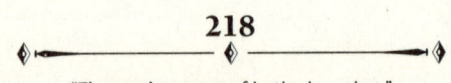

"The overdone sense of justice is a crime."

§ § §

Wurtz's Howl rips through the valley from high in the sky, like a crazed wolf baying at the moon.

We've tried a few methods of provocation, and the sound of Wurtz's voice now dissipates. We wait for a while, but there is no response.

It seems they can't hear him. I open my eyes and scowl as I address Amelia, who had been plugging her ears.

"They're not hearing him. Let's change locations."

"Is there any point to this?"

"There is. If their ranks have already left Golem Valley, then it would be meaningless, but the chance of that is slim."

Werebeasts are prideful and have extremely wild tendencies. Their response to Wurtz's first Howl is proof of this. But why hadn't they shown themselves instead of simply howling back?

There's a chance they held back out of self-control, but—more likely, their companion stopped them from retorting. Different races of werebeasts possess different temperaments, but in general, it's the tough types that show their feral side the most.

I have already surmised that there are at least two of them, with at least one having the capacity for flight. Any werebeast that can fly will typically be a paltry warrior. He must be the one holding the other back.

If that's true, the rest is a cinch. We'll just keep casting lines until they bite.

Fishing for werebeasts is easier than catching fish. Their intellect is similar to a human's, so I can predict their actions. I yell out to Wurtz, who's taken position in a rather conspicuous spot on top of the cliffs.

"Wurtz, it doesn't seem like they're here, so let's move to the next location!"

"I really don't think it'll be that simple...," Amelia grumbles uneasily, even though it was her idea originally. No worries; as far as I know, werebeasts are pretty simple creatures.

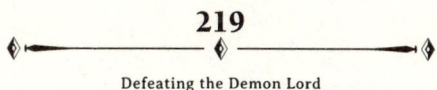

219

"We haven't seen a single monster yet today. And yet, my detection reveals that there are still some present."

Just as Amelia says, compared to yesterday, we haven't seen even one monster so far.

"They might be on guard due to Wurtz's Howl."

"Do golems even have the intellect required to make that decision?"

I look toward Wurtz, who's walking beside me. He catches my drift and slowly shakes his head.

"And yet…there are many things about this region's golems that remain unknown. It's certainly a possibility."

Wurtz's remark brings to mind the group of metal golems we encountered previously.

"…Hmm… Well, at any rate, it doesn't matter now. Nothing will come without a fight."

"…Good point."

The three of us head toward our next location with our map open. Our plan is to cover as much of the area as possible using Wurtz's Howl. When we reach our next destination, Wurtz gargles water to clear his throat and climbs the cliff side alone.

"Did you really think I wouldn't appear again, you diminutive pissant? You, who lack even the guts to challenge me—you are no warrior! If you mean to flee with your tail between your legs like the vermin you are, then I have no intention of giving chase! However, should you have even an ounce of pride left, then come and fight me, fair and square!"

His words rip through the valley. He is certainly a thespian…then again, he might be entirely serious. I remember the first time I met him. At the time, Wurtz Beld was impetuous, on par with the werebeasts themselves.

As I cross my arms and ponder, a strong gust blows from the side. Looking up, another Howl resounds in response to Wurtz.

"—Ergh—AAAHH——AHH———AAHH——!"

One second, two seconds, three… It's vastly longer than yesterday's response. It seems they're angry. I don't know where they are, but

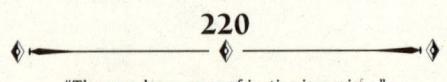

"The overdone sense of justice is a crime."

gauging from our current location, we'll be able to sniff out their approximate whereabouts.

The stark contrast in power between living beings gives me goose bumps. I furrow my brow just in time for another eruption from above.

"OOOOUUUUGGGGGHHHHHHHHHHHH!!"

Wurtz Howls again. It is meaningless, a pure intimidation tactic.

The cliff wall shudders from the force of his voice. Someone of low level might actually be adversely affected, their brain rocked to the core by his Howl.

Some time after it dissipates, another Howl rings out in response. Amelia has her ears completely plugged.

We won't leave to search for them immediately. We need to shake them up a bit. That's all it takes to catch a werebeast. No matter how much intellect they possess, werebeasts are unable to control their impulses.

They exchange Howls for some time, before Wurtz's Howl ends the long call-and-response session. His encampment is in plain view. If his provocation works, they'll likely come straight for him.

We wait for a while, but no action is taken. It seems they've managed to keep their cool.

However, their responses have gotten more and more severe. Just a bit more to break their equilibrium.

Wurtz climbs down from the cliff. He must be worked up from using his voice so much—his breath is ragged. I say to him curtly, "...I've worked out their approximate location. We'll provoke them again tomorrow."

Impatience is forbidden. Our provocation is working. A werebeast's pride will not permit it to flee.

I want information on our adversaries. No matter how many golems spawn, there will be high-level golems coming, to the extent we can handle them. I have no intention of losing, and I will raise our winning percentage. I turn to Wurtz and Amelia.

"We'll see if any information remains on our enemies. If we can determine their origins, we can pinpoint just what level of power we're dealing with."

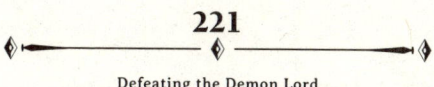

We'll finish them off slowly, like spider's silk slowly constricting around their necks.

§ § §

The party moves slowly, ever so cautiously forward. At the same time, they must remain vigilant of their surroundings.

Stephenne's senses are attuned to a level she's never experienced before, to the extent that she's not even bothered by Cacao running around her feet. Of course, Cacao is not playing around. Its typical goofy look is replaced by a stern expression, lips pursed tightly. It's keeping close watch on its surroundings alongside Stephenne.

Thanks to this, Stephenne has not tripped and fallen once today. Stephenne is grateful to get a chance like this once in a year, maybe. At any rate, the earth spirits have always blessed her, and she's always had a strong affinity for them.

The party has been walking around outside the town for an hour. Toudou, who's leading them, turns around to look back. Usually, someone will run into her if she stops suddenly, so she does so slowly, cautiously. She cocks her head to the side, a dubious expression on her face.

"…Hmm… Don't you think there are surprisingly few monsters today?"

"Yes, you're right… We've been walking an hour already, and we've only had one encounter."

Aria suspiciously surveys the area. As always, the valley stretches onward serenely.

Suddenly, she comes to a realization:

"? Hmm? Stey, you're oddly on point today… You haven't caused any trouble, not even once."

"…Just what do you think of me, Aria?"

Aria averts her gaze. Toudou and Limis keep silent. Then, Stephenne takes the chance to proclaim loudly, "It's because I'm on my A game today!"

"You should be on it *every* day…"

"Okay—onward and upward! You can count on me!"

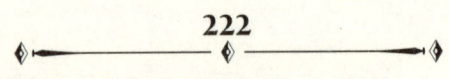

"The overdone sense of justice is a crime."

This is a serious responsibility. If a werebeast or other enemy that the Holy Warrior can't handle appears, Stephenne has been told to attack them without hesitation.

In other words, that means she must protect Toudou. Stephenne knows how important a job it is to protect the Holy Warrior. She takes her assignments seriously at all times, but this is a task she can't help feeling fired up about.

Toudou's dubious glance aside, Stephenne and Cacao both raise their fists in the air and shout *Hurrah!* before continuing forward.

§ § §

I am not a warrior. I do not have the mental disposition that comes with knighthood. If the end justifies the means, anything goes.

We find the werebeasts' tracks easily. As expected, they are within reach of Wurtz's voice—inside a single cave.

I examine the endless claw marks in the cave wall. I can't feel their presence close by, but they were definitely here, not long ago. Amelia traces the marks, which look similar to sword slashes, and stares at the cave floor.

Werebeasts are all of the same lineage, but depending on the amount of beast spawn they contain, their abilities vary wildly. The more they contain, the more they look like beasts, and their physical prowess is subsequently very high. At the same time, their feral tendencies are heightened, and as such, these types of werebeasts are rarely seen among men.

The marks on the wall are in sets of four long scratches. Claws are a werebeast's foremost weapon. Depending on their lineage, their claws can be sharper than most blades and are even used as the raw material to forge swords in some instances.

Wurtz is investigating next to me. He growls gutturally.

"...It's strong."

The cave still emanates an aura of something extremely powerful having inhabited it. Beings with high life force leave a noticeable trace

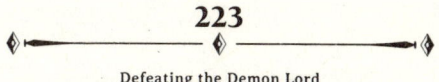

behind. If they are highly emotional, those traces become even more prominent.

The razor-sharp claw marks indicate that this is not a werebeast of standard lineage. It is likely of highly feral and fearsome stock. Its entire body should be covered in fur, but there isn't a single strand to be found on the cave floor.

Beings of such specialized physical capacity are the natural enemies of priests. Wurtz is a half giant with elevated physical abilities, which makes it a bit better for him…

Wurtz must be feeling the same as me, having gauged the werebeast's power. He growls, a grim look on his face. "It's feline," I tell him.

"…What do you mean?"

Wurtz looks perplexed, and Amelia also seems at a loss. I trace my finger along a claw mark on the wall.

"That's the key word for our next provocation."

However, our strategy won't change. Our foe is the outstanding threat to humanity: the Demon Lord's army. We've already assumed the extreme nature of their battle prowess.

"We're up against a feline werebeast, likely of extremely high level. I don't know if it's a tiger or a lion, but werebeasts of this lineage absolutely hate being ridiculed as lower-level beings. This one's already about to snap. We'll reel them in with our next move."

"Ares… Do you really think you can take it down?" Wurtz asks.

My level is 93, but I am a priest. A warrior of similar level would lose eight or nine times out of ten. However, when it comes to taking down a werebeast, possessing the greater brute strength isn't necessary.

Amelia and Wurtz are waiting on me with bated breath. I can't let them feel anxious. My reply is emphatic.

"Yes."

However—I will not be doing the fighting.

I look toward Wurtz, his giant body and massive skeletal frame. He comes from a race of warriors; if he were the same level as me, he

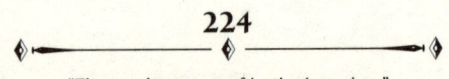

"The overdone sense of justice is a crime."

would be exponentially stronger. I stare deep into Wurtz's eyes before continuing.

"However, Wurtz— It'll be you and Amelia facing off against it."

I am not a warrior. I do not have the mental disposition that comes with knighthood. If the end justifies the means, anything goes.

§ § §

This place reeks of blood. The blood rushing in my head has seeped through my skin and is wafting toward my nose, Sapo thinks.

For the highly revered steel tiger, who's never been at the whim of anyone to ridicule him, a simple provocation—a trap—is akin to pure poison.

That pent-up poison has corrupted his brain, and now the fighting instincts dyed into the fabric of his very being are all that remain. Felsa's narrowed golden irises pierce Sapo's soul. His face twitches as Felsa crushes a rock underfoot.

Under normal circumstances, the resulting sound would be barely noticeable. But now, it's almost as if Felsa is trying to make his presence known. This isn't simply an alternative way of letting off steam—and as far as Sapo can tell, it doesn't contain any specific meaning.

"Calm down and cool your head, Felsa. That was a trap. There's nothing more to it."

"Hah?! Are you saying that I... That I, Felsa, do not look calm?! You son of a bitch!!"

His tone indicates he will not accept any rebuttals. From Sapo's perspective, getting Felsa to calm down after the previous provocation would be nothing short of a miracle. There's not a soul out there who can stop a steel tiger on the warpath.

Felsa's stomach rumbles audibly. Pangs of hunger—the last thing keeping him from losing control. They should be receiving provisions before long. And when that happens, Sapo will have no recourse in stopping him.

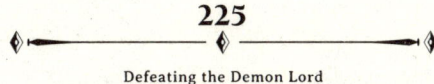

Sapo has accepted this. Their mission is top secret, but that is no reason to let those tracking them off the hook. No one in their midst should be capable of taking down a pure steel tiger.

"Your hunger will soon be sated. That will mark your chance to repay them for their pitiful trap."

"Tch…"

Felsa bares his fangs and wordlessly increases his pace. Sapo follows closely behind, keeping an eye on their surroundings. Destroying a golem would curb Felsa's impulses slightly, but just their luck—there are no monsters in sight.

For now, Sapo will have to continue to keep the feral feline beast at bay using only his wits.

Felsa's anger is blatant, even as Sapo tags along from behind. He's a ticking time bomb.

There's nothing more terrifying than taking a risk with a steel tiger. That would be a foolish move on Sapo's part.

Additionally, once Felsa has eaten, Sapo will have to join in the fight against whatever enemy he discovers. Sapo is a seasoned blackwing warrior. For any opponent incapable of flight themselves, any powerful attacks launched from the sky will prove just as formidable as going head-to-head with a steel tiger. Sapo clasps his hands around the golden amulet hanging from his neck and ponders the possibilities that await him.

The amulet is known as a cicada shell pendant—able to ward off detection magic, it's a superior magical tool handed to Sapo directly from the Demon Lord himself.

It is a sign of his lord's expectations for him. It has the power to keep the short-tempered and violent Felsa at bay in these lands. The fact that his lord gave it to him means that he must genuinely trust Sapo. Without it, Sapo would have likely given up on the idea of joining forces with Felsa.

As he recalls their long and arduous days, Felsa comes to an abrupt stop in front of him. Sapo addresses his companion, stopped stiff as a board.

"? What's the matter?"

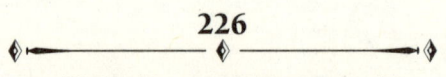

"The overdone sense of justice is a crime."

"…"

"?!"

Sapo swallows a lump in his throat, having spoken out loud instinctively. Felsa is no longer enraged. The ire that was prevalent not only on his face, but in his whole body, has completely disappeared. Instead, he appears to be…in a trance.

Sapo completely loses his train of thought at this bizarre development but soon rushes to Felsa's side and shakes his shoulder.

"Hey—what's going on?!"

He hasn't taken an attack. No to mention, no golem in this region could even pierce the hide of a steel tiger. Felsa's ears are twitching involuntarily. He turns ever so slowly and looks at Sapo.

An unknown sense of foreboding rushes through Sapo's entire body, from his toes to the top of his head.

Felsa's pupils have expanded to the maximum, flashing brilliantly. Sapo can see his face reflected in them.

§   §   §

The biggest difference between a standard warrior and a crusader is their experience level.

Warriors and monster hunters only join in fights they know they can win. Crusaders, on the other hand, must delve into battle by order of the Church, no matter who or what they come up against. I've cut my teeth battling werebeasts on many occasions in the past.

The most important thing is preparing the battlefield. Knocking a werebeast off a cliff will not be enough to defeat them. I choose a spacious battlefield when concocting our battle strategy—a place that will not allow any unexpected tricks, with ample vantage points. There is a massive, perfectly placed boulder ideal for Amelia to hide behind jutting out from the edge of the field. That said, I've already surmised that Amelia will not be harmed during this battle. Werebeasts take great pride in their strength. If you propose a one-on-one fight, they'll likely accept.

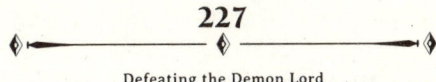

227

I carefully cast a bevy of buffs on Wurtz as he breathes deeply in the center of the cliff-side arena. Feline werebeasts are highly agile, so Wurtz won't have time to cast healing magic on himself. All his healing will come from the Regen spell I've cast.

Wurtz is level 65. Given his half-giant heritage, you could even say his own abilities are 10–15 levels higher than the average human's. Plus, those abilities are now enhanced by the buffs I've cast—equal to about a 5- or 10-level increase.

There's no standard for how much one's stats increase according to their level, so Wurtz won't literally have the power of a level 90, but even Golem Valley's high-level enemies shouldn't be a problem.

However, I've taken this into account and estimated Wurtz's opponent's abilities to be of maximum potential, putting him at a disadvantage. Giants are extremely powerful, but Wurtz is a half giant. Pitting him against a pure werebeast is to his detriment.

Wurtz opens his eyes slightly. His brown irises smolder silently, his eyes bloodshot in the thralls of the imminent battle.

Warriors do not fear death. Even if supremely outmatched, they will fight to the bitter end. As Wurtz calls my name, he shoots me a glance so steely that for a moment, I forget he's my ally.

"Ares—"

"Take him down. I know you can."

That is the only thing I can say. One's raw stats don't directly correlate to victory or defeat.

Wurtz furrows his brow, lined with wrinkles. At the very least, I can give him some advice as a parting gift.

"Keep it fair and square, and go for a one-on-one fight. Wurtz, this should be your specialty. Amelia will be watching from the edge."

"Ares, is there any point to me being here? Shouldn't I be with you?"

"There's something I need to do myself."

Wurtz's cheek twitches at the words *fair and square*. This is a fight made for a giant.

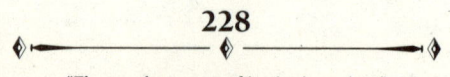

"The overdone sense of justice is a crime."

"Amelia, Wurtz—if you go against it two-on-one, it will immediately try to pick off the weaker of you two. More likely than not, Amelia would die."

And die in vain. Wurtz alone cannot fend off the highly agile werebeast and keep Amelia safe at the same time.

"Amelia, all you have to do is watch from the side. Your support won't be needed, which means you'll stay safe."

"……In other words… I should be relaying the status of the battle to you? That's it?"

"Not necessary. You should just stay put."

Our enemy will be aware of Amelia's presence just by her being there. It'll throw them off, if by a small margin. Also, for Wurtz—if he knows his loss will also cause Amelia's death, he'll give this fight every ounce he has.

Wurtz must understand my ploy—he scowls at me with force. Nonetheless, I will do anything I must to increase our chances of winning. Victory on the battlefield is decided by the smallest of margins.

"I have other business to attend to. When I'm far away enough that you can no longer see or detect me—that's your cue to begin the fight."

§ § §

Wurtz loves to fight. The stronger the opponent, the better. The second he defeats a powerful enemy is the greatest chance to verify his own prowess. The vast majority of half giants use the blessing of their bodies to make battle their livelihood. The reason Wurtz fell outside this description and converted to the priesthood is because he found a foe more powerful than himself.

By nature, Wurtz tends to believe it's easier to act than to think. Of course, he hasn't had many chances to fight since joining the Church, but this aspect of his disposition hasn't changed.

Wurtz has always believed himself to be a warrior. Ares is different;

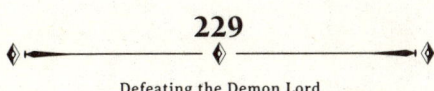

he only lives for the result. This makes Ares's sudden and flaky departure all the more troubling for Wurtz.

It's already been a number of years since Wurtz was last on the battlefield. His discipline has not waned, but his battle intuition has likely dulled. And today's foe will certainly be one that he couldn't have been sure of defeating, even in his heyday.

Ares's buffs are extremely potent. The holy techniques of a high priest easily turn one's abilities on their head. Even with that in mind, the scent left behind in that cave was menacing. There is no questioning the fearsome nature of Wurtz's foe.

He hasn't said it out loud, but Wurtz gives himself a 30 percent chance of coming out on top. That percentage could easily be reversed depending on his foe's condition, but for Ares, 30 percent is certainly a number to be concerned about. If Wurtz knows Ares as well as he thinks he does, there's no reason he should have said "fair and square" in the first place.

Wurtz's concentration lapses for a moment, but he soon refocuses. Amelia, who Ares left behind, asks him, slightly hoarse, "Wurtz... Will you be okay?"

"...Yeah."

Wurtz recalls his experience training the Holy Warrior:

"—*I refuse to take the chance of losing, no matter how slight.*"

His words to the hero were genuine. Wurtz became a priest so that he would never have to lose again—he cast aside the swordsmanship that he cultivated to acquire a new form of strength.

However, the only thing burning within Wurtz in this moment is the fire of battle lust. In the years since becoming a priest, he has made efforts to regulate his instincts, but the only thought occupying his mind now is how badly he's itching for a fight.

Per Ares's instructions, Wurtz waits for him to disappear, then looks to the heavens. There isn't a cloud in the expansive blue sky above.

This is a fine day to meet a powerful adversary. Even though his enemy is not before him yet, his entire body is replete with fulfillment.

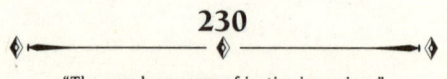

"The overdone sense of justice is a crime."

"I still have much I want to do in life, so please win this," Amelia calmly tells Wurtz.

"...Okay."

Wurtz only needs one word. Speaking any more could cause the power welling within him to dissipate, if only slightly.

Amelia nods slightly, satisfied with his assent. She moves to the boulder just near the edge of the battlefield.

Wurtz takes a deep breath and lines up Ares's provocation in his head.

Ares is no warrior. The reason being, he considers all potential options before acting. Ares is so impossibly hard for Wurtz to comprehend. Yet, there is just one thing that allows them to be friends and work so well together.

That one thing is—strength. All warriors respect strength.

Ares possesses devilish strength, and to this day, Wurtz does not understand the reason behind it—even since becoming a priest himself.

Wurtz inhales deeply and unleashes a ferocious Howl, intending to reach as far and wide as possible.

"This is your final notice! If you truly take pride in your skills as a warrior, come out and fight me fair and square! One-on-one! To the death! If you run with your tail between your legs, I won't chase after you, you gutless pussycat scum!!"

There's an immediate shift in the atmosphere. The air sizzles, and Wurtz instinctively takes a step back.

Unlike last time, there is no Howl in retort to Wurtz's provocation. However, Wurtz understands from instinct that he has been heard. He doesn't know where his adversary is, but his presence is ever more palpable, and wholly unusual.

Step on a cat's tail, and this is what you get. Wurtz adjusts his stance, preparing to face the madness coming his way.

When he casts a fleeting glimpse at the surrounding area, he sees the typically stoic Amelia withering on the spot.

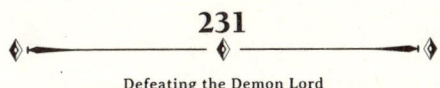

Defeating the Demon Lord

Wurtz may have said "fair and square,", but he still has absolutely no idea where his foe will come from.

—Just then, the opponent shows itself.

The soft sound of its leap sends ripples through Wurtz's ears, and in the next moment, it appears.

Despite his precautions, Wurtz's opponent appears right in front of him. Wurtz stands tall and unflinching.

A heavy scent of blood wafts on the wind.

Giants have the largest physiques among all demi-humans. The werebeast before Wurtz is a whole size smaller than him. Nonetheless, Wurtz braces himself. He now understands that Ares's assumptions were correct. This is unmistakably a top-tier warrior, even among werebeasts.

Underneath the golden fur, its perfectly sinewed muscles alone are weapons of destruction. Its paws are splayed casually on the ground, and its razor-sharp claws, each like individual blades, are dripping with dark blood. Its golden eyes are quiet, yet teeming with endless rage.

The thick bloodlust filling the air threatens to swallow everything whole. Wurtz raises his gauntlets and clashes them together. They haven't even traded blows yet, but Wurtz can tell from the overwhelming power he feels that this is hands down the first or second most powerful adversary he's ever encountered.

Wurtz silently revises his perception of their difference in battle prowess and ponders the upcoming fight. He's strong. More so than any werebeast he's ever encountered. He's been prepared for this since the moment he felt their presence in the cave, but beholding the enemy in front of him, he realizes he had no idea.

Wurtz cannot afford to take any attacks from the beast's claws. At the least, he must make sure they only make contact with his armor. Wurtz's gauntlets are created from a special metal alloy. They will be able to trade blows with such claws, but his body armor and chest piece are made from metal of a lesser grade.

Wurtz can't imagine that his armor will be able to stop the werebeast's claws. A portion of any damage received will quickly be healed

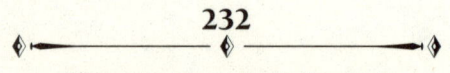

"The overdone sense of justice is a crime."

by the Regen spell Ares cast on him. Wurtz's gauntlets also provide protection from shoulder to elbow. No matter how fast his adversary, he's confident he can fight back his blows, especially now with his heightened senses.

The werebeast quickly glances toward Amelia before immediately turning its gaze back to Wurtz.

"You've finally shown yourself, werebeast—soldier of the Demon Lord's army."

Wurtz recites the line Ares practiced with him. There's an imperative to collect information here also. There's no chance of putting the werebeast into submission. When Wurtz throws out the words *demon army*, the werebeast doesn't take the bait for a second and remains emotionless. He merely growls back. Perhaps he'd just eaten, because his sharp fangs smell of blood.

"The steel tiger Felsa."

Each and every one of his nonchalant movements screams bloodlust. The only reason he hasn't attacked already is to further inflate his already bloated pride. This, Wurtz understands full well.

Yet, the beast continues before Wurtz has a chance to understand what they actually said. He sees nothing but a deep, unfathomable void in his opponent's eyes.

"That is the name of the one who will kill you."

They may belong to different races and factions—not to mention the differences between their entire life stories—but there is no denying the resemblance between Wurtz and Felsa.

Slowly and deliberately extracting information from this creature, who seems like he'll attack at any instant, will be impossible. Wurtz must assume a battle formation immediately or face being devoured. Though he may appear calm, the werebeast in question is anything but relaxed, and Wurtz knows it.

His provocation was perhaps too effective. Yet, he doesn't regret it. Wurtz licks his dry lips and replies, "I am Wurtz Beld, a giant warrior. That woman is simply a spectator. We may begin whenever you like."

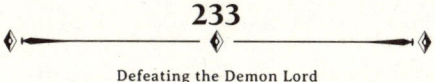

Felsa looks toward Amelia again but loses interest immediately and stares back at Wurtz. He clearly understands that no matter what happens, Amelia will not be joining this battle. That means there won't be any chance of Amelia getting attacked so long as Wurtz is in the fight. Taking hostages is a sign of weakness and a behavior unsuited to the werebeasts.

Wurtz raises both arms in the air and readies his fists. Felsa slowly splays his claws.

The battle begins.

Felsa's golden eyes flicker ominously. Wurtz and Felsa have starkly different physical constitutions.

However, there isn't a shadow of doubt in the murderous rage that lies in Felsa's eyes as he glares up at Wurtz. It also tells of a long history of battle and conquest.

Felsa's werebeast eyes threaten to eat Wurtz alive. Cold as ice, yet burning with raging fire.

Not a moment later, Felsa's claws flash out, and droplets of the blood glistening on them flit through the air.

This is clearly a preliminary strike, void of true bloodlust. Wurtz takes a step back and swings his gauntlets down. Felsa's attack is like a single sword strike, and as Wurtz brings his gauntlets down, they collide in a shower of sparks.

Paltry. But no—Wurtz quickly dashes his impression of this first attack to the wind. It's not paltry.

Werebeasts have different capabilities according to their lineage. Felsa clearly possesses superior agility, making him the antithesis of Wurtz.

Looking into those feline eyes from up close, Wurtz thinks he must be thinking the same thing. The fact that he didn't even attempt to land a blow but instead tested him is proof that he's also on his guard.

Whoever harbors the most contempt is at an advantage. Excited by this, Wurtz breaks into a Howl.

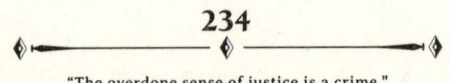

"The overdone sense of justice is a crime."

"OOOOUUUUUGGGGGGHHHHHHHHH!!"

This Howl isn't simply loud. It bears true force and tears into Felsa, who has superior auditory senses. His face warps into a grimace.

Wurtz takes that moment to approach Felsa. A giant's greatest weapon is their physical dominance. This makes them especially adept at military tactics that involve war axes, war hammers, and greatswords. Attacking with such weapons alone generally doesn't allow their opponent to get close.

Wurtz doesn't have a weapon today—aside from his arms and legs. They will be enough.

The ground shakes as Wurtz charges forward. He brings his fists down from directly above, but Felsa sidesteps to the right.

Felsa saw right through Wurtz. His movements are heavy and intense, and Felsa is simply faster. Wurtz's fist whiffs through the air. Next, his kick—which would obliterate a high-level golem—just barely misses Felsa's chin.

Wurtz is very long-limbed. Felsa's hands and feet have long, sharp claws, but even with those in his arsenal, Wurtz's limbs are still longer. Nonetheless, his repeated blows continue to miss their mark. Felsa moves silently, calmly watching Wurtz's limbs as he avoids each blow in the blink of an eye.

A combat technician. Birthright, aptitude, experience, and intent. Felsa has them all—a natural born soldier.

The earth shakes from Wurtz's attacks, but Felsa doesn't falter one iota. Wurtz quickly gives up on attacking further.

He can't land a single blow on him. Doing so would result in reasonable damage, but unless luck is on his side today, there's no chance of that happening. Felsa doesn't even need to block—he simply evades everything. And with ample breathing room, at that.

From his gaze, Wurtz surmises that Felsa might think he's slow-witted. But that is a mistake. Wurtz is anything but dim. This is a giant's fighting style.

Wurtz is prepared to take blows. Felsa has superior speed and

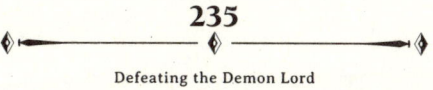

perception, but Wurtz is winning in terms of regenerative power—largely boosted by Ares's Regen spells—and his pure physical dominance. Not to mention the sheer toughness that runs in his giant blood.

If Wurtz can put Felsa's body or limbs into submission, he can win. Any other method is going to prove highly difficult.

Wurtz's body rages, a fire consuming him. Ares's buffs have given him a seemingly inexhaustible supply of energy.

Felsa leaps high in the air and flips over, bearing his fangs and staring into Wurtz's eyes.

Felsa's grim expression is highlighted by his bloodred tongue, just visible at the back of his throat through his slightly open mouth.

"I see now—you're strong."

Felsa spits out the words, but they aren't laced with vitriol. It sounds more like a statement.

His legs are enveloped in sinewy, taut muscle, and his claws pound the earth flat as he tramples it. The glint in his eye pierces through Wurtz as he speaks again—a simple expression, yet full of strength.

"But make no mistake—I am vastly more powerful!"

Felsa's body shimmers like a blast of hot air over flame and disappears from Wurtz's field of vision. He brings his gauntlets down reflexively and they bash against Felsa's claw sideswipe. The sharp sound of metal resonates and his arms shudder from the vibration.

Wurtz's arms, armored in a special metal alloy, also function as a massive shield. Felsa's strike was lightning quick, but his physical structure isn't anything more impressive than a human's. Wurtz was able to predict his attack.

"—Hng!!"

Wurtz grits his teeth and blocks attack after attack—from above, below, the side. Each claw swipe is as sharp as a strike from a blade. His gauntlets don't let them through, but each attack resonates sharply through his arms.

Felsa's claws are sharper than imaginable, coming at Wurtz like a storm of razor blades. The golden-furred beast becomes a flash of golden wind.

"The overdone sense of justice is a crime."

There are very few gaps in Felsa's consecutive blows, almost like a dance. Attempting an attack would leave Wurtz open to being slashed immediately. However, every sequence of strikes will eventually come to an end. During a pause in the din of attacks, Wurtz can hear Felsa's breath.

What agony. Wurtz is still stifling the bloodlust he just experienced in each of Felsa's attacks, breathing raggedly. Yet, during their battle, his sense of awareness is being sharpened like a sword. The sounds of battle, his own breath, and surges of golden fur become Wurtz's entire world.

Suddenly, Felsa pauses. The next instant, Wurtz's half-ton body is levitating slightly. A numbing impact belatedly rushes up his arms, and by the time he realizes it, a blade is flickering toward him.

Wurtz brings his right arm crashing down on the piercing attack that slips through his arms and gauntlets. He throws it off its axis, but the tip of one of Felsa's claws grazes his chin. A sharp pain rushes through him, and he takes a step back to realign his stance.

"Tch—!!"

Felsa rushes in, and Wurtz's field of vision is filled with the talons on Felsa's feet closing in.

It's not just his arms that are strong, though. Werebeasts are part human and part beast, and just like their human counterparts, their legs possess far more strength than their arms do.

Wurtz's solid guard is broken, but his chin is soon healed from the Regen buff. Felsa's eyes grow wide, but his movements are undeterred.

This is a poor choice for a battlefield. Nothing to hide behind, and so spacious. There's nothing Wurtz can put to use. This will be a fight determined by true potential. And a fight determined by true potential leaves Wurtz at a disadvantage.

Should he buckle down for the long haul? Or wait for an opening? As he ponders, Felsa again disappears from view. Then, Wurtz feels a shock flash through the back of his head, and he immediately spins around before smashing his fists down onto the ground.

This chance maneuver of Wurtz's manages to deflect Felsa's attack

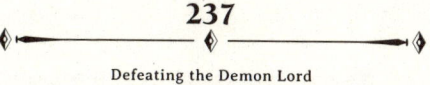

from behind, and Wurtz notices Felsa click his tongue in exasperation. Wurtz didn't see the attack coming; the only reason he was able to spin around and block the attack was due to his experience.

Their give-and-take begins again. However, Wurtz's mind-set has now shifted.

He knows the battle won't last long on its current course. Felsa moves like the wind. To a spectator, their movements might not look that different, but taking him head-on, Wurtz understands full well: His attacks are slowly, yet steadily, ramping up in speed.

Clearly, Felsa's not a slow starter, but he definitely hasn't reached top speed yet.

This is a clear indication of the werebeast's superior muscular structure. It isn't any manner of technique or skill—he's just fast, pure and simple.

Wurtz is a terrible match for Felsa, yet the corners of his mouth turn up into a grin. He understands why Ares asked him to battle Felsa. Now, he gets it. Although Ares is high level, as a more vulnerable member of the human race, and a priest, his aptitude for fighting Felsa is the absolute worst. It wasn't even an option for Ares. That's why he asked Wurtz.

He's still at a disadvantage, but Wurtz can now feel the blood surging within him, giving him newfound strength.

His arms and legs are becoming fatigued and his breath is ragged, but his spirit is alive. He brings his foot down heavily and crushes the ground, sending gravel flying in all directions. Felsa is forced to retreat a number of steps to avoid the barrage of stone fragments.

In that instant, Wurtz channels his entire being into a ferocious, red-hot Howl.

"OOOOOOOOOOOUUUUUUUUUGGGGGGGGGHHHHHHH HHHHHH!!"

Wurtz will be victorious. He is not so deeply indebted to Ares that he owes him his life.

Yet, he will defeat Felsa, for that is his command. Even if he exerts every ounce of strength in his body and falls into disrepair. That is the pride of a warrior.

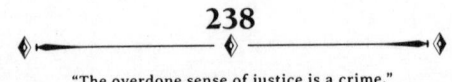

"The overdone sense of justice is a crime."

The entire world—the sky, the earth, the air—shudders from Wurtz's Howl. Felsa smiles fiendishly in response.

Then, Wurtz begins to attack, putting all his force into the first blow without pondering the second. He crushes a boulder underfoot and raises his right arm high in the air, swinging it down on Felsa. He puts the entire force of his gigantic body weight, of all its gravity, into his single right fist.

An explosion rips through the air from his fist alone. Even if it misses the target, a mere graze would flatten and pulverize anything in its way. And then—

—Felsa does not evade the blow but receives Wurtz's swooping, armored fist.

He hasn't pulverized flesh. Wurtz can feel a groaning sensation underneath his right hand.

For a moment, Wurtz is completely at sea. How has this transpired? Felsa blocked his blow, his mighty fist, with his own two hands.

The sound of Felsa's claws scraping against his gauntlet falls dead on Wurtz's ears. One fist was not enough—both of Felsa's palms continue to groan underneath it. Felsa's footing crumbles and his fur is matted, but he has clearly not suffered bodily harm.

Wurtz's confusion dissipates, and he continues to put all his force into his right fist, which Felsa has blocked. But it won't budge.

Wurtz's face turns a deep scarlet as he continues to push down on his opponent.

"You feckless grunt, did you possibly think you were more powerful than I?" Felsa growls in a muffled tone.

Wurtz's, and in turn Felsa's, arms both continue to creak and groan.

From the tone of his voice and the sound emanating from his arm, Wurtz knows that Felsa is overworking himself. His words were lies—he doesn't have that much left to give. Nonetheless, he blocked Wurtz's blow. He chose, deliberately, to block it, to show Wurtz that he

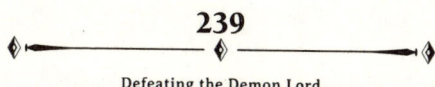

can, even though he clearly had the option to evade it. This is exemplary of a werebeast's warrior pride.

This is a matter of neither prowess nor technique—Wurtz feels the intended threat. Recklessly cutting someone down is simple, but a sure sign of a hero's mentality.

Wurtz inhales deeply and musters all his strength. Felsa grits his teeth in opposition.

At the start of this battle, they were struggling for supremacy. But Wurtz's attacks have been losing momentum ever since his first blow. He raises his arms slowly, gradually. Felsa could easily evade him by taking a few steps back, but he shows no sign of any intention to sidestep.

Felsa speaks to Wurtz, his voice rough. He's not angry. He's simply expressing his battle lust.

"I will pulverize you. One-on-one, face-to-face, I will annihilate you."

Wurtz once more feels his own will to fight surging through him, red-hot.

One single blow. Why would Wurtz give up the fight after having one single blow deflected? He's the one who wished for a formidable opponent to do battle with. That one attack, which he poured his entire being into, was blocked. What's more, his chances of prevailing may be thin, but what does that matter?

Although he's already summoned all his strength, Wurtz manages to thrust more power into his right fist. The golden werebeast licks his lips.

Wurtz can fight. He still has it in him. He's utterly exhausted, but his body can still move and will continue to do so until it falls apart entirely.

The moment Wurtz furthers his resolve, the sound of something colliding pierces his auditory senses.

Directly in front of him, Felsa stares up at Wurtz, his eyes bulging wide.

What was that sound…?

Wurtz furrows his brow, and in that instant, the force underneath his right arm vanishes. Without anything to support it, his arm plummets downward and smashes the boulder below.

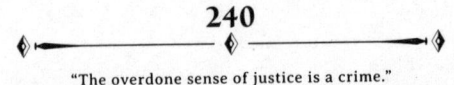

"The overdone sense of justice is a crime."

As the cloud of dust subsides, Wurtz can see Felsa falling back, a look of astonishment on his face.

"…What?"

Felsa's ferocious growl has been reduced to a subdued whimper. Several black objects stick out from various places amid his velvety fur—in his ankles, shoulder, and elbow joint. Finally, he spots a single knife on the ground and realizes what the objects are.

Knife handles. The blades piercing his body slide cleanly out— although he hasn't touched them—and fly through the still air, along with the knife on the ground. Black blood oozes from the wounds and stains his golden fur.

Wurtz is floored. He traces the path of the knives into the sky. Just in front of Amelia, staring at Felsa with extreme perturbation, stands a shadow that had concealed all traces of its presence—a veritable god of death.

Ares spins a knife that's returned to his hand and addresses Wurtz, his voice utterly devoid of warmth.

"Well done, Wurtz. You put up a better fight than I anticipated. I'll handle the rest, so…you take a breather."

Felsa grabs his ankle, his eyes boring into Ares with inexorable hatred. His ragged breath shows evident signs of anguish. But that's not the reason he's rendered completely speechless.

Ares gets within ten meters of Felsa and draws his mace, shrugging his shoulders.

Like Wurtz, Amelia must be similarly floored by this unexpected turn of events, as she stares at Ares, wide-eyed.

"Gregorio's technique was pretty good… These knives would've missed had I not thrown them directly, but being able to retrieve them like this is incredible. These are invaluable blades."

Amid everyone's confusion, Ares continues on as if he's making small talk.

He says his next words coldly and without feeling. He retrieves a shady mask the color of black ink from his chest pocket and puts it over his face.

241

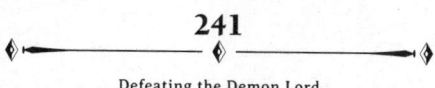

"It's a pleasure to meet you, Felsa. My name is Ares Crown. I am your worst enemy—the one person you have been so desperately searching for...the Holy Warrior."

All that remains visible behind the mask are Ares's eyes and mouth, making his expression impossible to read.

§ § §

The werebeast that calls itself Felsa turns to me with a demonic gaze that he did not show to Wurtz.

Werebeasts are a powerful species, but in general, they're below followers of darkness in terms of the danger they pose. This is the reason why: There may be differences between individual races, but their weak points are exceptionally vulnerable.

In my hand, I twirl my knife, which I've covered in scraps of the demon skin Gregorio sent me.

There's nothing more terrifying than a wounded beast. Keeping Felsa's agility in mind, I stop ten meters—or one pause length—in front of him. Both ankles, his shoulder, and his arm. All vital points. Although not mortal wounds, for Felsa, whose primary weapon is his agility, this definitely puts him at a major disadvantage.

Wurtz remains stupefied as he opens his mouth to speak.

"Ares—"

"Yeah, I know what you want to say. I'll listen later, so just be quiet for now."

I've done something terrible. Using Wurtz and Amelia as a decoy is an affront to humanity itself—however, if I'd been honest with him, Wurtz would have rejected the idea completely. That said, even if he didn't reject it, he would have known that I was lying from my behavior.

I am not a righteous man. I only live for results. If Wurtz and Amelia place all their pride on winning a fair-and-square battle from a place of decency, then it is my job to do whatever it takes to win.

"Felsa. You are a tremendous warrior. I estimate the appropriate

level to take you down to be…seventy-five. Of course, that's in terms of an entire party against you."

A mage and a priest, plus a healthy vanguard and plenty of long-range physical damage weapons—a party of six that isn't too particular about how they win could finish him in five minutes.

Conversely, taking down Felsa one-on-one would be a massive challenge even at level 90. Felsa's prominence would be too much for one single warrior to handle.

Given how Wurtz was losing hand-to-hand despite mustering every last bit of his strength, the Demon Lord was quite prudent in dispatching Felsa. Not that he should even have a warrior of this level to send to a place like this… If Toudou and his party had come across Felsa, they wouldn't have lasted a minute.

"Holy…Warrior… Impossible— Why here—? Wait— Level seventy-five, you say?!"

Holy Warrior. The fact that Felsa repeated the words greatly increases the chances that he's connected with the Demon Lord.

Felsa gets to his feet, but his center of gravity is amiss. I've aimed for his tendons. He won't be able to stand properly.

"This is called a party play. Learned something today, didn't you? Taking you on by myself would require too much effort."

As I speak, I launch one of the knives with all the force I can summon, aiming for Felsa's eye.

It races like a bullet toward his face, but he breezily strikes it down with his claws. Werebeasts are highly resistant to physical damage. Ideally, you'd need a mage to properly take them on.

His body is covered in golden fur, alongside razor-sharp claws and fangs. His long tail points straight to the heavens as if the very embodiment of his rage.

Felsa stumbles toward me. I stare into his eyes, which are rife with violent derision, and speak again.

"You're a steel tiger. Golden fur stronger than any armor, claws sharper than any sword. Born with a steel muscular system and the most

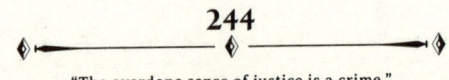

advanced race of all werebeasts—a mighty warrior with the strength of a thousand men."

"Tch... And you're—"

Felsa's brow perks up, and he bares his fangs, threatening me. This behavior confirms my suspicions. From the moment I knew we were going up against a werebeast, I made a guess as to what type it was. Steel tigers are the strongest of all. I've fought against two of his ilk in the past, but neither of them were quite the individual he is.

A mighty warrior of Felsa's repute can't be taken down by even a sizable troop of ordinary soldiers. Had he shown up in a more frenetic battle, he'd likely amass a mountain of corpses in his wake.

"Very lucky."

"...?!"

I lift my mace and point its spiked ball at Felsa in provocation.

"I am so very lucky to be able to exterminate you here today. Being the hero comes with baggage. I have to fight each and every hideous creature I come across, no matter how ghastly, and protect my party at the same time."

"Rrgh... You bastard—I'll kill you!!"

Felsa's voice is rife with resentment and malice. He seems to have steadied his faltering balance. He's mustering his final ounce of strength—these blazing, fierce eyes are not the sign of a beast that's been critically wounded.

I can't imagine he'll last much longer, but he can likely still exhibit the same speed he showed earlier.

I switch up my game plan. He'll only last a few minutes, if that. Even if he can move forward, I doubt he'll be able to do anything precise. I'll likely come out ahead in this game of tag, but...there's just one thing that concerns me. I've got the general idea, but—

"Ares. This is my—"

Wurtz puts a damper on my werebeast duel as he opens his mouth again. I ignore him and focus on Felsa, who's watching me like a hawk and focused on ripping into my jugular.

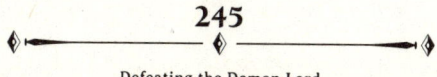

"Hey—what happened to your friend?"

"…Huh?"

Felsa stops dead in his tracks at my query, and his eyes go wide.

I pay close attention to him while I look up at the sky. There's nary a cloud or shadow within it.

"Your friend. I was keeping watch on him. He's around, right? You know the guy—highly capable, able to fly. He's just a little bit smarter than you."

"…"

The color suddenly drains from Felsa's eyes, and his ears twitch restlessly. I continue to address him as if in admonishment.

"I was honestly paying more attention to him than I was to you. Besides, it'd be quite difficult for you or I to attack him, given our lack of wings. If he's set on fleeing, chasing after him would prove difficult. The more I think about it, the more I realize the guy's a pain in the ass. I was late to your battle here because I got so wrapped up in tagging him. Taking both of you on by myself would be a challenge, after all."

I'm lying. It's true that I was tracking his companion, but only because I figured that in most cases, provocation would lead to catching just one of the two.

The reason being, if the smart one of this pair were still alive, he would have tried to stop Felsa from doing anything reckless. In other words, the steel tiger in front of me is now sorely companionless.

I've been camped out far below these cliffs, concealing my presence and watching things play out. I left Amelia here to create one point of intrigue in an otherwise blank battlefield. That alone turns the tables in terms of who's keeping on guard.

I had decided either to take out the enemy while he had yet to notice Amelia, or to let him inevitably become careless from keeping an eye on her. I went with the former and launched a surprise attack.

Felsa mumbles, looking around restlessly before screaming, "Sa… po… Yes, that's right! SAPO! COME HERE!"

"Hmm? You think he's alive…?" I ask, playing dumb.

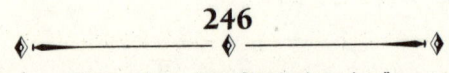

"The overdone sense of justice is a crime."

If he's still alive, then whose blood do I smell, wafting from your mouth and claws? Felsa doesn't seem to have a firm grasp on things, so I help him.

"Just as I expected, you came here after you devoured your companion."

"...Ah... Mmm... Wha...?"

Felsa utters a noise of utter bewilderment, like he can't believe what he's hearing. I walk toward Felsa, fully caught in a trance, and raise my voice so that he can hear me.

"Hey, it's a tale as old as time. You forget yourself, and you give in to base instincts. This tends to happen to your kind, right? It's certainly not unheard of for someone like you to eat one or two of your allies. There's no reason for you to get down on yourself! If anything, I ought to thank you for lightening my load of annoying enemies."

I knew it was possible. Not exactly probable, but certainly within the realm of feasibility. Every possible outcome ran through the back of my mind. The situation we're currently facing is the most advantageous one I came up with.

At any rate, you could just say that Felsa had a falling out with a werebeast who had the rare capability of flight, and he settled the score. That his movements are now dulled from the shock is icing on the cake.

"Ares... You heretic," mumbles Amelia, looking repulsed.

Look, if being a heretic means saving the world, then sign me up.

"Preposterous... You think I would...eat...Sapo?"

"Was he tasty?"

"SILENCE!!"

Felsa staggers and leaps toward me instinctively, but he's lost considerable speed.

I wind up with my mace and clock the werebeast in midair with one swing. I feel a dull sensation through my mace as if knocking into something metal.

I only claimed to be the Holy Warrior for good measure. I have no intention of letting Felsa live to tell the tale.

Felsa bounces on the ground like a rubber ball before landing

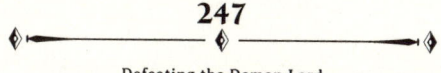

247

facedown. I rush toward him and lift my mace high over my head, aiming for his skull. In that moment, Felsa covers his head with his hands—surely a survival instinct. This beast is terrifying as long as he can still move. However, werebeasts have terrible regeneration capacity. There's no way he'll heal during the span of our battle.

"Did you eat him or not? You should be able to feel it in your gut, no?"

I continue to rile him up as I bring the mace down on his now wholly immobile body.

I would finish him off more easily if I had lethal poison handy. If I had paralysis poison or a means to restrain him, I might've even been able to capture him myself.

But I don't. Not enough personnel on hand. Just when I might've had the chance, my only option now is to kill him.

Felsa's golden fur scrapes along the ground and becomes dingy, dark. However, his eyes are well and truly alive. He's definitely still in shock from learning that he ate his companion. Yet, I can tell he has some fight left in him.

Felsa raises his arms to attack, but I swing my mace directly on top of him, blasting through the arms he lifted to block me and smashing directly into his skull.

"Urgh—"

"Did you actually think I would be weaker than Wurtz?"

I can think of some reasons why—my posture, my weapon, my level. But even now, he's still mocking me.

"I abandoned my battle plan…because I knew it was the optimal solution."

He's still rock hard. It goes to show just how much of a threat his defenses are, even without wearing armor.

I don't give him a chance to stand up, approaching again to bash him back into the boulder with my mace. I'll scramble his brain and pulverize his muscles.

Yet, Felsa continues to match me. He's still highly vigilant—I'm looking for an opening and keep throwing knives, but he's still blocking it

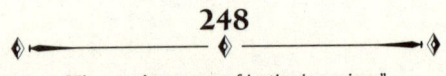

"The overdone sense of justice is a crime."

all without fail. His endurance is frightening. You could scarcely believe that he hasn't used a buff or Regen.

Goddammit—I can't believe I'm facing adversaries of this level when we're still within the Kingdom of Ruxe's borders!

He must have some brain damage by now—a line of blood-mottled drool hangs loosely from Felsa's mouth. I can't fathom how he's still conscious, how he still has the will to fight, or why he hasn't begged for his life.

"But I'm glad you're here! Without producing results, we would have never made it to the next stage."

He's alive. What a truly remarkable will to live. But he's getting weak—he won't last another ten minutes. I must put him down. If he somehow escapes, that could become a huge problem. The simple thought of being hunted by a werebeast of this rank turns my stomach.

As Felsa tries to stand up yet again, I bring my mace down on him once more. In that instant, a powerful gust of wind blows between the two of us. I unconsciously take a step back.

"?!"

Looking up at the sky, I realize the gravity of my mistake. It wasn't the wind—there's a massive bird soaring through the sky, roughly the same size as me and gray in color. A golden pendant dangles from its neck.

Lying on the rock-hard earth, Felsa turns a muddled eye to the sky and just barely squints.

Amelia calls out to me. "Oh no… Ares, look!"

"…Shit, you're right. It wasn't the two of them—there were three…"

A different breed of demon…? No, it must be something of strong werebeast origin. With its giant wings, it hardly resembles a human, but a closer look reveals that its body is indeed humanlike. Furthermore, it seems to have some form of intelligence from the way it eyeballs me from the sky.

It's either a messenger or supply troop. I thought Felsa's companion might have been performing both functions, but it looks like there was a third party involved.

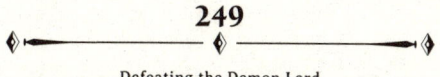

249

I had considered the possibility, but no one would have thought that two flight-capable troops might be deployed to the same place. The bird creature observes Felsa and I for a while before retreating. It flies away smoothly, flowing through the sky like water. I might be able to catch it if I jump high enough.

Is it trying to escape or inviting me to give chase? At that size, it could lift Felsa and fly away without issue. Did it refrain from trying because it knew that doing so would hinder its speed and altitude? If it made that decision independently, it's definitely smarter than Felsa.

...No matter. I may not have expected it to show up at this juncture, but the battle has been won.

Wurtz remains largely undamaged. He could easily take down the injured Felsa now.

I lower my arms and tap Wurtz on the shoulder. He's stiff as a board.

"Wurtz, I'll chase after that thing. If you can finish this now, then by all means."

Word of Felsa's death will eventually make its way to the Demon Lord. However, reducing our number of flight-capable adversaries will also pay dividends. Even small victories like this lead to substantial results.

"You and Amelia work together to wring the final breaths from Felsa's throat."

"Hmph..."

Wurtz grunts softly but not in agreement. I can see he's vacillating and that he's displeased with me. Yet, I've conceded enough. Truthfully, I'd like them to pick Felsa apart for his fur and bones, which make excellent defensive implements, but I haven't asked them to—largely because I can sense how Wurtz would feel dishonoring a worthy opponent.

Wurtz still looks dumbstruck, and I tell him, "This is business. If you let him go, there's no telling how many people will die as a result. Don't you dare forget—we'll never be able to take full responsibility if that happens."

So pour your entire heart into it. No matter what the outcome, at least take some pride in your actions.

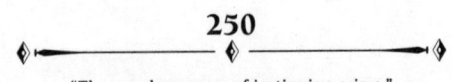

"The overdone sense of justice is a crime."

Wurtz remains rooted to the spot and doesn't move a muscle. Amelia steps out from his shadow.

"Ares, I'll take care of it."

"All right. It's on you."

I would be worried leaving Wurtz alone with Felsa, but having Amelia there, I know she'll stir up the gumption in him.

I look away from Amelia and head toward the bird creature in the distance, running as fast as I can.

§ § §

"Sa...po..."

His world is on end, the ground spinning in every direction.

Pain shoots throughout his body. Likely due to the deep wounds in his ankles, he can't stand no matter how hard he tries. Felsa has never experienced this before, but even worse than the pain, that man's words are digging deep into him.

He ate him. He ate Sapo, according to that man.

Felsa is a steel tiger. Sapo may be of a different race, but they serve the same lord.

And that man claims Felsa ate him. Yes—the man who claims to be the Holy Warrior.

Felsa mumbles to himself and looks up at the sky.

Sapo was weak. Far weaker than Felsa. Even so, he had powerful wings that allowed him to traverse the skies, and his cunning intellect in devising strategy was something Felsa respected. Above all else, he understood Felsa. Their lineage was different, but they were companions.

He looks to his bloodied claws. It's not his blood. It's not Wurtz's blood. He wants to deny it, but he cannot.

He has no recollection of the act. Before he knew it, he was face-to-face with his opponent. The last thing he remembers is hearing the provocation—the Howl—and the blood rushing to his head, consuming his entire being. That is all.

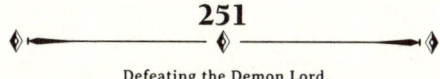

Defeating the Demon Lord

His belly is full, his body replete, and the smell of blood lingering on his claws and fangs indicates the validity of that man's claim.

I see… So I did devour my companion. The words finally enter his head. They were thrown at him in the heat of battle, and he refused to ingest their meaning. Now, he silently marvels and understands it.

He puts both hands on the ground and gets up slowly. The pain is unbearable. The fatigue. The inexorable pain threatening to rip his body asunder is a welcome friend. Felsa did not become a warrior simply by being born of a superior race—he did it through trial and tribulation.

Felsa wipes blood from his eye with his paw. He is enraged, filled with hopeless resentment. But he refuses to vocalize it. It's a waste of strength to speak.

He knows what he must do, what he must accomplish above all else. After devouring his own companion, he will not simply lie down and perish—doing so would bring him utmost shame as a steel tiger.

Felsa stands up wearily, and pain shoots through his ankles. He's been injured in vital points, but if he can withstand the pain, he can move for at least a limited period of time.

And if he can move, his battle-ready claws can tear anything in his wake to ribbons.

His life essence still burns brightly. Felsa knows this full well: He is stronger than ever when his life is at risk.

The woman notices his movements and furrows her brow. She calls on Wurtz, who reacts accordingly and looks down at Felsa.

The Holy Warrior is not here, but he is guaranteed to come back. Wurtz purses his lips and raises his fist.

The woman takes a few steps back. No matter—after he kills Wurtz, he'll eat her, too.

Felsa stands steadily on his haunches and stares at his enemy with pure malice. Perhaps it's the endorphins coursing through his brain or his sense of resignation, but the pain assailing his entire body has completely dissipated.

Felsa stomps on the ground using every last ounce of strength

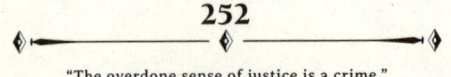

"The overdone sense of justice is a crime."

he has left. He has to kill the Holy Warrior, Wurtz, and that spectator woman—or he'll never be able to face Sapo in the realm of the dead.

§ § §

"It's over, then..."

"Welcome back. Did you catch up to it?"

"No, it was no use."

The creature's daunting speed and precise movements proved they're also an accomplished warrior. Hopefully, losing track of them this time won't have any ramifications in the future...

The battlefield is in worse shape than when I left. Felsa must have put up quite the fight at the end.

The ground is shattered and riddled with scratch marks everywhere. Wurtz groans in agony. His priest's robe is shredded, and a deep gash runs along the right side of his abdomen. I cast Heal on it as I gaze down at Felsa lying on the ground.

He looks like he's sleeping, but there's no doubt—the werebeast is no longer breathing.

Even the devil himself would be unlikely to take it this far, biting and thrashing at their opponent, truly murderous intent seeping from their bones until their last breath. Felsa's golden fur is spotted with blood, and his limbs are splayed out in every direction from overexerting himself.

Resisting his adversary to this degree, despite being at death's door, proves how truly fearsome a warrior Felsa was.

I so desperately want to skin him...but I guess I'll have to resist. Wurtz is staring at Felsa's corpse, facedown on the rock-hard earth.

"Let's head back. It won't be long before the golems return in droves," I say to him.

I have to consult with the Church about how to proceed next. I'm confident we unearthed the source of the unusual phenomena plaguing Golem Valley, but there's still a chance the Demon Lord will dispatch a new breed of horror soon. It's a slim chance, but still...

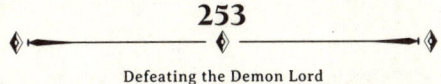

Defeating the Demon Lord

Just before I go to climb down the cliff face, I turn to Wurtz, who's still kneeling.

"Wurtz, finish this up quickly."

"...? Finish...what?"

Wurtz lifts his head with a sluggish motion. He looks awful... I bet he'll get a scolding from the madam for this.

"A service for the dead. There are no allies among the fallen, right?"

"The overdone sense of justice is a crime."

Epilogue

And Thus, the Priest Demands the Very Best

"Incredible work, Ares. The information you've gathered will be closely examined and passed on to the Kingdom."

As always, Creio responds to my report with meaningless thanks.

In all honesty, the battle with Felsa was extremely arduous. I didn't have enough supplies, let alone personnel, for that matter. Above all else, I still can't believe that such a horrifying creature showed up in Golem Valley. It's uncommon for someone of my level to face such a close battle. The Demon Lord's army is advancing at a far more inconspicuous pace than the Church previously thought. I didn't have a chance to ask questions, but let's say for instance that the Holy Warrior did destroy the mother golems, then we will have to be more vigilant about who he goes up against.

"I'm short-staffed. Send me more personnel."

"I'll see what I can do."

I made my demand crystal clear, but Creio's tone doesn't indicate any sincerity. I need a firm commitment. A priest with the God of Order does not tell lies, but I also cannot trust claims that are open to interpretation.

Creio must realize I'm ready to retort, as he adds incredulously, "But Ares, you take the easy route, do you not?"

"Hey, I'm a priest!! In what world could you find a priest who can single-handedly take down a steel tiger?!"

"No, you're not a priest. You're a crusader. And you came out on top, didn't you?"

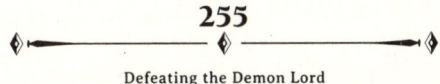

He's right on both counts. In terms of supplies and commands, I have been treated relatively well. But I'm not omnipotent, dammit!

Creio continues, obviously trying to placate me.

"Ares. You are a top-class crusader. You have defeated more followers of darkness than anyone before you. This is why you receive the most difficult assignments. Resources are limited, but you still bring the greatest results through the least expenditure. We're able to divvy up surplus resources among other crusaders, and as a result, we can keep other factions of the Church quiet."

"I told you we won by the skin of our teeth, didn't I?"

"Ares, I have full confidence that you, Ex Deus, will overcome this hardship as well."

Creio's tone is perfectly serene, and I give up on trying to persuade him any further. In these instances, he's truly hardheaded.

Thankfully, I have another option available. I'll use Stey to put the pressure on Cardinal Sylvester.

"...For the time being, the threat is behind us. We'll continue to remain vigilant and level up here in Golem Valley."

"Understood. If something goes awry, inform me immediately."

The transmission cuts out, and I sigh deeply.

I have enough priests on hand. Next, I want someone with scout capabilities in the fold.

Amelia has been quietly waiting in a corner of the room during my communications with Creio, and she now starts to approach me, saying, "Well, at least things have calmed down a bit, haven't they? Besides, it will take the Demon Lord some time to plan his next move."

"Good point... Let's withdraw Stey and devote ourselves to raising the party's level."

I'm concerned about the werebeast that got away, but all I can do is keep an eye on things. Just then, the door flies open, and a familiar cheery voice fills the room.

"I'm baaack! Oh, Ares, you're here, too!"

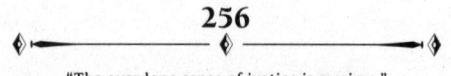

"The overdone sense of justice is a crime."

"Oh, so you're back. I assume you don't have much—"

—*to report*, I start to say. But the moment I turn to face Stey, I lose my train of thought. She hops toward me with a spring in her step and makes a peace sign with her right hand.

"I finished all my work!"

"......What happened to you?"

Stey is covered in soot, black from head to toe. Her nose is darker than anywhere else. Something has obviously happened. Amelia puts her hand to her forehead and asks, "...What in the world did you—?"

"? Um, nothing in particular?"

Quit lying and bring Cacao out!

"...Stey. Tell me everything, starting from the beginning."

"? I finished all my work, that's all."

I've already heard that many times. Logically speaking, there's no damn way you came out looking like that from nothing!

That said, I doubt she has the self-awareness to realize she's fibbing. What should I ask her to get the truth?

"In other words...today was completely uneventful? Toudou raised his level without any problems?"

"...No, he didn't gain any levels. He couldn't take down any golems today."

Stey looks at the floor as she answers. *Okay, this is a dead giveaway—you know that, right?*

I grow weary as I stare at her. She quickly becomes flustered and blurts out in a high-pitched tone, "B-but, I did exactly as you told me! I put a bind on the bird werebeast thing, just like you said—"

"Whaaaaa?!"

This is futile... There's absolutely no way I can get through to her. Stey is obviously flustered, and as I stare at her, my stomach aches for the first time in a long while.

Just like that, we find ourselves departing Golem Valley.

"Thank you for everything, Madam."

"Heh-heh-heh, don't you worry about it one bit. Supporting the next generation is my duty."

I'm back at ever-so-nostalgic First Town church. The madam replies to me calmly, but her words are weighty. Just one of the reasons why she is so deeply respected here.

"Please keep an eye on Wurtz for me."

"Fear not. He's very sensitive... I'm sure there will come a day where you see eye to eye."

In the end, I was unable to reconcile with Wurtz. Of course, I knew that a genuine warrior like him would never accept my plan. I knew he would harbor ill feelings toward me, but it's not like I hadn't considered that beforehand.

I could try reasoning with him, but there's no point in me trying to force him to feel differently.

The madam's reassurance is a true saving grace for me. The clergy of Ahz Gried do not tell lies—if someone as cunning as her truly believes this, then she's right—Wurtz and I will come to an agreement, someday.

I say my good-byes and leave the church. Amelia and Stey sensed what was going on and waited outside for me.

Looking at my face, Stey seems disheartened as she asks me softly, "Am I...f-fired?"

"No, Stey, I'm not firing you. I still...have work for you. I will forge you in the fire and temper you in the flame."

"Y-yes, sir! I'll d-do my best!"

"Ares, are you sure about that? You can fire her anytime, you know."

Amelia's barb cuts as deep as always. Stey grabs her by the sleeve and yanks on it.

"Wh-whyyy would you say such a thiiing?!"

Stephenne Veronide's greatest flaw is in the disparity between her thought process and that of those around her. She has tons of other flaws, like tripping and falling all the time, or quickly losing concentration, but it all comes back to that fact. She has no idea what I'm thinking.

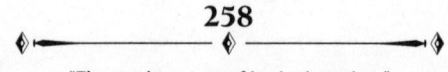

"The overdone sense of justice is a crime."

For instance, discovering a werebeast while out with Toudou is well within the realm of what I asked her to report—yet, she failed to include it. Further, she never mentioned to me that she knows the reason why Limis can't contract with the other seven elemental spirits. Stephenne has absolutely no sense of what is truly important—she's only capable of doing exactly as she's told.

Stey is a moron, but her blunders are entirely due to my inability to properly educate her.

"Is there anything else you didn't include in your report?"

"N-no, nothing else. I'm sure!" she answers without hesitation. Her credibility remains low, but all I can do is plug away at educating her.

I pack my belongings into the runner lizard. Our next destination is the city of Cloudburst—outside the Kingdom of Ruxe. It will be a long journey.

Unfortunately, I've never been there, but it's a famous city. I can more or less tolerate our reasons for going there. Cloudburst—the water capital—is only a third-rate location for leveling up. No matter how vigilant the Demon Lord is, the chances are slim that his reach extends that far already. This should prove to be a good chance to throw him off our scent.

It's a shame that we couldn't get Toudou's level quite as high as we wanted in Golem Valley. Just as I get lost in thought packing my things, I hear a voice I hadn't been expecting.

"Lady Stephenne, at last we meet again."

"…Huh? Wh-what are you doing here?"

The two people who were with Stey when I first took her under our wing approach us with hardened expressions. It's a man and a woman, the two chamberlains who have looked after Stey since she was a child… Barnard and Vilma.

It's been over a month since they saw her last, when Stey joined us in Purif. Vilma ignores Stey's confusion and takes a step toward me. Barnard looks at me silently, lugging a massive trunk with him.

"What's this about?"

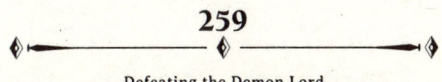

"We are indebted for your services."

Damn straight. I can't blame you for pushing her onto me, but leave an instruction manual or something, would ya?

Vilma bows cordially before continuing.

"We sincerely apologize for all the trouble that Stephenne has caused you. Ares, sir, I'm sure you knew beforehand—"

"Skip the introductions. I'm a busy man. Nor do I need your apologies. State your business."

"Understood... To put it frankly, we have come here on Cardinal Sylvester's orders to take Lady Stephenne back with us."

That's what I figured. Two chamberlains who have been largely set aside until now wouldn't have any other business.

"...What?!"

Stey cries out hysterically, her eyes wide as saucers. Vilma doesn't flinch and keeps her eyes on me.

"We are truly grateful for everything you've done. This was surely a valuable experience for Lady Stephenne as well."

God, what a load of bullshit. Spare me. I couldn't get rid of her when I wanted to, but now you've come to claim her? Her and Cacao?! Now you're just screwing with me.

"You're here to take her back, *now*? I refuse. Apologies, but we have plans in motion."

Like hell I'm giving Cacao up.

Astonished and even more wide-eyed than before, Stey quickly hides behind me, pressing her head into my back as she says, "A-Ares... I knew I could trust in you... I love you..."

"...May we ask your intentions?"

Vilma furrows her brow and gazes up at me. I doubt she was expecting this. It's unlikely that anyone has ever said they don't want to give Stey back. But even I can polish a turd. Stey is most certainly a steaming pile of garbage, but with Cacao, and her status as a cardinal's daughter, she definitely retains two undeniable merits.

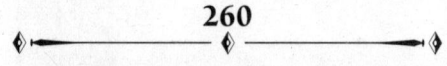

"The overdone sense of justice is a crime."

"I have no intentions. I will make good use of Sylvester's daughter. Tell him to let her go."

"...Ares, you are truly reckless," mutters Amelia from behind me, but I am a crusader—I don't yield to authority.

If they have a problem, they can take it up with Creio, who dispatched her in the first place. That said, I don't plan on returning her even if Creio tells me to. If he wants to make a compromise, then there's gotta be something he'll offer in return, no? Superiors have an obligation to take care of their subordinates. If they don't, they'll soon find themselves bereft of loyal men.

Vilma lets out a brief sigh and takes out a small bag, offering it to me. I accept.

I remove the contents, rough against the palm of my hand. Amelia raises her eyebrows at their peculiar shine.

"Mythril buttons. From her robe... We've brought them with us."

"I see. What about them?"

"They're for you. Now, will you please allow Lady Stephenne to come with us?"

I see how it is... Not unexpected, coming from a mercantile big shot like Cardinal Sylvester. I am well familiar with the world of transactions.

Of course, I want the mythril so bad I can taste it. However—

"Are you saying I should sell my subordinate for a mere bauble?"

"...Ares... I *adore* you..."

Stey nuzzles her face into my back and says what I hope is a joke.

I don't need love and adoration! You're terrifying me! Just get to work!

Vilma shudders in response and looks at me again, searching for an opening.

"Let me be even more blunt. How much is she worth to you?"

This language I understand—very much so. I decide to go for an easily understood reply.

"Are you saying I should sell my subordinate for money?"

"Yeah, take that! Ares would never sell me!"

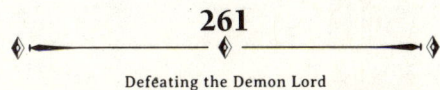

Defeating the Demon Lord

Stey pokes her head out from behind me and sticks out her tongue. She really doesn't grasp her place in all this...

Vilma must have read my next move, as her cheeks begin to twitch.

Sylvester is a former legendary merchant. He has more money than he knows what to do with. I don't need him as my enemy, but he would do anything, regardless of expense, for his beloved daughter. A single bag of mythril is a drop in the bucket.

"I see unprecedented value in Stey. She's high-level and extremely talented. She's gorgeous, and although still immature, she has some definite assets. I've already devised plans that depend on her involvement."

"Wha? Whaaaat?! Ares, you love me, too?! Does this mean it's mutual? Will you marry me?"

Stey is prattling a bunch of nonsense, and Amelia is staring at her like she wants to rip her in half. I ignore them entirely and state my demands loud and clear.

"I want mythril. Plus one hundred million lux. That's my final offer."

"...We have half of that with us at the moment. Will you accept the remainder in installments?"

"Huh????!!"

Barnard opens the trunk without a word. They must have assumed what kind of guy I am—the trunk is loaded with a mountain of gold.

Stey turns to stone. She rams her head into my back repeatedly, clearly feeling betrayed.

Damn—with one hundred million lux, I can employ top-tier mercenaries for the long haul. Stey has definite potential, but I already have a priest on deck. No matter which way I slice it, taking the gold is more advantageous than trying to foster Stey's true potential. Money makes the world go round.

Well... This is it, then. Satisfied, I make a show of nodding my head.

"This is an offer I cannot refuse."

"...We appreciate...your kindness."

Thinking of all the times I struggled dealing with Stey, this is obviously

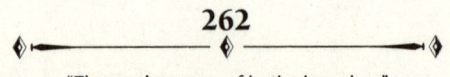

the sound decision. Lux gold currency is highly stable and easily exchanged in other countries.

Vilma glares at me angrily but nonetheless bows deeply. She's probably deeply regretting having let Stey go so easily in the first place. *Serves you right.*

As I receive the trunk of gold, I peel Stey off my back as she shakes her head back and forth, truly in shock. At the end of the day, there's no denying that she'll be happier leading a quiet, calm life at the Church headquarters, rather than taking part in a potentially deadly journey.

I muster the tranquility I haven't felt for some time to address Stey in a friendly voice.

"Stey, take care of yourself back home. I won't forget you."

"N-no, I don't wannaaa. I wanna be with you, Ares!"

"That's not happening."

"?!"

Vilma comes forward, dead-eyed, and grabs Stey by the arm. That's when I remember something.

"Ah, by the way, I'm only selling Stey. Cacao stays here."

"????!!!"

Stey is incompetent, but Cacao more than makes up for her. It's the only thing keeping her conscience afloat.

Stey finally realizes what's happening and glowers at me with tears in her eyes. She can barely pronounce her words as she lays into me.

"Um, Ares?! Cacao and I come as a set, y'know! With me included, we're a real bargain!"

"What is this, some kind of sketchy back alley deal?"

"What's that supposed to mean?! Oh! Cacao, no! Don't go with hiiim!"

Stey's scream could shatter glass. Vilma and Barnard fidget restlessly as people begin to stare. I was only half joking. Neither Amelia or I can actually see Cacao, but it appears that it's come toward us. Just what can you do without your covenant-bearer, Cacao...?

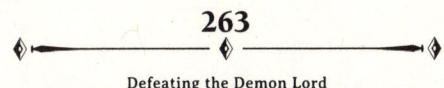

Stey grasps at thin air as she hollers in disgrace.

"Nooo!! Ahhhhhnnnngh! H-how are you two so friendly with Cacao?! You big ol' cheater!"

"...Take her away."

At my orders, Stey's chamberlains grab her by the arms and quickly drag her away. She's just as loud now as when she joined us— In a way, she's a bit like her own walking circus.

Her screams linger in the air before trailing off. Silence finally returns. Amelia simply asks, "Are you okay with this?"

What's that supposed to mean? For better or worse—makes no difference to me.

"It'll be really lonely without Stey around, but we have important business to attend to. Our journey is just beginning."

"That's pathetic."

And here I tried so hard to consider Amelia's feelings, only to get an acerbic response in return.

Cacao may be invisible to us, but I get the feeling it's dancing around near our feet.

The Holy Warrior, Naotsugu Toudou—currently level 40.

Our next destination—the water capital, Cloudburst.

Our goal—capture a powerful water spirit.

§　§　§

Stephenne believes that she can accomplish anything she sets her mind to. That's why she put more effort into Ares's assignment than anything she's ever done before.

Acting as personal escort, all by herself. She absolutely could not afford to mess it up. Her nervousness must have helped—she didn't make any small mistakes like usual, and her escort duty went exceptionally well.

None of the golems that usually appear had spawned, and Toudou and the others seemed highly suspicious of such circumstances. But for

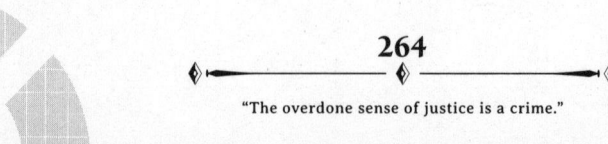
"The overdone sense of justice is a crime."

Stephenne, that was neither here nor there. Ares has taught her that she's not a capable multitasker—a stunning yet accurate revelation.

As she tended to her escort duties, Stephenne kept on walking, ruminating over one thing, and one thing only—making sure not to mess up, no matter what.

"If Toudou runs into a werebeast, or a high-level golem he can't take on, I want you to use earth magic to stop them dead in their tracks, okay? If you can completely bring them down, then by all means, go for it."

If Toudou ran into a werebeast or a high-level golem, she would stop them dead in their tracks. And finish them off.

Stephenne was extremely invested in keeping watch on the party as she marched onward. It's no surprise that she immediately noticed the giant birdlike werebeast flying high above their heads. When it appeared, she stopped it dead in its tracks, just like she was told. It was just the tiniest speck of a shadow, and Stephenne instinctively used her magic before she realized it.

It was a gravity-enhancement spell that she had just finally remembered the other day. Thankfully, the spell worked perfectly, and the werebeast flying high in the sky crumpled like something had grabbed both of its legs, before plummeting to the ground.

Toudou and the others made a ruckus at the sudden strange noises, but Stephenne simply put a serious look on her face and counted on her fingers to figure out what her next move should be. Just as Ares had said, she borrowed Cacao's skills to stop the werebeast. That meant next, she needed to finish it off. If she could completely bring it down, then by all means, she had to go for it. That was her responsibility.

"Wh-what the—? What was that?"

Limis was bewildered. Stephenne couldn't simply leave her in the dark, so she pondered for a moment before explaining. She hadn't been ordered to keep any information secret—aside from Ares's name.

"This is my job! I've been ordered to defeat any of the Demon Lord's underlings if they appear!"

265

"Wha… Whaaaaa?! Really, Stey? *You?*" Aria was beside herself with shock.

"Yes, that's right! Me!"

Stephenne nodded, clearly a bit proud. She promptly made her next move and headed down the cliff, making extra sure not to trip on the way. An unexpected sight had been awaiting her when she arrived.

Five metal golems, their steely bodies curving elegantly, as they surrounded the downed werebeast. Arranged in something like a military formation, the golems turned to Toudou and company, who still didn't understand what was going on. Meanwhile, Stey immediately sprang into action.

They possessed immense power—as a mage, Stephenne could feel it. From her estimation, these were high-level golems. Much stronger than Toudou and her party. If Toudou ran into any high-level golems she couldn't take on, Stephenne had to fight them herself. That was her command.

"If Toudou runs into a werebeast, or a high-level golem he can't take on, I want you to use earth magic to stop them dead in their tracks, okay? If you can completely bring them down, then by all means, go for it."

First, stop them dead in their tracks. Then, bring them down if she can.

Oddly, Cacao had been shaking her head as if refusing to help, but Stephenne ordered her to channel every bit of their magic into an Earth Gravity spell and unleash it on the werebeast and all five golems.

"Ugghh… Where did I go wrooong? I did everything as I was told…"

Well, that's because you didn't defeat those golems…, she admitted with some hesitation.

Honestly, she couldn't help it. Earth elemental spells simply aren't that powerful in terms of attack power. The fire spell that Limis cast afterward barely damaged them, too—obviously, her earth magic was destined to fail.

She felt she followed her orders to the letter, but Ares still sold her

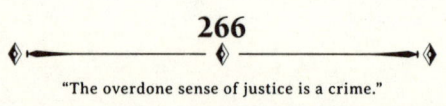

off to Barnard and Vilma. She couldn't believe it. He had been speaking so highly of her just seconds before… He changed his mind way too quickly.

Barnard picks up Stey with an experienced hand and puts her onto their horse carriage. Vilma chides Stephenne, her eyes glazed over.

"…Yes, yes. I'll listen to your excuses later…"

"Ares even called me reckless…"

"Yes, yes. You can complain and moan to your father as much as you want—later."

Suddenly, Stephenne is hit with a revelation and claps her hands together.

"…Oh… Of course! I just need to persuade Papa!"

Stephenne is very close with her father. The reason she got the operator job was thanks to his intervention. She perks up immediately, but Vilma makes the same face she did when negotiating with Ares.

"?! …C-come, come now, we're going home! You must be tired. When we arrive at the Church, you can rest aaaall you want."

"Huuuh? I'm not tired one bit! It's sooo unfair—Cacao gets to have all the fun!"

Stey protests and kicks her legs as the horse carriage starts down the bumpy road.

§ § §

It's hard to believe this is the room of a church. The scent of some unidentifiable incense lingers in the air, making Toudou's brow twitch. An older woman sits in the center of the dimly lit room with a suspicious smile creeping across her face.

Toudou can still remember her first impression of this woman as if it were yesterday—that this is no ordinary human being. Standing silently next to the cunning madam is Wurtz, and Toudou gives a slight bow of her head.

"Thank you so very much."

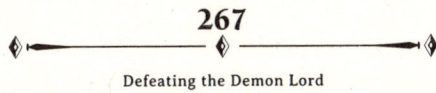

267

"Heh-heh-heh, not at all. As a member of the Church, assisting the Holy Warrior is my duty."

It was a short period of time, but the training sessions really boosted Toudou's prowess. She owes everything to Wurtz and the madam.

If she could have exactly what she wants, Toudou would love to stay here and level up further, but a new destination awaits her.

"I hear you're headed to the water capital, yes?"

"...Where did you hear that from?"

Toudou's question brings a grin full of hidden meaning to the madam's face. She likely doesn't intend to answer. Gathering her thoughts, Toudou finally asks something that's been on her mind for a while.

"...Madam, was it you who sent Stey—Stephenne Veronide—to our party?"

Tripping, falling off cliffs, constantly forgetting things—the girl was a real ditz. Stey caused Toudou and her party a lot of trouble, but there's no denying her powerful elemental spells and high level.

And Toudou can't forget her final words—that she'd been tasked with repelling the Demon Lord's underlings.

"No, that wasn't me, dear. However—it's true that she was dispatched to you by the Church."

In Toudou's eyes, Stephenne isn't a very competent human being. She's not a bad person, but if possible, Toudou wanted her out of the party sooner rather than later. Her entire party recognized this—that's why they went to such lengths to level up.

However, if Stephenne only joined the party to protect them, then that changes everything. Looking back on it, there was something unnatural about her behavior—so much so that Toudou can't believe that she never thought it was out of the ordinary at the time.

Stephenne has already left Toudou's party, meaning they have no means of confirming things—but thinking about it logically, there's no way someone could be that incredibly klutzy. Looking back on it all, every one of her moronic charades seems like an act.

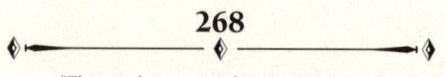

"The overdone sense of justice is a crime."

She brought a werebeast that appeared out of nowhere to its knees and then drove off a group of five metal golems single-handedly, when Limis—who boasts the most powerful fire magic Toudou's ever seen—couldn't even damage them. She carried out this mission and then left.

Could some ditzy young girl actually do all that? Not a snowball's chance in hell.

What's more, she even went so far as to give Limis advice on how to improve after she got down on herself when her fire elemental magic didn't work.

"If you find someone as tough as Gar-Gar, I bet you'll be able to form a covenant with them, for sure."

"I'm going to contract with a water spirit next. Cloudburst ought to have powerful ones inhabiting it."

Garnet is the most powerful of all fire spirits. There aren't many examples of one contracted spirit influencing another. That said, if Limis can find a spirit as strong, or stronger, than Garnet, she should be able to form a covenant with it.

Without a doubt, the only reason Limis realized this is because of what Stey told her.

Although the Friedia family claims a prestigious elemental magic heritage, that doesn't mean they have innumerable high-level spirits at their disposal. Limis has never had a chance to contract with an elemental spirit as strong, or stronger, than Garnet.

She doesn't know if she'll be able to form another covenant—it's not an easy task in itself. But she determines that it's worth a shot, and Toudou is fully on board.

Until now, Limis always thought that with Garnet by her side, she would have no issues. Maybe she was just in denial. However, her experience in Golem Valley, including seeing Stephenne's mastery of earth elemental spells, made her realize that she can't stay the same any longer. The party chose the water capital as their next destination in part because

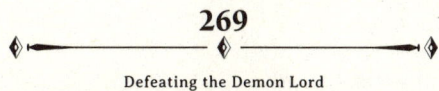

a water elemental spirit is oppositional to Garnet, a fire spirit, and Limis believes it's her best chance at forming another covenant.

Wurtz has remained silent thus far, but now he looks at each member of Toudou's party in turn before speaking.

"Holy Warrior. The water capital lies outside the Kingdom of Ruxe. If anyone there learns of your affiliation, you may find yourself wrapped up in a whole lot of trouble. Even in these times, when the menace of the Demon Lord looms, humanity will not gather as one. For better or for worse—your reputation as the Holy Warrior reaches far and wide."

"…Yes, sir."

Every town they've visited thus far has been within the realm of the Kingdom of Ruxe. They've been able to inform each respective town's headman of their arrival and receive ample financial support and supplies. They've been provided with maps, tips for leveling up, and even some intel. But this is all because the party has remained within the Kingdom's sphere of influence. Leaving its borders means that influence will plummet sharply.

Wurtz continues, his voice full of vigor.

"Yet, no matter which kingdom or town you visit, the influence of the God of Order, Ahz Gried, will remain strong. If you find yourself in need, please trust in the Church. They will be able to help you."

"…Understood."

Golem Valley has provided the group with so much.

Powerful monsters and terrain they'd never seen before. Glacia joining the fray of her own accord. The group received training to acclimate to their newly heightened levels, along with a particularly idiosyncratic yet powerful new party member from the Church. In the end, they got a glimpse of another fearsome side of the Demon Lord's army, although they have yet to understand exactly what they saw.

They may have gained several levels, but their achievements don't end there.

Toudou opens and closes her hands, confirming the power resting within them. She can still move, and she's surely become stronger, bit by

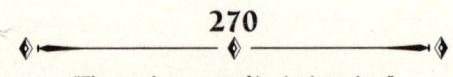

"The overdone sense of justice is a crime."

bit. Not a single shadow of doubt is cast on her resolution to defeat the Demon Lord.

Wurtz smiles mildly and forms the sign of the cross with his thick fingers.

"And with that, may you go. Brave Holy Warrior, sir, as you face the journey ahead—may you receive the blessings of Ahz Gried."

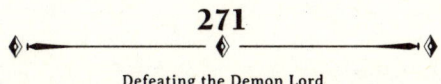

Part Four

Still Continues

I Won't Make the Same Mistake Twice

I can feel contemptuous stares swirling around my entire being.

The room is cramped and flooded with hazy light. Human figures crowd around a few dingy tables in the windowless barroom, and the bartender wears a mask just a bit more stylish than mine.

A few of the tables are lined with liquor bottles, but I can't smell alcohol or tobacco smoke. The indistinct aroma of herbs wafts toward me—it's a deodorizer. Calling the rabble underneath the dim lamplight *mercenaries* would be entirely banal. They're completely different in appearance from the mercenaries and monster hunters I've seen in Vale Village or Golem Valley—they're either overwhelmingly massive or lack any sense of fear whatsoever.

This is a place where mercenaries come to unwind. Like Thira back in Vale Village, these locations have a special back entrance for those who meet special requirements. Towns that are big enough will always have one, but this place is different. It's a members-only tavern, the kind only seen in big cities. It looks like a bar, so everyone calls it "The Bar."

It's not your average watering hole—it's something more exclusive, with members clearly not of the normal party deviation. They're all hired mercenaries, cream of the crop, real-deal types. The majority of them have earned enough money to live in decadence for an entire lifetime, yet, they're still gathered here.

It's as if they're searching for especially difficult commissions, something that will give them meaning.

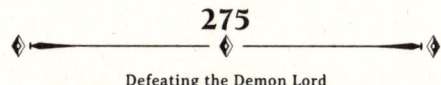

Before leaving for the water capital, I head to the only bar in Ruxe's own royal capital.

Back in Golem Valley, I was way too low on capable party members. Particularly when tracking Felsa, things would have been a lot easier if I'd had someone with a special set of skills.

I won't make the same mistake twice. Fortunately, I have plenty of money from selling off Stey.

It appears that I'm the only paying customer around. The Bar is strict when it comes to letting in members. The only reason I got in is due to a connection from back when I belonged to a mercenary party.

The second I enter, I hear nothing but the patrons' hushed voices. That, and the echoes of the secret codes they're tapping out on the tables. There are only a few people in the room, but I can't tell what voice belongs to which person. High-level individuals who specialize in espionage and secrecy excel at such techniques. Even though I'm high level myself, I have a hard time understanding what's being discussed.

The information and experience they hold sets them apart from the average mercenary. One of the voices says:

—*Check out the black ring on his left hand. Episcopal earrings, the mark of a priest. He's a black sword of the God of Order.*

A hoarse voice seems to respond:

—*A battle mace made of orichalcum. A young man with silver hair and green eyes—it's Ex Deus, Out Crusade first order, Ares Crown. No doubt about it.*

—*He's a high priest, and a former member of the A-class monster hunter party "Endless Blade."*

"..."

...For some strange reason, they seem to know my name instantly.

—*Just over a year ago, he was level eighty-seven. Now, he could easily be over ninety. One of the strongest priests in existence.*

—*He's exterminated more followers of darkness than anyone before him, and all by himself. The man is insane.*

Pretty harsh, but that's the kind of thing we crusaders tend to get.

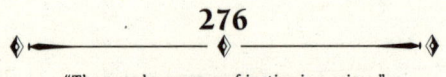

"The overdone sense of justice is a crime."

How do they know my level, though? I never include it in my reports to the Church, and I can conduct level-up rituals by myself, leaving few opportunities for anyone to find out. Of course, Creio knows, but the chances of him leaking such information are awfully slim.

It's not something I go to particular lengths to hide, so I suppose it leaking isn't the end of the world. But why the hell do they know the level of a guy who literally just walked in?

This is my first time at the Bar. I knew it existed, but at any rate, it's pretty expensive.

I give a slight shudder, and soon another voice chimes in:

—*He reeks of the winds of Golem Valley.*

"…You can't be serious."

It's been over a week since I left Golem Valley. Even if the winds there had a particular scent, there's no chance it'd still be on me at this point.

—*I can also smell the Great Forest of the Vale and Yutith's Tomb on him.*

"…You're kidding me, right?"

Come on, this has to be a joke. This goes beyond having a sharp sense of smell.

However, the patrons seem fully convinced of their assumptions. The ones speaking must be highly credible.

—*Why would a top crusader visit such low-class battlefields?*

—*The royal castle summoned a hero, so I'm told. Creio Amen was in charge and the Saint of Light, Tilt, executed the order.*

—*The hero summoning.*

—*So they mean to vanquish that calamity, huh?*

—*The summoned hero has black hair, black eyes—*

Where is this information leaking from?

However, these people are Ruxe mercenaries. Not to mention, they're of formidable repute, and they have sway over the aristocrats. There are many individuals involved in summoning the hero. There's a gag order in effect, but it's not surprising that there's been a leak.

At any rate, this is not good. I have to stop any further chatter, so I clap my hands loudly. The room falls silent.

"I'm in need of good men."

—*...That's a tall order. This is the stuff of legend.*

—*I can smell the stress and conviction on him.*

—*There's proportionate risk, too.*

—*But he's dead broke!*

I heft my trunk up in front of me, containing fifty million lux, and a hand-signed promissory note for the remaining fifty million. It contains the signature of Cardinal Sylvester, former merchant of legend, which makes it extremely credible. Anyone would give it the okay.

"I have gold."

Silence fills the room after I speak. Then, the voices begin again.

—*That's the sound of lux gold bullion. I'd say nearly fifty million. And... there's a promissory note for another fifty million. A hundred million in total.*

—*This is an attempted spending cut. These bastards don't know what money's worth.*

—*That's the price of our world, eh? One hundred million lux.*

—*Now I can smell the agitation on him. You should all keep your mouths shut. This is heresy.*

I'd like to bludgeon all these assholes with my mace. They'd probably survive.

Perfect timing—just as I feel the power surging through my hand, the bartender breaks his silence.

"Just what sort of men are you after?"

My irritation is slightly abated by his calm voice. I haven't even reached the water capital yet, but this is the moment of truth, in a way. The difficulties I face on my next mission are riding on the kinds of skilled mercenaries I can employ here.

I take a deep breath and compose myself before stating my demands.

"I'm seeking someone with the proper battle prowess and scouting skills capable of taking down a steel tiger only a party over level seventy can defeat. In addition, I need two girls cute enough to make anyone fall for them, who won't balk in the face of demon foes, and both with a strong tolerance for stress. Their level is not a concern."

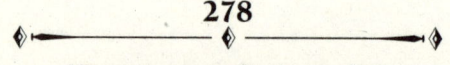

"The overdone sense of justice is a crime."

"..."

The masked bartender falls silent, utterly speechless.

—...*Tryin' to wine and dine them, eh? You've got your work cut out for ya.*

Whoever spoke doesn't know just how perfectly they've described it.

Stephenne ☆ Ditz Supreme

They say it's no use crying over spilled milk. In other words, regretting something that's a done deal doesn't change anything. So you better be careful the first time around.

They also say that prevention is better than cure. This means that if you don't shirk your responsibility in making the right preparations, you won't have any problems when something goes awry down the road.

Putting both of these adages into practice, you may wind up with a black-haired girl wobbling her head to and fro. Her eyes are unfocused, and her face looks like a perfectly formed apple, sweet and red. Her expression is fixed into a gentle smile, like she's stuck in some sort of euphoric dream. Unfortunately, there's nothing euphoric about this sight.

It's the face of someone full-on drunk. Amelia sighs deeply, seated next to the drunkard.

"See? I *told* you not to give Stey alcohol… Ares, you big dummy."

Amelia is sulking, and her words don't suit her. Bewildered, I reply, "…Hey now, I only gave her a spoonful!"

I regret the one time I got Amelia drunk, so I took care to only give Stey a minuscule amount. I meticulously chose a fruit liqueur with a low alcohol content and mixed it with soda—a literal teaspoon. One single teaspoon. This is nothing like the time Amelia fell in love with the wine bottle and wouldn't let go.

Not to mention—Stey said she can hold her booze! I didn't intend to take her word for it, yet, this time around, I realized the truth—lightweights always brag about how much they can drink. Amelia warned me in advance, but this is beyond the pale. Stey's a complete featherweight.

Stey grins foolishly, and Amelia's face stiffens as she says, "Stey is always ditzy, but this version of Stey is really getting up there."

"You mean…she gets even worse than this?!"

It's my own damn fault for giving her alcohol as an experiment, but I really don't want to see how bad it can get.

I can't tell if Stey is listening to our conversation or completely oblivious, as she starts to pull on the hem of her skirt.

Amelia's eyebrow twitches. The next instant, Stey makes a grand show of ripping a button off her dress. The button, engraved with the cross scale, falls on the floor. She contorts her body and takes off her dress. Without hesitation, she moves her hand to the buttons of her slip, but Amelia quickly pins her arms behind her back.

Stey has completely lost it and announces, her face beet red, "Isso hot. I'm takin' it awf."

Hearing this brings to mind the time Amelia got drunk. I instinctively erupt at Stey.

"You already took it off!"

"Stey is a terrible drunk, Ares!" screams Amelia as she struggles to contain Stey. I want to tell her, *Takes one to know one!* but Stey has truly eclipsed her. At least Amelia had the decency to take her clothes off *after* announcing it to the world.

Stey is now stumbling forward while trying to get naked and, perhaps having realized that Amelia is subduing her, twists her neck around to look her in the eyes.

"Amelia… What're… What're you tryna do to meee?"

"I should be asking you!"

"But Amelia… It's just that… I love you sooo much…"

Stey twists her neck around and puts her lips on Amelia's cheek. It was a sudden move, but Amelia dodges her deftly, like an expert martial artist. She releases Stey, who promptly loses her balance and falls on her ass.

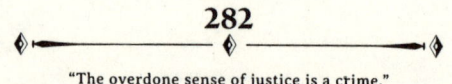

"The overdone sense of justice is a crime."

"Damn, Amelia, that was impressive…"

"W-well, I just have prior experience…"

Prior experience…? So this has happened to you before?

I grow weary as Amelia looks at me. Desperate not to be misunderstood, she shouts in a panic, "N-no—it was on my cheek! On my cheek, Ares, not my lips. Don't get any ideas!"

Uh, I never even asked in the first place.

Amelia is agitated, and Stey definitely takes notice. She's always a complete airhead, but now, she leaps to her feet with unbelievable dexterity and latches onto Amelia from behind—likely revenge for what was just done to her moments ago. How the hell is she so much more agile now that she's drunk?!

"Eek!"

"Hee-hee-hee, I gotcha now…"

Amelia squirms frantically to break free, but Stey must have a perfect lock on her—she can't resist at all. Stey may be a hot mess, but she's a *level-72* hot mess. She squeezes Amelia tightly and says, practically in ecstasy, "Ooh, Amelia… You smell so good… And your body's so soft, what tasty bits you have."

"Um, umm… Ares… Could you give me a hand here?"

Amelia's timid plea brings me to my senses. Yes, I should help her. I was enjoying this so much that I didn't realize.

I stand up and go to put my arm out when Stey looks at me and smiles languidly.

"Hunh? Ares, you wanna bite, too?"

"Whaaa—?"

"Eek! Stey, wait! Don't—"

My hand stops of its own accord. Stey opens her palms wide and grabs both of Amelia's breasts from behind. Amelia squirms and lets out a little squeal, but Stey doesn't flinch as she starts groping Amelia's breasts.

"Da meat gets softer if ya tenderize it, Ares. Today's speshul cut is… breast meat."

"Are you a chef or something?"

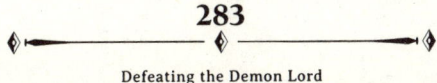

"Um, Ares?! What are you talking abouuu—"

Amelia's face is red as a barn door as she elbows Stey, who remains unfazed.

"Amelia, you're so skinny, but dis spot is suuuper meaty. 'Fyou treat it properly, it'll aaalways be there for ya!"

"You... You're so dead, Stey. I'm gonna kill you!! Mmph?!"

Stey's fingers have reached Amelia's dress buttons, and she opens the first one with ease. Amelia's scarlet face is now turning different shades. Her lips tremble, but she can't seem to find any words due to the shock.

Stey has only managed to undo the middle button of Amelia's dress, so I can't see any skin or her panties, but still... This is way too far. Who knew someone could be such a terrible drunk that they try to strip someone else naked?

Yet, before Stey can go any further, I step in and drag her off Amelia from behind. She tries hard to fight back, but I'm a much higher level than her and peel her off easily.

Amelia rushes away from Stey, closing her button with a shaky hand. She glares at me with tears in her eyes.

"I told you! I *told* you not to get Stey drunk..."

"...You're right, I'm sorry."

"...A-Ares... If you hadn't been here...she would've attacked me."

It almost sounds like a joke, but Amelia looks absolutely serious.

Her breasts, freshly kneaded and groped by Stey, heave up and down with her breathing. She must have noticed I was looking, as she takes a deep breath and says emphatically, "I think you've assessed the risk... quite thoroughly enough."

"I'm glad I gave her booze here, at the inn. And I'm glad we were the only ones around. It would've been a damn mess if we did this at a bar."

"Th-that's not what I'm talking about!"

"But hey, at the very least... I feel like you've grown from this experience."

As I reply, I look at Stey, who's calmed down now that I've subdued

her. Abilities are one thing, but implying that Stey's shortcomings could lead to someone's improvement is…completely absurd.

Amelia mumbles hopelessly, "…Yes… I've learned so much…"

"Ares, lemme gooo. I know whut ta do… I know whut ta do!"

"The hell are you talking about, you dumbass?!"

Stey seems obedient, but she's still slurring like crazy. I can't quite catch what Amelia is trying to say since Stey is so loud.

Before I can ask Amelia to repeat herself, Stey lifts her neck as high as she can and moves her head. Her hair brushes my hand, and her pale throat sticks out right in front of my eyes. She must still be really drunk, because she gives me a coquettish look and says, "Ares, 'fyou dun want Amelia's meaty bits, y'can have mine."

"What?"

"My hands or feet or shoulders or tummy or boobies or butt—take whatcha like. I'm feelin' real good today so y'can have the whole banquet to yerself."

"…You're a really shitty drunk, Stey."

If just one teaspoon of alcohol mixed with soda gets her this absurdly wasted, how would she deal with a regular drink? If Amelia's seen this before, I can understand why she thinks she can hold her alcohol—Stey is the world's biggest lightweight.

As I continue to restrain her, Stey starts to nuzzle me like she's some sort of cat. Through her thin slip, I can feel her warm, pulsating body against mine.

"I'm nawt a prime cut like Amelia, but I got faith in my meat quality. See, seeee!"

Without a trace of modesty or embarrassment, Stey grinds her whole body against me. She feels so incredibly soft. *Hmm, she's not wrong. This is some high-quality meat…*

I'm strangely impressed, but just then, I hear a voice cold as ice ring out:

"**Recovery.**"

Amelia places her hand on Stey's forehead, and a pale-green light

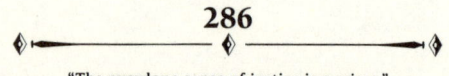

seeps into her skull. Her eyes refocus, and she blinks repeatedly before gazing up at me like she's just woken from a dream.

"Huh? What's going on? Why are you holding me?"

Amelia ignores Stey and fixes her stern gaze on me.

"…Wh-whaaat are you doing, Ares? Are you sexually harassing me?"

"…I'm sorry. I promise to never give you alcohol ever again."

Stey is the ditz to end all ditzes. Let's call her the ditz supreme.

It's no use crying over spilled milk, and prevention is better than cure. As I nod, content with the results of my experiment, Amelia mutters to herself—not for Stey's ears.

"…I'll learn from this, for next time."

CHARACTER DATA

NAME Stephenne Veronide

【**Level**】: 72

【**Occupation**】: Holy Mage
(elementalist + priest)

【**Gender**】: Female

ABILITIES

Physical Strength: None

Endurance: A Bit High

Agility: Regular

Magical Energy: Kinda High

Holy Energy: Kinda High

Will: High

Luck: High

EQUIPMENT

Weapon: None (too dangerous)
Clothing: Custom-fitted robe (black, which hides dirt; the buttons are now wooden)

EXPERIENCE UNTIL NEXT LEVEL   77,777,777

A transmission magic operator with the Church, and Amelia's junior. The daughter of a cardinal, she is supremely talented and highly sociable, but her klutziness is her fatal flaw, and she lacks any self-awareness. Nicknamed Stey. Takes her clothes off when she gets drunk.

AFTERWORD

TSUKIKAGE

Thank you so much for picking up this copy of *Defeating the Demon Lord's a Cinch (If You've Got a Ringer)*.

Expanding on Volume 2, which was originally published on the website Kakuyomu, this is the edited and revised third volume of this series.

Volume 3 is characterized by its new characters, chiefly Stephenne Veronide, nicknamed Stey. She's a hopelessly klutzy sister dispatched by the Church to assist Ares in Golem Valley. She also happens to be the most powerful character in this book, in a sense. She's always tripping and forgetting things, but she's a very strong presence, just like her fellow holy caster Amelia. I encourage you to hold your head in your hands like Ares does as you read along.

In this volume, we get a glimpse of the Demon Lord's army's movements from the first book onward. The series has focused on internal struggle thus far, but I will continue to detail the Demon Lord's army and their developments moving forward.

Of course, I must continue to acknowledge everyone who's supported me, including the amazing illustrator bob, who brought the naturally ditzy and hilarious Stephenne to life better than I could have imagined. Thank you so much! I must also express my gratitude to my editors, Shukutani and Kawasaki, who work so hard to prepare these books for publication. I'm so sorry I keep going over the word limit. Next time...I promise to be careful. Last but not least, thank you to everyone who's supported this series since its beginnings on the web, and to those who started with the published book. I express my deepest gratitude to you all.

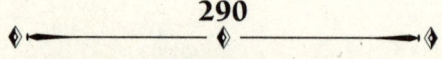

"The overdone sense of justice is a crime."

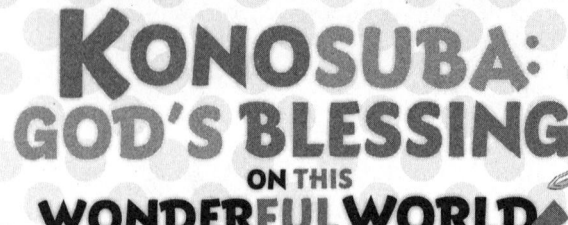

Read the light novel that inspired the hit anime series!

Re:ZeRo
-Starting Life in Another World-

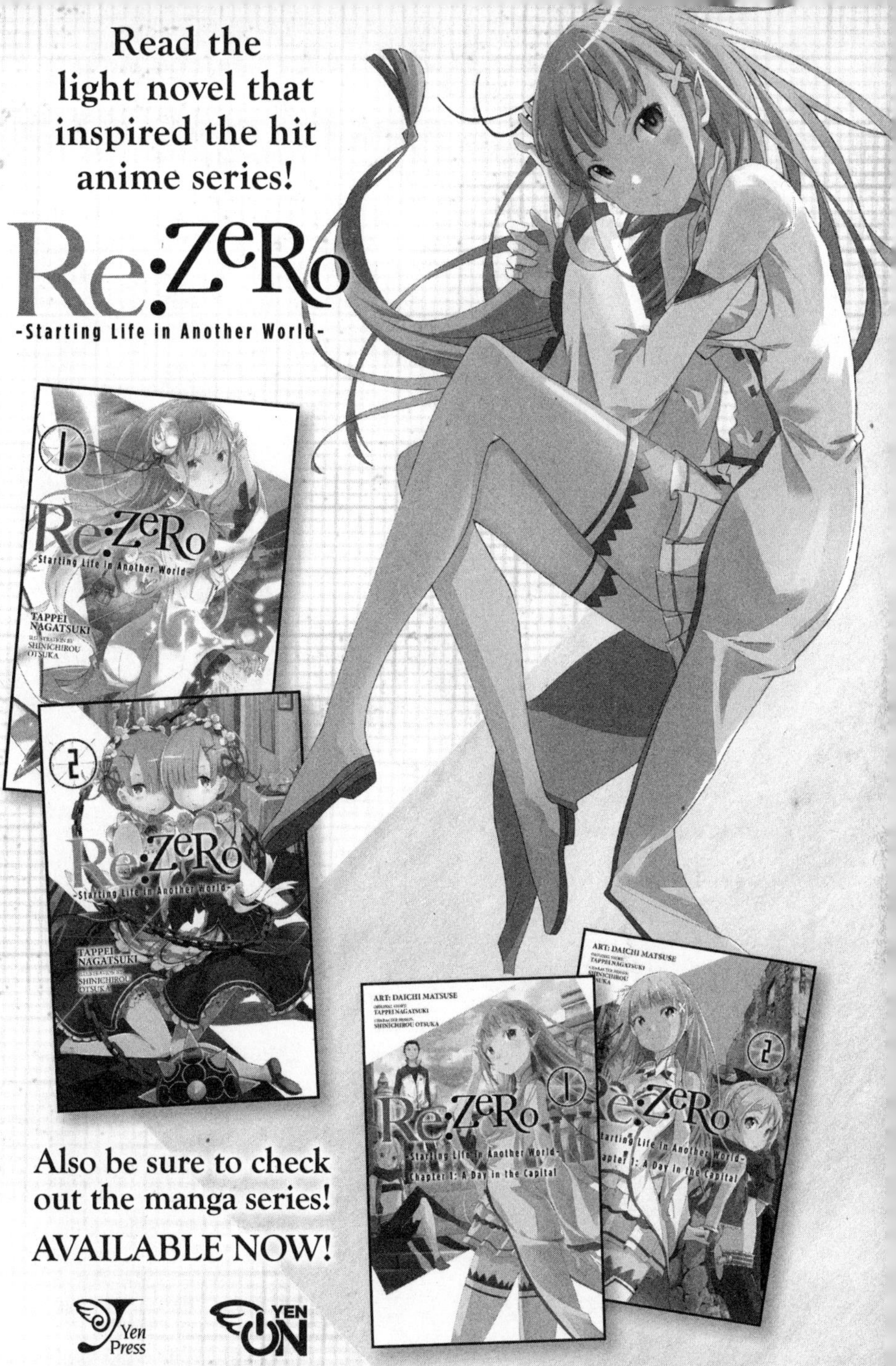

Also be sure to check out the manga series!

AVAILABLE NOW!

Yen Press

YEN ON

www.YenPress.com

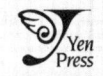

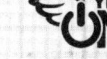

Discover the other side of Magic High School—read the light novel!

The Irregular at Magic High School